NEXUS MOONS

Book One of the Tales of Graal

Ron Root

An Epic Fantasy

Nexus Moons
Book One of the Tales of Graal

Copyright © 2020 by Ron Root
All rights reserved

Book cover artist: RLSather
SelfPubBookCovers.com/ RLSather

Cover design by Vickie Duchscherer

ISBN: 978-1-09830-935-0

This book is dedicated to my grandchildren:

Brooklyn, Jackson, Savannah, Alyssa and Logan
Hayden, Nate, and Taylor

Contributors:

Catherine Evleshin, Chrissy LaVielle, Jessica Morrell and Vivienne Boogaard

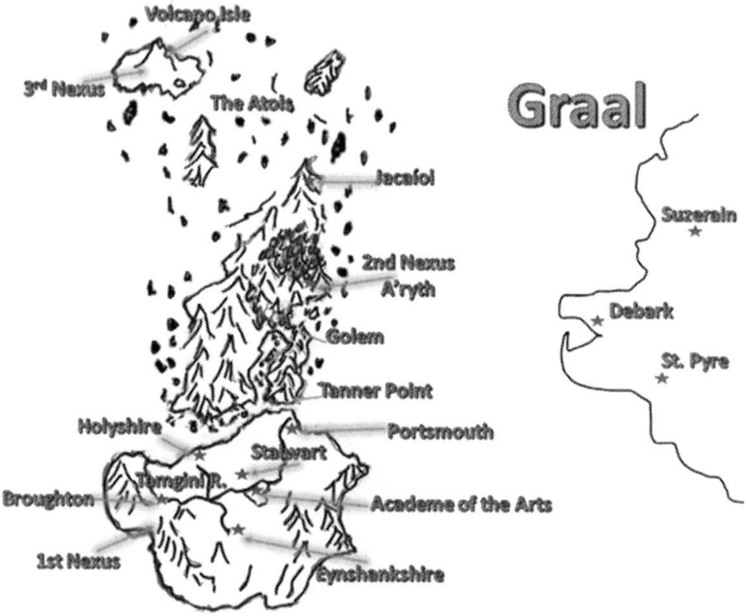
Volcano Isle
3rd Nexus
The Atols
Graal
Jacafol
Suzerain
2nd Nexus
A'ryth
Debark
Golem
St. Pyre
Tanner Point
Holyshire
Portsmouth
Stalwart
Tamgini R.
Broughton
Academe of the Arts
1st Nexus
Eynshankshire

Arrival

The helmsman guided the ship past the final buoy and into port. "Boom two points abaft the beam, starboard side!" came a cry from the crow's nest. The sails dropped and the ship slammed against the pylons. The loud grating of wood on wood spawned a flurry of dockside activity. Mooring lines were tossed to waiting dockers who looped them around bollards and the vessel was secured.

Jarek stood watching from atop the ship's deck, his magus robes flapping in the breeze. His plan had been to change into something more practical before debarking, but by the time he boarded, his belongings had already been stowed. The Captain had ordered the crew to treat them with extra care—to place them where rough seas wouldn't damage them. That 'extra care' had them buried them so deep in the hold that the ship's cargo would have to be offloaded before the crew could reach them.

He took in the scene before him. Like all seaports, Portsmouth reeked of offal. He pinched closed his nose in a vain effort to thwart its stench. Why his sister had chosen this island to birth a child was beyond him. Perhaps she picked it because of its remoteness. It made sense, given that Damián was mundane. Ever was it frowned upon for a magus to marry an ungifted for fear it would diminish chances of their offspring inheriting the Gift.

If isolation was Bronwyn's plan, it worked. It had taken Jarek nearly two decades to discover her whereabouts, long after her abduction by Chevaliers, the One Church's men-at-arms. Whereas the magi believed any person so gifted was free to practice the arts as he or she saw fit, it was not so with the One Church. They claimed exclusive domain over any aspect of the arts dealing with a man's soul. For anyone but one of their Clerics to practice such arts was deemed heretical, and it was the Chevaliers' sworn duty to enforce those laws. Had that been Bronwyn's crime? Had practicing forbidden arts precipitated her arrest? He sighed. After all this time, the answers to such questions were of secondary concern; he was here to find his nephew.

The gangplank fell, its loud bang shattering his reverie. A helmeted, sword-clad, bodyguard guided a pair of wealthy benefactors down to the dock. Attired in latest Suzerain fashion, the portly man was bedecked in brightly colored tunic and leggings, loose-fitting breeches, and a chaperon cap. His wife's garish attire made her husband's look tame.

Porters arrived, gathered their belongings, and escorted them to a waiting carriage. They boarded and left. Jarek watched their departure with envy. Had the crewmen recovered his baggage in timely fashion, he'd be on that carriage too.

With the gentry's departure, the more modestly dressed common folk disembarked too. Soon all passengers were off the ship but him. "You!" he hollered at the nearest porter, "Have they gotten to my belongings yet?" The young man's eyes darted about, hoping it wasn't he that Jarek had hailed. Ever did sorcerer's garb intimidate the mundane. "Come," Jarek encouraged, motioning the lad to come join him, "I wish you no ill, I'm simply anxious to be on my way."

The young porter approached, his dread obvious, as if some horrific spell was about to be cast upon him. "Apologies, Magus, but me fears it'll be some time yet afore the boys be reaching your things."

"So be it," he muttered, shaking his head. "Secure them on deck once they're finally recovered. I'm going ashore to bide my time. I shall return anon to fetch them."

"Yes, Magus." Looking relieved, the young swab scurried away.

Jarek scanned the town, hoping to spot some worthwhile means of passing time. Row upon row of merchant shoppes dotted the harborside, their open doors welcoming patrons. Cobbled alleyways parceled the town into sections. Haphazard rows of wattle-roofed crucks filled the area behind the shoppes, likely the abodes of the locals. The dawn sky glowed a soft orange above them. A sheriff's man bedecked in intimidating armor, sword at his side, strode among them, his presence assuring peace in a place that otherwise might be lawless mayhem. Ever were port cities dangerous.

Although Portsmouth bustled with commerce, it would get little of his coin. His plan was to head inland as soon as possible and begin his search for his nephew. He shook his head, still struggling to grasp the idea of having kin again. With his parents' passing and his sister's disappearance, the idea of having family seemed a treasure forever lost. To learn his sister had birthed a son on this remote island was almost unfathomable. But that's what the document proclaimed, and only a fool questioned the veracity of a Royal Library scroll.

He descended the gangplank and was heading toward town when he spied two oddly dressed sailors coming his way. Draped in fur with animal bones dangling from their long blonde locks, they looked fearsome. "Sirs," he hailed as they approached, "perchance could you tell me where I might hire a coach?"

They stopped, the larger of the two eyed Jarek's purse. "*Taka penningr?*" he asked of his companion.

But it was Jarek's robes that had the second one's attention. "*Æva, dārǣ!*" he said, with a shake of his head. "*Man hafa feldr sîða!*" The two scurried away, looking as if something of greater import had suddenly arisen.

A voice from behind startled him. "They were about to rob you, Sir." Jarek turned to find a portly young man with unruly brown hair sitting atop a wagon, holding its reins. "But fearing you might be a witch, they decided to seek easier prey."

"You understood them?"

The lad shrugged. "Enough to grasp their meaning. They were speaking Nosarian—one of many tongues you'll hear on these docks."

"And how is it you understand Nosarian?"

"My father's a merchant. As a boy, I travelled many lands and learned many tongues—a necessity if one wishes to successfully trade."

"I am in awe of your skill young man." He glanced toward the town, "I'd be even more impressed if you could direct me someplace where I might secure a carriage inland."

"That would be at the carriage post, sir. It's next to the livery."

"Ah, I see. And where, exactly, would the livery be?"

"How daft of me. Of course, a stranger wouldn't know that either." He looked toward town. "The post isn't far. I could take you thither if you'd like." He scooted over, making room for Jarek. "Just be aware, my comfortless wagon is hardly a proper conveyance for a Royal Magus."

Jarek had said nothing of his rank, yet the lad knew. How? There was more to this young man than met the eye. "Our meeting wasn't accidental, was it?"

"I… a… no Sir. I saw your robes as you walked down the gangplank. Knowing only Royal Magi wear black with a red sigil, I wanted to meet you."

"How is it you know so much about the magi?" he asked, climbing aboard.

"I once studied to be one."

Jarek had forgotten the island had an Arts school. "You're full to the top of surprises, aren't you? May I know your name?"

"It's Hagley, Sir."

"Well met, Hagley," he said, settling beside him. "I'm Magus Jarek Verity, and as you so astutely observed, a Sorcerer of the Court. So, where did you study, and why aren't you wearing robes?"

The spark left the lad's his eyes. "At the island's arts university. But I failed both my trials, so was refused them. Now, instead of being the university's student, I'm its wagoner."

"Failed them twice, eh? Are you aware a third test can be granted if circumstance warrants it?"

The young man shrugged. "I guess mine didn't warrant it."

"Where is this university of yours?"

"Just outside of Stalwart. I'll return there once I finish my errands," he said, spurring the horses forward.

Soon they were among the shoppes. The rankness of fresh blood assaulted Jarek's senses as they passed a butcher's shoppe, only to be replaced by the even more offensive fetor of a fishmonger's stall. Next came the livery stable, and finally, the carriage post. Hagley let him out and went on about his business.

Jarek headed inside. A grizzled-looking fellow stood behind the counter poring over a stack of journals. He glanced up, eyeing Jarek. "Yes?"

"How soon is the next carriage to Stalwart?"

"It just left. It'll return by nightfall, but won't leave again until the morrow," he said, returning his attention to his journals.

"Hells! Surely there's more than one carriage?"

The clerk glanced up from his journal, looking indignant. "You're no longer on the mainland, Sir. We islanders number few. Two carriages a day would not be profitable."

"Apologies for my curtness, it's just that I'm most anxious to reach Stalwart. Is there another means of conveyance you can suggest?"

His conciliatory tone seemed to mollify the man. "You might try the livery. Although they could provide a horse, bear in mind that Stalwart is a half-day's ride." He smirked. "Waiting for tomorrow's carriage would be far more comfortable, say nothing of more penny-worthy."

Tomorrow wouldn't do. "Gramercy," he said leaving, departing for the stable next door.

He approached the nearest groom. His hair was every bit as gray as the carriage post clerk's. "Good sir, how much to rent a horse to Stalwart? And perhaps a pack horse to carry my belongings."

He spit out a wad of chew, exposing blackened teeth. "That depends on when you be bringin' 'em back."

"I was thinking more in terms of leaving them in Stalwart."

"Ha!" the man bellowed. "Then you be talkin' buyin,' not rentin'. A silver each ought to cover it."

"A silver each!" Although cost wasn't really an issue for Jarek, paying that much to spend half a day with his arse doing battle with that of a horse seemed outlandish. Ever was he a poor horseman. "I fear that won't do."

Leaving, he wandered the town, pondering his plight, trying to come up with another option. The town's shoppes were colorful if nothing else, say nothing of noisy and aromatic, from the jarring clang and blistering heat of the blacksmiths and farriers, to the far softer tamping of tannery by cobblers fashioning their leather. Since none offered a means of getting to Stalwart, he resigned himself to searching for an inn.

While passing a tinker's wagon he was accosted by its driver. "Let me read your palm, kind sir," she said, struggling down out of its seat. One of her feet was mangled. Using a sawed-off tree limb for support, she limped toward him. "Just one chink learns your future," she said, flashing a toothless grin. "A bargain for such a boon."

Jarek doubted she was a true seer; those who could soothe were extremely rare. But he couldn't find it in his heart to refuse one burdened by such ill fortune. "Of course," he said, fishing out the requested chink.

Taking it, she led him into her wagon. Sitting facing him, she took hold of his hand and began her reading. Her augury turned out to be the very type of babble he expected—until she suddenly sat up, frowning. "Most unusual," she said, running a fingernail along a Y-shaped crease in his palm. "See this line?" she said, looking up. "It portends something most unusual."

Her remark roused his curiosity. "How so?"

Clasping his hand in hers, she looked deep into his eyes. "In days soon to come, you are fated to experience both great joy and extreme dismay."

Her pained expression was unsettling, making him wonder at her portent. Was she a true seer after all? "Such a profound augury is worthy of more," he said, handing her a second chink.

Leaving her wagon, he walked away, wondering at her prophecy. Did it pertain to his nephew? If so, he'd best find him soon. As he passed the next alleyway, movement caught his eye. He looked. Two shoppes down he spied Hagley, loading goods into his wagon. "Praise the Gods," he whispered, and headed down the alley.

Hagley looked up as Jarek approached. "Magus Verity, good to see you again. Did you book your carriage?"

"No, I've chosen another option."

Hagley's brow furrowed. "What other option is there?"

"I'm riding with you."

Stalwart

After retrieving Jarek's belongings, the two were soon Stalwart bound. "Since you've so kindly offered a ride," Jarek said, "I can do no less for you. Introduce me to your headmaster and I'll do my best to get you that third opportunity to pass your trials."

Hagley's eyes lit up. "You'd do that for me?"

Choking back a smile, Jarek glared. "Are you questioning a Court Sorcerer's word?"

"No sir! I'm sorry, Sir."

Jarek broke out laughing. "It was a jape, Hagley. Don't you recognize a jest when you hear it? Now tell me about this university of yours, and how it is you failed your trials."

Hagley recounted both his failures. Jarek was surprised at the level of detail he provided. The lad had a keen mind, making his inability to pass his trials all the more puzzling.

After exhausting the topic of Hagley's woes, their conversation ebbed. Jarek sat contemplating his upcoming task. He thought back to the day he'd first heard of the existence of his nephew. He'd been researching in the library on a wholly different matter when the Archivist came to him, telling of a parchment he'd found that alluded to a sorcerer named Verity, wondering if it might be a kinsman. Since Jarek and Bronwyn were the family's only practitioners, it had to pertain to her.

The document turned out to be a recounting of Bronwyn's husband's posthumous trial. It read: Damián Smithy, Stalwart village smith, died hindering the arrest of his heretic wife, Bronwyn Smithy, born Verity. Care of said persons' male infant was given over to local clergy.

Although the scroll shed little light as to Bronwyn's fate, it proclaimed the all-important news that Jarek had living kin. How many winters had passed since he could last make that boast? He clenched his jaw, realizing the same miscreants who abducted his sister and killed poor Damián, were now raising his nephew. Had they already poisoned his mind with their perverse doctrine? Could the lad be extricated from their clutches, or had they already created a disciple of his own flesh and blood? If so, would he even like the boy? No, not a boy; he'd have celebrated nineteen winters. More importantly, what would this young man think of some stranger showing up after all this time claiming to be kin? Pondering these possibilities had Jarek's stomach astir. It roiled even more when a town came into view.

Hagley pointed to the fortressed village appearing on the horizon. "There it is, that's Stalwart."

The town seemed to increase in size as their wagon drew closer. Its fortified walls stood a good twenty cubits high, five times the height of a man. Soon their horses' hoof beats were echoing off its buttressed walls. Their wagon rumbled beneath a giant gatehouse portcullis; past a pair of pike men; onto cobbled streets that lead to the village proper. His chest tightened at the possibility of finally finding family.

"Where can I take you?"

Jarek surveyed the surroundings. "My business is with the town parish. Are you familiar with it?"

"Yes sir." Hagley pointed. "See those two buildings?"

Jarek shaded his eyes, squinting. "Yes, but neither looks very churchlike."

"Nor are they. The one on the left is a cadet institute where soldiers train. The other is an academy for highborn ladies. If you look in between them, you can make out the tip of the parish's spire."

They wove their way through the crush of artisans jamming the roadway. Hagley slowed as they approached a spot where the wheel-rutted gatehouse road intersected the cobbled avenue that split the town in two. Market Street was emblazoned on the crossroads stone. To one side were a myriad of shoppes, inns and tenements, and a foundry. Had Damián worked there?

A marketplace was on the other side, with denizens and merchant tents so numerous only someone on foot could weave through the crowd. Livestock were there—the stench of their dung overwhelming. As Hagley's wagon climbed the hill, their view broadened. Inside Stalwart's walls was a fortressed garrison with its own set of abutments. Filling the wide gap between the inner and outer walls were the shanties of the common folk, and row upon row of wagons, likely some caravan making a stopover.

Once past Market Street they made good time, and Jarek soon found himself standing outside the parish. "Who is the church's thane?"

"Prior Rigby. All here know him." Hagley pointed to a nearby trough. "I'll water the horses while you tend to your business. When you're done, I'll drive you back into town."

"A kindly offer, but I don't know how long this will take me. I'm sure I'll have no problem finding my way back to town."

"I really don't mind, sir. Besides, your bags look too heavy to carry."

His bags! In one was the gift he'd brought for his nephew. "You're right," he said, picking up the knapsack that held it. "This alone would be too cumbersome."

He headed for the entrance. A brown-clad clergyman greeted him, looking none too friendly.

"I'm here to see a Prior Rigby."

The man eyed Jarek's robes. "What matter has a godless sorcerer in a house of worship?"

And what business is it of yours? "It's a personal matter." He offered up a faux smile, hoping to diffuse tensions. "Now, if I may, the Prior?"

The clergyman stood silent a moment, looking him over. "As you wish," he finally answered. He eyed Jarek's knapsack, "May I relieve you of your burden?"

Jarek hugged it to his chest. "A most gracious offer, but I can manage."

The grim-faced clergyman led him down a long corridor. Rooms lined its sides. The people inside them eyed his robes with similar distrust. Guiding Jarek into one of the rooms, his escort nodded. "Wait here while I fetch the Prior."

With two elegantly decorated chairs and a table, the room was well-furbished. Deep red tapestries woven with intricate golden accents adorned the walls. The chairs were of matching silks. Disdaining the room's finery, Jarek remained standing.

The dour clergyman returned, escorting a short, pudgy, white-haired man in a brown robe. Wrinkles framed his mouth, hinting of a man who often smiled. "I'm Prior Rigby," he said, his eyes trained on the royal signet embroidered on Jarek's collar.

Jarek offered his hand. "I am Magus Jarek Verity, Sorcerer of the Court."

"Well met, sir." The churchman's eyes drifted back to Jarek's signet. "If I may ask, what concern has the Court for our small island parish?"

"None. My presence here is unofficial. I seek an orphaned kinsman whom I've never met. Recent documents I've uncovered suggest he may have been raised here within your grounds."

The Prior cocked his head. "Apologies, but we have no resident here named Verity, nor have we ever."

"That's to be expected; my sister's marriage name was Smithy."

The priest blinked. He looked Jarek over, appraising him. "That would have to be Gresham Smithy."

Jarek's pulse quickened. Did this man know his nephew?

"He attends our cadet institute." Jarek found that surprising. Typically, only sons of the wealthy were trained as military officers—never heretic orphans. "They're quartered within walking distance. If you'd care to make yourself comfortable," he gestured to a sofa, "I'll send for him."

"That is most gracious of you. Gramercy."

Jarek watched the Prior leave. The fellow seemed affable enough, especially for a churchman. But how many not-so-amicable clergy were running about? He peeked down the corridor but spotted none.

He paced the room. On the far wall was a mural portraying the One Star showering the world with its aethers. Its plaque read: 'The Blessed God Star.' He shook his head. What other distortions of truth had been taught to his nephew? The sooner he left this repository of misinformation, the better. He resumed his pacing, but it did little to settle his unease.

Prior Rigby returned, escorting a young man dressed in red tunic and black leggings. He had a sword strapped at his side. Jarek had seen others similarly dressed on his ride here. He guessed this must be standard cadet attire. Tall and broad of shoulder, he had pleasing features. Not surprising, given his roots. If this truly was his nephew, Bronwyn would be proud.

"Here's your visitor, Gresham. Meet Magus Jarek Verity, of the Royal Court."

The young man's heels snapped together. "Sir. Cadet Gresham," he said, his expression a mix of wariness and perplexity. "You wished to speak with me?"

Gresham. Had Bronwyn named him that, or was it the Church? He was well mannered. Jarek liked that. When they shook, his grip was firm, and although Gresham had Damián's physique, he had his mother's eyes. So much so, it made Jarek's heart ache just looking at them. Yes, this truly was his nephew. "You're built like your father."

Gresham's eyes widened. "You knew my father?" he asked, incredulous.

"I met him only a handful of times. It's your mother I know well. She is—was—my sister."

Gresham stiffened and stepped back, appraising Jarek, looking skeptical. "You claim us family?"

Jarek laughed. "If but one man can constitute a family, then yes, I make that claim. Your grandmother died birthing your father, leaving him an only child. And I'm your mother's only first kin." He placed a hand on Gresham's shoulder, "I can't begin to express my joy at finding you."

Reaching a hand for the chair behind him, Gresham sank onto its cushion, his expression softening. "If what you claim is true, your joy pales compared with mine." He sat, staring at Jarek, shaking his head. "I have family. Can you tell me of my parents, and what became of them?"

Jarek sat beside the lad. "Of course. Your father was a blacksmith; your mother a sorceress." Gresham's eyes flared at that statement. Jarek went into great detail about his sister, sprinkling his tale with what little he knew of Damián. As their talk progressed, his nephew relaxed enough to chuckle when told how his mother used to chase Jarek with garden snakes, knowing how he feared them. "Snakes, heights, enclosed spaces; I could never abide any of them."

Jarek paused, having forestalled the inevitable long enough. "You ask what became of them. I've no firsthand knowledge of the incident, but I've studied your father's trial notes in depth. The One Church charged your mother with heresy, most likely for practicing forbidden arts." He studied the boy's reaction, wondering how he'd respond to this subtle reproach of the very institution that had nurtured him, but Gresham seemed too hungry for information to react. "When the Chevaliers came to arrest her, your father intervened. Armed only with his smithy's hammer, he faced five armed men. When the fracas ended, three were dead; including your father."

This telling pained Jarek, as if he were witnessing the encounter firsthand. He could only imagine its effect on his nephew, who sat frozen, listening, showing no outward emotion. "The Chevaliers seized her. Where she was taken, I cannot say, or even if she yet lives. I prefer to believe the latter. I've made it my life's mission to find her and gain her release." He gave Gresham a sheepish look. "A task at which I've thus far failed miserably."

Gresham ran his hand through his hair. "Until this day I believed myself to be without family. Now, not only do I have an uncle, but my mother may yet live too." He met Jarek's gaze. "If that is true, I'd like to help with your search."

The idea of teaming with the lad was something Jarek had never contemplated. It appealed to him, surprisingly so. Eyes watering, he swallowed, wetting his throat. "I relish that prospect. If I gain knowledge of her whereabouts, rest assured, I'll come fetch you," Jarek placed his hand on Gresham's knee, "and we'll seek her together."

Gresham's hand found Jarek's. "I'd appreciate that, sir."

He was starting to like the lad already. "According to the trial notes, when your mother was taken, Prior Rigby's orphanage took over your rearing. The rest you know better than me."

Jarek glanced at the knapsack he'd brought, then strode to the door. After checking to ensure no one was within earshot, he returned to his seat. "This is from your father's trial," he said, carefully emptying the knapsack's contents on the table. "When a life is lost during an arrest, the Law requires a hearing." Sitting, he lifted a parchment out of the pile and handed it to Gresham. "This is a copy of those proceedings."

Gresham's voice caught as he read its opening line. "Damián Smithy and his wife Bronwyn." He looked at Jarek. "Before today I'd not known my parents' given names; such knowledge makes them more real. Thank you."

"There's more." Jarek picked up a small box. "As you see, this box bears your father's name." He slid it toward Gresham. "It's yours now. Show it to no one, for I violated uncounted laws in taking it."

Gresham looked inside at what were likely the only surviving remnants of his heritage. Many was the time Jarek had studied those contents. It contained Gresham's parents' rings and his father's hammer and belt. The young man's mouth opened as if to say something, but then closed. He picked up the larger of the rings and slipped it onto his finger. "My fingers are larger than most, yet my father's ring fits me perfectly."

Jarek picked up a smaller ruby-crested ring with an image of the One Star embedded in its center. "As I said, I've found nothing of what became of your mother, but this was hers," he said, handing it to Gresham. "Only magi achieving the rank of Master are issued rubied rings like this. Have you ever sensed the Gift in yourself?"

Gresham took the ring. "No sir, I'm but a simple soldier. The arts are beyond my ken."

"Perhaps not. We should assess you. There's a test they conduct at arts universities. I understand there's one near here."

"Thank you, sir, but what use has a soldier for the arts?"

Jarek shrugged. "You might be surprised, but it's your decision. Let me know if you suffer a change of heart."

Jarek stood. "I've taken enough of your time and have a young man outside waiting for me. I have other business to attend while I'm here." Had the Spymaster arrived yet? If so, what assignment did he have? "Once that's done, how about we dine together?"

Gresham stood. "I'd like that, sir."

Jarek shook his head. "No more sirs… call me Uncle. I'll contact you as soon as I've attended my tasks."

Smiling, Gresham squeezed Jarek's hand. "Until that supper—Uncle."

Gresham escorted Jarek out of the building, bid his goodbye, and with knapsack in hand, returned to his soldier's hall. Jarek paused, lighting his pipe, thinking how astonishingly well things had gone with his nephew.

He was about to seek out Hagley when Prior Rigby hailed him. "Magus Verity, how went your talk with Gresham?"

"Far better than I could have hoped. I'm in your debt. Gramercy."

Prior Rigby shook his head. "You've nothing to thank me for." He shrugged. "It's too bad you arrived when you did, you narrowly missed an opportunity to meet our Grand Inquisitor."

Jarek frowned. "Grand Inquisitor? That's a title I've not heard before."

Prior Rigby touched his palms together. "Apologies. The title is new. It's how we are to address the new head of the Chevaliers."

The Chevaliers! So the bastards had a new commander. He'd best learn more. "Do you know this man's name?" he asked, feigning politeness.

Prior Rigby clasped his hands together. "It would be improper for one of the clergy to address him by anything but Your Grace. However," he said, cocking his head. "I do seem to recall having once heard... ah!" He snapped his fingers. "Kolton; that's his name. He's due to arrive here later this week," Prior Rigby said, beaming ear to ear.

Rance Kolton! That obsequious ass now headed the Chevaliers? No wonder Suzerain had so readily granted Jarek leave to come search for his nephew. They wanted him here to spy on his old nemesis. Who better than a former schoolmate? Jarek felt like a token in a great game of castles. It did, however, explain the Spymaster's pending arrival. "I'm curious, what interest has he here?"

"Each year the Chevaliers come to recruit from our graduating cadets." He pressed the fingers of each hand together, "Who knows, maybe Gresham will have the good fortune to be chosen."

The Prior's words brought to mind the gypsy's augury, 'In days soon to come, you are fated to experience both great joy and extreme dismay.' Was she right? Jarek couldn't imagine a more horrible prospect than finding kin only to lose him to the clutches of the Chevaliers. "We can only hope for such an honor," he said, looking around. The clergyman who'd first greeted him stood not far away, scowling his way. Ever were churchmen the bane of the magi, and Kolton and his Chevaliers were on their way. "Alas, the hour is late," he said, smiling at the Prior, "and I've yet to secure lodging."

He left in search of Hagley, finding him at the troughs. "Where to now, sir?" Hagley asked as Jarek approached.

"I need to find an inn. Is there one you recommend?"

"Most mainlanders prefer the Sleeping Dragon."

"The Sleeping Dragon it is then," he said, hopping into the wagon.

As they headed for town, he pondered all that had just transpired: The joy of finding his nephew, offset by the deplorable news of Kolton's pending arrival; and even worse, the prospect of Gresham becoming a Chevalier.

"Sir?" Hagley said, interrupting his thoughts, "In Portsmouth you mentioned something about speaking with my headmaster about a third trial."

"Ah, that I did, that I did. But not this day. I am travel weary and in need of rest."

"Tomorrow then?"

Jarek found Hagley's insistence amusing. But then, with the prospect of gaining his robes at stake, he could hardly blame him. "How about you come fetch me after I break my morning fast?"

A Promise Kept

Lavan turned the page, taking care not to damage the delicate sheepskin. His eyes roamed the parchment, absorbing its author's every word. Reading Great Age history was like rummaging a treasure trove; if you weren't diligent you risked overlooking some gem of wisdom. This tome chronicled the Sorcerers War and the havoc brought on by the ancient's reckless use of the arts. It resulted in constraints still in place today—restrictions Lavan considered wholly unnecessary. Arts, when coupled with caution, need not be dangerous.

Hungry to prove his point, he probed each page, looking beyond what was written for secrets unsaid, hoping to find a good argument for easing those rules. A knock disrupted him. A young man stepped into his library hoisting a sheathed weapon. "Your pardon headmaster, a courier just delivered this. Master Kagen said you'd want to see it straight away."

Lavan's breath caught. Turpin's sword had finally arrived. He'd received word of the precious find a fortnight earlier, along with the scroll found with it. He hurried to relieve the young man of what was the first Great Age relic unearthed since Lavan had succeeded old Kagen as the university's headmaster.

He eased the blade from its sheath. Rotating it, he examined it. Fashioned from opal, the pommel balanced the weapon perfectly. Dragons embossed its hilt and twisting serpents crawled down its blade, their tongues lapping at the tip. Its polished sheen gave testament as to why it had taken so long to arrive—the scholars had been attentive.

"Thank you—that will be all." Dismissed, the young man bowed and turned to leave. "Wait! Have Mistress Genevieve meet me in the relic vault." Responsible for logging the university's relics, she'd need to catalog this latest acquisition.

From the damaged scroll delivered earlier, Lavan knew the weapon was enchanted. Now, with sword in hand, perhaps he could sleuth out its secrets, something rarely done with Great Age relics.

What secrets did it hold? Finding out would require diligence. Anxious to begin, he headed for the relic vault.

Once a high lord's estate, the university now served a higher purpose as training ground for aspiring young sorcerers. His footsteps echoed off its stone-wrought floors as he wound through the university's labyrinth of corridors. Carved window holes dotted its walls, their only adornments. Built with protection in mind, iron bars blocked any opening wide enough to crawl through. Lavan reached the darkened, windowless stairwell that led down to the relic vault. Buried below ground, its designer's intent was to make its discovery difficult.

He muttered an incantation. Instantly a ball of light burst into existence, hovering above him. He continued down the sloping pathway until a prickly tingle crawled up the back of his neck, making his hairs stand; the signal he'd reached the hallowed room. He stopped. A reveal spell exposed its hidden doorway and he stepped inside. Light from his globe danced off the relic-laden counters, casting a kaleidoscope of colors across the ceiling. The chill from its masonry walls mixed with the acrid stench of centuries-old sorcery to assault his sharply honed senses. He held his breath, waiting for the feeling to wane. It was the toll the gifted paid upon entering the vault.

Once his trembles ceased, he intensified his globe and the colors faded. A library of scrolls filled one side of the room, tables of relics the other. He walked its aisles, assessing the room's treasures. The university had been collecting relics for decades. Theirs was the greatest collection of its kind, and as its headmaster, their mysteries were now his to fathom, to hopefully restore some lost art or knowledge to the present day and perhaps accomplish something worthy of his office.

One table held rings and amulets, each harboring its own special knack or enchantment, none of which he had so far comprehended. He stopped at a bench to fondle two tiny orbs. Thumbnail sized, this matched pair allowed its bearers to mind-speak with one another.

The next table held weapons. He laid Turpin's sword next to its scroll he'd placed there earlier. He ran his hand along its sheath, wondering at its secrets.

A knock disrupted his concentration. "Yes?" he called; his gaze fixed on the weapon.

Mistress Genevieve entered. "You sent for me?"

He glanced her way. "Turpin's sword finally arrived. You'll need to record it."

"Of course," she said, nodding. "Also, you've a most important visitor waiting—a Sorcerer of the Court. What should I tell him?"

"Bring him here!"

She looked around the room. "Are you sure?"

"Of course. What secrets here can't be shared with a Court Sorcerer?"

Minutes later Genevieve was back. She gestured to her side as if to introduce someone, looking baffled. No one was there. Then, before their eyes, a man suddenly appeared out of nothingness, grinning from ear-to-ear. Genevieve jumped back with a screech.

"Jarek?" Lavan asked, looking every bit as stunned as Genevieve. He hadn't seen his friend in years.

"None other," Jarek said, spreading his arms. He turned to Genevieve, "Mistress, may we have some privacy?"

Composed now, she gave Lavan a questioning look. He nodded. "As you wish."

Lavan studied his old schoolmate. His once-black hair had surrendered to streaks of grey, and he'd added twenty-plus years of post-school girth to a frame that was already taller and broader than most. Perhaps Jarek was thinking much the same of him. He lacked Jarek's size and paunch, but his hair was just as grey, albeit, he had far less of it.

Jarek's eyes widened as he stepped into the room.

"It happens to anyone gifted who enters the vault, likely because of the concentration of aethers here. It passes quickly." The two men embraced. "I see you've not lost your sense for flair—or jests. That was quite the entrance you made. I feared Genevieve might piss herself. I know I would have had you appeared beside me out of nowhere. I'm curious, how did you do that?"

"I merely released the cloaking spell I was using. After the Mistress told me who her headmaster was, I simply couldn't resist the prank."

Lavan shook his head. "Your knowledge of magic's intricacies exceeds me."

Jarek guffawed. "Hardly! But my discipline does. You should consider it sometime."

"Ah, so you're here to evangelize discipline; I've often wondered how royal lapdogs fill their days."

Jarek scowled. "Lapdogs! A Court Sorcerer's duty is to protect his king and do his biddings, as opposed to doing whatever one pleases—as some do." He looked around. "Such as playing with this collection of toys you've garnered here."

"They're hardly toys. And I don't 'play' with them—I examine them with the hope of learning their secrets."

Jarek picked up one of the relics—a jeweled dagger. "I suspect there's more play involved than you admit; you were never one to abide by the rules."

"And you were ever afraid to break them," Lavan said, taking away the knife and placing it back where Jarek had gotten it. "We both made our choices: you, the propriety of the Suzerain Court; me the freedom of the isles."

"Choices need not be forever." Jarek countered, picking up another relic.

Lavan took this one from him too. "How about we go to my study and renew acquaintances over a game of Castles?"

"Why? Ever did you beat me at it."

Soon they were in Lavan's study, staring at one another across a game board. "So," Jarek asked, making his opening move, "what have you been up to these many years?"

"As of late," Lavan said, countering Jarek's move, "I've been studying the Great Age magi. I've concluded their vast powers weren't innate, that they achieved them by focusing the aethers."

"And what, pray tell, does focusing aethers mean?"

Lavan paused, formulating his explanation. "If our world attracts the aethers, it follows that other heavenly bodies do too. Every few years our three moons align. When this happens, I believe their collective pull might focus the aethers to a common point. If one were to stand at this nexus, I believe the strength of his Gift would be magnified to something akin to that of the ancients. I've devised an experiment that I hope will prove it."

Jarek made another move. "Why in demons' hells would you want such power? Have you forgotten those Great Age magi nearly obliterated themselves?"

"Bah! Having knowledge and misusing it are two different things—if I exercise proper caution, I'll be perfectly safe. I simply want to study the aethers in their concentrated form."

There was a pause in their prattle as each made a series of moves. "Ha!" Jarek whooped, capturing one of Lavan's pieces. Grinning, he leaned back. "Your curiosity has always exceeded your prudence. Why are you never content leaving things the way they are—why must you constantly seek out something new?" He shook his head. "Assume your theory to be true, were you to touch such power, it would be sensed by everyone gifted within leagues of here. I just heard the Chevaliers are coming to your isles. Do as you plan, and their Clerics will sense a disturbance in the aethers. You'll have them pounding your door claiming you violated some holy law, and likely charge you with heresy like they did with Bronwyn. This experiment of yours plays right into the One Church's hands."

Lavan's gut constricted at the mention of Bronwyn, despite the passing of years. "You were ever the worrier," he said with a dismissive wave. "Every headmaster before me has in some way bettered the arts. This experiment you so readily belittle, could very well be my contribution."

"Go on," Jarek said, studying the board move Lavan just made.

"Each moon will create a new focus point—a nexus of its own. The first one happens tomorrow night, with two more to follow shortly thereafter. It takes place not far from here. It's too great an opportunity to miss. Instead of making disparaging remarks, why don't you be my friend of old and assist me?"

Jarek let loose a laugh. "Tomorrow, eh? I still think it's folly, but you're right, friends should help one another."

"Then you will?" Lavan said, driving his knight's sword through Jarek's king.

Jarek sighed. "Why do I even play this with you? You win every time." He leaned back, shaking his head. "Yes, my friend, I'll help you."

Lavan grasped his hand. "Thank you."

"Truth be known," Jarek said, seeming like the Jarek of old. "I rather like the idea of us working together once more. It evokes fond memories of our university days."

Lavan laughed. "I'm sure Master Gil's twisting in his grave at that prospect. Remember that imp we loosed in his quarters?"

"How could I forget? It took us days to put things back in order."

"Yes, but doing so kept us from getting expelled."

The two took turns recounting the various pranks they'd played to torment their old mentor, several bringing peals of laughter. When it finally died down, Lavan asked, "I'm curious, if you didn't know I was headmaster here, what brought you?"

"Right after my ship docked in Portsmouth, I met a most interesting lad who claimed he'd studied here but failed both his trials. In talking with him, he seemed shorter on confidence than talent." He lay his king down in surrender. "I promised him I'd speak to his headmaster to see if I could get him a third trial. His name is Hagley. A nice fellow, the sort who could prove a credit to our guild."

"I'll speak with the schoolmasters about him. If they agree with your assessment, I'll grant him that chance." He moved his game pieces back to their starting positions. "That explains why you came to the university, but not what brought you to the islands."

"I found out Bronwyn had a son, back before she was taken—on this very island. I came to find him."

Lavan's gut tightened once more at the mention of her name. He'd loved her dearly. "Was the father of this boy the same fellow who caused her to break off our betrothal?"

"Yes," Jarek said, looking anguished, "Damián was the boy's father. I wish she'd chosen you over him—we'd be family now if she had."

Lavan grasped Jarek's hands. "I feel as if we are, anyway."

"As do I."

Bronwyn had been so beautiful; way too much so for a homely man like him to covet. "The gods had other plans for me. Instead, they brought me here to do what I love. How can a man be angry at that?" He reset Jarek's game pieces too. "I'm curious; why wait all these years to seek him out?"

"I only just learned of his existence—from a parchment in the Royal Library."

"I can't believe she never let you know."

"She didn't correspond with Suzerain. You know how the Magi Council feels about the gifted marrying the mundane. Still, I'm saddened she didn't let me know she was with child." Jarek pursed his lips. "Perhaps she was waiting until she'd safely delivered, and her arrest somehow foiled her plans." Jarek stood, his face lighting up. "The good news is that I found him! His name is Gresham. He's training to be a soldier right here in Stalwart."

"What marvelous news," Lavan said, clapping his hands. "When do I get to meet him?"

Jarek winked. "Right after we conduct this damned experiment of yours. If this Nexus of yours happens tomorrow, when do we leave?"

"It's a full day's travel to get there. Dawn would be best."

"I'm not sure I can get here from Stalwart that early."

"Stalwart? Nonsense! You're spending the night here as my guest."

"Then dawn it is." Jarek placed a hand on his shoulder. "With the two of us teaming again, what could possibly go wrong?"

Havoc

Jarek inhaled, savoring the crisp morning air. He was at the stables bedecked in riding attire, finally out of those damned robes, waiting for Lavan. "I want you to look like a representative of the court," Spymaster Booker had insisted the morning Jarek left Suzerain. He supposed he'd find out why once Booker arrived. Kolton likely figured into the puzzle somehow.

He scoured the area. The only other person here was a man repairing a broken wagon spoke. Jarek spied a stick propped against a nearby post. Since it was roughly the size of a sword, he picked it up, thinking how remiss he'd been about practicing his fencing. Pointing it toward the post, he stepped through the required poses. Engarde; lunge; ballestra; parry; riposte. Over and over he repeated the moves, his vigorous efforts forming sweat on his brow. Engarde; parry; riposte.

"Gods, Jarek, stop before you frighten that poor post to death." It was Lavan, arriving late as usual.

Twisting around, he pointed the stick at Lavan. "Beware of your taunts sir, or after I dispatch that post, you'll be next."

Lavan raised his hands. "I yield, please spare me that poor thing's fate." He lowered his arms. "Tell me, are royal sorcerers so lacking in the arts they must rely on mundane skills?"

Jarek lunged his stick at Lavan. "A wise protector needs more than one tool in his arsenal to defend his liege. Fate may not allow time to cast a spell." Jarek lowered his stick, looking it over. "Why, if pressed, this stick might even suffice. Besides, swordplay is invigorating—it keeps one in fighting condition."

Lavan pointed at Jarek's stomach. "Then you've clearly been remiss as of late."

Jarek grabbed his ample belly and laughed. "That I have; that I have."

"You seem in unusually good spirits."

"And why not?" Jarek answered, looking around. "It's a glorious day, and I've shed those unwieldy robes you so love to wear." He looked down at his tunic and leggings. "I find this far more fitting for conducting an experiment."

"Ahh, possibly more fitting, but far less comfortable." Lavan said, shaking his loose hanging robes. "Are you ready to undertake our adventure?"

"Most definitely. In fact, I'm getting impatient."

Lavan glanced toward the man fixing the wheel. "As soon as Goodricke has our wagon ready, we leave. In the meantime, I have something to show you I think you'll enjoy."

He pulled a necklace out of his robes. It held a pendant. Whereas most magi embedded their Master rubies in rings, Lavan had opted for that pendant, maintaining a ring could disrupt one's spell casting, inviting ill fortune. For a man whose beliefs were otherwise steeped in logic, Lavan's superstitions where luck was concerned had always baffled Jarek.

Lavan snapped open his pendant's bail, pulled out his ruby, and removed one of two thumb-nail sized crystals he had stored behind it. He handed one to Jarek. "Place this behind your ruby."

"To what end?"

"Just do it."

Jarek no sooner had it in place when the words *Now aren't you glad you did?* blasted his mind. "I heard that!" he said, giving Lavan a wide-eyed stare.

"Of course you did," said a beaming Lavan. "Now you try it."

"How?"

"Simply direct your thoughts toward me... ...*like this.*"

Like this?

"Bravo! See how easy that was."

Jarek stood, mouth agape. "Amazing."

"Isn't it? Since today's journey's a long one, I thought we could while away its drudgery experimenting with these."

Jarek studied his orb. 'It's too bad Master Gil is no longer with us. These could have provided great sport." Goodricke's approaching wagon caught his attention. "Perhaps we still can. How well does your man take a jest?"

Lavan guffawed. "I'm thinking he's too large a man to trifle with, but then, so are you."

"Are you ready, milords?" Goodricke asked, climbing off the wagon.

Lavan hadn't exaggerated. The wagoner stood a full hand taller than him. He was trim and well-muscled, his long blonde hair reminiscent of the two Nosarians Jarek encountered on Portsmouth's dock. Lavan was right, Goodricke wasn't a man to be taken lightly. "And here I thought I was tall."

"This is Goodricke, my man-servant," Lavan said, then gestured toward Jarek. "Goodricke, this is my friend Jarek Verity, Magus of the Suzerain Court."

Goodricke tipped his head. "An honor, milord."

Lavan climbed into the wagon. "Come. Time is fleeting, and we have a long journey before us."

It was a two-horse wagon. Thrice a man's length and half that wide. The driver's bench would normally seat three, but with two as large as Goodricke and him, there was no way they'd all fit. With Goodricke driving and Lavan guiding, Jarek dutifully climbed in back.

"We're going to those wastelands beyond Pembok, Goodricke," Lavan instructed. "The Nexus will focus right along its coastline."

Once everyone was settled, the wagon team ambled out the main gate, Lavan's experiment officially underway.

Things went smoothly until they left the well-travelled roadways near Stalwart. Bump after bump now rocked the creaking wagon, banging Jarek against sideboard and backboard, quickly making him rue his seating choice. Worse, he had to either kneel on the hard, wooden floor, or sit facing backwards with no view of the road ahead.

Judging from the comfortable chatter up front, neither of the other two men shared his discomfort. Bored and uncomfortable, he decided on some mischief. *You ready to play with these toys of yours, and have a little sport with your manservant?* he asked, directing the thought toward Lavan.

All right, let me take the lead. "Goodricke, I should warn you to keep your thoughts shielded, lest Magus Verity read them."

Goodricke chuckled. "Now that's one you've not tried on me before, milord, but I've been around long enough to know when I'm the target of a jest."

"What, you doubt me?" He nodded at Jarek. "Ask him something he couldn't possibly know, and I'll wager he'll come up with the right answer."

Goodricke gave Lavan a dubious look. "I'll not wager, but I'll play along." He twisted around toward Jarek. "All right, sir, what did I do before serving Master Lavan?"

The game was afoot. Work or not, their game would at least take his mind off his misery.

He was a sailor. I bought his indenture.

Keeping in character, Jarek pressed hands to temples and closed his eyes. "I see ocean—and a ship." He paused, as if in deep thought. "Ah, it comes to me now. You were a mariner, but not wholly by choice. You were indentured."

Goodricke's eyes widened. He cast a suspicious glance Lavan's way.

Lavan shrugged. "I told you. Ask him something else."

Goodricke contemplated a moment. "All right, milord, besides driving the wagon, in what way did Master Lavan think I could assist him?"

He has this seafaring instrument that reads the stars. It will help us pinpoint the Nexus.

Jarek scratched his chin. "You brought something with you— from your seafaring days. A device that will help hone the Nexus' location."

Goodricke's jaw dropped. "How…" he muttered, shaking his head. "Only sailors know of tritants." He shook his head, eyeing Lavan, "I've no idea how you're doing this, milord, but you'll not convince me Magus Verity is reading my thoughts."

It was late morning when they reached Pembok, where they stopped briefly to sup. Later, a few miles short of Broughton, they angled off the road and headed into the wastelands. Small woody plants and stunted trees littered the terrain, forcing a meandering route. They successfully circumvented every obstacle until they reached a canyon. A crevasse, perhaps a hundred feet deep, stretched side-to-side as far as they could see, leaving them no choice but to backtrack. "Turnabout Goodricke—find another route, and quickly, lest we be late."

"I see you're planning skills are as fine as ever," Jarek chided.

"If I want a cockalorum's opinion, I'll ask for it."

They eventually skirted the canyon—albeit, after losing precious time. Their alternate route wasn't significantly better. Endless ravines forced a serpentine path over rough, rocky terrain. Boulders were everywhere, one even breaking a linchpin. Fortunately, the wagon carried a spare, and after yet another delay, they were able to press on.

Jutting rock formations dotted the landscape, slowing progress. Worse, the skies were darkening and moons rising. Juno had crested the horizon, well on her way to joining Ceres and Minerva. Their convergence would trigger the Nexus. They needed to hurry.

Around dusk they reached the coastline. "Praise the gods, we're here," Lavan shouted, hopping off the wagon, surveying the surroundings. Jarek joined him.

They were atop a bluff overlooking the sea, the crashing surf audible despite being far below them. Dark, windy and foreboding, the place appeared lifeless. A waft of brine and prairie sage assailed Jarek's senses. Despite it being early summer, the night had the crispness of autumn, and a deepening mist threatened to block their view of the emerging moons.

Fighting the buffeting winds, Jarek walked to cliff's edge and dared a peek. His head spun. The dizzying drop spelled sure death. How he hated heights. An icy gust caused him to lose his balance. He fell to his knees, grasping rocks, soil, even grass, desperate for any handhold. Heart racing, he crept back from the ledge.

"There!" Lavan shouted, pointing toward an arch that bridged the gap between two nearby cliffs. "Quickly Goodricke, calculate where it will focus."

Scurrying to the back of the wagon, Goodricke retrieved his tritant. Roughly the size of a crossbow, he placed in on the wagon seat and aimed it skyward. Sighting something of interest, he began adjusting dials and levers. After repeating this process several times, he pointed. "There, about fifty cubits beyond where you stand."

Lavan scoured the area. "Jarek, look," he said pointing. "On the far side of that archway, nestled in those shadows. It's the only possibility."

Squinting, Jarek looked. "All I see is a rocky cliff."

"There, just below Juno. A cave! It's the only thing within fifty paces, so it has to be the nexus point."

Jarek still couldn't see what Lavan did, but his night vision had never been good.

"Come, we haven't much time," Lavan urged, hustling back to the wagon. Grabbing a pair of knapsacks, he slung one over his shoulder, and handed the other to Jarek. "Let's get to that cave."

They'd have to cross the archway to reach it. The thought of doing so had Jarek's head spinning. "I'm not good with heights. Perhaps I should stay with Goodricke."

"Nonsense!" Lavan barked, stepping onto the arch, edging his way across. "Come on," he insisted, motioning Jarek to follow. "You know as well as I do, you're too curious to stay behind."

His friend knew him well. After a day of anticipation, there was no way he'd miss this Nexus, especially after coming all this way. Taking a deep breath, he eased his way onto the archway, careful to avoid any downward glance. "If I fall to my death, may my ghost come back to haunt you."

"Ghosts, bah! Who believes in such things?"

Jarek did. A facet of his Gift was speaking with the recently dead, something he'd done on more than one occasion; something for which the Chevaliers would happily charge him with heresy.

After what seemed an eternity, he finally stood safely beside Lavan, directly in front of the cave. The rising moons were close to merging now, creating a strange light that washed over them in waves, distorting his vision. It's dizzying effect was strangely reminiscent of what he'd experienced stepping inside the relic vault—where the aethers had been so overwhelming.

They entered the cave, following a path that spiraled downward, losing itself in darkness. They eased forward, the steep gradient and loose gravel making footing chancy. Lavan hadn't taken twenty steps when pebbles broke from beneath his heel. He fell, sliding down the embankment. Jarek reached out. "Grab my hand!"

Lavan took it. "Praise you!" he said, struggling back to his feet. "Step with care."

The two trudged deeper. The farther they went, the darker it grew. There was no way they'd be able to see the moons from in here, no way to test Lavan's Nexus. Were they even in the right place, or were they squandering their only chance to view it? How trustworthy were Lavan's calculations and Goodricke's instrument?

Light appeared, shining from a hole just ahead. They peered down at a vertical drop to a moonlit beach below. Several cubits deep, a fall here could prove fatal. Gods how he hated heights.

"Any ideas as to how we get down there?" Jarek asked. "Perhaps roping ourselves together?"

Lavan scoffed. "The very sort of mundane solution I'd expect from a royal lap dog. Is that the limits of your art?" He held out his hand. "Take hold and grip tightly, let me show you how a real magus deals with such situations." He chuckled. "Although its theory is sound, I'd be remiss to not point out that I've never tried this before."

Jarek rolled his eyes. "Of course."

"Do you want to see this Nexus or not?"

"Just do it!"

Lavan chanted, and a sense of weightlessness swept over Jarek. His stomach lurched as he and Lavan lifted off the ground. He held his breath, heart palpitating, as they drifted out and downward, floating feather-like toward the moonlit patch below.

Moments later they were standing in a small ravine, their feet once again on solid ground. "And you said I was one for flair," Jarek mumbled, trying to regain his equilibrium.

The strange moonlight was even more intense down here. And although they were out of the wind, it felt cooler here. Wherever a rock stuck out, a shadow formed beneath it, giving the tiny gorge an eerie look. Its stone walls were layered with orange, interspersed with tan. Lichens and small shrubbery scaled their craggy walls to either side, which merged at a pond that gave the place a dank smell.

Jarek walked to the waterhole. Kneeling, he dipped a hand into its waters and smelled it. It was freshwater not brine, likely what sustained the nearby plant life. He looked around. His duties had taken him to many exotic places, but none compared to this one. Had other Nexuses occurred here before to create this marvelously unique setting, or was this the first of its kind?

"Hurry, the Nexus happens soon," Lavan urged, upending his knapsack. A large stone and several crystals tumbled out. Roughly the size of a man's head, the stone's surface was filled with sparkling agate motes. "These crystals are Celestine. Exposure to the aethers makes them glow. The more concentrated the aethers, the brighter they shine."

Jarek emptied his pack. It held a pair of hammers.

By now shadows were dancing on the surrounding crags, heightening the canyon's strange feel. Off in the distance he could hear the crashing of surf—they were almost down to the sea. Blowing air on his chilled hands, Jarek's gaze sought the heavens. Minerva and Ceres now overlapped, and Juno was drawing close. Lavan's Nexus was imminent.

Lavan picked up the crystals, giving half to Jarek. "I'll stake this side of this pool; you do the far side."

Jarek waded through shallow waters to the far side of the pool. Running his fingers through his hair, he scouted out where best to place them. The two men set about tamping the crystals into the sand until the pond was encircled.

Done, Lavan sat back on his haunches and lit his pipe, his shaking hands barely allowing him to do it.

"I've never seen you fret so. What's the purpose of the stone and crystals? How is this experiment of yours supposed to work, anyhow?"

"I'm fretting out of dread that my experiment will fail—that we've trudged all this way for naught."

"Not to worry old friend—your theories always bear out. Now, about that explanation…"

"Once the Nexus begins, I'll levitate this stone over the water, keeping my aether flow constant. If as predicted, the Nexus focuses the aethers, the strength of my spell should increase, thus driving the stone skyward." He rotated the stone. "I chose it because of its reflective motes. They'll serve as a visual measure of the ebb and flow of the aether's strength. It's the same with the crystals; the brighter they glow, the greater the concentration of aethers."

Jarek shook his head. "You've thought of everything, haven't you?"

Light suddenly flared from the crystals. Color cascaded everywhere, as if a rainbow had shattered above them and was falling from the sky. Jarek sat staring in awe. What sort of thing was a Nexus, anyway? He rubbed his arms. The place had gotten dramatically colder. But despite the chill and that awful float down, seeing this amazing sight made it all worthwhile.

"It's begun," Lavan yelped, tossing the stone at the pond. Before it could hit, a waggle of his fingers pushed it to the center where he hovered it in place. Glancing Jarek's way, Lavan pulled out his amulet and he kissed his ruby. "For luck." Arms extended, he chanted. Swirling mist engulfed the stone, spinning it within a cloudy maelstrom. As the crystals burned brighter the glowing agate rose. It was now at shoulder height.

Jarek sat there, fascinated by what was unfolding before him.

The crystals exploded in a burst of light, and the agate leaped higher. "Yes!" Lavan yelled, hoisting his fists, watching the stone rise. Puffing his pipe, he gave Jarek an I-told-you-so grin.

Jarek simply gawked at the cavorting rock. Apparently, his friend had the right of it—maybe he was witnessing magic akin to that of the ancients.

The Nexus continued to strengthen Lavan's spell. But what were they learning here? Would this discovery indeed be the legacy Lavan hoped for?

Jarek's musings were suddenly interrupted by strange murmurings in his mind. What in all hells? It sounded like speech, but not any language he'd ever heard. Dim at first, it grew louder. It was a voice! He looked over at Lavan, who stared back at him looking every bit as confounded as he was.

Are you making those noises? Lavan asked.

No!

Who speaks? asked the mysterious voice—now speaking Common.

Jarek sat up, his heart pounding. Someone—or something, had joined them. He looked around, but saw no one.

Lavan was also looking. He'd heard it, too. *An excellent question. Who does speak, and where are you?* Lavan ventured.

The pond churned, bubbling, glowing an iridescent blue green. *I am here.*

Lavan backed away, looking aghast, as did Jarek, his skin crawling. The ripples faded, replaced by a macabre image of a face! A ghoulish one, buried deep within a cowl. The strange visage slowly filled the pool's surface, with no body visible. The creature was appalling.

Yes, I see you. Lavan answered. *Who and what are you, and how is it you appear before us?*

Shrouded under its hood, the thing's face was barely discernable. Enough showed however, to see a pair of glowing red eyes take in their surroundings. The beast's gaze flitted from Jarek to Lavan. *I'm a fellow practitioner of the arts, and if I may be so bold, one of no small merit. Knowing so little of those to whom I speak, I am reluctant to say more.* Its gaze settled on the crystals. *Who are you, and what antics are you about with those fiery gems?*

Jarek remained silent, trying to fathom the shimmering abomination before him. He could see right through its ghost-like image, down to the sands below. The wraith's gaze met Lavan's, waiting.

Jarek shook his head in a silent plea for his friend to say no more.

I'm headmaster of an arts university, he answered, paying Jarek no heed. *These 'antics' test this zenith of power before us, but you must answer my questions if you wish me to share more.*

The creature took Lavan's measure, as if the two were engaged in a game of Castles, each of them contemplating the other's next move. *A fair bargain. The first is simple; you may call me Zakarah.* Jarek wondered at the name, so unlike any he'd heard. *Divulgence of my location is… difficult. Think of it as 'elsewhere,' an alternate existence to your own. This 'zenith of power' as you call it, has removed the cumbers between our worlds, allowing my presence. So... ...whom do I address?*

The cowl masked Zakarah's expression. Jarek knew his scholarly friend was dangerously intrigued by this beast. *I am called Lavan, he's Jarek of the King's Court. Your turn, what brings you to this place?*

Shadowed images appeared at Zakarah's sides. Arms! He held them out, palms up, just below the water's surface. *The same agglomeration of aethers that drew you. How is it you assess it?*

Lavan looked toward Jarek. Puffing his pipe, he looked equal parts wary and enthralled. Jarek shook his head no. Lavan smiled, nodding yes. *We test our conjecture that an alignment of our moons will focus the aethers here, amplifying the Gift.*

I can assure you heavenly bodies do focus aethers, a postulate I have oft demonstrated in other elsewheres. Gnarled fingers of one hand touched those of his other. *Perhaps we might pool our knowledge... ...what say you to that?*

How so?

I would know more of those glowing shards, and of this university of yours.

Jarek thought the latter an odd request, one lacking good reason. His every instinct said to have no part of this repulsive creature. *Stop this folly,* he directed Lavan's way.

Zakarah's head snapped toward Jarek, giving him a hateful scowl.

Jarek's attention flew back to Lavan, who had crept back to pond's edge. *Are you sure of this?*

Lavan met his gaze. *It's all right.*

Save for his wandering eyes, Zakarah's image remained unmoving; his blurry countenance unchanging. It was as if he found this sort of encounter commonplace. What kind of creature was he? What powers were required for him to project himself here? Despite Zakarah's odious appearance, there was knowledge to be learned, an allure he feared his learned friend would find irresistible.

Lavan knelt by the pool and pointed at a crystal. *These gems gauge the aether's strength. As for the university, it's a place of learning. We store relics there, hypothesize magical theory, and train young sorcerers.* The crystals exploded light, blasting the agate higher. *We must hasten. Share what you will sir, but quickly!*

A smile painted the vile-looking visage—the first show of emotion since Zakarah's surprise appearance. *Good fortune blesses you, for kinesis is both my skill and my passion. Assist me and I'll show you its full potency.*

The agate now soared so high it was barely visible. *What would you have us do?* Lavan asked.

Quickly then, immerse one of those gems in the water.

Lavan upended a crystal, squinting against its intense glare. Shielding his eyes, he dipped it under the water's surface.

He screamed the instant it touched the water. With the spell levitating it disrupted, his agate plummeted, splashing into the water, disappearing beneath its surface. The resulting ripples blurred Zakarah's image.

Grabbing his hammer, Jarek splashed through the shallows, rushing to help. Grabbing Lavan's arm, he pulled him to his feet, but one foot remained ankle deep in the water. Gossamer threads entangled it. Jarek knelt, hammering at them. Instead of breaking, the spider-like webs encircled his wrist too.

A laugh echoed through his head. *Mayhap 'Jarek of the King's Court' is not so mighty as he thinks.*

Twisting the hammer, Jarek managed to break free, but by now, the strange netting had completely enveloped Lavan's leg. Grabbing Lavan by the wrist, Jarek rolled backwards, trying to pull him free.

Instead, some force pulled Lavan the opposite way. Lavan's hand slipped out of Jarek's grip. "Gods! Help me Jarek!" Lavan screamed as he slipped beneath the water's surface.

Jarek scrambled to his feet. Zakarah pointed a hand at him. A spell blasted his mind. Muscles twitched and gave way, collapsing him to his knees. Laughter flooded his mind—evil, hate-filled laughter as more diaphanous tendrils appeared, ensnaring his friend, pulling him ever deeper.

Lavan's dread was palpable as he slipped deeper and deeper into the watery abyss, his hand reaching, beseeching Jarek's aid, his expression was one of utter terror. *Gods Jarek, help me!*

It was Lavan's last plea.

His image shimmered, then faded into nothingness, his terrified mind-wail echoing briefly before it too, faded from Jarek's mind. "Lavan!" he screamed. "Gods Lavan, say something! What's happening?"

He tried using the orbs. *Lavan! It's Jarek—answer me*!

That plea too, went unanswered. He fell face-first in the sand. "No-o-o!" he screamed, sobs wracking his chest as he rocked back and forth, positive the look on Lavan's face would haunt him forever.

He heard footsteps pounding toward him. "Are you alright, milord?" Goodricke had somehow made his way down the shaft. "Where is Master Lavan?"

Jarek sat up, scanning the area. The crystals had dimmed—the Nexus having ebbed. He looked up. "He's gone! Seized by the foulest of beasts!"

Strategizing

Jarek sat in the wagon beside Goodricke watching the sun crest the ridge, but the dawn light failed to brighten his mood. Lavan gone—taken by that monster! How did that odious creature manage it? What powers did it wield? More importantly, where had it taken Lavan? In order to rescue him, Jarek needed answers, and right now he had none.

Thankfully, the university was in sight now. He'd gotten almost no sleep—poor Goodricke had gotten none. They trotted through the main gate. "Get some rest, milord," Goodricke urged, "I'll attend the horses. We've used them poorly."

Weary to the point of exhaustion, Jarek didn't argue. It was all he could do to open the university's heavy oak door. A sleepy-eyed acolyte greeted him. "Magus, may I assist you?"

"There's been a terrible incident. I need to speak with whoever's in charge in your headmaster's absence?"

"That would be Master Kagen."

"Then take me to him. It's urgent."

He followed the lad through the maze of corridors that connected the university's rooms and outbuildings. The young man stopped before an open door. "These are Master Kagen's quarters."

He spotted an old man poring over a tome. Dozens more cluttered the room. Some lay on tables and chairs, but the bulk of them were strewn about the floor. The room's only clear pathway led to a wine rack.

Jarek's escort left, and he stepped inside. Apparently hard of hearing, it wasn't until his shadow shaded Kagen's parchment that the white-haired old man realized he wasn't alone. Startled, he looked up. "I recognize that sigil on your tunic. You must be Lavan's Suzerain friend."

"I am. My name is Jarek Verity."

"Yes, yes, Lavan mentioned you. He said you'd be helping with his experiment. How did it go?"

Jarek cleared the books off the nearest chair and sat. "Disastrously."

Kagen spun his chair around, frowning. "Tell me."

Jarek proceeded to recount the experiment gone awry. Kagen sat silent, listening without interruption. "He just vanished, eh?" he asked once Jarek finished. "Where to, do you suppose?"

"To some elsewhere."

"Where and what is an elsewhere?"

"I've yet to work that out, but the beast spoke of elsewheres as if they were alternate planes of existence. It's consistent with The Law of Infinite Universes, so I find it plausible. I believe he somehow tapped the power of the Nexus to transport Lavan there."

Kagen's brows crinkled. "Even if you manage to locate this elsewhere, how do you propose bringing Lavan back?"

"I've been mulling that question since Zakarah took him. Lavan said each moon would generate its own Nexus, that two more would soon follow. If the power of the first one drew this creature, the others might too. I plan to be there to confront him, to find out what he's after; to see if there's something he'll take in exchange for Lavan."

"Not a great strategy, but at least it's a plan. Is there some way I can help?"

"Was anyone privy enough to Lavan's plans to tell me when and where the next Nexus will occur?"

Kagen stood. "I fear not. But Lavan's study has all his drawings. Perhaps there's enough there for us to puzzle it out."

Soon the two were poring over astral charts, mapping trajectories and calculating interceptions. By mid-day they'd concluded the second Nexus would occur seven days hence. The third would happen five days thereafter. All that remained was to pinpoint their exact locations.

Kagen spread a map over his table. Translating Lavan's notes, the two began mapping the moons' trajectories. "If I'm interpreting Lavan's scribbles correctly," Kagen began, "the upcoming Nexus will focus between these marshlands and that mountain range." He leaned close enough for his fading eyesight to read the map. "Some cataclysm must have created those mountains," he said, dragging his finger across the map, "and likely these atolls as well. Perhaps an eruption on this volcanic isle where the third Nexus will take place."

"Zakarah will either be at the second one or not. The location of the third one is of no consequence."

"Well, either way, both sites are in our islands. But getting to either place is equivocal at best. I've seen those atolls. They make any sea approach too dangerous to consider. That means crossing this marsh, not a journey anyone would covet. No wonder maps of this area are scarce. I'll have Genevieve check our annals for any information we have on these locations." He hollered out the doorway. "Hagley!"

Moments later Hagley poked his head through the doorway. "Sir?" His eyes widened when he saw Jarek. "Magus Verity, good to see you again."

It was Master Kagen's turn to look surprised. "Hagley, please fetch Mistress Genevieve, we've need of her services."

Hagley left and Kagen shuffled to a nearby bench. Groping, he eased onto it. "I'll likely need help standing again, but not too soon if you don't mind. So, how is it you know young Hagley?"

"He provided me transport from Portsmouth. During the ride, I got the impression you'd expelled him. I told him I'd do my best to get him a third trial. Lavan promised to look into the matter, but now…"

"Hagley expelled? Hardly. It's true, however, he failed both his trials, despite a mind keener than most. I've tested him several times. His results are erratic. On some occasions he lights up the prism like few others can, but in times of stress—like facing the reviewing magi, there's nary a flicker. You know how critical confidence is in spell casting. Until he gains it, I fear he'll never earn his robes. Worse, he considers himself a failure. The irony is that he might even be extraordinarily gifted." Kagen shook his head, "But try as I may, I can't seem to isolate his facet. I've hired him as wagon driver. He thinks I did it out of pity, but unbeknownst to him, I'm subtly teaching him. I leave ever more complex spell books lying around in obvious places. They always disappear, only to reappear on my shelves days later."

Jarek cast a dubious glance at the room. "Shelves?"

Kagen waved his hand. "Well, wherever he found them. Anyway, he thinks to fool me, but it's really the other way around." He winked. "I'll make a sorcerer of him yet."

Jarek chuckled. "I have no doubt you will." He wandered over to the wine rack and hoisted a wineskin and smelled its contents. "Ah, a Roberdavy if my nose doesn't deceive me. It's the rage in Suzerain right now." Picking up a glass, he looked back at Kagen, "Do you mind?"

"Not at all. Please pour two. My greatest fear is that I die before I empty my cellar."

Jarek brought Kagen a drink and hoisted his own. "Here's to finding Lavan."

Kagen clanked their glasses together. "And to bringing him home."

They'd finished them by the time Hagley returned with Mistress Genevieve. "You sent for me?"

"Yes, we're wondering if you have anything documenting an area we're examining." Kagen showed her Lavan's map and the area in question, making no mention of his disappearance. She studied it. "This may take a while—it's not an area I'm familiar with."

"We're most urgent to see whatever you might find. Let's hope it won't take too long. When you return, bring Turpin's sword, Magus Verity has use of it."

"Do not worry, I'll find you something, even if I have to work through the night. The annals are sure to contain something useful."

Exhausted, Jarek returned to the quarters Lavan had given him. "Take heart my brother," he whispered. "I'm coming for you."

Lavan lacked all sense of time, place, or direction, save for spinning and tumbling. Despite his struggles to orient himself, the vortex he was caught in defied him. Where was he? Why was he alone? Where was Zakarah?

His confused turmoil ended abruptly when a deluge of liquid inundated him. He punched through its wetness, emerging above it like a surfacing whale. Momentum lost, he splashed back into water. Rising on trembling legs, he found himself waist-deep in a pond not unlike the one he'd just left. Thankfully, all hint of the strange webbing that had ensnared him was gone.

Despite being drenched, the surrounding heat seared both skin and lungs. Water drained off his face, clearing his vision. He scanned the area, struggling to deduce his whereabouts.

His mote-laden stone lay half-buried in mud at the water's edge. Although the pond seemed a twin to the one at the Nexus, nothing else looked familiar. Void of plant life, the place stank of sulfur. Jagged rocks, streaked with hues of brown and red, surrounded him. Heat waves rippled off them, distorting the surrounding air. Crimson skies overhead added to the place's alien sense. Was it even sky? Lacking sun, moon, or stars, it seemed more like a shimmering roof. What sort of hell had Zakarah taken him too, anyway?

"Look up there long enough and you'll find yourself dead—but only if you're lucky. Capture is far worse."

The voice came from behind him. Lavan wheeled about. There stood Zakarah. Half again as tall as a man, he had greenish skin awash with reddish-brown blotches that extended below elbows and knees.

Zakarah pushed back his cowl. His mouth stretched into a grin, exposing rows of jagged teeth and a forked tongue that seemed to probe the air with a mind of its own. Arms trembling, it was all Lavan could do to draw a breath. Despite the intense heat, cold crawled up his spine—Zakarah was a demon. He truly had been taken to hell.

A large cave loomed in the background a stone's throw away. Cages lined its walls, too many to count. Each held a captive, none any type of creature he'd seen before. Some looked dead, most others not far from it. All appeared bony and gaunt. Worst were their vacant stares, at least on those few who had the will to look Lavan's way.

Hissing, Zakarah made his way into the pond, his red eyes boring into Lavan. "Welcome to my elsewhere, Headmaster." The demon's laugh died abruptly as he scanned the skies. "Let us retire to my cave lest prying eyes discover us, something neither of us would enjoy." A gnarled finger propelled Lavan toward him. "Come," Zakarah encouraged, his tongue flitting about, "we have much to discuss."

It was only then Lavan noticed an empty cage with an open door—the one they were headed for. Zakarah's ensuing cackle evoked shudders that even a master sorcerer was helpless to bridle. Moments later he was in that cage—its door slamming behind him. As he looked around, that same look of helplessness he'd seen on the other prisoners' faces washed over him too.

Pursuit

Jarek sat picking at his morning meal, too worried about Lavan to have any real appetite, when Hagley burst into the refectory. "Magus! Master Kagen beckons you; Mistress Genevieve found something."

Foregoing the remainder of his meal, Jarek followed Hagley to Lavan's study. Kagen waited there, next to a cluttered table. "Ah, you're here!" he said, motioning Jarek over. "Question: as a child did your parents frighten you with stories of the Boggarts of Ariath?"

"I've not heard that tale."

"Here in the islands it's a common bogeyman tale. Ariath is the watery abode of ghastly beasts who, in the dark of night, whisk away misbehaving younglings and eat them."

"On the mainland the tales are of ogres, not boggarts."

Kagen handed him a scroll. "Genevieve found this. Based on what I just read, Ariath may actually exist."

Jarek looked at it. "I'm not versed in this ancient script. What does it say?"

"It's a scholar's account of the early exploration of our islands. Malg was the author's name. He was the ship's map maker and historian, charged with charting newly found lands. His scroll describes his encounter with a people from a place called A'ryth."

"Are you suggesting Ariath and this A'ryth are one and the same?"

Kagen nodded. "Its peculiar name simplified over time."

"That seems a bit far-fetched. If these A'rythians truly exist, surely someone would have encountered them again by now."

"Not necessarily," Kagen said, raising a finger. "I found one part of his recounting particularly interesting." He ran his finger down the scroll. "Ah, here it is. It chronicles Malg's exploration of that desolate bay across from Portsmouth. Listen to this: 'Much to our dismay, we found this freshwater inlet infested by beasts so vicious our crewman dubbed the area Foul Marsh. We lost several sailors to its brutes." Kagen looked up. "Here we have it, boggarts and Ariath sharing the same tale."

Jarek looked at the scroll. "A small coincidence doesn't make a tale true."

"There's more," Kagen said, setting it down. "Malg disdained his fellow crewmen, portraying them as marauders more interested in plunder than exploration. To support this opinion, he cites the violation of two A'rythian women by them. When the A'rythians demanded justice, the ship's captain refused. The following morning the mutilated bodies of the two sailors were found, their male parts severed. The A'rythians were never heard from again. Perhaps they remain isolated out of choice?"

"Even assuming that's true, what has it to do with finding Lavan's next Nexus?"

"This," he said, laying Malg's map beside the one they'd drawn their calculations on.

"Gods!" The locations of A'ryth and the upcoming Nexus were one in the same, and Malg's map showed far more details. It depicted an area even more rugged than they'd first surmised. "What a marvelous find. What are the chances of getting this copied? Malg's journal too."

"Our scribes are working on it as we speak."

※※※

Hagley scanned the corridor. Confident no one was watching, he slid the cinder slab aside, slipped into the concealed passageway behind it, and closed the block behind him. He conjured a light globe, one of his few reliable spells, and headed down the stairs—into his private world.

It was common knowledge that the university had once been some baron's manor, but few knew noblemen's households had hidden passageways that granted servants access to attend its rooms. It was his special secret.

So far, his explorations produced two considerable finds. The first was the tunnel that opened into a small canyon behind the university—his personal gateway in and out of the school. The other was learning the corridors had spy holes that allowed you peek into rooms.

He'd just overheard Master Kagen and Goodricke talking about a trip to Portsmouth. Their hushed voices hinted of something secret. Finding out about it was too tempting to resist.

He found the spy hole into Kagen's room and ever so slowly opened its slider. He peered inside. The two were there arguing with Magus Verity. "This undertaking is way too dangerous to involve Goodricke," Master Verity barked. "I'm going alone—on horseback if necessary."

Master Kagen shook his head. "Look at Malg's map," he said, pointing. "How are you going to traverse that swamp on a horse? It'd just become fodder for Malg's beasts. You need a boat!"

"I don't know the first thing about boats."

Kagen bounced his finger on the map. "Which is precisely why you need Goodricke. He was once a seaman."

Their talk of beasts and swamps quelled Hagley's interest. Although trips to Portsmouth were always adventures, what they were talking about sounded dangerous—and danger was something he always steered clear of. He closed the peek hole.

"Hagley!"

It was Kagen. Had he moved the slider too fast? Even if he had, how had the old coot known he was the one peeking through it?

"Hagley!" Kagen repeated. "Where is that boy? He was supposed to organize my books this morning."

He exhaled. He hadn't been caught after all. He had, however, forgotten his promise to set Kagen's library right. He slipped out to the corridor and rushed to answer Kagen's summons.

He opened the door. "I'm here to fashion your books, Master Kagen."

"Ah, there you are." He motioned Hagley inside, "Attend to the books later. Magus Verity is returning to Portsmouth. I want you to drive him. Goodricke will be going with him. While there, drop by the guild; my supplies need restocking. I'll make you a list of ingredients." He grabbed his quill and started scribbling. Hagley stood waiting. "Here," he said, handing Hagley the list. "By the time you've readied the wagon, the scribe will have a letter of authorization drafted too."

Hagley stuffed the list into his pocket and slipped out the door. As soon as the door closed behind him, he let out a whoop. A letter of authorization! Unless you'd earned your robes, the only way you got into the Sorcerer's Guild was with a letter of authorization. Several of the spells in his latest book required special ingredients. He'd been agonizing over how he'd practice without them. Now all he had to do was add them to Kagen's list and they were his. With a hop in his step, he headed for the stables.

He brought the wagon to Magus Verity's quarters and helped Goodricke load gear. Finished, he returned to Kagen's chambers for his letter of authorization. The old man was alone now. "It's there on the table. There's also a bag with adequate coin. You may keep anything extra."

Hagley's eyes widened. Kagen had just solved Hagley's problem of how to pay for his items. "Gramercy Master Kagen, you're most generous."

"Bah! No need to thank me, just take care, the port city is full of ruffians. Return as soon as you can. I don't want you spending even one night in that jeopardous place."

"Sir, it's not as perilous as you make it to be."

"It is. It is. I'll abide no argument. The cooks are packing travel rations. Stop by the kitchens before you leave. Now hasten lest you keep the Magus waiting."

Hagley left, pondering Kagen's warning. Portsmouth truly was a dangerous place, but he could defend himself. Maybe not with fisticuffs or weaponry, but he had his arts—even if he couldn't always depend on them. Besides, any show of the Gift usually frightened off trouble. He'd impressed the ungifted with spells before. Of course, his wellbeing hadn't been at risk any of those times.

He found Magus Verity and Goodricke waiting at the wagon. After a brief stop at the kitchen, they were on Kinsmen's Highway, Portsmouth bound.

At first, travelers were plentiful, but not after they distanced themselves from Stalwart. It was then the Magus began. "So,

Hagley, Master Kagen says you have sufficient gift to pass your trials, but you lack confidence. Do you agree?"

The comment gave Hagley butterflies. Did this mean Master Kagen thought him capable of earning his robes? "Well Sir, I'm not sure if it's confidence, it's just that sometimes my spells work, other times they don't. I never know which it'll be. The same is true with my prism tests, sometimes it shines brightly; other times, nothing. I'm fortunate that Master Kagen was kind enough to enlist my wagoner services. The prospect of returning to my father as a failure is not something I relish."

Jarek patted Hagley's knee. "Not all is lost yet. I'm guessing Kagen has the right of things. Have you memorized the Laws?"

"Yessir."

"Recite them."

"Well, the first is the Law of Knowledge."

"What does it state?"

Gads, I'm being tested by a Royal Magus. He thanked the gods for his excellent memory. "That knowledge is power. With understanding comes control. The more that is known about a subject the easier it is to gain control over it."

"Excellent. And the second?"

"That of Self-Knowledge. It means know thyself; that you need to know your own strengths and weaknesses in order to control your art."

The Magus twisted to face him. "Do you know yourself, Hagley? This law is about believing in yourself. Kagen thinks that's the crux of your issue. Remember, the moment you begin to doubt yourself, you're doomed to fail. Isn't that the essence of the seventh law?"

"I never thought of it that way."

"State it."

"The Law of Perversity says that if a spell goes awry, it will do so in a most calamitous fashion."

"Precisely. The key here is not to allow something to go wrong. And isn't that what's happening to you? When your spells fail, what's going through your mind at the time?"

"Mostly how foolish I'll feel if they fail."

"Tell me this, when you practice by yourself do your spells work?"

How did he know? "Mostly, except when I'm first learning them."

"Next time you cast a spell in front of a gathering, imagine yourself practicing. Clear all else there from your mind."

Thankfully, the Magus shifted his attentions to Goodricke, and their plans to go to some awful-sounding place called Foul Marsh, and Erth, or some name like that.

As they grew nearer to Portsmouth, travelers became commonplace again. Many were on foot, laden with heavy baskets. Hagley didn't envy them.

Once inside Portsmouth, Goodricke directed him where to go. "The Sailor's Guild is in Pirate's Cove, south of the main docks."

Pirate's Cove was considered the most dangerous part of Portsmouth. It smelled of fish remains—and danger. Would-be cutpurses and wag-halters eyed them as they approached the wharf, but the sight of magus robes kept them at bay. The south pier had room for only one ship, and sailors and dockers were busily unloading it.

Goodricke pointed, "The sailor's guild's over there. We'll need to go there to book passage."

Hagley waited in the wagon while Jarek and Goodricke went inside. His heart nearly stopped when he spied a disheveled seaman, leaning against a nearby bale, staring right at him. Judging from the number of daggers dangling from his belt—he was some sort of brigand. Was he about to rob him? Or worse? Hagley looked away, praying no ill would come to him before his protectors returned.

Hagley nearly jumped out of his skin at the sound of a deep voice, "The captain won't be able to take us aboard until the ship has unloaded." It was Goodricke.

Doing his best to avoid the cutpurse, he didn't notice his passengers' return "The harbormaster says there's an abandoned lodge not far from here where we can stow our things while you attend Master Kagen's chores." Left unsaid was that Hagley dare not leave a wagon unattended anywhere in this town.

They found the lodge a half-league or so up the bay. From the outside it looked ready to collapse, but inside it was quite serviceable. Gear unloaded, Hagley headed for Guild Street, trying to retrace Goodricke's route. Pirate's Cove was new territory for him. Dastardly looking scoundrels lurked everywhere, most staring, none looking friendly, and he no longer had a robed magus sitting beside him to discourage them.

Even after he'd cleared the docks, he kept peeking over his shoulder, expecting to find some ruffian ready to jump him. He didn't relax until he'd made it to the guild.

He showed his letter of authorization and was granted entrance. Inside it was far smaller than he'd imagined, cramped even. It reeked of aethers, the pungent smell reminding him of the time Kagen had shown him the university's relics room. Its walls were lined with shelves. Some held herbs and minerals or animal parts. Others held wands and staffs and various other apparatus used by the guild's members. Although he could scarcely contain his joy at being alone inside the guild, another part of him was keenly aware that of the patrons present, he was the only one not wearing robes. He was certain the guild owners saw him for a charlatan and would deny selling him anything.

One-by-one he loaded list items into his knapsack. It took him a while, but he eventually found every item Kagen had requested—as well as those he needed for practicing his spells. To his delight, no one challenged his purchase. He could finally attempt his newest spells. Best of all, after paying the reckoner, he had a few leftover chinkers.

As he approached the docks, weapon-wielding ruffians could be seen lurking everywhere, many eyeing his approach. Would one rob him? His delight over his newly gained wealth faded.

The roadway branched. Which direction had he come from? He made a guess. The street soon narrowed so much that his wagon barely fit, bringing the buildings on either side far too close for his liking. Anyone of ill intent could drop into his wagon and slit his throat before he could react. His palms grew sweaty as he scoured the road ahead. Concern turned to panic when a group of foul-looking ruffians emerged from out of nowhere, blocking his path. He counted five in all, each armed with a cudgel, all eyeing him. Why hadn't he stayed with the Magus and Goodricke?

Their leader offered up a toothless grin. "Look what we 'as 'ere boys. This laddie done brought us a wagon. Right friendly of him, eh?" Encouraged by his comrades' cackles, the man continued. "Climb off lad, 'n live to breathe another day."

Should he surrender the wagon and avoid harm, or try to make good his boast that the ungifted feared the arts. If he lost the wagon, he'd also lose any lingering confidence the Masters had in him. He'd never earn his robes—he'd be sent home to face his father. He inhaled and sat up straight. "Beware sirs, a formidable sorcerer sits before you. Be gone and I shall not harm you." He gripped the reins tighter, hoping his trembling hands wouldn't give him away.

"Har! Boys, we gots us a wizard afore us. Best run for your lives." His remark brought the anticipated howls. He flipped his cudgel to one of the other men and unsheathed a saber. "Now boy, off the wagon I says, lest I use this on ya."

Hagley flashed back to the Magus's advice. *You need to believe something is possible for it to happen.* Closing his eyes, he mentally recited the spell, one he'd never tried before. *Put your mind in the right place*, he reminded himself. *This is just practice; a chance to successfully cast a new spell on the first try.*

He started weaving his fingers in the intricate pattern described in the book. Standing on shaking legs, he offered up his friendliest, most confident look. "Fellows, why waste your time and considerable fighting skills over the likes of this old wagon when there's a soldier's hall just up the way? One full of purses and fine weapons of all sorts, just lying there for the taking. Think of what you could do with them."

His fingers continued their pattern, spinning faster now. "I demand no share. But my wagon blocks your path; let me pass and I'll leave the spoils to you."

The leader's eyes glossed over, and he smiled, until his men's shouts disrupted Hagley's charm. Shaking his head, the man blinked. Just as Hagley was convinced he was about to die, the man turned to his men. "Step aside, boys! This wagon be's in the way of soldiers sittin' on a king's ransom. It be there for the takin' for lads as brave as we."

Weapons high and cheering, the men looped around his wagon and set off down the road, raucously bragging of the plunder they'd soon own. Miraculously, Hagley held his spell long enough for it to serve its purpose. Apparently, greed won out after his charm no longer held sway.

Fearing to remain any longer, Hagley yanked on the reins and let out a loud, "Heeyahh!" The horses bolted, tumbling him backwards, and raced hell-bent up the road. Had he escaped one fate only to suffer a worse one under hooves or wagon wheels? He clung to the reins, heart hammering as they raced from the wharf, sure he was about to die.

Master Verity and Goodricke must have heard the galloping hooves, for both were outside staring down the road, watching him approach. Fortunately, Hagley had finally calmed the excited animals.

"Trouble, Hagley?" Jarek asked.

Hagley exhaled. "Nothing I wasn't up to."

Jarek shook his head. "And Kagen says the boy lacks confidence. I daresay he's brimming with it right now. Good job lad. Now, let's be about loading this gear, we've a ship to board."

The trip to the docks was short. Hagley wished them luck and goodbye, and hurried back to Kinsmen's Highway, anxious to distance himself from the dangers of the wharf.

The Spymaster

Sully drew a long, slow breath and tightened his grip on the sword—the one the king had given him. He tiptoed along the cave's wall, staying in its shadows, sneaking closer to the sleeping dragon. Keeping close to the wall, he timed his footsteps to the beast's snores. He dare not wake it. He shivered—the place be terrible cold. He peeked ahead, finally able to see into the cavern. The beast lay sleeping atop a gigantic pile of glistening gold and sparkling jewels—all soon to be his. Just one fast stab with his sword through its heart and he'd save the princess. He supposed she'd mostly want to marry him then. It'd probably be the will of the people, anyways.

"Sully! You out here?"

Sully lowered his stick; it was Zele, screeching at him again. What'd she want now? Why did Keep have someone as noisy as her in a place called the Sleeping Dragon? No one could sleep through her yelling.

"I be down in the cellar working the barrels like Keep said." Stepping away from the wall, he zigzagged his way past the ale barrels. Stepping in something wet, he cursed. A keg be leaking. Moaning at the prospect of patching another barrel, he made his way up the steps to where Zele stood waiting.

"Working the barrels? More likely you be play acting again—as always. Come boy, Keep be calling for you."

"Don't call me boy!"

"Oh! I forget, you be nine winters old now. That be a man by any reckoning," she said, ruffling his hair as he stomped past her. "Hurry along now, he's in the saloon with some highborn soldier." She was looking toward their table with that look a woman has when she fancies some man. As if a highborn would even notice the likes of a tavern wench. A soldier, and highborn. Thinking this interesting, he scurried into the saloon.

The tables was mostly empty. Keep be serving the soldier ale. The soldier be kind of old. Well, not so much as Keep. Maybe Zele fancied him because he was as old as her. Sully judged his looks were all right except for a crooked nose. But she was right about one thing, he had the look of a highborn; likely an officer with all them buttons and badges on his uniform.

The soldier was talking to Keep. "What did he look like?"

"Big fella. Had on robes like them sorcerers at the university wear, 'ceptin' his was black, not grey."

"That's the man."

"Odd thing is, he paid for a week's lodging, but only spent one night here. Ain't seen him since."

Sully cleared his throat, drawing their attention. "Zele says you be looking for me. I been busy stacking the kegs like you said. One be leaking."

"Ah, there you are, laddie," Keep said, fingering his beard like he always did when was nervous. "Forget the kegs for now. This here is Marshal Booker, the garrison's new commander, come here all the way from Suzerain."

"Suzerain? Wow! Do you know the king?"

"Sully!" Keep warned. "Don't be speaking unbidden!"

The Marshal laughed. "It's all right. I don't exactly know him, but I serve him."

"Beauteous!"

"Marshal Booker be asking after that man your friend took someplace the other day. He's wanting to know what he's up to."

"Hagley said the man had visited Prior Rigby about some lost kinsman."

The soldier nodded. "Yes, that's why he came here. Is there a chance I could speak with this Prior Rigby regarding his whereabouts?"

"I could send someone to fetch him if you wish," Keep answered.

"Yes, I would. Much obliged."

"In the meanwhile, laddie," Keep said, looking at him, "you go up and ready the highborn tables so the Marshal can have a bit o' privacy."

"Aw, Keep," he moaned.

"Sully!" Keep said, giving him that look that meant he was near to getting swatted. "Get along and do as told. And don't let me catch you pestering the Marshal here with a bunch of silly questions."

"Yessir."

The highborn tables were upstairs. Whenever they supped or stayed at the inn, Keep made sure they didn't have to sit with the commoners. The balcony circled the commons. You could watch the goings on from up there. He supposed highborns must like that.

Sully trudged up the stairs and started arranging chairs and wiping off tables. Just seven of 'em, so it wouldn't take hardly no time. He even replaced the burned-out candles.

He was setting the last table when he heard boots on the stairs. It was the soldier. "No need to do anything more, son. It's already tidier than the quarters I shared with the gabbling old friar I came here with." The soldier plopped into one of the chairs. "What's your name again?"

"Sully, Sir. I'm going to go adventuring on a ship someday."

"I fear you'll find adventuring is far less exciting than you think. So, Sully, I've a copper for you if you'll tell your innkeeper I'll have some of that stew he bragged about."

"A copper! Yes, Sir!" he said, skipping his way down the stairs.

Sully started when the door suddenly flew open. In walked another soldier. "I'm here to see a Marshal Booker."

"He be upstairs. I'll take you to him."

They found the Marshal leaning back in one chair, his feet resting on another. "Yes?" he asked.

The new soldier saluted. "Sir! Cadet Gresham Smithy here. Prior Rigby said you were asking about my uncle."

"Well I'll be… so Jarek did have kin here." The Marshal sat up, his chair legs clanking to the floor. "Pleased, Cadet. I'm Marshal Booker. Your uncle was to have met me here by now. Do you know his whereabouts?"

"No sir. Truth is sir, I know little of him. I only just met him days ago. He did say he'd contact me after attending to some business, that we'd dine together, but I haven't heard from him yet."

"Well, when you do, please send him to me—here at this inn."

"Of course, sir," Gresham said, turning to leave.

"Don't go yet!" Gresham turned back around. "Are you familiar with a Captain Dyson?"

"He's Captain of the Guard and commander of our cadet school. I don't know him, but I do know his son Quinn. He's favored to win our upcoming tourney. I hope to best him."

The Marshal smiled. "Do more than hope; surpass him. I persevered to beat what I thought were long odds in my own tourney. A good soldier never sells himself short. Remember that."

"Yessir."

"Well, I wish you well, but I now command your garrison, not the good Captain. Once I finish my meal, perhaps you could show me to his headquarters."

"Yessir."

"Good." The Marshal leaned back in his chair again. "Sit a spell Cadet," he said, gesturing to a nearby chair. "I have a few questions you might be able to answer." He waited for Gresham to sit. "I've only just arrived here and have little knowledge of this place. Tell me about Stalwart and the island's other cities, like who is in charge. And I'd know more of this Prior Rigby fellow."

"Stalwart was founded by Baron Stalwart, who passed long before I was born. The island has five other villages, but none as large as Stalwart. I was raised in Prior Rigby's priory, so know him well. I find him a good man. He's as much a king's man as a church man. I know he dislikes the Chevaliers persecution of the heretics. He feels that's the One God's duty."

"I agree. Such matters should be left to the gods." The Marshal sipped his ale. "I hope I don't offend your religious beliefs young man, but the Chevaliers go too far. They're zealots who punish any who worship other than they do. They seize the King's citizens, and seizure violates King's Law. One of my duties here is to assure that doesn't happen in Stalwart."

He took another swig of ale. "As I was telling the serving boy earlier," he said, smacking his lips, "I've just arrived here from the mainland. I paid the ship's captain extra to assure I arrived ahead of the Chevaliers' new Inquisitor. Rumor has it he may try to arrest a few of the island's good citizens. My advice is to give him and his people a wide berth, and whatever you do, do NOT let on you're the nephew of a Court Magus—ever have those two factions been at odds."

He hoisted his empty mug. "Boy! My mouth is parched. Have your innkeeper bring me another ale—and one for this lad too. Oh! Here's your copper." He flipped Sully a coin. "Well done."

"Yessir. Many thanks, sir."

Sully skipped down the stairs, leaving the soldiers to their conversation, grinning and squeezing his coin the whole way. He found Keep in the kitchen badgering Cook about the stew meat. Hearing the Marshal's demand, they left to fetch the ale. Soon the two of them were tramping back upstairs.

The Marshal and Gresham were still talking. "What do you know of your island's magi and their university?"

"Nigh onto nothing. In fact, before my uncle arrived, I would have said nothing."

"Good. The less you appear to know of them if you're questioned, the better."

Seeing Keep and Sully return, the Marshal waved them over. "Innkeeper! I'm wanting information about the magi at your university. Who runs it?"

Keep laid their drinks on the table. "That would be Headmaster Lavan, Sir. He's newly appointed. Headmaster Kagen preceded him, but he was recently pensioned."

"Tell me about this headmaster."

Keep scratched his chin, thinking. "He's bald, skinny and slumped at the shoulders. Although his youth is lost, he's too young to be called wizened. I'd say someplace middling. Otherwise he's like any other man. Not his manservant though. Goodricke's a full head taller than most and has that deep voice. You can't miss him. He's usually with the headmaster, but every so often comes to The Dragon to partake of some spirits. Would you like me to tell him you're interested in meeting his master?"

The Marshal raised his mug. "I would."

Sully had an idea. "Maybe you could talk to the man what got penched?"

Keep scowled. "Sully! This be none of your affair. Off with you. Go finish stacking those barrels. You said you have one to patch."

"Aw, Keep."

Keep pointed down the stairs, giving him that look again. "Do as told, boy!"

Fearing a head cuff, Sully left. Moping, he returned to his chores. A thousand hundred kegs later he was done. The soldiers were long gone by the time he'd finished. Normally he slept in a loft above the inn, but if there were vacant rooms—like tonight, Keep let him and Zele sleep in them, provided they straightened them up in the morning.

***

Zakarah scanned the saffron skies, searching for Greater Demons. He'd barely survived his last encounter with one, exhausting far too much magic in the process. With no threat in sight, he had time to raid another lesser world and replenish his expended magics.

He stared at his scrying pond, focusing his thoughts. A waggle of fingers brought the Lavan-creature's world into view. He was fortunate to have captured one so gifted. Mayhap there were others there like him. Although his captive had divulged nothing worthwhile so far, Zakarah could tell his spirit was weakening—that he'd soon be picking this human's mind for useful information. He momentarily nursed pangs of regret, fumed even, angry at himself for letting that second wizard escape. Hastiness had cost him. It wouldn't happen again.

Reaching forth, he fanned his fingers, seeking distant waters. He spied another human sitting atop a beast as it drank. This one radiated the Gift, too. Were all creatures of this world so blessed?

He was about to project his image when he sensed something lurking beneath the water. Curious, he waited. This new arrival burst into view. Massive jaws opened and enveloped the riding beast's head. Blood spewed everywhere. A suctioned arm looped around the human as it tried to flee, only to be ensnared by other suctioned arms. The stalker dragged both its victims underwater and vanished.

Zakarah smiled. Although it had stolen his intended quarry, this hunter had provided sport. It would make for a great pet, but to ensnare something that large from so far away he'd need power; like that found at the Lavan-creature's Nexus. Were such events common in his world? A conjecture worthy of investigation. He knew who could provide him answers. He went in search of his human.

Sully tossed and turned—having another bad dream. This one about a grey monster disappearing a man into a pond. He looked around. He'd never slept in this room before, and strange places were always scary. There be shadows everywhere. This one be too scary.

Slipping out of bed, he crept to the door and peeked down the corridor. With no beasties in sight, he tiptoed to Zele's room, lifted the latch, and slipped inside. Closing the door, he made his way to her bed.

He shook her shoulder and her eyes opened. "What are you doing here?"

"I just seen a boggart eat a man and his horse—I think maybe it was Ariath."

She hugged him close. "You just be having a nightmare. Besides, Ariath ain't a real place, so it can't be having no monsters. Folks just tell little ones the stories to scare them into behavin'. You be too old to be believin' such things."

"No, I seen it—it really happened!" He looked around the room, checking the shadows.

"Come, sleep with me then. Boggarts be like men; neither be gracing my bed, whether I be wanting 'em to or not."

Sully crawled into bed and cuddled close. In no time Zele was snoring. He surveyed the shadows one last time and slid beneath the blanket. If you couldn't see bad things, they couldn't see you neither.

Vainglorious

Shivering, Quinn pulled his cape tighter, but the chilly mist was not to be denied. He loathed Portsmouth. He was here because his father had assigned him as part of an honor guard that was to escort some dignitary back to Stalwart. His father said he wanted to acquaint Quinn with men of importance. He couldn't care less. All he wanted was to be someplace warm.

Bedecked in purple finery, the luminary in question was talking to one of his Clerics, watching the grooms offload their horses. A half-head taller than the Cleric, the Grand Inquisitor's barrel chest exaggerated their size difference. Although grey of hair, his carriage was that of a much younger man. His gaze flitted over the surroundings. Anyone caught by its piercing scrutiny looked away. When it came Quinn's direction, he too felt compelled to glance in another direction.

As soon as the horses were unloaded, a white stallion was brought to the man. Mounting, he urged the steed forward, coming Quinn's way, with the Cleric and eight mounted Chevaliers trailing behind.

"Quinn!" His father whispered, "let go of that cape and sit up proper—the Inquisitor's coming." The Inquisitor reached them. "Your Grace," his said with a bow of his head. "I'm Captain Dyson, officer in charge of your escort."

"Thank you, Captain, but as you can see," he said, gesturing toward his Chevaliers, "your men are not needed."

"One cannot be too careful," his father offered, "the wharf is a dangerous place."

"I assure you I am capable of dealing with whatever dangers it presents. In fact, it is my divine duty to unleash the One God's wrath on any who defy him. Since He fears no man, I don't either."

"Of that I have no doubt," his father said, bowing his head. "Still, I would be honored to guide you to Stalwart."

Quinn gritted his teeth. Gods Father, stop fawning over this haughty ass, you lickspigot. You embarrass yourself.

A cry rang out from farther up the wharf. "What do you suppose that is?" the Cleric asked.

"Let us go see," the Inquisitor said, spurring his horse to a trot. Both Chevaliers and honor guard followed. The Inquisitor's demeanor and garb reeked of such authority, none of the townspeople dared to meet his eye. Instead, they scrambled out of his way.

They found the source of the bustle a short way up the wharf. A crowd had surrounded a boat beached on a dock ramp. One was a mother with two young children, one sobbing, the other with its face buried in her skirts. A man standing close to the boat was wrenching.

Despite the townspeople's fascination with the boat's contents, the approach of heavily armed Chevaliers had them backing away, clearing a pathway to a dinghy, presenting the party with a view of two hideously disfigured carcasses.

The Cleric crossed himself, "Blessed be He that watches over us."

The Inquisitor simply stared, expressionless. Dismounting, he went for a closer look. One of the corpses was human, albeit missing its face. The other, grotesque beyond description, was some sort of beast. With massive jaw and long claws, it was half again the size of the man. The Inquisitor cast a glance at the crowd, his gaze settling on the closest churl. "What devilry is this?"

The man's eyes flitted about. Only when he realized it was he who'd been spoken to, did he answer. "This boat be found floating near the lagoon that lies across the bay, Yer Eminence. Those what found it, brought it here. That be all any of us knows."

Pointing at the dinghy, the Inquisitor faced the crowd. "Look closely. See the fruits of consorting with evil. Only by following the One God's righteous path will you be saved. Look and choose."

Eyes darted back and forth between the Inquisitor to the ravaged carcasses.

Grimacing, the Inquisitor turned to one of his Chevaliers. "Procure a wagon. Place these remains atop it for all to see. We take them with us."

Quinn shook his head. Thanks to this hufty-tufty, he'd be forced to endure this rotting stench all the way to Stalwart—a good half-day's ride.

They made their way through Portsmouth, their grotesque acquisitions producing the Inquisitor's desired effect on all who saw it. Although some shied back from the gruesome display, most were drawn in like insects to a flame, unable to resist its morbid appeal.

It was late afternoon when they reached Stalwart. Despite having left the sea soon after obtaining their grisly cargo, it had taken Quinn a full hour to finally warm up.

The crowds in Stalwart reacted to the ghastly spectacle much as those in Portsmouth had, and the Inquisitor's evangelizing sounded no different. Enthralling the crowd with endless oration, the Inquisitor led his procession through town and up the long hill that led to the Cadet Institute where the churchmen were to billet.

Done at last, Quinn was quite sure no duty could have been worse. That was before he was ordered to oversee the delivery of a wagonload of books to Prior Rigby. Delivering books was peasant's work! Worse, he'd have to abide the company of the two lowborn cadets who'd been assigned the same duty. One was an orphan totally lacking pedigree, the other the son of a sheriff. How had persons of such low pedigree become cadets anyway?

Sun breaking through the afternoon clouds sculpted shadows across Rayna's path, painting the garden pathway in hues of yellow and orange. Delightful fragrances wafted her way, like perfume adrift in the wind. It was the beauty of taking the garden route out of the academy. Yudelle was with her, looking stunning in a full-length blue dress with silver headband that drew everyone's eyes to her marvelous golden locks. Despite Yudelle being dearer to her than any other, the woman's presence made her feel drab, despite having worn her favorite green dress—the one people said accented her eyes.

Tomorrow would be their final day at the academy. They'd have their roses pinned, designating them as maidens worthy of marriage—of bearing some nobleman's child. Unlike her father, she'd treasure the idea of having a family. Another year had passed without him, making her feel isolated and alone. Thank the gods she'd made friends with Yudelle. But tomorrow Yudelle would return to the mainland, leaving her friendless once more. It seemed too much to bear. Stopping, she took hold of her friend's hand. "I so hate to see you go. What will I do without you?"

Yudelle caressed Rayna's cheek, eyes watering. "I feel the same way."

"Has your father's ship made port yet?"

Yudelle nodded. "Yes. It anchored in Portsmouth yesterday. Has yours?"

Rayna stiffened. "No, but I'm sure his lackey will soon show, anxious to do my father's bidding by ushering me someplace new." Each year Robard arrived to escort her to whatever place her father designated—to where she'd once again become the stranger no one knew.

Yudelle pinched her lips together. "I forgot your father rarely visits."

Rayna opened the gate and started down the hill toward town. "Not rarely—never!" She supposed as a babe he'd tolerated her presence. If so, it was too long ago to remember. What misdeed—what wrong, had she committed to make a father unable to abide the presence of his own daughter?

Yudelle's eyes widened. "Never? I thought he pays your tuition and boarding costs."

"He does, but never in person. His stipends arrive from the mainland through a reckoner without as much as a note." Everything about her father was kept secret, and she'd never once heard mention of her mother. What she didn't share with Yudelle—what she was too ashamed to admit, was that she didn't even know her father's name.

"How horrid for you." Yudelle's expression brightened. "Enough doom and gloom," she said, tugging Rayna's arm, "a caravan arrived on the yester, chock full of interesting things." She flashed that gorgeous smile of hers. No wonder the men were always smitten with her. "Who knows, maybe some handsome cadets will be there."

That prospect lightened Rayna's mood. "Speaking of cadets, how many have volunteered to pin your rose?" Tradition dictated that a graduating cadet did so for each lady graduating from the academy.

"None as yet." She clapped her hands together. "But I think Quinn means to."

Rayna flinched. Quinn was the cadet all the girls fancied, save for her. Ogling Rayna whenever Yudelle wasn't around, Quinn made her uneasy. She feared the self-centered cadet might ask to pin her rose, which would break her friend's heart. He was insensitive and self-absorbed. "How wonderful," she offered, starting down the hill.

Engrossed in conversation, Rayna didn't realize they'd reached town until boisterous laughter caught her attention. Nearby, a portly friar stood lecturing a dozen or so townspeople. Whatever he was saying had them cackling non-stop. "What do you suppose that's all about?"

Yudelle stood on tiptoes, peering at the gathering. "I don't know. Let's find out."

They were welcomed with a broad smile. "Ladies, ladies, join us in our prayers. I'm Friar Luc, the people's Prior."

One of the listeners cupped hands to her mouth. "More like the pantry's Prior from the looks of ye."

Her riposte garnered hoots and catcalls from those around her. The friar laughed along with them. "Alas, to treat God's messenger so. You wrong me, good lady." He handed a cup to the closest spectator. "Good sir, mayhap you could pass this back to that boisterous wench. Perhaps He will overlook her trespass against me were she to tithe a bit of her day's earnings."

Before the man could pass the cup, Rayna elbowed her way to his side and dropped in a silver. Smiling, she handed the preacher his cup. "Perhaps this will soothe your wounded pride, good friar."

"You are most generous, milady," the friar said, facing her. His grateful expression transformed into one of puzzlement. He stared at her. Disquieted, Rayna stepped away and hurried back to Yudelle.

"Did you see the way he looked at me?" she whispered.

Yudelle simply shrugged.

They resumed their walk. It seemed as if the whole village had turned out to see the caravan. It was so crowded they had to weave through the mob. It was always so when a caravan was here. Tents and pavilions lined Market Street, and the din of the barkers' promises had her anxious to see their wares.

One voice suddenly drowned out all others. "Ladies!"

Rayna turned to see a horse-drawn wagon driven by two cadets heading their way. Waving from the horse beside it was Cadet Quinn. It came to a halt beside them.

Rayna recognized the driver as one of contestants from the cadet tourney—the one with the sandy hair and piercing gray eyes. She'd only seen him from a distance before. Up close he was quite handsome. Tall, broad-shouldered with a thick neck, the other contestants surely found him intimidating. Fearing he'd catch her staring, she turned to Quinn.

"What brings such beauty down amongst this rabble?" Quinn asked, dismounting.

Rayna cringed. He'd addressed her, not Yudelle.

Yudelle offered her hand. "Cadet Quinn, how good to see you. Rayna and I are on our way to see the caravan's spoils. It leaves soon, and we simply must visit it before it departs."

Quinn seemed not to notice her outstretched arm. He waved at the nearby throng. "Unescorted, with ruffians lurking about? I insist you allow me to escort you."

Yudelle tossed her head to one side, bouncing her flaxen curls—a practiced move that never failed to draw men's attention. "Why thank you, milord, you're most gracious."

Such was life with Yudelle. Although the men in the wagon were clearly captivated by her blatant flirting, Quinn seemed oblivious.

"Smithy! Kendal! Take care of the wagon while I attend to the ladies' safety," he said tying his reins to the wagon.

The passenger hopped off the wagon. "You're sure, Quinn? I was thinking maybe you and Gresham could unload the wagon while I escort the ladies."

The driver laughed and rolled his eyes. Quinn was far less amused. "You forget your station Kendal. These ladies are highborn."

The driver sneered. She wondered at his name; Quinn addressed him as Smithy, yet his friend called him Gresham. "Yes, Kendal, you're being remiss. Fortunately, we have Quinn here to remind us of our life's lot." He and Quinn locked eyes, neither flinching. "Do your business Quinn, we'll deliver Prior Rigby's load."

Quinn smirked, then looked at her. "So, Rayna, has a cadet offered to pin your rose yet?"

This was it—the moment she'd dreaded, and Yudelle was here to witness it. Her gut twisted. How could she fend off his overture? She cleared her throat, stalling. "Why, yes." She turned to the wagon driver. "Your friend here presented himself to me only this morning."

"What?" Quinn looked at the wagon driver as one would a leper. "Him?"

She wasn't sure which of the three cadets was most shocked by her statement, but to the driver's credit, he gave nothing away. "I still ponder my answer." Turning so Quinn couldn't see, she gave the good-looking cadet a pleading look. "I promise an answer on the morn. Where should the runner deliver it?"

Smithy-Gresham answered without missing a beat. "The main hall at the cadet quarters. A duty clerk mans the desk night and day."

Quinn recovered quickly. "Ah, good. Perhaps Yudelle and I will see you at the pinning ceremony." He dropped to a knee in front of Yudelle, "providing my lady would allow this unworthy cadet the honor of pinning her rose."

Yudelle could hardly contain herself. "Why Cadet Quinn, I for one will not make a gentleman await his answer. I accept."

"Thank you, milady, you've fulfilled my fondest hope," he said, rising. "To the parish, cadets, and stable my stallion afterward."

"We live to serve, Quinn. Come Kendal, there's lowborn work to be done."

As the driver grabbed the reins, Rayna raised her hand. "Please wait. I've turned my ankle coming down the hill. It's painful to walk on it. Could I enlist a ride with you as far as the Lady's Academy? Besides, I'm sure Cadet Quinn and Yudelle have much to discuss."

The driver tipped his head. "We'd be honored, Lady."

She held her hem as Cadet Kendal helped her onto the buckboard seat and hopped into the wagon behind her. She waved to Yudelle. "Enjoy the caravan."

She endured an awkward silence as the wagon made its way up the hill. She so envied Yudelle's ease with words, but alas, shyness was an integral part of her solitary life.

When they reached the academy, Smithy-Gresham jumped out and offered his hand. Taking it, Rayna braced her free hand on his muscled shoulder and hopped down. He towered over her. She smiled up at him. "I can't find words to thank you for what you've just done." Would he grasp her innuendo?

He nodded. "I'm sure I speak for Cadet Kendal as well as myself in assuring you it was our pleasure, Lady."

She beamed. "I shall send you my answer as soon as I break my morning fast."

He bowed. "Alas, it seems I shall have to wait until then."

"Just one more thing."

"Yes?"

She leaned close, whispering. "Do I address it to Cadet Gresham or Cadet Smithy?"

He laughed. She loved its timber. "Cadet Gresham will do nicely. For reasons that escape me, it pleases Quinn to call me by my surname."

She offered up her best smile. "Cadet Gresham it is then."

With a nod, she headed for the building. Halfway there, she realized she'd forgotten to limp. She shuffled the rest of the way to the door. Once inside, she fell against the door, giggling.

Gresham said nothing as they drove away, but the astonished look on Kendal's face made maintaining this pretense difficult. Finally, unable to restrain himself any longer, a flurry of questions burst from Kendal's mouth. "Where did she come from? What possessed you to ask a highborn if you could pin her rose? How did you ever work up the nerve? Why didn't you tell me about her? And those eyes. She's the most gorgeous creature I've ever laid eyes on."

"Most gorgeous?" Gresham rubbed his chin. "I don't know. I found Quinn's lady rather striking too. I'd consider them equally attractive."

"Heavenly light man, how do you even know this enchantress? Why didn't you tell me about her?"

"What, and spoil this moment? You should see yourself."

Gresham spent the remainder of their ride fending off questions, none of which he could truthfully answer. It was great sport nonetheless. As he half listened to his friend carry on, he couldn't help wondering what the woman had been up to. Kendal had the right of it about her being comely. She'd taken his breath away when he first saw those cat-shaped green eyes of hers. They could capture a man's soul. Their contrast with her ebony hair seemed to make them glow. And she was so tiny. How could he not have noticed her before? Where did she keep herself? She'd clearly concocted her yarn to put off Quinn, but why? Since it wasn't likely he'd ever hear from her again, he doubted he'd learn those answers, but it had been great fun upsetting that ass Quinn. He laughed aloud, puzzling poor Kendal even more. Quinn would likely get his revenge at their tourney, but this day was one Gresham would savor for a long time to come.

Since the parish was within walking distance of the Lady's Academy, their trip was short. Work was at hand. Most of their wagonload was books. Prior Rigby had purchased an entire lot from a caravan wagon. The old bookworm would be in One God's heaven with all this to read.

Gresham offloaded a few books, stacking them beside the wagon. Could he carry one more? He grabbed another and dropped it with a yelp. It tumbled to the dirt.

Kendal gave him a quizzical look. "A problem?"

"I think something bit me when I picked up that book. It made my hand tingle."

"Right! More likely thoughts of that girl bit your brain."

"No, really." He bent down and picked it up and felt the same prickly sensation. "It did it again. Do you think it's poisoned or something? Here!" He tossed the book to Kendal.

Kendal leaped away. "Gods! If it's poison, why throw it at me?" Kendal stared down at the book. After a moment, he scooped it up. "Tingle my ass. If you ain't the trickster today. Liked to have wet my breeches with all that poison talk." He scanned its cover. "It says Battle Strategies and Actions. Here," he tossed it back to Gresham, "poison yourself."

The instant Gresham caught it that same tingle shot up his arm. The sensation lasted briefly and faded. "You're sure you didn't feel anything?"

"Enough foolery; let's finish our job."

Gresham placed the book at the top of his stack and lugged it into the parish. As soon as the door closed, he plopped down his load and picked up the book. The prickly feeling returned. Was this sorcery? If so, why didn't it tingle for Kendal? Was his uncle's conjecture correct—was he gifted?

He flipped through its pages. All were full of strange characters, the likes of which he'd never seen. They looked more like pictures than lettering. Making sure no one was looking; he hid the book behind a vase. He'd retrieve it later and hope his uncle could explain what had happened.

Tourney

Gresham sat resting on his cot, whittling the final touches to his carving, when Kendal hollered through the doorway. "You'd best get to the stadium Gresham, lest you forfeit your match with Quinn. We wouldn't want you to lose to that bounder."

Right, just beat the institute's finest swordsman. Gresham had won the archery and survival competitions, getting him to the competition's finals. To no one's surprise, his opponent was Quinn.

But as important as this match ought to be, he'd given it little thought. It was Rayna dominating his thoughts, not Quinn. He'd received two notes from her since their first meeting. The first had to do with his alleged request to present her graduation rose. 'Dear Cadet Gresham, I regret to inform you that I cannot accept your kind offer to present my rose.'

Although he'd expected as much, it still disappointed him—until he read her next sentence: 'After all, since you never actually asked me, what have I to accept? If you choose to rectify that, contact me at the Lady's Academy by day's end. Yours, —Rayna Kent.'

He'd laughed aloud when he read it, but she wasn't the only one capable of gamesmanship. He'd have loved to have been a weevil on her wall when she read his return letter: 'My dear Lady Rayna, as appealing as I find the idea of being your presenter, I fear it would be ill advised to pay court to someone about whom I know nothing. How would I address the inevitable questions regarding our presumed friendship? However, were we to spend some time together beforehand, say to finish that trip to the caravan we cadets interrupted, I would know you sufficiently well to pin your rose. I anxiously await your reply. Earnestly, —Cadet Gresham Smithy.'

Her second note was an acceptance of his proposal. They were to meet on the morrow, after midday meal.

Setting down his knife, he blew away the last of the shavings and admired his handiwork—a rose for Rayna. Courting a highborn had him out of his depths. Kendal told him that courtly speeches and lead-up gifts were an important part of the rose presentation. To that end, he'd carved her this flower. He planned to present it to her right before his bout with Quinn.

Tucking the carving into his waistband, he headed for the stadium. He entered the theater, the site for the final contest. Rows of tiered seats surrounded the performing arena, their nearness offering the audience a close-up view. He scoured the stands for Rayna, spotting her in the third row with her blonde friend. Trying unsuccessfully to quell his butterflies, he walked over and presented himself. "Although this one can't be pinned, please accept this early rose, milady," he said, bowing from the waist as he offered her his handiwork.

"That is most gracious of you Cadet. I shall treasure it," she said, her green eyes sparkling.

He was feeling rather proud of his courtly manner—until Quinn arrived. Handing Yudelle a jeweled rose, he dropped to one knee. "Lady, the more I drink of thine sweetness, the greater becomes my thirst. What need have I of sunshine when I can bask in your radiance?"

Yudelle absolutely glowed. "Although unworthy of such praise, I shall nonetheless savor it. Rise, good sir." Removing her scarf, she handed it to him. "Wear this. May it bring you victory," she said, with a disparaging glance at Gresham.

The tourney horn sounded, sparing Gresham further chagrin.

At center ring, the two performed a short ceremonial greeting that ended with their forearms clasped, raised to the crowd. The audience roared as the two men faced off.

It took only a few strokes and parries to discover Quinn's prowess. Parry left, parry right, lunge, disengage. No matter what Gresham tried, Quinn countered with a faster, defter maneuver. The man wasn't even sweating. To make matters worse Quinn wore a condescending grin the whole time.

"What's the matter, Smithy? Your style's clumsy. Who's your sword master, anyway?" He followed with a flurry of complex slashes that sorely challenged Gresham's defenses. "Ah, that's right, lowborns have none." His tone shifted, suddenly menacing. "You're no match for the likes of me and you know it."

His next attack drove Gresham backwards. He lost his balance. Quinn lunged, and his blunted weapon touched Gresham's gut. One point, Quinn. A cheer erupted from the crowd.

Chest heaving, Gresham tried to compose himself. Matters were worse than he'd anticipated. As arrogant as the man was, Quinn had the right of it; his fencing skills far outstripped his own. All this with Rayna watching. The first to seven touches would be declared winner. At this juncture Gresham wondered if he'd score a single point. It was time for caution, to defend well and hope for an opening.

That opening finally happened, but by the time he'd scored his first point Quinn had four. Moments later it was five to one.

Quinn kept up a non-stop banter the whole time. "It's hard to believe that Lady Rayna accepted your court." He followed with a series of vicious pokes and parries. The crowd roared. "Or maybe I should drop the Lady and simply call her Rayna. Keeping company with the likes of you dishonors not just her, but all proper folk."

Even though Quinn's attempts to goad him were obvious, demeaning Rayna sparked Gresham's anger anyway. "You're an ass."

The two unleashed a series of attacks and counterattacks, displaying a viciousness rarely seen in gentlemanly competition. Gresham flipped sodden hair from one eye and grinned, pleased that sweat now dripped from Quinn's brow, too. He sucked in some much-needed air and circled left, to Quinn's weaker side.

"You shame her Smithy, but I'm curious, how far has she sunk? Does she now rut with lowborns, has she lain with you yet?"

Quinn's crude taunt sparked some beast within. Rational thought vanished, replaced by unbridled rage. But it brought with it something queer. Somehow he seemed to be floating outside his body, watching their skirmish from above. In this strange vision, it was just the two of them, the crowd gone. From his elevated vantage point any subtle movement became obvious, making it easy to anticipate Quinn's moves—to block and counter them. All awareness of his surroundings surrendered to but one thought—he must destroy this man standing before him. He charged, roaring like a madman. Gone was any hint of technique. Instead, he wielded his sword as if it were a club, taking broad, brutal swings.

Quinn's expression went from concern, to shock, to something approaching fear, as Gresham pressed his bestial charge. Five to two. Five to three, then four, then all even. His advance continued, unrelenting. He was invincible. No longer content to win, he needed to hurt. To maim. To punish. Six to five, his favor.

Quinn backed onto a small mound, seeking the uphill advantage. The gravel under his foot gave way. He slipped, falling, his sword clutched in both hands in a desperate defense.

Hurt! A wild swing jarred Quinn so hard a hand slipped off his weapon. Mangle! Two brutal cuts nearly clipped the man's face. Quinn raised his sword to protect himself. Gresham batted the weapon from the lone-handed grip. It landed well out of arm's reach. He raised his sword, visualizing the killing thrust.

"Smithy! I yield! Gods, don't stab me!"

Quinn's words flipped some switch inside of him. He was within his body once more. He lowered his weapon, his face burning, blushing at what he'd nearly done. He stepped back. "I won't. I would nev… forgive me." Some distant part of him acknowledged the crowd's cheers, but his imagined moment of glory had transformed into one of ignominy. What just happened? Not only did he want to win, he also wanted to destroy. He turned and stepped away, staring at the ground, ignoring the crowd's cheers.

Lost in thought, he still heard approaching footsteps, and Captain Dyson's angry voice. "You yielded! Only cowards yield! You shame our good name before everyone!" Gresham turned to see the Captain castigating his son. "You're weak like your mother. Weak! I am loath to call you son."

Gresham would never have imagined he could feel sorry for Quinn, but seeing the devastated look on the man's face, sympathy overcame him. "Captain, he lost his weapon. He had no choice."

The Captain turned, snarling. "Silence! I'll not tolerate insolence from some witch's get." He wheeled about and stormed off the field.

Witch's get? What in the gods' names did that mean? Events were exceeding Gresham's comprehension. First the mysterious appearance of a sorcerer uncle, followed by the book with a seeming magic that touched only him. Then he defeated a man in a swordfight against whom he stood no reasonable chance and had done so by turning into a madman with mystical vision. And now his commanding officer had just accused him of being a witch's child. In a day and a half his world had twisted upside down. What was happening to him? He needed his uncle's counsel. Without as much as a glance at Quinn or the crowd, he followed the captain off the field, past the viewing stand, back to the soldier's hall.

◦◦◦

Rayna left the stadium without Yudelle. The silly woman wanted to console Quinn. After his humiliating loss to a commoner, Rayna doubted the pretentious cadet would be in any sort of mood for Yudelle's prattle. But that was their affair. She was more concerned over what she'd just witnessed, vacillating between a strange sense of pride in Gresham for having won the tourney, and concern over his curious behavior. She chided herself. The matter was between the men. It had nothing whatsoever to do with her.

The duty girl hailed her as she entered the academy. "Prior Rigby left this for you," she said, handing Rayna a note. "Apparently you have a visitor waiting at the parish."

Rayna's breath caught. Had her father come to her graduation after all? Would she lay eyes on him for the first time since she was a babe? She walked to the nearest looking glass and combed fingers through her hair, doing her best to make herself presentable. Frowning, she shook her head. Fretting over it possibly being her father was stupid, why not just go see who this visitor is.

Blunderer

The sun was setting by the time Hagley made it home from Portsmouth. A shock awaited him. A group of robed horsemen—the ones called Chevaliers—were gathered in front of the university blocking the entrance, leaving him no choice but to stop. He edged the wagon as close as he dared—and listened.

Judging by the everyone's expressions, this encounter wasn't cordial. All but two wore white tunics. One wore blue, the other purple. The man in blue was speaking. "Sir, do you know to whom you deny entry?"

Barring their access stood Master Vardon, the university's Battle Master. Hagley had always admired the man. Ever did he seem in command. Hagley so wished he could be like him. With legs wide and arms folded across his chest, his stance sent a clear signal that he wasn't one to be easily intimidated. "I do," he answered. "He's your Grand Inquisitor."

"Precisely! His Grace demands to see your headmaster."

Vardon gave a patronizing smile. "As I already told you, the headmaster's away."

"Are you second in command?"

"We are a school, not a military. We have no chain of command. I am, however, responsible for ensuring the university's security."

The churchman made no effort to hide his frustration. "Surely there's someone in charge?"

Master Vardon spread his hands. "I'm sorry Sir, we have but one headmaster. I realize I repeat myself, but he's not present."

The man scowled. "I find it difficult to believe there's no one in authority here. Who's your decision maker?"

The spokesman's threatening attitude made Hagley nervous, but to his credit, Master Vardon stood undaunted. "You could speak with our former headmaster. He no longer speaks for the university, but perhaps he can serve your needs."

The man in purple finally spoke. "Fine, bring this man." The Inquisitor's voice positively brimmed of authority. Here was a man used to being obeyed.

Master Vardon remained unbowed. He whispered something to the young man beside him, who immediately ran off. Hagley sat waiting with the others, intrigued by the scene unfolding before him.

A while later he spotted Master Kagen, bedecked in his former headmaster robes, slowly making his way to the gate, studying the visitors as he approached. "I'm Master Kagen. How may I be of service?"

The spokesman started to speak again, but the Inquisitor raised a hand. "Master Kagen, is it true you used to govern this school?"

"Govern? No, but until recently I was its headmaster."

"You shall suffice then. Escort me to your training rooms that I may observe the manner in which you teach the use of His Gift."

Master Kagen smiled. "I'm afraid that won't be possible, Your Grace. It would be a direct violation of the standards we assure our student's patrons when they place them in our charge. And even if I could allow you inside, what we do here at the university is our concern, not the One Church's. We don't ask how your Clerics utilize the Gift. We expect the same courtesy from you."

The Inquisitor tensed. "Beware Sir, I take umbrage at your belligerence. Violation of Church Law is heresy."

Master Kagen spread his arms, palms up. "Such is not my intent. You speak of Church Law, Sir. Tell me, which one do I break by rightfully refusing you entry to our grounds?"

The Inquisitor straightened. "Do you mock me Sir?"

"Mock? All I ask is what law we defy."

The Inquisitor scowled. "You've broken no laws—yet! Word of your insolence shall spread. We will meet again, 'former' headmaster," he said, reining his horse to face one of his soldiers. "Corpsman, keep your squadron here. Watch these people's activities. The rest, with me."

Just as he appeared ready to leave, the Inquisitor turned to Vardon's messenger. "You, boy! What's your headmaster's name?"

"That would be Headmaster Lavan, Sir."

Oddly, the Inquisitor smiled. "Describe him."

"He appears as any other man, but his gold collar identifies him as headmaster."

"Thank you. Your manners exceed those of your masters." He looked over his shoulder. "All right corpsman, you know what to look for." Without as much as another glance at Vardon or Kagen, the Inquisitor urged his horse to a canter and rode off, followed by his men, save for the four who'd been ordered to remain.

Vardon's chagrined messenger turned to Master Kagen. "I'm sorry Sir; I should never have spoken. Now I bring the Church's wrath on the headmaster."

Kagen put an arm around the young man's shoulder. "Don't worry yourself, we have it on good authority that this man is an old acquaintance of the headmaster's. He's simply a zealot. Not all churchmen are so, but these Chevalier fellows seem to have more than their fair share of them."

Once everyone vacated the gate area, Hagley drove inside. As he rode through the gate, the portcullis dropped behind him, and the gates were bolted, something he'd not seen before. He shuddered, wondering which was worse, having Portsmouth's ruffians track him here, or dealing with trouble stirred up by this man they called the Grand Inquisitor. He peeked back through the bars at the remaining church troopers. Their presence did not bode well.

The next morning he dressed, ate, and headed to Master Kagen's quarters. The old man seemed pleased to see him. "How went the trip? Did the Goodricke and Magus Verity sail?"

"The last I saw they were lugging their gear up the gangplank." He plopped his pouch atop one of the tables. "Where would you like your guild purchases?"

"There on the table is fine." As usual, Kagen had his nose in a scroll. "Ah, Church Law, here it is." He looked up at Hagley. "With these churchmen stirring up trouble, I'll likely be tied up all day. The morning is yours. Do with it as you please." He ran his finger down the parchment. "I just wish this had happened while Lavan was here, so he could contend with it."

Hagley knew better, the old goat loved to feel needed. He was likely in blessed heaven over the whole affair. A morning free of duties! Now he had both the time and the components to work on new spells.

Making sure no one was looking, he walked down his special corridor, opened its hidden door, and made his way to his secret exit. Winding the crank, he lifted the tiny gate that led outside. Other than getting here via his secret tunnel, the only way to get to his practice place was to hike down a boulder-strewn ravine. During heavy rains the small canyon flooded, perhaps explaining why no one ever ventured here, allowing him to practice free of prying eyes.

Sunlight warmed his skin as he thumbed through the latest tome he'd borrowed from Kagen's study. It dealt with summoning spells. They appeared to cause objects to materialize out of nothing; which was impossible. They'd puzzled him at first, until Master Kagen explained that, whereas most spells required only the proper words or the ritual to be cast, summoning spells required the added use of a physical component.

The first spell to catch his eye was one to conjure up bellytimber—the perfect remedy for hungry times. He planned to summon bread. Its required component was a kernel of wheat. He placed a kernel on each of four rocks he'd laid out before him. He reviewed all laws that might apply. Every law you brought into play increased your likelihood of success.

Two laws came to mind. Since bread comes from wheat which comes from kernel, the Law of Association would logically apply. The Law of Similarity purported a spell's effect had a connection with its component. He ran through the Twenty Laws of magic one last time but found no others that applied. He was ready.

He reread the spell one last time and eyed the first wheat kernel. *I'm alone; no one will laugh if I fail. I—will—succeed.* He closed his eyes and chanted. He heard a loud popping noise. He looked. Sitting on the rock where the kernel had been was a small stalk of wheat. *Damn the Law of Perversity anyway.*

He moved to the second kernel and tried it again. Another wheat stalk. *Of course, the Law of Cause and Effect—he'd hadn't varied a thing; no wonder he had the same result. What could he do differently? Perhaps it would help if he first envisioned his goal.* He'd seen the cooks prepare bread in the kitchen many a time. He replayed the process in his mind. Closing his eyes, he stood over the third kernel and recast his spell.

He opened his eyes and screeched. The third kernel had become a rapidly growing ball of dough. He'd violated the Law of Balance. Control a spell too little and a magus loses control altogether. Had what he summoned been dangerous, he could have killed himself. The dough ball continued to grow. His heart started pounding. Was he about to die anyway, smothered by a giant glob?

Frantic, he reviewed the remaining laws. Polarity! Any spell could be split into opposing patterns, each the essence of the other. He invoked the counter spell and the white glob exploded, painting the vicinity in white dough, much of it on him.

As he was wiping off his clothing, he heard a noise. Someone was coming down the canyon! He froze. Visions of the dockside ruffians flooded his mind. Had they traced him here? He scoured the ravine but spotted no one. Who could it be? Perhaps whoever was coming was ungifted and could be easily frightened. He stretched to his full height. "Hold! Come no closer. Be warned that I am versed in the arts and will not hesitate to use them against you." He nearly lost his bladder when a head appeared beside a large boulder.

"Hagley, it be Sully! Please don't be using your arts on me." Sully crawled over the rock, dusted off his pants, and looked around. "This place be a mess."

His heart pounding, Hagley exhaled. "Don't sneak up on me like that. You frightened me something awful."

Sully ignored him, staring at the goop. "What be all that white stuff?"

"Another failed spell. I tried to make bread."

Sully gathered a bit of the dough on with a finger and sniffed. "You almost did it. This be bread dough like what Cook uses."

Hagley spread his arms, shaking his head. "Masters make bread, not dough. I'll fear I'll never earn my robes."

Sully gave a pleading look. "You got to. You said when you become Master we'll go adventuring. You know, killing monsters and saving princesses," he said, licking batter off his finger.

Hagley sighed. "I know I promised, but I'm afraid you're counting on the wrong magus."

"No!" Sully shook his head. "That ain't so, you be a great magus. I seen it lotsa times." He patted Hagley's arm. "You just need your lucky person with you. I'm here now."

Sometimes it seemed that way. Virtually every time his little friend was with him, his spells worked. "I wonder why?"

Sully gave him a toothy grin. "I know."

Hagley laughed at the little braggart. "Really? Pray tell, what's so special about you?" Sully looked hurt. "I mean, aside from you being my lucky person."

Sully gave him a fatherly pat. "Because I be your friend, and you don't be nervous around me like with other people. That be as plain as your nose to see."

That was the same thing Kagen and Jarek had told him. He draped his arm around his little friend. "Maybe you have the right of it."

Sully grinned. "I can prove it. Try your spell again."

"All right." Hagley looked at the last wheat kernel, shut his eyes, and ran through the laws. *My lucky person's nearby.* He cast.

"I told you." Sully bragged, pointing. "There's your bread."

Stooping, Hagley picked up the bread, shaking his head. He tasted it. It really was bread. He split the loaf and gave Sully half. "I guess I'll have to start calling you Lucky instead of Sully," he said as they munched the conjured meal.

Hagley spent the rest of the morning experimenting with new spells. All worked on the first try. He'd accomplished a lot. He glanced skyward. The sun was straight overhead. "It's time for afternoon wagon duty. Want a ride back to town?"

"Sure."

Hagley retrieved the broken portcullis bar he'd hidden in the brush, inserted one end under the gate, and placed the other over a rock. He leaned his weight onto the bar, and the levered the gate rose. "All right, meet me at the main gate."

Sully peered into the tunnel. "Can't I go your magic way? I always be wanting to."

"You can peek inside, but I can't take you into the building with me. If I did, everyone would know about my secret passage."

"Aw, just one time?"

"You heard me," he said, slipping inside. He lowered the gate and headed down the tunnel leaving Sully to sulk. The boy was right, somehow Sully made Hagley's magic work. But Sully wouldn't always be at his side. Masters rely on skill, not luck. He'd been lucky at the wharf yesterday. Next time that might not be the case. The Law of Perversity meant the price for failure could very well be his life.

Foul Marsh

    Goodricke stood at the ship's bow watching a pair of squawking gulls squabble over a catch. Wind buffeted his hair, waggling the sails overhead, the ever-present smell of brine evoking fond memories of days past. He missed the seaman's life. It had been exciting, every port a new experience, but it was also lonely. Had he a woman he could share that life with, things might have been different, but few women coveted the seas. Such wistful thoughts were pointless; he knew he was lucky to serve Master Lavan. He led a good life—he shouldn't dream of more. But if that good life was to continue, they had to bring his patron home.

    Magus Verity was below decks, battling seasickness. Their ship had crossed the bay from Portsmouth, and dropped anchor. The Captain stood beside him shouting orders as the crew lowered Goodricke's skiff. It nearly clipped the ship's rail. "Careful with that thing, damn ya!" After a bit more cursing and sweating it was safely in the water. "Bosun! Get the Magus topside."

    The Captain's eyes scoured the inlet to their port side. "The two of ye be mad to be settin' down here." He pointed, "Just look at that shoal. Skerries be scattered all around it. Like as not their rocks is gonna bust ya up afore ye can even get halfway into that lagoon."

    Goodricke took measure of the cove's entrance. What the Captain said was true. Long jetties jutted from both shorelines creating a dangerously narrow, rock-strewn opening. Maneuvering past it would be risky. "You'll hear no argument from me, Captain, but the Magus is committed, so we're heading in."

    "Daft them sorcerers is—the whole lot of 'em. Hate to lose a good seaman as yerself over some madman's folly."

    The bosun arrived with Jarek. Soon they were aboard their skiff watching the ship lift anchor. "Have you gained your sea legs, milord?"

    Jarek tucked his cloak around his chest. "Somewhat. My stomach's settled, but this wind is blowing right through these old bones."

"It'll die down once we're inside the cove." Goodricke grabbed the oars. "Let's get out of this gale and check provisions." He spun the boat around, their stern facing the bay. "I need to row backwards to fight this current, so you'll need to scout our course."

Jarek warmed his hands with his breath. "I can do that much."

It took all of Goodricke's strength and seaman's skill to safely guide them past the shoals that rimmed the lagoon, but as predicted, once he'd maneuvered into the inlet, the winds tapered off. The shallow waters were placid, void of any current. Grass and reeds poked above the surface in all directions. Save for the few small specks that hinted of distant islands, the marsh was flat as far as the eye could see, and the once-invigorating aroma of the seas had been replaced by one far more putrid.

Jarek loosened his cloak. "Praise the heavens. That wind was unbearable."

"But typical of coastal waters." Goodricke shipped the oars and grabbed for the wooden mast laced to the side of the boat. "And don't thank the gods prematurely. We want some of that wind, milord. Sailing will save us both time and effort."

"It's just the two of us now. Feel free to address me as Jarek, not milord," he said, helping him lash the mast. They kept its canvas furled while they inventoried gear. Goodricke picked up two packs. "We'll wear these once we're out of the marsh. He held one up. My tritant and gear are in this one. I'll take our bearings tonight." He handed Jarek the other one. "This holds your gear, and the scribe's map and scroll."

Dropping his pack, he grabbed a pair of bags. "While in the boat we'll keep our gear dry in these. They're cow bladders," he said, picking up a third one, "this one holds our drinking water. If we use it sparingly, it should get us to A'ryth. If not, we'll need to find fresh water along the way." He reached for the sail. "And I'll drink less if we use this."

Jarek stopped him. "Wait!" He fished through his gear. "I've something for you. Kagen and I have grave concerns at exposing you to Zakarah." He handed Goodricke a scabbard. "Here's some protection."

Goodricke unsheathed a sword, marveling at its finery. "It's magnificent. But what good is iron against a wizard who's not even of this world?"

He pointed at the designs embossed on its blade. "This is no ordinary sword. Forged by a magus of the Great Age named Turpin, it's ensorcelled."

Goodricke hoisted the sword, rotating it, the sun glistening off its metal. "Ensorcelled? How so?"

"Every creature capable of reason tends toward good or evil. Many gifted can sense the nature of these tendencies, and although we don't know how Turpin accomplished it, this sword senses them too. In short, it warns its bearer when evil is present."

Goodricke lowered the weapon. "Such things exceed my ken. What I do know is that it's a craftsman's marvel. I'm at a loss as to how to thank you."

Jarek placed a hand on his shoulder. "You already have, by helping me find Lavan."

Goodricke stowed the sword in his bag. "What of you? What protects you?"

"I have this," he said, pulling out a short sword. "And a spell or two Zakarah won't find to his liking. If one is to become a successful Court Sorcerer and watch over those he's charged to protect, it's imperative that he learn a trick or two."

Goodricke unfurled the sailcloth, tied it off, and loosened the jib. He grabbed the rudder. "Let's turn this wind to our advantage." The boat lurched as a gust filled the sail.

Jarek fished the parchments out of his pack and handed one to Goodricke. "You study Malg's map while I review his journal."

One glance at the map told him the marsh was too large to cross in a single day. It showed a large island marked as Devil's Isle near its midpoint. Squinting, he spied an island, but it was far too close to be the one depicted. If the map didn't show it, what else was missing?

Jarek tapped the journal. "Kagen read some of this to me earlier, but he left out its most important passage. Listen to this. It has to do with this very cove. 'Much to our dismay, we found the freshwater inlet infested by beasts so vicious the crewman dubbed it

Foul Marsh. Several sailors fell victim to its brutes. We named the most perilous of these monsters The Lurker because of how it concealed itself in the shallows, waiting for its prey. When someone drew too close, it rose out of nowhere to ensnare him in its tentacles, like those of an octopus. Some it dragged beneath the murk. Others it slaughtered where it caught them. We now steer clear of that heinous lagoon.' He looked up. "If that's true, we'd best avoid the shallows."

"Aye, deeper waters it is."

The morning passed uneventfully. Around midday the winds died off. Fog drifted in, dropping the temperature, forcing Goodricke to batten the sails and row. Although backbreaking work, it kept him warm. The same couldn't be said for poor Jarek who couldn't find enough wraps to fight the chill.

Come sunset, they'd failed to find their island. "Milord, I fear we'll not find this Devil's Isle. Should we drop anchor and sleep in the boat, or look for land?"

Jarek's teeth chattered. "I fear I'll catch some malaise without a fire to warm me. Let's find an island."

Goodricke looked around. "Easily spoken, but how do we find one in all this haze?"

"Where there's land, there are living creatures. Large or small, I can probe for their presence. Once I find one, we can use it as a beacon."

He fell into a trance. Despite how many times as Goodricke had seen Lavan cast spells, he was still ill at ease around the arts.

Jarek pointed. "That way."

He rowed while Jarek directed their course. Glancing down, he could see bottom. "Milord, these waters are shallow. What of this lurker?"

Jarek shook his head. "A creature its size would give me a much stronger signature than what I sense. These are small, perhaps squirrels or birds or the like. We're safe."

True to Jarek's boast, they were soon rewarded with the sound of chirping birds. Using their song as a beacon, they quickly found land. Goodricke thanked the gods they'd begun their search before the birds had nested for the night.

They beached. Goodricke tied off the boat and they unloaded gear and pitched camp. Looking over the desolate island, he wondered if they were the first humans to have ever set foot on it. It was a mix of sand, rocks and grasses, the foliage matching the dull gray of the clay soil. Small trees were farther inland, likely where the birds nested.

With deadwood plentiful, they soon basked in the warmth of a roaring fire. However, the heavy mist spoiled any chance of getting a trident reading. "If this fog doesn't lift, I won't be able to fix our location. We're bound to have strayed off course."

They bedded down. Tired from the day's rowing, Goodricke was asleep as soon as his head touched his blanket. Despite his fatigue, he tossed fitfully, dreaming he was back in the water, his feet stuck in mud, unable to move. Bird-like creatures haunted the vision. Gathering in ever greater numbers, they circled overhead. Gone were those gentle chirps of the earlier birds, replaced by ever more raucous squawks. As if spurred on by their collective cries, the birds suddenly dove, one after the other, talons flexed, swooping down on Goodricke. Unable to move his feet, he clung to his boat, wondering what to do.

A loud thrumming shattered his dream. Waking, he looked around. It was the sword! He drew the blade. It was vibrating; glowing a brilliant blue.

Jarek yelped.

Goodricke scrambled out of his bed roll, sword in hand. A half dozen dark shadows flapped about just above the Magus's head, their squawks matching those of Goodricke's dream. A shrieking form veered away, diving toward him. Instinctively, he raised his weapon and struck. He felled it. Stepping over its thrashing carcass, he rushed to Jarek's side. A bat-like creature with protruding eyes and long pointed fangs was perched on the Magus's shoulder. It took off before he could kill it. He spun about, sword raised, but all had fled into the night sky. He lowered his weapon. Silent now, it ceased to glow. He looked at Jarek. "Milord, are you all right?"

Jarek touched the back of his neck. "I believe that creature bit me."

Probing, Goodricke found a cut. "You're right, there's blood." He removed his sash and dabbed at the wound.

Jarek shooed him away. "Did you see Turpin's blade?"

"Yes, it glowed. It hummed, too. That's what woke me."

Jarek conjured a light globe. "Let me see it?" Goodricke handed him the weapon. Jarek rotated it, examining it top to bottom. "How can this be? Mindless beasts lack the wit to have humors, good or evil, yet the blade responded as if they did."

Goodricke gathered wood and soon had the fire blazing again, and washed and bound Jarek's wound. Done, he retrieved the carcass of the creature he'd killed. It looked like an ugly bat with oversized fangs. "Look at this," he said, handing it to the Magus.

Jarek's eyebrows rose. "A red bat? I've never heard of such a thing." He sniffed. "It smells fishy, likely its usual prey." He held it up, examining it from every angle. "It hasn't been dead very long. Since the sword only reacts to evil, I should check for an aura."

He slipped into a trance. Moments later he snapped out of it. "The sword told true; this thing has an evil residue." He looked around. "Someone, or something, has used the Gift to pervert this creature. Is this Zakarah's deed, or is there some other evil at work here?"

Goodricke scanned the nearby bushes as he climbed back into his bed. Does some other evil lurk here, too? He shook his head. As if Zakarah weren't threat enough. He'd get little sleep this night.

Calamity

Goodricke woke to the pleasant twitter of birdsong, a sharp contrast to last night's bat attack. He sat up and was instantly overwhelmed by an awful stench. Foul Marsh had been aptly named.

The sun had burned away most of the fog, but a thin mist still hovered just above the water. Islands dotted the landscape everywhere, some only a short distance away. Jarek was awake too, looking around. "Malg's map isn't very detailed is it?"

"You've the right of that. I'm not sure how we'll ever discern which is Devil's Island." Worse, closely nested islands meant plenty of shallows. "The lurker could be anywhere."

Jarek climbed out of his bed. "You worry too much. Its signature would be huge. If I sense it, we'll give it a wide berth." The grasses swayed as a breeze blew through their encampment. "And won't this wind be good for sailing?"

"Aye." Goodricke rekindled the fire and they shared a morning meal of beans and bread, listening to the whisper of dancing tree leaves.

While loading the boat, a sudden hush fell over the island. Only the gentle buzz of insects defied the eerie silence. Goodricke scanned the area, his hand on Turpin's sword. A loud squeal pierced the quiet. A large boar-like creature came charging through the shallow water, spraying them as it raced past their camp, squealing in terror.

Curious yet wary, they followed its trail of rippling water and fading squeals. They'd walked less than fifty paces when they heard a horrific roar followed by a mournful bawl. Alarmed screeches erupted from all over the island. The sword vibrated.

Waves rippled across the nearby water, washing over rock and bush, bending any plant caught in its wake. The water settled. The whole island had gone deathly still. Goodricke exhaled ever so slowly, "What do you suppose that was?"

"I don't know," Jarek whispered, "nor do I wish to find out. Me thinks the sooner we leave this place, the better."

They made a hasty retreat to their encampment and finished loading their gear. Goodricke launched the boat and made for deeper waters, casting skittish glances at the water as he rowed.

Only when the water was too deep to see bottom did he drop a rock tied to a rope overboard. He lowered it until he ran out of twine. The rope was four times his height and the rock hadn't touched bottom. He hoped these waters were deep enough.

The breeze picked up enough to resume under sail, careful to steer clear of any island. Their morning was uneventful, but like the day before, around midday they lost their wind, forcing them to furl the sail.

Even though the day was warmer than the previous one, Jarek sat with knees cuddled to his chest, shivering. "Are you all right, milord?"

"I fear I'm with fever," he said through chattering teeth. "Likely from that vermin's bite."

"Should we make shore and get you to bed?"

Jarek hugged his chest, shaking his head. "We dare not lose a day. I just need rest."

Concerned, Goodricke foraged through the Magus's bag and tossed him his blanket. "Wrap yourself in this."

Jarek slid to the flooring and snuggled into it. "All right but wake me every once-in-a-while so I can probe for the lurker."

Later, Goodricke tried to wake him. "Milord, it's time for a probe." Jarek's only response was a moan. When further efforts fared no better, Goodricke decided to let him sleep. It just meant he'd need to stop every so often and use rock and rope to test the water's depth.

The repeated stops to check their depth slowed his progress. As the afternoon wore on, the landscape changed. Instead of occasional large islands with long stretches of open water in between, they were now smaller and more plentiful. Giant cypress trees sprouted out of the water everywhere. If their roots could find soil, the water wasn't deep.

The fog was gathering. Dusk was upon them. His back ached. He needed to find a camp spot. The fact that islands were plentiful now worked in their favor. Taking out his spyglass, he scoured the marsh, seeking one large and dry enough to be habitable, but between the gathering darkness and growing mist, seeing was difficult. He picked the nearest one of consequence, took its compass reading, and rowed in its direction.

The moist fog had him shivering, despite working the oars. He hoped Jarek's blanket was keeping him warm.

The island he'd spied through his glass came into view. Nearing shore, he heard only water splashing over rock, not birdsong. He thought back to how silent the marsh had gotten when the pig was killed. Was it quiet now because the lurker or some other equally loathsome beast was at hand?

He veered for the splashing sounds, sighing with relief as the bow thudded against the shoreline. He roused Jarek, albeit barely. Doubting the man could walk, he scooped him up, blanket and all, and carried him ashore. Propping him against a tree a safe distance from the water, he bundled him up. Shudders wracked the poor man's body. His forehead was on fire. Goodricke decided to scout to see if the island was camp worthy.

The place lacked any semblance to their previous camp. He'd walked only a short distance before the rocky soil gave way to rancid mire. Uncounted stumps poked through the thick green quagmire in unsuccessful attempts to become full trees. None were dry enough for fuel.

Stopping, he studied one of the mud pools. Mostly quicksand, it smelled putrid. Strange lumps were scattered over its surface. One moved; then another. They were alive. He searched his pockets for the jerky he'd snacked on earlier. He tossed a piece into the pond. It hit with a splash. Frenzied growls erupted from the nearby lumps. Long flat-winged creatures leaped at the serving, snarling after the spoils. Hungry eyes blinked from behind other distant lumps. He shuddered. This place would never do.

Even though the sun had set, daylight lingered. Taking out his spyglass, he climbed atop a boulder and scanned the area, finally spotting a grove of alders. After taking a compass reading, he returned to Jarek.

He gave him a sip of water and poured some on his fevered forehead. "Just one more channel to cross, milord, and then I can cook up a warm broth and tuck you into a proper bed."

Jarek nodded. "I'm awake, just help me stand."

Goodricke helped him into the boat, hopped in after him, and aimed for the channel. The quickness with which they crossed it surprised him. He took solace in knowing the day's ordeal would soon be over.

A sudden churning of the water doused that sense of relief. He scanned the area.

Jarek's warning broke his concentration. "It's very large, and very near."

A huge dark form swam past them, just below the surface. Waves rocked the boat as the creature sank from sight. It swam back and forth—to and fro. A giant gray back broke the surface, looking much like the great whales Goodricke had seen in his seafaring days. He rowed faster.

The beast rose out the water a fair distance away, staring at them through monstrously large eyes. Its head was twice the size of a man. Rows of jagged teeth rimmed its mouth. Several octopus like arms waved above its head, each with suctions spanning its length. It hovered briefly and then dove, the icy echo of its plunge reverberating across the water. The resulting wave caused him to miss a stroke. He struggled to regain his rhythm—they had to move. And quickly!

The lurker burst out of the water directly behind them, its roar reminiscent of the one they'd heard just before the boar's pathetic death cry, the smell of its rancid breath washing over them. It bellowed, poised above them, eying them. He flailed at the oars, frantic to reach the island. In his haste, the boat ricocheted off a submerged rock and tipped. He tumbled overboard, landing flat on his back. Pain ripped through his ankle. His foot was caught in the bowline. He grabbed it and freed his foot just as the rope lurched, the force of it nearly tearing the twine from his grip. His head popped above the surface. The boat was moving. Jarek was at the oars. Each stroke jerked the rope forward. Each jerk dunked Goodricke under water.

He clung to the rope, knowing it was his lifeline. He couldn't see the beast but knew the safety of shore was only boat lengths away. Then something slithered past him. A moment later the boat was flipped airborne. Turbulence sucked him underwater, tumbling him to the muddy bottom. He thrashed about in a sea of blinding, swirling murk, swallowing rancid water. A knee touched bottom. He grabbed handfuls of mud to stop his spinning. Struggling to his feet, his head broke through the surface. He was stomach-deep in water. Gagging, he spewed fetid liquid from his mouth and wiped water from his eyes. He drew Turpin's sword. It was aglow, vibrating.

Long choking tentacles ensnared the shattered fragments of their boat. Jarek was nowhere in sight. The lurker's grotesque face hovered above the wreckage. Roaring, it lunged, its jaws splintering what remained of their skiff. Both boat and beast disappeared beneath brownish foam.

Fighting muddy footing and turbid water, Goodricke struggled toward shore. Something grabbed his foot, knocking him off balance. He sliced his weapon at his unseen assailant. The sharp blade struck something solid and his leg broke free. An instant later the monster's head appeared above him, swaying, its mouth open like a snake ready to strike. He splashed through the shallows, desperate to reach the beach, all the while waiting for that inevitable strike that would spell his doom.

That strike never came. Miraculously, his feet found dry sand. He ran far up the shoreline before daring to turn to see what had become of the lurker, to learn how he'd been spared.

It was bobbing and weaving, hovering above the wreckage in some sort of trance. Only paces away stood Jarek, knee-deep in water, arms outstretched and fingers dancing. Seeing Goodricke safely out of the water, he stopped casting and scrambled ashore and ran to join him.

Coming out of its trance, the lurker roared its displeasure, its bellow echoing throughout the marsh. With its prey having escaped, it sank underwater and didn't resurface.

Jarek arrived, panting. Using Goodricke's shoulder for support, he eased down beside him. "Heavens preserve us, it doesn't seem able to come ashore."

Goodricke sprawled onto his back, drained and spent. Jarek thudded down beside him. They lay there, propped on elbows, watching the lurker resurface twice more, before finally swimming away.

"Are you all right, milord?"

Jarek slapped Goodricke's shoulder, grinning. "I think I shall live—barely!"

Goodricke flexed his limbs. Although bruised and battered, he detected no serious injury. A remnant of a lurker tentacle still stuck to his ankle. He tried to rip it loose, but the suction wouldn't release. It hurt to try. Despondent, he stared out at the water. "Without a boat, we're stranded."

Missive

Stuffing Prior Rigby's note into her pocket, Rayna made the short walk to the parish and rang the bell. A manservant greeted her and led her to a sitting room with two cushioned chairs and a table scattered with books. "Please wait here, Lady. Prior Rigby is entertaining an important guest. He should be available shortly."

Was Prior Rigby talking with her visitor? The waiting rooms had no doors, allowing her to hear them talking in the adjacent room. Sitting straighter, she listened.

"But Your Grace, the magi acknowledge The Effulgence as the source of their magic, how could such use be deemed heretical?"

It was the Grand Inquisitor, here at the parish! Wait until Yudelle hears!

"It's not what they use, but how they use it. Rest assured, if any crime is descried, I'll not hesitate to prosecute them the same as I would any other heretic."

"As you say Your Grace, but I assure you it's unlikely. I know many of them. All are good men."

"Perhaps, but if you prove wrong, I'll show them no more mercy than they deserve. Our ship's dungeons await any who profane His Gift."

Their voices shifted to the corridor, growing louder—they were heading her way. Rayna grabbed a book, pretending to read it. She glanced up in time to see the men walk past her doorway.

A short time later Prior Rigby walked into her room and smiled. "My apologies for keeping you waiting my dear, but I too, had a visitor."

Setting down her book, she stood to greet him. "You've no need to apologize."

He motioned for her to follow. "Come, your visitor awaits you." They headed down a short corridor. She inhaled, trying to calm herself. Who would it be? Robard? Her father?

They entered another waiting room, a twin to the one she'd just left. Her visitor spoke. "I assumed correctly then." It was the fat monk, the one who had the townsfolk laughing at his sermon.

"I'll leave you two alone," Prior Rigby offered, withdrawing.

Rayna approached the man. "What is it you assumed, Sir?"

The friar stood. "Ah, forgive the vagaries of an old man. When I saw you in town, I was sure it was you. Please," he gestured toward a chair, "have a seat and let me explain."

She sat. "It's Friar Luc, isn't it?"

Smiling, he nodded and seated himself. "Your memory is excellent, my dear."

"Sir, aside from our chance meeting at the market, should I know you?"

"No, no." He paused. "Where to begin? Maybe it would be best to be direct. I was sure it was you because you're the very image of your mother."

Her heart thudded! She'd expected to someday find her father, but her mother! This was something she had never dared to dream. "You know my mother?"

The friar shrugged. "It would be more precise to say I knew her. The last time I saw her she was your age, and you were but a babe." He leaned back, studying her face. "Were the image I see in my shaving glass not so obviously aged, you look so like her, I would swear I'd gone back in time and you were her."

I look like my mother! What else? Questions flooded her mind. "But where is she? Who is she? Why has she never contacted me? And what of my father, why does he ignore me? What is my crime to have been abandoned so?"

"Fair questions all. I'll try my best to answer them." He chuckled. "Firstly, babes do not commit crimes. As far as I know, you're innocent of any wrongdoing." He raised his eyebrows. "If you know otherwise, confess as much to Prior Rigby, not me."

The friar pondered a bit before continuing. "I only knew your mother a short while, but long enough to gain respect and a certain fondness for her. Although I don't know your father, I do know he's very highly placed. He shrugged. "But I digress." The friar flexed the chubby fingers of one hand against those of his other.

"Your mother was foreign-born, for she spoke with an accent. At the time we met I was Prior of a small country parish not far from St. Pyre, a town of some size on the mainland."

St. Pyre—I must remember that name.

"Your mother appeared at my doorstep one night, flush with fever. Clearly ill at ease, she kept peering over her shoulder. Although likely an unwise decision, I couldn't turn away anyone so ill, no matter what the source of her dread.

"My church was small, with only my room, a kitchen, the prayer room and a drawing room, which I proffered her. She wept at my offer.

"The next morning, curious to know what sort of artifice I'd embraced, I asked who or what it was she was fleeing. After much coaxing, she confessed that, despite being the wife of a Lord, the Church had declared her foreign beliefs to be heretical. She was fleeing to avoid ruining your father's name. I've seen what such allegations can do to the standing of noble families, as had your mother. Since you're a noble's daughter, it would have been a cardinal crime for her to take you with her."

I'm the daughter of a noble—one who cares nary a whit for his offspring.

"Around midday she fell into fevered delirium, raving in some foreign tongue. It lasted for two days, after which she seemed weak, but more her true self." Pausing, he placed his hand over Rayna's. "I don't feel I'm being overly bold in saying during this time each of us came to view the other as friend. I daresay I found myself rather smitten with her."

Riveted by the friar's tale, Rayna listened in silence, envious of this man who had spent time with the mother she so longed to know.

"On the day your mother departed she handed me two items, one a sealed missive, the other a list of names. 'I have a daughter' she said. 'She's but a babe in her father's care. I've been forced to leave these two people I hold most dear, to return to my homeland. I'll likely remain there, but I would have my child know something of her mother.' She handed me her list. 'The first of the names is that of my daughter. She's celebrated but one winter. The second name is of an inn in St. Pyre. The last is my manservant and friend. His brother owns the inn. I know I ask much of you, but when she reaches her majority—long after news of me would ruin her good name, could you deliver this letter to the innkeeper and ask that he get it to my daughter?'

"I accepted the request and stowed these..." He said, pulling a parchment from his pocket and handing it to her.

It was her mother's list. "St. Pyre, then? My father lives there?" She asked, looking up, sure she wouldn't rest until she confronted him. "And this man..." her finger trailed to the third name, "...Jagger, he lives there too, near this King's Inn?"

Friar Luc nodded. "Yes, and he's still in your father's employ."

She shook her head, wondering at all she'd heard. "But how did you know how to find me?"

He chuckled. "Little did I know at the time of my promise how daunting a task I'd undertaken. Realizing this was your year of majority, I set out for St. Pyre, some two moons back. I found the innkeeper and established that this Jagger was indeed his brother. I told him I bore an important message and asked if he would deliver it. A prudent man, he refused, but promised he'd speak with his brother. He asked that I return the following day.

"When I arrived, Jagger was there. I asked him to deliver this to you." The friar held up the missive. "He sat quiet for a long time. 'I'm sorry, I cannot do that, but be here this evening and perhaps I can tell you where to deliver it.'

"When I returned, he made good on his promise, telling me you were here attending this island's Lady Academy. I had long since left my little parish to wander God's country delivering His message to the people. Since I'd never visited your island, I decided I would undertake to earn the passage to get me here."

Rayna reached for her purse. "Oh, good friar, my father's reckoner keeps my purse well fed. Please tell me your costs and I'll make good on them."

He shook his head. "Nay lass, I did this out of respect for your mother. Consider it a labor of love. I found a merchant ship that booked occasional passengers," he held out his hands, palms up, "and now I'm here.

"Milady, such is the tale of how I got here, but not why. Here," he handed the epistle. "This is from your mother." His smile was gentle. "Oh!" He pulled a golden key from his pocket. "I'm to give you this, too."

As he passed the key it fell from her trembling grip, clanging to the floor.

"Allow me, milady."

Wheezing, he bent down and grabbed it with his pudgy paw. Wrapping her quivering hand in his, he folded her fingers over the key. "I shall leave you to your privacy, Lady. You're as beautiful as your mother. I hope her message is one of love."

He stood. "I must leave for your port city, now. My captain was to dock for but a few days before returning to the mainland. I wish you the best." He kissed her hand. "It has been an honor. Rest and compose yourself now. I shall see myself out."

Rayna remained sitting, limbs shaking, staring at the friar's back as he left the room. Finally, drawing a deep breath, she slipped her finger between paper and wax, but couldn't bring herself to break the seal. Would its tidings be ill or good? The reading of its contents could never be undone and might change her life forever. Did she truly want that? Deciding not knowing was the worst thing possible, she broke the seal.

It held a letter and a leather map sketched in charcoal. The map listed two townships, Portsmouth and a place called A'ryth. Was this the Portsmouth she knew, or was that name given to many a port city? If so, this map could be of these very islands. The map included a drawing of a man with a key on his forehead, its shape matching the one the friar had given her.

She opened the letter.

> My dearest daughter and love of my bosom, you don't know me—or mayhap even of me, but I am your mother. Leaving you behind was grievously painful, but to stay would bring shame, or worse, to you and your father. Because I love you both, I have returned to my place of birth where my reputation cannot harm you.

Tears blurred Rayna's vision. Her mother had loved her. Wiping her eyes, she resumed.

> It is my hope that someday you'll find a way to forgive the mother who abandoned you. It would grant my fondest dream to lay eyes upon you one more time. Your father's people look unkindly upon mine, without tolerance or understanding. That is why my people stay hidden from Outlanders. Trust me in this and show no one this map. It will lead you to me should you choose to come.
> I love you. Your mother, —Akaisha.

Akaisha. The friar hadn't mentioned her name. Yes, very foreign sounding. She'd expected to someday find her father, but her mother? She'd spent her whole life knowing nothing of her parents and suddenly in a single conversation she'd learned where each lived. She wiped nose and eyes. "I'll find you both." They were accountable to her. Someday she'd look each in the eye and demand to know why they'd abandoned her so.

Prior Rigby entered the room. "I understand the friar left us."

She glanced up, blinking away tears.

He frowned. "Did he upset you, my dear?"

She stood, smiling as she wiped her eyes. "No, not at all. This is as good as I've felt in many a moon. The friar and I had a most interesting discussion, but he had to leave. I should do the same." She tucked the letter and map into her bag and walked over and kissed Prior Rigby's cheek. "Thank you for sending for me."

He rubbed the spot she'd kissed, grinning. "I shall have to invite you here more often."

She hugged him. "Please do."

She departed, her dread of Robard's pending arrival vanquished. She wouldn't be here when he arrived; she'd be off pursuing her mother. Although she had no idea how she'd decipher her mother's map, she also knew hell's own demons couldn't prevent her from trying. *My mother wants to see me!*

Allegations

Gresham walked into the garrison on his way to Marshal Booker's offices, hoping he'd know his uncle's whereabouts. He was still reeling, struggling to comprehend that strange sense that had come over him in his duel with Quinn. The Captain had called him a witch's get. Was the Captain right? Was he possessed?

An aide greeted him as he entered the office. It was a waiting area with two chairs and the aide's desk. Behind it was an office, its door open.

"Yes?" the clerk asked.

"Cadet Gresham here to speak with the Marshal."

"Did he order you here?"

"No, sir."

The aide laughed, shaking his head. "Cadets do not simply march into an officer's command post and demand to see him. Come back when the Marshal has requested it."

"Please. This has to do with my uncle—he and the Marshal are acquaintances. It's important."

"Important to you, or him? In my duties I hear many such requests. Unfortunately, inquiring about uncles does not rank high among them. I'm sorry Cadet, but I cannot grant your request."

He'd feared as much, but it was nonetheless disappointing. "Gramercy," he said, turning to leave.

"Stay!" came a command from the doorway. It was the Marshal. "I was about to summon you. I've a matter of my own I want to discuss with you—perhaps they're even one-and-the-same. Join me in my office."

The Marshal motioned for Gresham to sit. He leaned back in his chair, looking grim. "I gather you're here to inquire about your uncle?"

"Yessir."

"Later. I have other news to discuss first—bad news."

Bad news? What sort of troubles heckled him now? He waited, fearing the worst.

"Captain Dyson and his son are disputing your tourney win."

"What?!" This was the last thing Gresham expected to hear. "On what grounds?"

"They claim you used witchcraft."

"I can't believe this, not even of Quinn."

"Blame the father, not the son." The Marshal leaned forward. "More importantly, is there any basis for their charge?"

"I…" What could he say—what *should* he say? Would the Marshal even believe him? "I'm not sure."

The Marshal leaned back. "Tell me."

He listened as Gresham recounted the tale of his duel and his strange behavior, leaving nothing out.

"It sounds as if you fell into a berserker's rage."

"I'm sorry, Sir, I'm not familiar with the word. Does it mean I truly did use witchery, or that I'm mad?"

"Mad?" He laughed. "No, nor is it witchery. It's a form of battle rage triggered by events around you. Although rare, we have berserkers in the army. They are warriors without peer while in these rage-triggered frenzies. In the Nosarian War I saw a berserker engage seven foes and singlehandedly kill them all. He later explained that while in such a rage, there was no such emotion as fear, only the desire to destroy his enemies."

Gresham sat stunned. "That's exactly how I felt. Had Cadet Quinn's plea to spare him not brought me back to my senses, I fear I'd have done him serious harm."

The Marshal nodded. "So it was with this man."

"What became of him? Did he rise within the ranks?"

The Marshal pursed his lips. "His squad was ambushed. Seeing his comrades die triggered his rage. Although all his assailants died in the ensuing skirmish, so did he." The Marshal met his eye, "Take heed, Gresham, berserkers rarely die of old age."

Gresham sat silent, absorbing what he'd heard, pondering how best to control his newfound aspect. He met the Marshal's gaze. "How should I respond to the Captain's charges, Sir?"

The Marshal leaned his elbows on the desktop. "My first instinct would be to contest it." He sat back. "However, the Chevaliers' Grand Inquisitor is here in Stalwart. If he gets wind of witchery charges, and who your mother was, I fear he'll pursue the matter, something I'm sure the good Captain is aware of. As unfair as it sounds, my advice is to surrender your title, and perhaps revisit the charges once the Inquisitor is gone. Meanwhile, leave Stalwart; and soon. As long as the Inquisitor is here, you're at risk."

"I'll leave forthwith, but I'd like to speak of my uncle first. Do you know his whereabouts?"

The Marshal paused, eying him. "It is an important aspect of my duties to have eyes and ears everywhere. One such source informed me your uncle left on a mission on behalf of the university magi. What and where, I know not. I suggest you ask them." Picking up paper and quill, he scribbled a note and handed it to Gresham, "The highways are dangerous; if you're leaving, you'll need protection. This is a requisition for whatever supplies and weapons you need. May the gods smile on your efforts to find your uncle."

Gresham went to the soldier's hall and started packing, grateful for the Marshal's requisition. His knapsack would hold very little. What to take, and what to leave? He set aside two pair of breeches, a tunic, coat and shirt. He stuffed his parents' rings into his purse—he'd not leave those behind. He'd also take his father's hammer and belt; nothing more.

The morning was waning, and it was almost time for his promised meeting with Rayna. He'd have to let her know he wouldn't be around for her rose-pinning ceremony. Assuming she'd even be willing to see him after his strange behavior at the tourney. He left in search of her.

He found her waiting on the academy porch. "Good day, Lady."

She flashed one of those radiant smiles. "Good day to you, Cadet." She brought a hand to her mouth. "Now that you're no longer a cadet would it be overly bold to simply call you Gresham?"

He smiled. "Not at all, Lady."

"Then addressing me as Lady must cease too. Please call me Rayna."

He gave a mock bow. "As you please. So how goes your day …Rayna?"

Her smile faded. "I have something to discuss."

It was as he feared; she couldn't abide his behavior after seeing his duel. With him having to leave, it was probably best. "As do I." Perhaps hearing her out first would prolong their time together a bit. "How about we make our confessions as we head to the market, and get to know one another better as promised?"

Her face lit up. "Absolutely!" He couldn't decide if she smiled more with her eyes or her mouth.

They started down toward town. She agreed to tell why she fabricated her tale of him having asked to present her rose, but only if he'd share something equally personal about himself.

She related her tale. Learning she'd said what she had to keep Quinn from hurting her friend was comforting.

"I'd not seen you before yesterday. Are you newly here?" he asked after she'd finished her tale.

"Yes. My father moves me someplace new each year. Always being a stranger makes acquiring friends difficult, so I lead a secluded life."

"Perhaps that explains it. Yours is a face I wouldn't forget." His neck flushed. He was making a fool of himself. "I fear I'm not as practiced at little talk as you highborns."

Her eyes twinkled. "Had you not told me I'd be completely fooled." She cocked her head. "Your turn. Tell me about Gresham Smithy."

He related growing up as an orphan here in Stalwart. By the time he was done, they'd reached town, and were weaving their way through throngs of people. Barkers' cries echoed along Market Street, extolling their wares. "Stop Sir! See this one! This will please her—buy it for your lady!"

Odd aromas wafted the area too. Food smells mixed with body odors, their collective reek powerful enough to water the eyes.

"So, 'no-longer-a-cadet Gresham,' what is it you wanted to discuss with me?"

The moment he dreaded was upon him. Stopping, her faced her. "I know it's tradition to have your rose pinned by a cadet, and that I promised I'd do it, but fate is forcing me to leave Stalwart, and before your ceremony. That means I can't be that cadet."

She broke out laughing. Did she think him a fool? "The gods are toying with us—I'm leaving too, and with luck, before my rose-pinning ceremony. So, what are these events beyond your control?"

"Suffice it to say it has to do with Chevaliers," he said, looking around.

"Oh." Her brow furrowed. "Tell me, did your soldiering include map reading?"

"It's a vital part of our survival training."

She studied the ground as they walked. "You asked of my plans." She looked up. "Please do not repeat what I'm about to tell you." She looked around, as if searching for someone. "I've been apart from my mother since I was a babe and have no memory of her. A man who once knew her has given me a map to where she abides. The map lists a town called Portsmouth. I'm wondering if it's the one here in these islands." She stopped. "If I were to show it to you, could you tell me if that's true?"

He shrugged. "I can't say for sure, but I suspect as much. Do you have it with you?"

"No, it's back in my room."

"Perhaps you can show it to me when we return."

Gresham started when he spied a trio of Chevaliers skulking about, challenging people, searching merchants' booths and waving crystal wands over their possessions. Pulse racing, he fingered the purse holding his mother's ring. Had the Captain told them of his witchery? Were they here looking for him? Was it too risky to even be here?

He was deciding how best to avoid them when a shout erupted from behind them. "You! Remain where you are!"

He could hardly breathe. Anticipating the worst, he turned to see who'd barked the order. Only paces away, three white-cloaked soldiers had surrounded a dark-skinned lady. They pushed the distraught woman to her knees, her eyes wide with fear. While two held her arms, the third waved his crystal wand over the necklace she wore. The crystal flared a bright blue. "Moonstone!" the man hollered. "In the name of His Grace, you are charged with heresy."

"No, please!" she cried out as they ripped off her neckpiece. They bound her hands and looped a rope around her neck. The crowd opened a wide swath, staring in rapt fascination as the Chevaliers half-pushed, half-dragged the pleading woman down the street. He shared her dread. One churchman stayed behind, eyeing the crowd. When his gaze settled on him, Gresham quickly looked away.

Rayna took his arm. "Perhaps we should forego visiting the caravan."

"Yes," he whispered. "Let's have look at your map."

They returned to her academy. She had him wait while she retrieved the map. Returning, she spread it out on a table.

"This is definitely a map of our islands," he said, looking it over. "That's our Portsmouth," he said, pointing, "but I've spent my whole life in the islands and have never heard of this place called A'ryth." He looked up. "What is it you'll do with this map?"

"Follow it and find my mother, of course."

He shook his head. "It's not that simple." He pointed. "See these marks, and these? They represent mountains and swamps. Although passage along the sea looks simple enough, A'ryth itself is deep in wilderness." He turned to her, "I'm sorry, this place you seek is no place for the likes of a lady."

Gifted

The next day Gresham trekked the long walk to the university. The hot day made it seem even longer. His spirits brightened when he spied an archway with 'University of Arcane Arts' embossed on it. That glee faded dramatically when he spotted a group of Chevaliers camped outside its walls. Dare he pass by them?

Feigning casualness, he marched right up to the gatehouse guard. "Kindly inform your headmaster that Magus Verity's nephew is here and wishes to speak with him."

The bored guard raised the gate, letting him in, and led him to the guard shack. "Wait here," he said, and disappeared into a building on the far side of the bailey.

Gresham surveyed his surroundings, a habit formed in his survivor training. The shack sported a single bench with several chains dangling overhead; likely pulleys for raising and lowering the portcullis. Lowered, its heavy bars and high walls would make the university impenetrable.

The sentry returned. "The headmaster isn't in, but Master Kagen has offered to speak with you." Gresham had no idea who that was.

He was taken inside to a room with books strewn everywhere. A white-haired old man sat waiting, appraising him as he entered. He smiled. "You must be Gresham."

"Yessir. How is it you know my name?"

"Your uncle is closely acquainted with our headmaster. It was he who told me about you. I am Master Kagen. Sit," he said, gesturing to an empty chair. "I presume you're here for news of your uncle?"

"Yes, among other things."

"He departed yesterday and will likely be gone for quite some time. Is there some way I can assist you?"

"You could tell me where he went."

"I'm sorry, I cannot share that information."

"I beg you sir, it's important that I find him."

Master Kagen sat silent for a bit. "You are family, mayhap that gives you the right to know. I'll have to think on it. In the meanwhile, you said 'among other things,' what did that mean?"

Dare he answer? Hells, share nothing; learn nothing. Opening his satchel, he removed his parent's rings and Prior Rigby's book. "Can you tell me anything of these, and what magic is—how it works?"

Kagen laughed. "Learn in one brief conversation what our students take years to learn, eh?" He picked up Gresham's mother's ring, examined it, then did the same with his father's. Lastly, he thumbed through the book. "You ask what magic is. Baldric Milos, a famous Great Age Scholar, defined sorcery as 'the shaping of the natural events through arcane means.' In other words, manipulating normal things and events through use of the One Star's aethers. We call such manipulation High Magic. A variant, known as Earth Magic, uses released aethers absorbed by the earth during daylight, that are released at night. Because it's strongest at night, it's often referred to as Moon Magic. Since the One Church considers its use heretical, you rarely hear it discussed."

Master Kagen's explanation was beyond him. He had no idea what anything the man just said meant. But thinking back on the Chevalier's arrest of that poor caravan woman for having a moonstone, the part about The One Church rang true.

Kagen picked up the rings. "What is it you wish to know about these items?"

"My uncle gave me those rings. They belonged to my parents. The book behaves strangely when I touch it. But only me, no one else. I wish to know why. Also, I was recently possessed, and fear I might be a witch."

He proceeded to recount his contest with Quinn, the sensations that came over him, the Captain's remark, and the Marshal's assessment of all that happened.

Master Kagen proved an attentive listener, waiting silently until Gresham finished. "I can certainly understand your curiosity; however, the answers could take a while."

This man has answers he thought, his heart beating faster. "Take all the time you need, Sir."

Master Kagen's account of the rings was pretty much the same as his uncle's, but what he said of the book was much more insightful. "The book is written in runes—the script of the magi. It describes warring spells. This reaction you're experiencing hints of attunement."

"Attunement? Is that some sort of bewitchment?"

Kagen chuckled. "No. Attunement is a rare form of the Gift. I know little of it, but we've a guest magus visiting from the mainland, a Master Vardon, who is well versed in the kind of spells in this book. What I do know is that attunement means you're gifted. Not surprising given your heritage. I can verify that if you're willing."

I'm gifted. "Uncle Jarek suspected as much. At the time I thought it farfetched, but now... you say you can determine if I'm gifted. How?"

"By putting you through what we call a prism test." He stood. "Come; this won't take long. Afterwards, we'll speak with Vardon about how the book affects you."

He was led to a small, roofless amphitheater. Sunlight flooded the room. At its center stood a waist-high table supported by four marble pillars. Sitting atop the pillars was the largest gem Gresham had ever seen. Ruby red and half the size of a man's head, it was pyramid-shaped save for its curved top. Other smaller jewels adorned the room's walls.

"How does it work?"

Kagen placed a palm atop the gem. Light burst forth, echoed by the gems on the walls. The old man smiled. "What you see are radiating aethers. It happens whenever the stone is touched by someone capable of channeling them. If you're mundane, they do nothing. Go ahead, try it."

Taking a deep breath, Gresham reached out and ever so cautiously lowered his palm. Light flashed. His eyelids fluttered, and his legs gave out. All went black as he sank to the floor.

Fingertips rubbed his temples. His dizziness slowly faded, allowing him to focus again. Master Kagen was kneeling over him, attending him. "You absorbed the aethers so quickly you couldn't contain them. You need training. As I suspected, your Gift is strong." He helped Gresham to a sitting position. "Now, if you feel able, we'll have that talk with Vardon."

They went to Kagen's chamber. He rang a summons bell, after which the door opened, and a plump wild-haired fellow about his own age poked his head in. "Sir?"

"Hagley, please ask Master Vardon to join us."

Minutes later they were joined by a trim-looking man not significantly older than Gresham. Dark-haired and of medium height, his coal-black eyes radiated intelligence. "You wished to see me?"

"Yes, come in. I've a young man I'd like you to meet. First however, would you bear with me in a brief experiment?" Kagen stood, holding a scarf. "This may seem odd, but I'd like to cover your eyes."

Looking puzzled, Vardon complied. Kagen cinched it tight and led him to the table filled with books. Burying Gresham's deep within the pile, he said, "Please choose the desired book from the table in front of you."

"That's not much to go on," Vardon said, blindly probing the stack. He picked up a book, shrugged, and set it back down. He did the same with book after book—until he found Gresham's. The instant he touched it he jerked his hand away. He removed his blindfold and examined it. "I gather this is your desired book." He looked at Kagen, "It made my hand throb."

The old magus joined him. "Have you ever experienced this before?"

"No, but I've heard of it. I believe it's called attunement." Vardon studied the cover. "Battle Strategies and Actions." He flipped through a few pages. "How did you come to possess this?"

Kagen pointed at Gresham. "That young man brought it with him. Since the boy reacts to it in much in the manner you do, I believe you've just verified the lad is attuned to the war arts."

Kagen waved Gresham over. "Gresham, meet Master Vardon. He specializes in combative spells."

Gresham nodded. "Pleased, sir."

Vardon studied him as if seeing him for the first time. "And me as well.

Kagen crossed his arms. "I tested him. He's strong."

"As one would expect of someone attuned." Vardon rubbed his chin. "So, you're a new student?"

"No, Sir."

"Then you studied the arts on the mainland?"

Gresham shook his head. "I've never studied them, Sir."

Vardon looked at Kagen. "That's surprising."

Kagen shrugged. "The question is, what do we do with him?"

"That's easy. With a Gift this rare, I'll tutor him." He smiled at Gresham. "What say you to becoming my student?"

Study under a War Mage; combine his arts with his military training. He felt overwhelmed. *I'm gifted—and rarely so?* But as much as Master Vardon's offer appealed to him, staying amongst Chevaliers was too risky. "A most generous offer, Sir, but circumstance is forcing me to leave Stalwart. For how long, I can't say. If your offer still stands when I return, I would be honored to accept it."

"Nonsense! Whatever this matter is, it can wait. Consider yourself my student as of now."

"Stop badgering him, Vardon. Give the lad time to think. You and I shall speak on it later. Right now, he and I have another matter to discuss."

"As you wish, but rest assured, you'll not dissuade me from mentoring such a rare talent," he challenged, then left the room.

Master Kagen eased into a chair. "You asked of your uncle's whereabouts. He's undertaking a quest on behalf of a mutual friend."

"What sort of quest? Where?"

"You wouldn't have heard it. Ancient documents refer it as A'ryth."

Did he mishear? A'ryth was the mysterious city on Rayna's map!

"I'm sorry," Kagen continued, "but I'm not at liberty to share the nature of his mission. Since he'll likely be gone for some time, I suggest you seriously consider Master Vardon's offer, he's very good, and as you observed, very insistent."

With Chevaliers lurking everywhere, there was no way he could do that, especially now that he'd learned where his uncle had gone.

A'ryth! If Rayna would take him on as her guide, he might not only find his uncle; but stay in the company of the most alluring woman he'd ever met. And be free of the Chevaliers' clutches to boot. It was fated. "I'll think on it and give him my answer tomorrow. Right now, I have other business to tend to."

"I understand you walked here."

"I did."

"That's a long walk. How about I have Hagley drive you home. We don't want you to be too tired to give our proposition due consideration. I'll have him meet you at the stables."

A short time later the fellow who'd fetched Master Vardon appeared with a wagon. "Are you Gresham?" he asked.

"I am," Gresham said, climbing aboard.

The driver offered his hand. "Hagley here. Master Kagen says I'm to take you to the soldier's hall in Stalwart."

As they rode, Gresham pondered all that had just happened. *I'm gifted—like my mother and uncle.* He'd never contemplated such a possibility. And Rayna and his uncle seeking the same city! Was this coincidence, or was it preordained? Perhaps the gods were using him for some end of their own? Would she consider him for her guide? "Hagley, is there any chance you take me to the Lady's Academy instead?"

Hagley did, and Gresham went inside to ask for Rayna, but the woman attending the desk was busily conversing with an older fellow. "I'm sorry, but Lady Rayna isn't here," she said, looking apologetic. "May I give her a message?"

"Yes, please tell her Robard is here. She'll know who I am. Tell her I'm lodging at that Dragon place."

"Yes milord."

Looking frustrated, the man walked away.

The clerk noticed Gresham. "May I help you?"

"I was looking for Lady Rayna too. Perhaps I…"

She raised a hand, watching Robard leave. As soon as the door closed behind him, she glanced up at the balcony and nodded. He looked. Rayna was standing there, watching from above. 'Come,' she mouthed, waving him up.

As he climbed the stairs, her gaze never left the front door. She led him into an empty room. "I dare not let that man know I'm here," she said, closing the door.

"Why? Who is he?"

She opened the door and took another peek. "Every year my father sends him to escort me to wherever I'm to go next," she whispered. "But this time I won't be going with him. Instead, I'll be searching for my mother."

His heart sank. "You found a guide?"

"I wish!" She sighed. "Truthfully, I don't know how to go about finding one."

"What would you think of me being your guide?"

"How? You said you did not know of the place."

"Nor does anyone else, but I looked into the matter. A'ryth is an ancient city only a few scholars know about. All I need to find it is your map."

"You looked into the matter?" she asked, smiling. "Aren't you the clever one." She studied him, as if seeing him in a new light. "I'm fully prepared to pay someone to guide me." Did that mean she was considering using him? "Would two golds be adequate?"

Two golds! Gods! That was 200 pence! More than two months' pay. Dare he tell her he'd gladly have done it for free? No, that was impractical. There'd be expenses to cover. "How about one gold before we leave—for buying supplies, and the other after we find your mother?"

"Agreed!" She spit into her palm and raised it. He did likewise. Pressing palms, they sealed their bargain.

"It's urgent that I leave soon," he said. "How quickly can you be ready?"

She glanced toward the door. "With Robard skulking about, the sooner we leave, the more pleased I'll be."

"Would tomorrow be too soon?"

"More like too late. How about you come for me at daybreak? Throw a pebble that window," she said, pointing, "and I'll come join you."

Gresham left, hardly believing his good fortune. Time was short, and it was up to him to get them supplied. He could buy most of what was needed in Portsmouth, but using the Marshal's supply requisition could save on expenses.

He headed for the armory. He entered and froze. Two Chevaliers were there foraging through gear. The supply clerk looked up. "One moment, gentlemen," he said, turning to Gresham. "What can I do for you?"

Tearing his eyes from the churchmen, Gresham laid the requisition on the counter. "I need three packs; the kind you can strap on your back. Oh, and a sword."

The clerk looked at it. "This doesn't indicate that many packs."

"Are you sure?" he asked, looking at the requisition. "When I talked with the Marshal, I was quite specific about needing three."

The clerk eyed him. "You spoke with Marshal Booker?"

Gresham nodded. "Yes, earlier this day."

The clerk looked at the Marshal's seal. His eyebrows raised. "Far be it from me to question a Marshal. Wait here."

Gresham eyed the Chevaliers, but they were paying him no heed.

"Here," the clerk said, plopping the requested items on the counter."

Thinking back on the map, at the wilds it depicted, he wondered if he'd need more than a sword. "How about one of those crossbows too?"

The clerk looked at him, then the requisition. "It's does say 'weapons,' and that's definitely the Marshal's seal." Shrugging, he brought one over.

Eyeing the Chevaliers, Gresham donned his sword, and tried to stuff the crossbow into a pack. It was too large. He stuffed two packs into a third, strapped the crossbow to it, put on the pack, and headed out the door.

⁓⁕⁓

Quinn was making his way to the garrison, his mood ill. He'd just endured another berating from his father for losing the tourney, getting reminded how his father had won his tourney, as had his father before him. Worse, Quinn had lost to a commoner, an intolerable embarrassment. What angered Quinn most was that Smithy had resorted to witchcraft to do it. At the time of the duel, he'd had been in such a state of shock he hadn't noticed. Fortunately, his father had. Smithy, a witch's get! In hindsight, it was obvious. How else could a commoner defeat a gentry? He smiled. His father's plan was sure to work. The title would soon be his.

Lost in thought, he nearly ran into Smithy as he burst out the armory door, a pack on his back. Was the coward running? "Going someplace, Smithy?"

"As a matter of fact, I am."

His answer was curt. Ever was the man ill-mannered. One who didn't even have the grace to show the proper deference due an obvious superior.

He spat, barely missing the Smithy's boot. "I've just learned about your mother. It must be as they say—that fruit falls close to its tree. You'd best hurry away witch boy, before we make known your crime."

His piece said, Quinn stalked away, feeling good for the first time that day. The Chevaliers knew how to deal with Smithy's ilk. Perhaps it was time he speeded matters along.

Marooned

Goodricke looked out at the shattered remnants of their boat. Bobbing beside it was the netting that held their belongings. "Look, our gear! Praise the gods, we still have our supplies."

"Don't be too sure," Jarek cautioned, "That netting looks torn."

Goodricke went over to retrieve it. Jarek was right; one entire side of the netting had been shredded. He pulled it ashore and started removing their gear, one piece at a time, examining each as he did so. The food bag was all but destroyed; they had barely enough for a single meal. And all but one water bag was gone, but the rest looked undamaged. He spotted Jarek's bag floating a few feet from shore, and waded out to rescue it. Stuffing it and anything else salvageable into the torn net, he dragged it up the beach. "We'd best pitch camp and build a fire. Everything's soaked, especially us."

They found a flat dry place farther inland. Dry brush was plentiful, and they soon had a fire blazing. A closer inspection of their salvaged gear revealed their map and parchments still intact, as was his tritant.

Jarek's shivering continued. Goodricke had him change into warmer clothing and crawl under Goodricke's bed blanket—the only one still dry. He parked him near the fire. The heat soon did its job, and Jarek's shudders subsided.

By the time he finished cooking their meal, the Magus was asleep. Thinking nourishment more important than rest, Goodricke roused and fed him. Still feverish, as soon as Jarek was done eating, he dozed off again.

Damp clothes and night air had Goodricke shivering too. To make matters worse, the lurker had torn the remaining clothing bag. Not only was the remaining bed blanket soaked, so were his clothes. He wrung them out, donned his wet coat, built up the fire, and strung a line to dry his clothing on. Wrapping the damp blanket around his shoulders, he hunkered down as close to the flames as he dare, watching the steam rise off the sodden gear. After rotating his blanket's wet side to the fire a few times, he had it mostly dried.

The evening offered one bit of good news. The skies had cleared. He got out his tritant and took a reading. These new settings would give them a decent bearing, even if cloud cover tomorrow prevented him from updating them again soon.

Strange-sounding animal calls filled the evening air. He stared into the darkness but spied no creatures. He heaped more fuel on the fire. Whatever was out there would likely fear fire. He huddled under his blanket shuddering; whether from dread or cold he wasn't sure. What he did know was that he'd get little or no sleep this night.

⁂

Jarek couldn't stop thrashing. Delirious, his only awareness was of burning heat. He drifted in and out of consciousness. He awoke drenched. Had his fever broken? The burning sensation had eased, as had his muscle pains. Grateful, he drifted back toward slumber.

Jarek!

Who dared disturb him? *Go away.*

Jarek, it's Lavan!

Some distant, lucid part of his mind forced his alertness. *Gods Lavan, is it really you? Where are you?*

In a cage, in Zakarah's elsewhere, or more accurately his hell. Beware, Zakarah is demon-kind!

Gods! Things just kept getting worse. *What's your condition? Has he harmed you?*

So far, it's been bearable—but only barely. Mine is one of many cages. Each holds a captive. Some creatures are sentient, but most are feebleminded. What we all have in common is the Gift. He's collecting sorcery. Once he drains a captive of its knowledge, that creature disappears. Knowing this, I resist him, but he's frightfully strong. I don't know how much longer I can defy him.

You must! I'm coming for you. The next Nexus is imminent. I'll be there to attempt a rescue, but I need your help. What is Zakarah's aim? What does he covet? What can I barter for you?

He rapes our minds, ravaging us for anything that has to do with the arts. We're unable to prevent it, and the pain of it is excruciating.
What has he taken from you?
Information about the university's relics. He's obsessed with them. He constantly probes my mind seeking more knowledge of them.
What have you told him?
I'm sorry. I must go. He comes.
Wait! Answer me first. Lavan?
Silence greeted his plea.

Zakarah stared at his shimmering reflection pool, relishing yet another discovery in this latest world. The image before him was female. Thin, and robed in black, her Gift was odd; powerful yet somehow tainted—perhaps reflective arts. Her wooded surroundings were so dark he could barely see her. She knelt before the quivering beast that lay before her. She touched it and its trembling stopped. Its body began transforming into a beast of a different sort; apparently one more suited to her liking. He smiled. Was she a collector too? This female interested him. Best of all, she'd ventured close enough to water to be gathered. The hunt was afoot. Whatever arts she possessed would soon be his.

He extended his arms, his fingers dancing, visualizing her trapped inside one of his cages. Once he harvested her, it would be her home.

He started. Instead of teleporting to his pool, she looked up, as if she could somehow see him. Hissing, she pointed a gnarled finger. His chest spasmed. Stunned, he watched the snarling female thrust her hand higher. His twitches turned to agony. He could scarcely breathe. With monumental effort, he broke his link to her world. His convulsions faded. Fear was an emotion he rarely felt, but it had just touched him. This one had power. He breathed deeply, calming himself, shaking off the memory of her touch. She'd surprised him was all; it wouldn't happen again. It was simply a matter of time before he collected her too.

Devil's Isle

Warm sunlight shining on Goodricke's face wakened him. Squinting, he looked up. The sun had bored a small hole through the cloud cover, providing a soothing respite from the swamp's unending gloom. He lay savoring its rays until drifting clouds blocked them again. Sitting, he surveyed their campsite. The fire had died, and dew had undone much of his drying efforts. At least he'd stayed warm. Despite its dampness, his thick blanket had preserved his body heat.

He crawled out of his warm cocoon and slipped on his boots. The lurker's tentacle still clung to his ankle. He examined the soft fleshy suctions that gripped his skin. Efforts to pull it free were both painful and futile. Somehow, he needed to get rid of it. Between it and his swollen ankle, he could hardly lace on his boot.

He hobbled over to check on the still sleeping Jarek. His hair was damp. Was it dew or had his fever broken? Jarek stirred as Goodricke felt his forehead, but didn't waken. He wasn't nearly as hot as the night before. Deciding to let the magus sleep, he re-stoked the fire, preparing to cook. Then he remembered they'd eaten the last of their provisions the previous night. How long could they go without nourishment? He looked around. Finding food here seemed unlikely, but somehow, he had to replenish their supplies.

He pulled his rum crock out of his gear and placed it in the embers. Once it warmed, he woke Jarek and got him to swallow a few sips. He re-checked the Magus's forehead. His fever was definitely down. Since they were far from the dangerous waters, he decided to risk letting him rest some more. "Milord, our food supply is lost; I need to restock. Will you be all right by yourself?"

Jarek nodded and closed his eyes.

Strapping on sword and hunting knife, Goodricke grabbed his coat and set off exploring. Sounds of wildlife were abundant. He wished he'd brought traps or a bow; something better suited for hunting than knife, sword and twine.

Patches of fog still lingered, especially over the occasional mud pools that dotted the landscape. Dispersed among scattered cypress and alders, they stank of rot. He'd hoped to snare a squirrel or rabbit but found nothing so ordinary. The island was populated with strange and repulsive creatures. Few had fur or feathers. Those he saw were covered with odd scales or had various deformities. Just as the bat had long fangs, these had two heads, two tails, or horns on their faces. Foul Marsh seemed the embodiment of the grotesque. What quirk of the gods created such odd creatures? Or maybe it wasn't the gods, but some malevolent being. After all, the Magus had hinted that someone, or something, had done this on purpose.

Tracks were abundant, and there was seldom a moment when strange cries didn't erupt from somewhere. He unsheathed his throwing knife. One of these creatures must be edible.

A terrified shriek startled him. A second followed, then all went quiet. He remained still, his pulse racing. What had cried out? More importantly, what sort of creature had frightened it? He crept through the brush, working toward the sounds. He heard some sort of a beast trotting off. He crouched behind foliage, waiting. Only after its sounds had faded did he risk a peek. There was a clearing several paces beyond him, he spied a log with a pair of carcasses slumped over it. Man-like in shape, they were brown, hairy and brawny. He pulled out his spyglass and scouted the area for signs of whatever had killed them.

Seeing nothing, he pocketed the glass and crept forth on hands and knees. Using brush for concealment, he crawled to the log. Blood oozed from both beast's mouths. Off in the distance came another horrific cry. He ducked behind the log and froze, afraid any movement might alert the mysterious marauder. Again, he heard what sounded like hoofbeats. Fading hoofbeats. Whatever it was, it was in full-out killing mode.

Convinced that the threat had gone, he rose and examined the carcasses. Large daggered teeth poked upward below their lower lips. One still clutched the half-gnawed carcass of a recent kill. With hairy face and bulging eyes, they were hideous. The smaller one was a miniature version of the larger. He probed their necks for signs of life, but found none. Both were dead, undoubtedly the result of the metal disks embedded in each of their skulls.

He removed one, examining what was some sort of projectile riddled with jagged blades. It was unlike any weapon he'd seen—and definitely man-made. If there was someone on this island capable of making this, they were also capable of leading Master Verity and him out of this accursed swamp. But would pursuing this assassin prove to be his salvation or his demise?

Pocketing the strange weapon, he followed the assassin's tracks. If he was to catch up with this person—or thing, he needed to make haste. Jogging, he set off in pursuit. Each stride jarred his injured ankle. He did his best to ignore the agony, but after a while, the pain became too great. Spying a log, he plopped down to examine his swollen ankle.

Something poked his backside. He looked for the culprit. It was a plant—a very normal looking plant. More importantly, it was green, growing in brown soil, not the gray clay he'd seen everywhere else. He scoured the area. All the plants here were the same deep green. Were any edible? He broke off a leaf and was about to taste it when he heard a loud snort, followed by a splash. Crawling toward the sound, he peered through the bushes. Ahead was a pool of deep blue water. Clear, it was in sharp contrast with the gray murk he'd seen at all other pools. Standing at its edge was a magnificent white stallion. What was such an elegant beast doing in this horrific place? And clear blue water?

Hearing more splashes, he decided to further investigate. He edged down the slope as quietly as possible. Having encountered enough dangerous creatures in this foul place to last him a lifetime; he'd scout this thing before announcing his presence.

He slipped behind a knoll that offered a full view of the pond. Its stunning rich blueness seemed so out of place in this otherwise dismal marsh. He scanned the oasis for signs of life. A submerged head popped above the surface and swam toward the horse. His mouth gaped as the swimmer trudged ashore. It was a woman. Long wet red hair hung down to her waist as she sloshed along the beach toward a pile of clothing. Was she the marauder's lady? If so, where was he, and how would he react to someone spying on his woman?

He crawled back up the hill. In his haste his knee crushed a small twig. It snapped. He froze, listening. Hearing nothing, he resumed his arduous journey hill. Spying the log he'd rested on, he rose and limped toward it.

He wasn't sure if he felt it or heard it first. It looped over his head with a swish, pinning his arms to his sides. He'd been lassoed. As he stumbled backward, he saw his assailant on a tree limb above him. It was the woman.

A jerk of her twine knocked him to the ground. *"Stop, nó cosnóidh sé tú beagnach,"* she shouted. He had no idea what she'd just demanded of him. Of greater concern was that she was spinning a long piece of rawhide. Embedded in its tip was a metal disk matching the one in his pocket.

Flight

Gresham was packed and ready to go when Hagley arrived the following morning. "Ready to visit the magi again?"

What Gresham really wanted was to leave, to be on the road with Rayna before Robard or the Chevaliers found them, but he'd promised the magi an answer. "A favor first, if I may?"

"I suppose that depends on the favor."

"I've someone I'd like to bring with me. She's waiting at the Lady's Academy."

"She?" Hagley asked, breaking into a grin. "Sure, no problem."

A quick loading of gear and he and Hagley were off to the Academy. Gresham scoured the area, checking for Chevaliers, or that fellow Robard, but saw neither. Very few people were awake and about this early.

"Wait here while I fetch her," he said when they arrived.

He walked around to the side of the building, scanning the area for observers. Seeing no one, he tossed a pebble at the window she'd pointed out. He missed on the first try, but his second one was true, striking it with a resounding clack. Rayna appeared in the window, waved, and disappeared.

He returned to the wagon. "She should be here soon."

Moments later she came out of the building bedecked in a black riding outfit that covered her from ground to shoulders. It clung to her tiny form. She wore a matching hat, alluringly angled to one side. She looked more like a duchess going on a fox hunt than someone about to take to the highways. She did, however, look dazzling.

Hagley let out a soft, slow whistle. "Is that our she?"

Gresham laughed. "Yes."

After looking around—likely for Robard, she stepped back inside, reappearing moments later with a travel bag. She vanished again—and again—each time returning with an additional bag, quitting after four—enough baggage stuff to fill half a dozen knapsacks. There was no way two of them could carry that much gear, but now was not the time to debate it—they needed to get out of Stalwart.

Hagley helped him load her bags, and they left for the university. Thankfully, Chevaliers no longer guarded the gate.

Hagley tied off the wagon and escorted them inside. After stowing their baggage in an alcove near the front entrance, they were taken to a small room with a single table and six chairs. It was perfunctory at best. "I'll let the Masters know you're here," Hagley said, leaving the room.

"Why are we here?" Rayna asked.

"I'm fulfilling a promise."

"Shouldn't we be aboard our carriage by now?"

Gods! How could he have forgotten something as important as booking a carriage? "I, uh, figured that would be the first place Robard would look for you once he learns you've fled."

"How would he even know I'm leaving?" She eyed him. "You did book a carriage, didn't you?"

"It's a part of my plan I've yet to get to."

"What!" Her look was one of astonished disbelief. "What kind of guide are you?"

He had no excuse. "Apparently not a very good one."

Rayna buried her hands in her face. "Gods, please tell me Quinn wasn't right about you."

As Hagley approached Kagen's study he heard the old man arguing with Master Vardon. "You can't force him to stay against his will, Vardon."

"I can, and I will. We can't let someone with this rare a gift wander off with no assurances he'll return. Keeping him here and training him properly is doing him a favor he'll be grateful for later."

Clearing his throat, Hagley knocked on the door, announcing his presence. "Excuse me, Sirs, Gresham is here."

Kagen looked at Vardon. "Say nothing to him on this matter until we've discussed it more."

"Providing we settle the matter today."

"Fine," Kagen told him. "Take us to him, Hagley."

Hagley returned with Kagen and Vardon in tow, unburdening Gresham of Rayna's unbearable silence. Vardon laid three books on the table. "Did you bring your attunement book?"

"Yes Sir," he said, fishing it out of his pouch.

Vardon thumbed through it. "Would you mind if I borrowed it? It contains spells I've not seen before."

"Of course, it's gibberish to me anyway."

"I'll return it in a few days." He pushed the three books he'd brought toward Gresham. "You can start your studies with these. They are the first an acolyte learns from."

Rayna gave Gresham a quizzical look.

"This one's a runes primer," Vardon said, tapping a book. "You'll need to master them in order to read spells. This one," he said, shifting his finger, "is written in Common. It's been translated for use by beginners. The last one contains simple warring spells, the perfect starter book for your training."

Rayna's eyes darted between Vardon and him, her expression a blend of confusion and dismay.

Gresham flipped through a few pages of the Common book. "Truth be known, even this beginner's book surpasses me." He glanced Rayna's way. "But since I won't be remaining here as your student, it makes little difference."

"Nonsense! Why would you not stay?"

"I've committed to Rayna to escort her on a family visit."

"A family visit! Apologies to you, Lady," he barked, facing her, "This young man's talent is far too rare to postpone for some 'family visit.'"

Seeing her shrink from Vardon's scathing rant, Master Kagen came to her rescue. "Vardon, if you'd give me a moment alone with them, perhaps I can sway them."

Master Vardon's gaze flitted between Master Kagen and Gresham. "See that you do," he said, then stormed out of the room.

"I'm sorry, Master Kagen," Gresham said, "no matter how angry it makes Master Vardon, my mind is made up."

"And why is that?"

"Are you aware of who my mother is?"

He nodded. "A sorceress arrested by the Chevaliers. Something to do with a heresy charge."

"Yes. Marshal Booker fears if this Grand Inquisitor fellow learns I'm her son, my freedom could be in peril too. He advised me to leave forthwith." He glanced at Rayna, who sat taking this all in. Would she think him an outlaw now? Or worse, a witch.

"I understand your concern," Master Kagen consoled. "But rest assured, Master Vardon won't. He's from Suzerain, bringing with him all the pride and arrogance that goes with his exalted station. He'll insist that you remain under his tutelage—regardless of what you or the Chevaliers might think."

Gresham squirmed, feeling trapped "If that's to be my fate, may I ask a favor?"

"Which is?"

"Lady Rayna is avoiding a powerful adversary of her own. One who would abscond with her against her will. Could someone somehow arrange a carriage for her to Portsmouth before he finds her? I have sufficient coin." Since Rayna had yet to pay him, he wasn't sure that was true.

"How powerful is this adversary?" Kagen asked of Rayna

"More so than you can imagine, Sir."

"If that's true, he'll likely hire mercenaries to track you down, and a carriage is the first place he'd look." He turned to Gresham. "The same is true of Vardon."

He and Rayna looked at one another. "It's not right to keep us against our will. Is there nothing we can do?"

"I'm sure I'll regret this later, but a chance to defy our haughty Suzerain friend is too good to resist." He waved them closer, whispering.

Gresham watched the tall, gaunt woman—Mistress Genevieve was her name, look Rayna over. "I see why Kagen sent you. Young lady, although I'm sure your attire is the latest fashion—it's an open invitation to every highwayman between here and Portsmouth to rob you. Bear in mind you'll be riding in an open wagon, not inside some guarded carriage."

Master Kagen had sent them to the Mistress. His plan was to have Hagley drive them to Portsmouth by wagon—with the lot of them posing as peasants.

Hagley entered the room with Gresham's knapsacks draped over his shoulders. Two servants followed behind him, bringing Rayna's belongings. Huffing, he wiped his brow. "This is all of it, Mistress."

The Mistress glanced at the pile, then at Rayna. "You can't possibly take all this with you. It would be a beacon for every highwayman out there."

"I…" Rayna stammered, leaving her retort unfinished. It took no more than a glance at the hawk-like Mistress to realize she wasn't someone to trifle with. Gresham was wise enough to stay out of it, but could have kissed the woman for having said what she had.

"Take only what fits in a single pack, the rest I'll have returned to your academy."

Rayna looked so forlorn Gresham almost felt sorry for her. Almost.

"I'll try."

"No, you'll succeed. Come with me," she said, leading them down a corridor, stopping next to two bundles of clothing. Placing her heel on one, she shoved it in Rayna's direction. "Change into these."

Her face twisted in disgust. "Those are servant's clothes."

Genevieve's back stiffened, her arms crossing her bosom. "Which is precisely why you're going to wear them, my dear." She picked up the bundle and thrust it at Rayna, leaving her no choice but to catch it. "These will make you look too poor to rob—say nothing of too insignificant for anyone chasing you to take notice." She opened a door behind her. "Now, since we have nothing left to discuss, you may change in here."

She handed the remaining bundle to Gresham. "This is your room," she said, opening a second door. "Put these on; and for the gods' sakes, hide that sword! Good luck on your journey," she said, leaving.

Gresham stripped to his linens and stuffed his clothing into his knapsack. After sorting through the clothes he'd been given, he donned his breeches, put on each of two long socks, and fastened them to his breeches. Picking up a faded brown tunic, he pulled it over his head and fastened the belt. Lastly, he placed the hat on his head and tied his knife and purse to his belt. He looked himself over. Although far short of fashionable, at least the clothes were comfortable. Grabbing his knapsack, he left the room.

Hagley stood waiting for him, similarly attired. "I'm guessing we're supposed to be ploughmen."

After a bit, Rayna appeared wearing a long brown dress, open at the neck and shoulders. She did, indeed, look like a serving wench. Accusing eyes bore through him, as if all this had somehow been his idea.

Their stay at the university over, Hagley picked up Rayna's knapsack and bade them to follow. Gresham easily managed the rest of their gear.

He led them down a long corridor, then suddenly stopped for no apparent reason. After checking to make sure no-one was watching, he bent down and pushed a cinder block aside, exposing a concealed opening. "No one knows of this passage but me," he said, slipping through it.

After handing their bags to Hagley, they climbed through too—into darkness. What happened next had Gresham shaking his head in awe. After mumbling a few incomprehensible words, a glowing ball appeared above Hagley's head. "There, now we can see."

"You're a magus?" Gresham asked, astonished.

Hagley laughed. "No. I tried to become one, but failed. I did learn enough to master a simple light spell however."

Rayna stared at Hagley, looking every bit as astounded as Gresham.

"'Ware your steps, milady," Hagley cautioned as Gresham led Rayna down a series of steps. Hagley's ball shed enough to see thirty or so paces in all directions. They now stood at the confluence of three separate tunnels.

"This way," Hagley said, heading down the center corridor. "It leads to a way to get out of the university unseen."

Sure enough, after walking a hundred or so paces, light could be seen filtering through one of the walls. There they found a small gate. Beside it, blanketed in cobwebs, were chain and pulley. Ancient looking, the gate was missing several of its iron bars.

Hagley set down Rayna's knapsack, brushed away some webs, and turned the crank. The gate rose, only to grind to a halt after lifting little more than a couple of feet. Hagley set the crank in the locked position, then lay down and rolled underneath it. Once outside, he looked back at Rayna, "Your turn."

Rolling her eyes, she got down on hands and knees and rolled out through the dust. Gresham handed out their gear, and crawled out behind her. They were in what appeared to be a dried-up creek bed.

"About a quarter league up this ravine you'll find a trail. It leads to a turnout on Kinsman's Highway. Wait for me there. I'll get my wagon and join you there." With that, he rolled back under the gate and cranked it closed, leaving the two of them standing there. Rayna gave Gresham a biting look. "I hope you follow directions better than you organize."

They headed up the ravine. Boulder-strewn, it had twenty-foot high banks on either side. Gresham helped Rayna climb over and around the seemingly endless stream of rocks. After a while the number of obstacles lessened, and the dusty terrain gave way to vegetation and far easier footing. Trees became more and more commonplace, and they soon found themselves in forest. More importantly, they stumbled upon Hagley's trail. In no time they were standing in a wagon turnaround on Kinsman's Highway. They found a place that allowed them to see the road, yet remain out of sight; dropped their packs; and sat down.

Rayna crossed her arms, clearly upset. "Commoner! You told me you were a commoner and I believed you. You, the poor little orphan boy who carved me a rose. How quaint. The next thing I know some magus is talking about you having some Gift that's so special we have to run away to prevent him from keeping you against your will. Gresham Smithy, you're the most frustrating man I know." She uncrossed her arms, "Except perhaps for my father."

"I don't blame you for being angry. I've made a mess of everything. Things just sort of got out of my control. Look, if you no longer want me as your guide, I understand."

"Gods!" she said, burying her face in her hands. After a moment, she looked up. "You're right, I am angry. I'm angry at my father; I'm angry at Robard." She tugged her clothing, "I'm angry that I have to wear this awful outfit. What I'm not, is angry at you." She buried her face in her hands again, rocking back and forth. "I just want to find my mother and lead a life like everyone else's, and the gods seem to be doing their all to prevent it."

He dared to feel hopeful. "Does that mean you're considering keeping me as your guide?"

She loosed a caustic laugh. "No, I plan to cart all this gear into the wilds by myself." She looked at him. "Yes Gresham, I still want you as my guide."

He breathed a sigh of relief.

Their exchange abruptly ended with the clip-clop of approaching horse hooves. They took cover and waited, relieved to see it was Hagley. They rushed out to greet him.

"I come bearing gifts," he said, pulling a bag out from under a large canvas laying behind the buckboard. He hoisted it. "Master Kagen suggested I stop at the kitchen and get us provisions. He lifted a second, smaller bag, and emptied its contents. Out tumbled four books, "Two for you; two for me," he said, looking at Gresham. "Master Kagen said I should teach you to read runes from this," he said hoisting one of the books. "That way you can learn from the spell book Master Vardon recommend while on your journey."

"Please return them. Tell him we're already carrying too much and have no room for books."

After stuffing their baggage under the canvas, they were on their way. Kinsman Highway was crowded that day, with carts and wagons heading in both directions. Dread washed over him when they heard a group of riders approaching from behind. Did Quinn and his father already have the Chevaliers out searching? He looked. Although the riders weren't wearing robes, they could still be mercenaries hired by Robard. Judging from Rayna's anxious look, she feared as much too.

The riders rode on by with nary a glance their way. Rayna sighed, and her features softened. He watched her out of the corner of his eye, marveling at how beautiful she was. Perhaps it was only wishful thinking, but he could swear she was sneaking peeks his way too, but every time he turned to see, she looked off in another direction.

After saying nothing for some time, she finally spoke to him. "I need to apologize for the way I spoke to you back there; it was most unladylike."

"No apologies necessary. After the way I've botched things so far, I deserved it."

Rayna was about to respond when a noise from behind startled her. She looked. Something was moving under their canvas. "Gods!" she screeched, jumping away.

Laughing, Hagley raised a hand. "Not to worry, Lady." Shaking his head, he stopped the wagon, and stood, facing the back of the wagon. "All right Sully, I know you're in there."

The canvas pushed aside and up popped a young boy. "How did you know?"

He gave Rayna an apologetic look. "He does this sort of thing so often I've come to expect it."

Sully had a hand over his mouth, giggling. "I been in here since you took them bags to the Lady place."

"Mistress Genevieve had me return your bags to the Lady's Academy," Hagley explained.

Sully climbed out from under the canvas. "Me and Hagley go adventuring lots."

Gresham's brow furrowed. "Adventuring?"

Hagley spread his hands. "Didn't you know that monsters haunt the highway?"

Sully's head bobbed up and down. "Yeah, Hagley and me be destroying them all the time. I be almost nine, so I be old enough to be doing that stuff." His gaze drifted to Rayna. "Are you a princess? You be pretty like one."

She gave him a warm smile. "Dressed like this? Hardly. No. But thank you for the compliment." She held out her hand. "Hi, I'm Rayna. And you are?"

"Sully, ma'am. Hagley and me sometimes save princesses too."

She laughed. "I feel safer knowing you're here."

Sully's eyes sparkled as he fixated on Rayna. Gresham knew the feeling well.

Hagley shook the reins, urging the horses forward. "No rescues today little man, I'm working." He turned to Rayna. "Lady, would you mind if Sully drove some, he's pretty good at it. That way I can tutor Gresham."

She glanced at the books, then at Gresham, and draped an arm around the boy. "Sure, Sully can be both my driver and my protector."

"All right, lucky person, get up here with your princess and make yourself useful."

The two men climbed in back. "Runes aren't difficult, they just require a lot of memorization. By themselves they're meaningless, but once you go through a couple spells, you'll see how the two fit together." Gresham eyed them. *Learn runes and go through spells; my first magic lessons.* Hagley picked up the spell book. "Hands and Arrows. Why these, I wonder?"

Gresham took the book. "Master Vardon said I was attuned to the war arts. Can you teach me from it, or is what's in the book not a specialty of yours?"

"I don't have a specialty. I was a student for two years, and in all that time no one could figure out what my facet was."

Hagley walked Gresham through the various runes, having him memorize their names and meanings. Only after he could recite them without error, did they switch to the spell book where Gresham struggled to grasp even the simplest of concepts. His hopes of becoming a magus faded.

After a mid-day meal of bread and warm ale they were back at his studies. Gresham was finally starting to grasp some of what he was being taught.

They hadn't travelled much farther when Sully pointed. "There be a wagon, with lots of them new type of churchmen."

Gods. They were Chevaliers.

Hagley raised a hand. "Everyone act normal. I'll deal with them. I've encountered them before." He handed Gresham his books. "Hide these. Old Kagen says the arts put them on edge." Gresham stuffed them into a bag. "Good, now use the bag as a pillow. Pretend to nap and let me do the talking."

They gradually closed the gap on the slower-moving party. As they drew closer Gresham could see the wagon carried barred cages with people inside them, likely heading for the ships' dungeons. As Hagley passed them, Gresham recognized one of the prisoners—the woman wearing the moonstone at the marketplace. Gresham looked away, feeling ill.

The lead horsemen blocked their passage. "Halt, we would talk with you." The remaining troopers surrounded their wagon. "Who are you, and where are you going?"

As promised, Hagley did the talking. While their leader quizzed him, the other soldiers scoured the wagon—and its passengers. Gresham stared at the floor, avoiding eye contact as Hagley deftly fielded their leader's questions. The men ignored Gresham, their interest clearly on Rayna. One took off his hat, looking her over as one would a piece of merchandise. Gresham seethed, choking back a challenge. Grinning, the man tipped his head. "May His protection be with you."

Interrogation over, they returned to their prisoners.

Gresham said nothing until Sully had their wagon well out of earshot. "How unnerving."

He scanned the road ahead, looking for more Chevaliers. Just because they'd made it through this encounter, didn't mean that would always be the case. He wouldn't feel free of their clutches until they were on their journey.

Feeling forlorn, he decided to take a nap for real.

Portsmouth

A hard jounce woke him. Sitting, Gresham stretched and peered around. The woods and farmlands that had dotted the landscape earlier had given way to thatch-roofed peasant huts. Such signs of civilization, coupled with a distinctive smell of salt air; told him they'd reached Portsmouth.

"Welcome back to the world of the living," Hagley chided, guiding the wagon around yet another pothole. "We're here. Where to now?"

An excellent question. He'd been so eager to get underway, he'd yet to formulate any plan. "How about we find an ale house and discuss it."

The one they chose was your typical dockside inn. Dingy and dirty, Rayna's grimace made it clear the place fell dramatically short of her standards, but dressed as shabbily as they were, going someplace nicer would only draw undo attention. Their plan was to not be noticed or remembered.

Fearing to leave their belongings unattended, they brought them inside with them, causing every patron to take notice. Most were gawking at Rayna. No matter what her attire, there was no disguising her beauty.

The men ordered bread, cheese, and ale, while Rayna opted for honey bread and Elderberry wine. Gresham paid for it out of his dwindling funds, a growing cause for concern. Rayna had yet to pay him her promised advance, something they'd need to discuss if they were to supply their trip.

"Time to get organized," he announced, trying his best to sound confident. "Harvest season is over, so the nights will get cooler." He turned to Rayna, "The blankets we brought are likely too thin. We'd best find a tanner and buy warmer pelts… and peat for fires; and water skins. Four should do it. Judging from your mother's map, I'm guessing the trip will take two to three days. To be on the safe side, we should buy food for twice that long." He smiled at Rayna. "And I'm guessing a nicer outfit is high on your priority list."

She rolled her eyes.

Now, to broach the topic of his advance. "We'll need to hire a boatman to ferry us across the bay. Its cost will surely exceed my present funds." He gave Rayna a pensive look. "Lady, could we discuss that advance we spoke of?"

"Of course. Here," she said, reaching for her purse.

Gresham grabbed her wrist. "Not here. Wait until we're someplace private."

Looking around, she released it.

"Hagley, you're familiar with this town. How about you show Rayna where she can buy clothing, and perhaps a small knapsack to carry it in."

"Of course."

"We should make a list of the supplies we still need, and shop for them. Bear in mind," he told Rayna, "it'll be just the two of us carrying whatever we take, so weigh need against size and weight. Also, that outfit you had on this morning, although stunning, would have been ruined in a day or two. A short hooded-cape with leggings beneath would better serve you."

"Rest assured," she said, crossing her arms and frowning, "I am perfectly capable of deciding what's best for me to wear."

Oops! "I apologize if I offend, but as your guide, it's my duty to advise." Doubting her sense for practicalities, he decided it'd be up to him to buy her something sensible; and give it to her later.

Once they'd completed their list, they spread Rayna's map out on the table. "Hagley, you're familiar with Portsmouth." He pointed to one of two X's on the map. "We need to get there," he said, pointing to one on the far side of a bay, "from here." He pointed to other. "Any idea where those might be?"

Hagley studied the map. "I don't, but the university maintains a livery here. It's just down the road. Its hostler could say for sure."

Meal done, they headed for the stables where they spied a grizzled, older man busily pitching hay. "Horace, how goes your day?" Hagley greeted.

The man looked up and smiled. "I fare well Hagley. You here to do more of the magi's biddings?"

"Nay, not this time. Any chance I could leave my wagon here while I show these grubbers around?"

Gresham frowned. Leaving the wagon hadn't been part of any plan.

The hostler nodded. "Surely. Leave the team by the stalls and I'll see to them. It's a bit sloped inside, so be sure to scotch the wheels."

"We have things in it that need watching—is that all right?"

Horace wandered over and peered into the wagon. "Pay the stable boy a chink and he'll be more than happy watch it for you."

"Oh, another favor," Hagley said. "You grew up in this shite hole, didn't you?"

"Ha! An apt a description as I've ever heard. Aye, born and raised in this stinkin' place."

"My man here," he said, resting a hand on Gresham's shoulder, "wants to do some fishin'. Some fellow sold him a map he claimed marked the best holes. Trouble is, we can't figure out where exactly they are."

"Lemme see." Gresham handed him the map. "See how the land juts into the water here by your mark? That has to be Pirate's Cove." Hagley stiffened at its mention. "That second mark is Tanner Point, a quay on the far side of the bay. It ain't used no more; the waters there be dangerous, and it's a long row to get there with little to show for your efforts. You'll want nothin' to do with that lagoon over there neither; boat bustin' rocks everywhere. Ain't uncommon for loobies who go there to never be heard from again." He met Gresham's gaze. "Hope you didn't spend much coin for this map, son, 'cuz go there and you're likely as not to wind up swimmin' with the fishes instead of catchin' 'em." He grinned at his clever play with words. "Best forget that place altogether. There be plenty of good fishin' holes on this side o' the bay."

Gresham tucked away the map away. "Gramercy. We'll take your advice."

"Well, good fishin'," he said, wandering back to his hay.

"Who said anything about leaving the wagon behind?" Gresham whispered once Horace was out of ear shot. "Why would we do that?"

Hagley raised a finger. "First off, none of you lot knows your way about this town, so you need my help. Secondly, Pirate's Cove is easily the most dangerous place in Portsmouth. Were we to leave our wagon there unattended, thieves would have it emptied and gone in moments."

"I hadn't thought of that," Gresham said, scratching his chin. "If this Pirate's Cove place is as bad as you say, I'd best take my weapons with me—disguise be damned."

While Hagley bargained with the stable boy, Gresham strapped his scabbard over his back.

Negotiations done, Hagley pressed a coin into the gleeful-looking lad's palm.

"You stay here," Gresham said, ruffling Sully's hair, "and keep the stable boy company."

"Aw-w!" he whined. "I want to go adventuring too."

"Sorry," Gresham said, "if Pirate's Cove is as bad as Hagley says, it's no place for a child." Turning a deaf ear to Sully's protests, the group headed for the wharf.

Sully hid behind the wagon, watching them go. Thinking there was no way he'd let them go adventuring without him, he followed, keeping out of sight. After a bit, they stopped to talk. Hagley pointed toward the bay, which was now in sight. Gresham headed that way, while Hagley and the princess went into a shoppe. Deciding whatever Gresham was up to had to be more interesting than buying stuff, Sully followed him.

He tracked him to the docks. Boats was everyplace. Gresham started haggling with a man there. After a bit, they spit in their palms and touched hands. A couple other men dragged a boat down to the water, and Gresham left.

Sully was about to follow, when some larrikin stepped out from behind another boat and joined the boat man, watching Gresham leave. Seeing the looks on their faces, Sully felt a sense of dread.

He crept closer. This new man was talking. "Who was the big fellow?"

The boat man laughed. "Some highborn posin' as a commoner, wantin' to rent a boat, but his words be way too fancy to fool the likes of me."

The new man pointed at the nearby boat. "Ain't that yers? Sure's ya didn't tell him you be lettin' him use that, did ya?"

The boat merchant grinned. He had one tooth. "No, Shay, he just thinks I did. Highborns have thick purses, and I be just the man to relieve 'm of it."

Shay drew his knife. "How about we get about doing it now, afore he gets away?"

The boatman raised a hand. "Hold on. I told 'em I'd row the boat up to the old Henley shack. He ain't payin' me 'til then. Let's make sure he's got his coin on him afore we feed 'm to the fishes."

Sully's heart pounded—these bad men were meaning to kill Gresham.

He ran after Gresham to warn him, but he was nowhere in sight. Dread washed over him. At a loss for what else to do, he raced back to the stable.

The shoppe proved a boon, and with Hagley's help, Rayna found everything on Gresham's list. Genevieve was right, she had packed too much finery, especially considering she'd be the one to carry it. Still, she had to do something about her outfit. Off the highways now, surely the need for disguises had abated. The clothes that chitty-faced Mistress had forced her to wear were an embarrassment, especially in front of Gresham. The man may claim not to be highborn, but everything about him said otherwise. He fascinated her like no man she'd known.

"Hagley," she said, handing him two silvers, "could you be a good fellow and pay for these? The shoppe next door had clothing in its window. You can join me there after purchasing our goods." Ignoring his bewildered expression, she headed out the door.

Once inside, the store was more than a little disappointing. Even the Shoppe's finest outfits fell far short of fashionable. But despite their poor quality, they were a noticeable improvement over what she had on. After a thorough search of the place, she found something marginally acceptable.

A sweating, grunting Hagley arrived with her goods. "Let's pay for that dress and go find Gresham."

When she handed the merchant her coin, he balked. "Sorry girlie, I can't be changin' no gold. You'll be needin' somethin' way smaller."

Girlie? The nerve! And here she was offering him a sale. Huffing, she dug out a smaller coin.

As soon as they were outside, Hagley grabbed her arm, whispering, "It's not streetwise to be flashing a gold piece. Doing so tells folks you're rich enough to rob."

"Oh!" Rayna blurted, putting a hand to her mouth. "I didn't think." She looked back over her shoulder. "What should we do?"

"Find Gresham and get out of here."

Gresham walked out of the shoppe feeling smug at having found Rayna a durable tunic and leggings—practical enough for their trek. He hoped they'd fit her tiny form. He found Hagley and her waiting at their agreed upon meeting place, looking worried. "Is everything all right?"

Hagley looked around, acting wary. "We fear we're being followed."

"Why, you look like paupers?"

"It's my fault," Rayna said, "I showed one of the merchants a gold piece."

"Gods no!"

The words were hardly out of his mouth when a band of knife-wielding ruffians emerged from behind the adjacent buildings. Gresham counted eight in all. Waghalters for sure, they looked filthy, mean and more importantly, dangerous.

"You boys go to either side and back now," the largest of them ordered, "in case them feels the need to run."

Gresham reached over his shoulder, groping for his sword.

"He's goin' for a weapon, Shay," one of them hollered.

Shay—their leader—eyed him, sneering. "Careful big feller, our eight little prickers be way better than that big one of yours."

Gresham matched his smirk. "Well 'Shay,' are you sure this motley band is ready to do battle the likes of a trained soldier and a magus?" he added, nodding toward Hagley.

Shay looked at Hagley. "I know you. You're that fat shit what tricked us into fighting them garrison troopers. A pox on you." He spat in the dirt. "You're a dead man, 'Magus.' You cost me four boys. Before you die, I'm cuttin' off one finger for each man we lost, you bastard. Lastlike, I'll cut out your eyes."

Hagley paled. Shay's gaze drifted to Gresham. "But you die first, soldier boy." He looked at Rayna, his eyes raking her body. "The wench we do last. Ain't never had me no highborn afore, no matter how she be dressing. She's a looker, that one. Me and the boys will likely have a bit of fun with her afore we slits her throat."

A loud ruckus coming their way drew everyone's attention. Charging hell-bent toward them were two large steeds, towing a wagon. Sitting in the driver's seat was a boy. Sully had brought Hagley's wagon. With dirt flying and dust spewing, he looked ready to mow them down.

Abandoning their quarry, the bandits scurried out of his path. Sully slowed as he neared his friends. "Hop in!"

Gripping the buckboard with one hand, Gresham grabbed Rayna's wrist and fell butt-first into the back wagon, pulling her on top of him. Hagley jumped in beside them. With everyone aboard, Sully snapped the reins, urging the horses forward. Before the brigands could recover, they were racing away.

Once they'd distanced themselves from their would-be attackers, Sully slowed the team. Hagley crawled to the front. "I'll take over," he said, relieving Sully of the reins.

A rattled Rayna gave the boy a hug as he crawled into the back. "Thank you, little hero, you rescued me, just like you promised."

Sully's grin put his every tooth on display. "That be pretty smart of me, huh?"

Gresham laughed. "Yes, it was." He climbed up front with Hagley. "Ever hear of a place called Henley's Shack?" he asked, checking for signs of the brigands. "I've arranged to have our boat delivered there."

"No!" Sully cried, "You can't! The man what sold it to you be waiting there to kill you! I heard him say it to one of them men back there."

"How could you possibly hear him?"

"I didn't stay at the stables," he said, looking sheepish, "I followed you."

Gresham gave the boy an exasperated look. "Thank you for the warning." He looked at Hagley. "You didn't answer my question. The boatman said I'd find our boat at the dock next to the old Henley Shack. Is it on this road?"

"I know of a shack, but I've not heard it called by any name."

"Good. Take us there."

Sure enough, there was a small dock not far from Hagley's shack with a small boat tied to it. "You three stay here while I look for this assassin. Put on those knapsacks and be ready to run. When I signal it's safe, come down to that boat. I want to be out of here before those ruffians decide to follow us."

Sword drawn, he crept down to the dock. The setting sun glistened off the water, making it difficult to see. He went to where the boat was tied off, and seeing no one, waved for his companions to join him. Seconds later he heard the familiar sound of a blade being drawn. He spun about. There, not ten paces from him, was the boatman, a cutlass in his hand. The man charged, swinging his weapon. Gresham parried the blow, and readied himself to do battle. Despite all his training, this was the first time he'd dueled for real. He doubted the same was true for the blackheart confronting him.

Fending the man one-handed, he drew his dagger. He preferred fighting with two weapons. Despite all his practice, he'd never faced such an awkward fighting style before, nor had he ever engaged a cutlass. Was this how pirates fought? After one or two exchanges, it became clear the man's skill was no match for his. That awareness calmed him. His attacker must have reached that same notion, for his once confident killer-to-be suddenly looked worried. Gresham paused his attack. He'd never taken a man's life and didn't want to now. "You're overmatched. Desist and I'll spare your life."

"We'll see the truth of that, lubber." The man said, slashing at Gresham's head.

Gresham parried, but didn't counterattack. He backed away, deflecting blow after blow. How could he end this fight without killing the man? That became the least of his worries when his heel found a patch of slippery moss. Footing lost, he fell to his back, exposed, and defenseless.

The man rushed him, cutlass held high. Just as he was about to deliver a killing blow, blood spurted from his mouth. Startled eyes went wide, then blank, as he slumped to the dock. Standing behind him stood Sully, holding Gresham's crossbow.

Rayna and Hagley came running down the pier. "The brigands are here," Hagley shouted. "We need to leave!"

Sully and Rayna climbed down the slip ladder, and hopped into the boat. Gresham handed down the remaining gear. Just as Hagley and he were about to join them, Shay and company came storming onto the far end of the dock.

They were way too many. "Hagley! Get in the boat! I'll hold them off as long as I can!"

Hagley simply stood there, mumbling something incomprehensible, weaving strange patterns with his hands. All of a sudden, the intruders started hopping about, spinning round and round, as if dancing. "YOU get into the boat," Hagley ordered. "Holler once you're in."

Seeing that whatever Hagley was doing was keeping their foes at bay, Gresham untied the bow line and slipped down the ladder. As he was doing so, Sully scrambled up it. "Get back here!"

"I will, I will," he yelled, crawling on all fours toward the dead pirate.

Gresham grabbed the oars and reefed. The boat lurched. "Get in now!" he screamed.

Hagley stopped casting and clambered down with Sully right behind him, clutching the dead man's cutlass. The boat was already moving as they leaped in. Rayna's grab of Hagley was all that saved him from tumbling overboard and possibly capsizing the boat.

Freed of Hagley's spell, the pirates raced down the pier. By the time they reached the ladder, Gresham was boat lengths away. Two dived in, giving chase, but Gresham's efforts widened the gap. The last thing he heard from the docks was the order for everyone to find boats.

The brigands abandoned the pier, racing back toward the wharf. Gresham shipped the oars to catch his breath. He turned to Hagley. "What did you do to them, anyway?"

Hagley looked embarrassed. "I haven't memorized very many spells. Usually I need to read them just before I cast. This one is an exception. I learned it a long time ago for a university festival."

"A festival?"

"Yeah, it compels people to dance."

Rayna laughed. "You saved us by making those horrible men dance?"

He gave a sheepish grin. "We had a lot of fun with it at the party."

Everyone cackled, even Hagley.

Gresham scanned the dock one more time, making sure it was empty. "They're gone. We need to get you two ashore and be on our way. I want to be long gone before those waghalters find boats."

Hagley looked stunned. "I can't go back."

"What?"

"You heard what that pirate said he'd do to me. No way I'm staying. I'm going with you."

Gresham could hardly believe his ears. "You can't; how will Sully get home?"

"I ain't going back neither," Sully protested, crossing his arms. "I'm going adventuring with you guys."

The other three exchanged glances. Sully had rescued them, surely angering the brigands. More importantly, he'd killed one of them. If they were to catch him, they'd likely do worse to him than what they'd threatened to do to Hagley.

Sully's lip quivered. "Please take me. Hagley be my only friend." He looked at Rayna, "'cept for you and Lady Rayna. I want to stay with you."

The orphan's impassioned plea struck a chord with Gresham. Rayna's wan smile likely meant she understood, too. Sully looked at Hagley. "You promised me Hagley. You always said someday we'd go adventuring."

Hagley looked at Gresham. "I did say that. Is where we're heading dangerous?"

Rayna answered. "I doubt my mother would have given me a map to get there if it was." She gave Gresham a pleading look. "We can't leave a boy alone in Portsmouth, it's way too dangerous. How would he get home?"

Gresham doubted he ever be able to say no to her. Sighing, he pointed at their knapsacks. "Everyone find warm clothing then. I plan to row this bay in the dark. It's the only way I can think of to get us away safe." He picked up the oars. "Search for my compass while you're looking—and Rayna's map. I want to get our bearings while there's still light. We can figure out how to get you two back to Stalwart in the morning." He looked at the young magus. "Ever row a boat, Hagley?"

"No."

"Don't worry, you seem a smart fellow, you'll work it out in no time. Our biggest problem will be keeping on course. Once that sun sets, I won't be able to read my compass."

"You forget who you're with." Hagley shut his eyes, mumbling. Suddenly a ball of light floated above them. He smiled. "The light globe is the first spell most magi learn. Just let me know when you need it." He snapped his fingers and the globe vanished.

Gresham shook his head. "Now that's useful. I wish I could do that."

Hagley slapped Gresham's knee. "I'll teach you tomorrow."

Hagley's offer shocked him, but why? After all, the prism had shown he was Gifted. It was time to change his thinking. "Have I learned enough?"

Hagley grinned. "There's only one way to find out."

He rowed them out to sea, thinking how dramatically his life had changed. He was gifted. Did that mean he might become a magus? A magus! Who'd have guessed? He broke out laughing. Sully had the right of it. *This isn't just a trip, it's an adventure.*

The shoreline gradually faded from view, as did the sun. They never spotted the wharf pirates. He labored onward well after the others had fallen asleep, wondering all the while what lay in store for him next; what awaited them all.

Arms aching, Gresham shipped the oars and looked around. The glowing skyline announced dawn's imminence. A gust of salty air lifted his collar, its chilling effect a reminder of the foolishness of rowing at night. But the wharf pirates had given them little choice.

His companions were wrapped in blankets, grabbing what sleep they could. Hagley had earned it. The two of them had traded off rowing duties over the course of the night. Sully had tried, but neither he nor Rayna proved strong enough.

He scoured ahead. Even in this dim light, Tanner Point was visible, the long row across the bay was near its end. Rejuvenated, he resumed rowing with a renewed vigor.

The boat rolled up a swell, splashing Hagley, waking him. He wiped his face and looked around. "Where are we?"

"We're almost there," Gresham said, pointing at the approaching quay.

Hagley looked. "You need to row seaward; we're getting too far inland."

"Would that I could," Gresham said, reefing on the oars. "This cursed tide keeps pushing us inland. I fear by the time we make shore it'll be a goodly tramp back to the quay."

Despite his efforts, the sea was unrelenting. Before long it had pushed them so far inland, they could no longer see Tanner Point. "Watch out!" Hagley yelled, pointing over Gresham's shoulder.

Gresham jerked his head around. A giant rock lay directly in their path. Reefing hard, he avoided it, albeit barely.

Hagley pointed again. "There's another!"

His shouts roused the others. Rayna sat up, rubbing her eyes. "What's wrong?"

"We're in a shoal. Rocks are everywhere. Everyone scout for hazards!"

While picking his way through the treacherous waters, Gresham spotted a lagoon off in the distance. Its waters looked calm. Partially blocking its entrance was a long expanse of boulders that ran all the way to shore. Unfortunately, the current kept driving him toward it. No matter how hard he rowed, Gresham couldn't alter their course. Closer and closer the boulders came. The incessant current pushing, thrusting, driving their boat toward inevitable disaster.
    "Brace yourselves!" he hollered, "We're going to hit!"
    The next swell slammed their boat hard against the seawall. Their craft high-centered atop a jutting boulder, accompanied by the horrific sound of splintering wood. Everyone held on as water inundated the boat, then washed back out to sea with such force they were nearly dragged with it. "The boat's destroyed!" he yelled, "Grab your gear and jump ashore!"
    They'd barely scrambled onto the rocks when the next wave rolled in. What was left of their boat disintegrated right before their eyes. "My pack!" Rayna screeched, watching her carefully selected purchases wash away—along with what little remained of their skiff. "It has all my belongings!"
    The four of them stood watching in stunned disbelief as the raging seawaters ripped apart their boat turning it into tiny pieces of flotsam, marooning them.

Guardian

Goodricke struggled to his knees, a difficult task with one's arms pinned. He ducked as hooves thundered past him, blanketing him in dust. The woman leaped from her limb, onto the horse's back, and looped her end of the lasso around her steed's neck.

Spitting grime, Goodricke stood, but quickly dropped to his knees when he heard the whoosh of her spinning weapon. He forced a smile, hoping a friendly demeanor would keep her from firing it. "Are strangers in this land always treated so? Am I to suffer the same fate as those beasts?"

Frowning, she stopped spinning her weapon. Her horse stepped backwards, pulling the rope taut, tumbling him face-first to the ground. Undaunted, he struggled back to his knees.

She glared. "Remove your weapons," she said, speaking Common. Her accent was heavy, unlike any he'd heard. He took off his belt. "Toss it far." He obeyed. "Does the Crone now get her henchmen from the Outland, or do her newest abominations simply resemble them?"

What was she asking? "You speak in riddles. I know nothing of crones or henchmen or outlands or abominations. I'm Goodricke Loddvar of Fort Stalwart. I have a companion nearby who is sick with fever. We mean you no harm, we simply seek something called a Nexus in order to save a friend." Impassive, she simply stared, saying nothing. "Perhaps if we could talk, we'd reach an understanding."

She pondered his words. "Your terms are strange; perhaps you truly are an Outlander. Answer my questions, but be warned, your answers determine your fate."

He spread his arms, palms up, daring to feel hope. "Ask."

"What is this Nexus, and why do you seek it?"

He cursed himself for having divulged so much in his moment of panic, but if he wanted to live, he had no choice but to offer more. "It has to do with the arts. I know little of them, so I can offer no better explanation. My companion and I seek a place called A'ryth, in order to save a friend."

The woman's eyes flared briefly. "If you seek such a place, why are you here in the swamps?"

Did that mean she knew of A'ryth? "The lurker destroyed our boat, stranding us here. Look," he pulled up his pant leg, "part of it still clings to me."

The woman leaned forward. "That is from a *beithíoch*. Heat will release it." She met his gaze. "You used other words. What are arts?"

"Arts are what the magi practice. Some call it magic, or sorcery."

She nodded, apparently understanding. It relaxed her enough to dare a smile. "You may call me Caitlyn, Goodricke Loddvar from Fort Stalwart." Her eyes twinkled as she collapsed her lasso and stowed it on her belt.

He sensed he was making progress. "Do you know of this place called A'ryth?" Her eyes flared again. *She knows*. "Will you lead us there?"

"Maybe I will leave you here for the abominations. Persuade me why this should not be so."

Her dismissal irked him. "Persuade you?" He threw up his hands. "I've crossed this accursed marsh just to find this city to aid one in dire circumstance. Do you realize what an undertaking that was?"

Her face hardened. "Be careful with your tone Outlander, it is you, not me, who bargains for help." She looked away, staring, before responding further. "I will lead you from the marsh, Goodricke Loddvar, and assist your friend. That is all I promise."

He bowed his head. "Thank you, Lady."

"We should leave now, I have duties to attend," she said, dismounting. He was surprised at how tiny she was. As he approached, she stepped backwards, looking wary. He stopped, studying her diminutive form. She wore the leather armor and leggings of a warrior. Her red hair was tucked under a rawhide helmet. Despite her mannish attire, he found her quite comely, and marveled that one so slight could be so skilled in weaponry. "Please take no offense, but are all your warriors so small?"

She gave an impish smile. "I am the smallest—but not by so much. Are all Outlanders so large as you?"

"Nay, I'm tall in any land." He winked. "But not by so much."

Then, without transition, she switched subjects. "We should see to your friend." She stepped toward her horse, but stopped. Frowning, she scanned the area.

Were more abominations coming? "What's wrong?"

"I perceive power." Caitlyn looked at him. "You brought that sense with you; it is what warned me you were here." She walked to nearby bushes and picked up his weapon belt. "It comes from this."

"Of course! Turpin's sword!"

She examined the sheath. "It is not yours?"

"Yes, it was a gift."

She studied it. "This is Lore Master's doing. Such a gift deserves better care." She brought it to him. "Take it Goodricke Loddvar, you may have need of it."

"In A'ryth?"

She looked up at him. "I do not take you to A'ryth; I lead you from the marsh." She mounted her horse. "Now where is your friend?"

"I fear I'm too lost to say, but if you take me to where you killed those two creatures, or abominations as you call them, I can find my way from there."

He sat behind her, riding double, heading back to the killing field. Her head came only halfway up his chest. The scent of her wet hair made him realize how long it had been since he'd made little talk with a woman. He decided to rectify that. "You speak Common with great skill. I would not have guessed it's not your first language."

She grinned back at him. "Thank you, but you do not lie so well, Goodricke Loddvar. Many words you say I do not understand. And you speak very fast."

"Apologies Lady, I shall try to speak more slowly." He gripped her waist as her mount leaped a fallen log. "We have many languages in the Outland, so people learn what we call Common so that when we speak, all can understand. Is it the same in your homeland?"

"Not so much, only Seekers learn your Common. Most there would not understand your words."

"Are you one of these Seekers? Is that why you speak my tongue?"

She looked back at him as if he were mad. "What a thing to say. I speak with my own tongue, Goodricke Loddvar, not yours." She explained that Seekers went to the Outland to study their ways, to understand what threat they pose. "Your people have given us cause not to trust them."

Once they found the abominations, he had his bearings and led her to his camp where he found Master Verity reading Malg's journal. Hearing their approach, Jarek turned, looking alarmed. His jaw opened when he saw who it was. "Goodricke?"

He dismounted, delighting in his companion's confounded expression. "You're looking much better, milord." He gestured toward his newfound guide. "Meet Caitlyn."

Caitlyn's steely countenance had returned, but she remained cordial, even insisting on examining Jarek's wound. "An *ialtóg* has bitten you." She fished herbs from a pouch on her belt and rubbed salve on the wound. "This will fight its poison." She made him swallow other herbs.

After tending Jarek, she started a small fire, heated a stick, and pressed the hot poker against the tentacle stuck to Goodricke's leg. The singed tissue peeled away.

She asked to see their boat. They escorted her to the beach. Flotsam was still floating near the shore. She wandered to the water and examined the area. "The *beithíoch* was very close, you are fortunate to have survived."

Goodricke interpreted. "That's the lurker's true name. She spoke as if they are many."

They returned to camp. Their belongings lay stacked in two piles. "I will call *capall* for you to ride, but you have much to carry. They may not be willing." She stared at their gear. "Do you need so much?"

Goodricke was sure he'd heard her wrong. "You can beckon the *capall*?" he asked, ignoring her question

She frowned. "Of course; how else would they know you wish to ride?"

Jarek answered her earlier question. "Our journey is long, Lady. I fear we need all the gear we've salvaged. As it is, we lost much with our boat."

She looked concerned. "I will call them now. But do not be too hopeful."

She pulled a carved reed from her belt and blew into it. Although Goodricke heard nothing, Caitlyn's horse reared. She rushed over, soothing it in low tones. Once it calmed, she returned. "When they arrive, you must ask to ride. Say these words, *'Cara na foraoise, is féidir liom turas tú?'* Remember them," she said, repeating it.

"What happens when we speak these words?" Jarek asked.

"If the capall accepts, it will lower its head."

While they waited, Goodricke stowed most of what they'd brought into knapsacks, but left some behind to appease Caitlyn. Packed, they sat and waited.

Although the wait was considerable, it did little to diminish the startling effect of seeing ten white horses thunder through the trees and halt just outside their camp. Save for their color, sinew and elegance, they looked like ordinary horses, but to find such stunning creatures in this dismal setting was nonetheless startling.

"*Fáilte róimh a capall,*" Caitlyn hailed as they danced in place, eying the humans. She turned to Jarek. "Ask."

He nodded. "Certainly, Lady." He faced the horses. "*Cara na foraoise, is féidir liom turas tú?*"

The horses snorted and pranced. Finally, one reared and trotted over to Jarek. Stretching one leg forward, it bent its other one. Goodricke could swear it was bowing.

Caitlyn nodded. "That is good, Lore Master; it accepts. You may ride now."

Goodricke grabbed Jarek's gear. "Climb aboard, milord. Once you're astride, I'll hand this up."

Jarek gripped the animal's mane and tried to swing a leg over its back. He slid too far and fell off the other side. The next try he managed to stay astride. Goodricke placed the gear on the horse's buttocks and fastened its binding around Jarek's waist. "That should hold."

Caitlyn tugged on Goodricke's sleeve. "Now you, Goodricke Loddvar."

Goodricke faced the steeds. *"Kara ne forouse, liam tarris?"*

Jarek winced. "Goodricke, if that's your ear for sound, you'd have made a poor magus."

"Try again, Goodricke Loddvar," she coaxed.

He did, again and again. The animals stared, unmoving. After his fifth try she stepped in front of him, choking back a grin. Judging from the shaking of Jarek's shoulders, he was enjoying Goodricke's chagrin as much as she was. She said something in her strange language, and a capall came forward and made the ritual offering. Although grateful, the fact he needed her help was embarrassing. He hoisted his pack to his shoulders and swung onto the animal's back, his long legs making it a simple matter.

The remaining horses trotted away. Caitlyn mounted. "Which way is this place you seek? We should leave the marsh in that direction."

Goodricke checked his drawing. "This map is crude, but I believe it's that way," he said, pointing.

She trotted over. "May I see your mapiscrude?"

"Of course." He handed it to her. "This mark is where Master Verity says the Nexus will occur, and we are here." He looked at her. "And apologies, I mean no criticism of your command of Common, but it is simply called a map. Crude means that the map is not a very good one."

She examined the drawing. "What is this writing by your mark?"

"It is how A'ryth is written in Common."

She was silent for a moment. "They are in much the same place."

"Our mark is only a surmise," Jarek explained, "but we suspect they may be the same place. Tonight, if the skies are clear, I'll use an instrument to not be so crude."

She handed back the map back to Goodricke. "Perhaps this is not so crude as you think."

She led them out of camp. Goodricke hadn't ridden bareback since boyhood, but quickly adapted. The same couldn't be said for Jarek, who nearly fell off his mount every time it lurched, jumped, or made any quick motion.

They wound their way through the sparse trees, working their way across the island. The gray-coated grasses and soil never changed, nor did the rankness of the mud pools. Away from the water, fewer beasts were heard, for which he was grateful. Still, his eyes flitted from underbrush to trees, searching for abominations.

Before long they'd reached the far side of their island. Other islets were visible; so many in fact, that it was hard to tell if the landscape was comprised of islands with water between them, or one land mass with innumerable ponds.

After scanning the waters, Caitlyn edged her steed into the water. She looked back at them. "Be watchful."

Memories of their narrow escape from the lurker flashed through his mind. He dreaded the thought of another such encounter. Judging from Jarek's expression, he felt much the same. Goodricke edged his horse forward, following Caitlyn as she veered for the next island. Fortunately, the distance between the islets was short.

He heard splashing! Three heads jerked toward the sound. Although Goodricke saw no hint of a lurker, that didn't guarantee other dangers didn't lurk just out of sight. He exchanged a nervous glance with Jarek as Caitlyn urged her horse forward. He prayed the woman knew what she was doing.

Their horses were rarely more than belly deep in water. Still, it wasn't until they'd reached the next beach that Goodricke breathed normally again.

This second island turned out to be one of many. Although they moved from island to island without mishap, Goodricke never relaxed. It was early afternoon when one island offered up a berry patch. Caitlyn dismounted and picked some. "Come, the *sméar dubh* will renew you. We are fortunate to have found some." She stuffed a mouthful and smiled. "They are very tasty."

They gathered berries and sat, passing their meal in conversation. Caitlyn was very respectful toward Jarek. The mage told her of Lavan's strange vanishing, and the upcoming Nexus, but all attempts to glean more about A'ryth were deftly avoided.

Although carefully avoiding the topic of A'ryth, Caitlyn was very open about the Crone and her abominations. This Crone apparently used the arts to change the marsh's creatures into the beasts Caitlyn called abominations. At least that was the opinion of her Lore Masters. Based on her description, Lore Masters were likely magi by another name. They conjectured that this was the Crone's hateful way to isolate her Haunt. Abominations abounded there, apparently more dangerous than the ones Jarek and he had already encountered. They emerged mostly after dark.

After eating their fill, they resumed their journey. It was late afternoon when they finally left the swamps and began a gradual ascent up a mountainside. The gray of the marsh gave way to brown soil and green foliage. Squirrels, songbirds, and other wildlife appeared, as did familiar-looking trees and brush. The gray of the marsh slowly transformed into a normal-looking forest.

They stopped every so often so Goodricke could check his compass. Caitlyn was keeping them on an unerring path. She and Jarek kept up their dialog. Goodricke let them do the talking, but his eyes seldom left Caitlyn. She had a way of keeping him off guard, treating him warmly one moment, only to become distant in the next. She captivated him.

At dusk they halted beneath a large bluff. "This looks to be a good place to sleep," Caitlyn offered, slipping off her mount. Since she hadn't bothered to scout the area, Goodricke wondered if she'd planned to bring them here all along.

Once he and Jarek dismounted, Caitlyn uttered something in her strange tongue, and the horses departed. She headed for the woods. "I shall find food."

After a while, she returned with two rabbits and a handful of herbs. Goodricke gathered rocks and kindling, formed a spit and built a fire, and watched her create what turned out to be the best meal he'd eaten in recent memory. "Caitlyn, this is delicious."

"Thank you, Goodricke Loddvar," she said, beaming.

That evening it was her turn to ask questions of the Outlands. Her fascination with their world more than rivaled theirs with hers.

She marveled over the idea of growing one's own food on farms, and of merchants who brought goods for sale and trade. Most astonishing was that a world existed where danger didn't lurk at every turn.

Jarek turned in early, but Caitlyn and Goodricke talked well into the night. Gone was any hint of her former aloofness. He couldn't say why, but their comfortable questions, answers, gibes and jests seemed uncommonly natural. Despite the dangers here, he couldn't remember the last time he'd felt so tranquil.

Finally, it was time to turn in. He fished out his tritant. "Before we sleep, I need to take a final reading. The Nexus must be close."

Caitlyn grew quiet as he set up his instrument. He took a reading. "Gods!"

"What is it, Goodricke Loddvar?"

"We're within a league of it." He looked up the hillside. "It must be just over this ridge."

She turned her back. "It is good you are so close." Her body language belied her words however, which were her last of the evening.

Goodricke crawled into his bed, pondering her sudden mood changes. He wondered which Caitlyn would awaken on the morrow, the one with the calming charm, or the hostile warrior with the deadly thong?

Jarek lay in his bed, unable to sleep. He twisted his ring. *Lavan, can you hear me?*

Yes! I'm here. Say nothing. I've done you a grave disservice my friend; Zakarah can see into my mind. He knows we are communicating, and that you plan an encounter at the upcoming Nexus. Tell me nothing of importance and beware his tricks. But not all news is grim. What Zakarah doesn't realize is that when our minds meld, I see his thoughts, too. I bring you warning. Something formidable disturbs him. It dwells close to the upcoming Nexus. Stay vigilant.

He comes! I must go.

Decisions

Rayna stopped to catch her breath. They were walking the jetty, slogging slowly toward land. Scaling its endless boulders was exhausting, say nothing of precarious. Many stood taller than her, and shallow water filled the gaps between them. They had to time their crossing of them, lest they get swept out to sea by some onrushing wave. What had begun as a joyous journey to find her mother had turned into a tedious disaster.

Gresham was leading the way, picking the safest route. Hagley walked behind them, ready to assist Sully or her if needed. Gresham navigated the boulders with seeming ease, despite lugging two knapsacks with a sword and crossbow strapped to them. She couldn't imagine carrying all that weight. She was fortunate to have chosen him as her guide, despite the journey's dubious beginning. Not only was he strong; he was smart, organized, and… well… very good looking. She found herself staring at him more and more often.

Their trek seemed to be taking forever, but the beach finally did come into view. A long wade through shallows had them standing on dry sand. She staggered over to where her exhausted companions lay spread-eagled on the ground and plopped down beside them. Their boat was lost. They were stranded; with the chances of finding her mother possibly gone. Worse, she looked a mess. It was all too much. She started to cry.

"What's wrong?" Gresham asked.

"What's wrong?" she squawked. "What is wrong! The better question is what is right? We're lost! Where, the gods only know. Half our gear is gone—including my clothing." She tugged on the rags Mistress Genevieve had forced her to where, "Leaving me nothing but these rags to greet my mother in. Assuming, of course, we even find her. And you ask what's wrong?" Burying her face in her hands, she started sobbing.

Gresham laid a hand on her shoulder. "Don't despair, we'll figure something out. In fact, I have something for you." He opened his bag. After foraging through it, he pulled out a bundle wrapped in black cloth. "It's a bit wet, but I'm sure you'll find it more to your liking than what you have on. I hope it fits," he said, handing it to her. "Although not nearly as nice, it reminds me of the outfit you wore when Hagley and I first took you to the university. And this one's far better suited for the wilderness."

Taking the bundle, she opened it. Inside were matching leggings and skirt and blouse, all made of sturdy leather. Although not elegant, they were a vast improvement over what she had on. She looked up, biting her lip, tearing again. "Thank you."

"Once they're dry, how about putting them on?"

She stood. "They can't be any wetter than what I have on. I'm putting them on now."

She wandered over to a nearby boulder, ducked behind it, and donned her gift. It did little to enhance her shape—something that seemed to be growing in importance to her as of late, but it was a vast improvement over what she'd been wearing. She combed her fingers through her hair in a futile effort to make herself look presentable, picked up her discarded rags, and rejoined the men. "Better?" she asked, slowly spinning in a circle.

"Wow!" Sully bubbled. "You be a princess again."

She laughed, "Only to you, little hero. Only to you."

She checked the two men. Hagley was staring wide-eyed. Gresham looked much the same. "That looks really good on you," Hagley offered. She'd never have guessed she could be this unkempt and still feel flattered, but there was no doubt she did.

Only three of their bags survived the boat wreck: Hagley's satchel; the bag holding their food; and the large one Gresham had lugged. "Let's see what's still usable," he said, upending his knapsack. Out tumbled clothing, weapons, and two water bags.

Hagley did the same. Out came the spell books the magi had given him. "At least I didn't lose these," he said, examining them one by one. "Like I did with the university's wagon and horses," he added, looking forlorn.

It was the first time it dawned on Rayna that this sweet man would grieve over having lost his magi's property. The pirates surely had it by now.

"Ah, it's here," Gresham said, hoisting her mother's map. "The water didn't damage it," he said, assuring her.

"Let's study it and revise our plan. Gather round," he said, coaxing the others over.

"Food and water are our greatest concerns. Two water bags won't last long; they'll need refilling. We only brought food enough to last two people six days. There are four of us now, likely not enough to get us where we want to be, so finding food will be a priority too."

Rayna marveled at how easily the man had taken charge. She'd chosen a worthy guide.

He spread the map out on the sand. He pointed to Tanner Point. "This is where we'd hoped to land." He slid his finger across the map. "Instead, we're here." Twisting around, he looked behind him. "Those cliffs jut way out in the water. Look how violently that surf pummels them. We were lucky to survive them in a boat. Without one, there's no way we can get to their other side." He turned back around. "Those cliff walls go straight up, making them too treacherous to try to climb." He sighed. "I'm sorry, but getting back to Tanner Point isn't an option. We have ocean behind us, and a lagoon to other side." He paused, his gaze settling on the beach ahead. "Our only remaining choice is to head up this beach."

Rayna's heart sank. "That means we can't follow my mother's map."

"In a way, we can." He ran his hands over the map, flattening it. "Our objective is to get to the far end of this peninsula—or island—or whatever is we're on, and find this man with a key drawn on his head." He bounced a finger on its image. "If we walk the side we're on, we'll eventually wind up at the same place."

Rayna wasn't convinced. "But we're supposed to go up the other side."

"True. I'm open to any suggestions as to how we might get over there."

"I…" she felt her cheeks flush, "don't have one."

"Then this is our plan."

He tossed the food bag to Hagley. "Magic-man can carry this. It's too heavy for Rayna. Let her carry your satchel. Do we really need those books? How about we leave them here?"

Hagley looked appalled. "These are rare and valuable tomes. There's no way I'm leaving them behind."

"It's all right," Rayna offered. "I don't mind." Having no idea how heavy they were, she hoped that was true.

"Sully, how about you be our soldier and carry the weapons?" he said, handing him the crossbow. "We'll tie them together and strap them to your back." He grabbed Rayna's discarded rags. "We'd best wrap that sabre in something before you stab yourself with it."

Sully's face lit up. "Sure!" he said with a little boy's enthusiasm.

Rayna studied the boy, wondering what it must be like to have killed someone. So far, it didn't seem to be bothering him.

Everyone donned their assigned gear and they set off up the beach. At first, all they encountered was flat sand, and sunny weather, making for an easy walk. But before long it clouded over and started to rain. Worse, they found themselves having to negotiate large boulders and jagged rocks. Her efforts had her sweating like some livestock animal. Her damp hair now clung to her forehead, despite the fact the rain had ceased. Worse, insects were everywhere, the red marks on her arms evidence of their incessant stinging and biting. Sure Gresham would hardly find her present state comely, she walked a good distance behind him. It was best he not see her looking like this. And Hagley's stupid, pointless books were proving far heavier than she expected. She sorely wanted to dump them out and leave them. But having seen how important they were to him, she couldn't bring herself to do it.

Lightning flashed overhead, followed in short order by the loud rumble of thunder. Next came the inevitable downpour, drenching her, head to toe. With her hair stuck to her face, she must look a sight. The good news was the rain had driven the bugs into hiding. That, and the outfit Gresham bought her was thick enough to keep her warm.

Her feet ached. She was sure they were blistering. Maybe Gresham's soldier training had readied him for something this strenuous, but nothing had prepared her. He'd periodically turn around and check on his brood, often giving her odd looks. Was he disappointed in her? Was she letting him down, making him sorry he'd offered to guide her? She had to be a fright to behold. Yudelle would have found some way to still look fetching under similar circumstances, but it was beyond her. And she needed to control her temper, lest she disappoint him further. Sighing, she kept on trudging.

The storm passed. Clouds parted, giving way to a warming sun, making the going less treacherous. Still, she kept slipping farther and farther behind. Even plump Hagley was well ahead of her. She no longer cared. Too exhausted to take another step, she leaned against a boulder, slid to the ground, and closed her eyes. It felt so good to rest.

Something tickled her, waking her. She looked. A huge spider was crawling up her arm. Screaming, she jumped to her feet, frantically slapping it away. Gods, she'd fallen asleep. For how long? She looked around. No one was in sight. She was alone in the wilderness. Heart racing, she ran to catch up.

This was Gresham's fault she thought, wiping away her tears. A good guide would have found a way to get her to Tanner Point, not strand her alone in the middle of nowhere.

※

Gresham turned, checking on the others. Sully wasn't far behind, and Hagley's head had just popped up from behind a rock quite a way back. He couldn't see Rayna, but she was usually not far behind Hagley. She was likely just out of sight. The two of them had been stopping more and more often. He knew he ought to wait for them to catch up, but dusk was falling and he'd yet to find a suitable place to spend the night. Knowing they were all too weary to go on much farther, he decided to scout ahead on his own.

He stopped when he stumbled onto a stream trickling down from above, only the third they'd seen all day. It produced enough water to nurture a small clump of trees and bracken near the swamp's edge. The area around was sandy, with enough flat spots for sleeping. A cave was visible a short way up the hill, likely the source of the creek. Deciding the odds of finding anything more suitable were slim, he dropped his pack and sat waiting for the others to catch up.

Sully was first to arrive, and Hagley shortly thereafter. "How far behind is Rayna?" he asked as Hagley dropped his pack.

"I don't know," he said, sinking to the sand. "I haven't seen her for quite some time."

"What!? How long?"

Hagley exhaled. "I don't know… a while."

"You two stay here while I go find her."

He'd hardly left camp when he spotted her. She looked ready to drop. He hoped the strain of this trip wouldn't dull her excitement at getting to meet her mother. He admired her for undertaking such an arduous trip. Very few highborn women would do such a thing. She had a goal and was willing to do what was necessary to achieve it. The same was true of Hagley and his quest to earn his robes. He envied their commitment. His own life lacked such purpose. Perhaps mastering the arts would fill that void. He hoped so.

"Here, let me carry that satchel," he offered as he caught up to her.

"Here!" she spat, tossing it to the ground. Giving him a withering look, she stomped past him without another word.

Whoa! This wasn't good. He rushed to catch up, "Wait," he said, placing a hand on her shoulder.

Jaw clenched, she pushed it away, walking even faster. Deciding it best not to press the issue—whatever it was, he kept quiet.

He followed her, listening to the seagulls squawk overhead. He looked up. Curiously, neither they nor the other seabirds ever ventured out over the lagoon. It seemed dead—it's only life being an occasional grotesque fish. Grotesque or not, they were still a source of food. Catching one would stretch out their sparse food supply.

Rayna's mood got no better when they finally reached the others. She stormed past Sully and Hagley without uttering a word, and sat by herself, brooding; obviously in no mood to discuss what was bothering her. Perhaps a fish dinner might thaw her outlook.

To that end, he broke off a nearby cat tail. Although not sturdy, it was sufficiently pointy to do the trick.

Sully's youthful energy had the boy up and exploring. "How about you search for bird's eggs," he told him, "while I try to spear us a meal."

The skies were darkening by the time he finally speared one. He cleaned it, started a fire, and dug his cooking pan out of his gear. Once it was fried, he speared a piece on his knife and took it to Rayna as a peace offering.

"I'm not eating that horrible thing," she said, turning up her nose.

"I'll get you something from the food bag, then."

After doing so, he joined Sully and Hagley by the fire. Hagley nodded toward Rayna. "What's wrong with her—she seems mad?"

"I have no idea," he said, shaking his head. It was then he noticed Sully looked even less pleased than Rayna. "What's wrong, little soldier?"

"I think this be the place where I seen a monster eat a man."

Gresham chuckled. "How could that be, you told me you've never been anywhere other than Stalwart and Portsmouth. How could you possibly have seen this place before?"

Sully scoured the water. "I seen it in my sleep."

This time Gresham laughed outright. "You mean you saw it in a bad dream."

"No!" Sully shouted, jumping to his feet, his anger genuine. "No, it was real! You'll see," he barked, stomping out of camp, heading up the hill.

Rayna finally joined them, warming her hands by the fire. She brushed her fallen curls out of her face. "Couldn't you at least humor him?"

Uh oh. At least she was speaking to him now. "Humor him? He had a nightmare. I was just trying to ease his fears by pointing out that it wasn't real."

She turned her face away.

"This isn't about Sully, is it? You're angry with me, aren't you?"

She sat quiet for a bit, before twisting to face him. "I thought you were my guide!"

175

He spread his arms. "Isn't that what I'm doing?"

She tucked her knees to her chest, glaring at him. "You left me all by myself back there. All of you did," she said, glaring at Hagley. "What if I'd fallen and hurt myself, or had some other mishap. You'd never have known."

Gads, they had deserted her, if only briefly. Rayna had confessed to having a temper, and this was the second time it had been directed it at him. He hoped it'd be the last. "I'm sorry, I wasn't thinking. I was so intent on finding us a place to camp before it got dark that I..." He stopped mid-sentence. "You're right. I'm sorry. It won't happen again," he said, placing a hand on her shoulder.

She brushed it away. "A promise too late."

Sully's shout from above disrupted their icy conversation. "This cave be beauteous. Anyone wanna search it with me?"

"Should we see what he's found?" he asked Rayna, hoping a distraction would calm her.

"You go; I'd prefer to be alone right now."

'Right now' sounded promising. Maybe leaving to explore the cave was what was needed. He climbed up thirty or so paces before reaching its opening. Seemingly as anxious to escape Rayna's wrath as he was, Hagley followed along. Not knowing what they might encounter inside, Gresham brought the crossbow with him. Maybe they'd find something edible.

From below, the cave looked like one would have to crawl on hands and knees in order to get inside, but it turned out to be overgrown brush blocking what was actually a rather tall entryway. Brushing it aside, he ducked inside.

His mouth dropped.

Hagley bumped into him, and looked too. "Amazing."

The cavern was four times his height. Most astonishing was the oddly shaped stone pillar that stretched from floor to ceiling. It had bulges like knotty wood on an old tree. Sully had already scaled it. He sat there, stretching his arm above him. "I can touch the top!" he bragged, pressing his hand against the ceiling.

"Here, this should help us see," Hagley said, casting a light globe, revealing a long hollow tunnel that stretched as far as Gresham could see.

Hagley grinned. "It's so good to have my magic restored."

Gresham found the comment puzzling. "What do you mean, restored?"

"I created so many light globes last night, it drained my aethers. One can only hold a spell so long before that happens. After that, you need rest to restore them. Sunlight makes that happen more quickly."

There was so much about the arts Gresham didn't understand, he doubted he ever would. That was for another time, however. Right now, the cave had his interest.

Thanks to Hagley's globe, they could see some distance down its tunnel. Light shimmered off its rounded walls, sparkling shades of black and gray. Sully jumped down and ran down it to explore. A rocky bulge ran the entire length of the walls on either side. Chest-high to Sully, it looked as if a river had flowed through the tunnel and suddenly turned to rock.

Sully looked back over his shoulder. "Can you be making more light, Hagley? I can't see no farther."

Hagley looked at Gresham. "I think Gresham should."

"Me?"

He laughed. "You heard me. You said you wanted me to teach you how to do it. What better time? You learned all you need to know on our trip to Portsmouth; it's time to try casting something."

Gresham took a deep breath. Cast a spell? Butterflies rippled through his gut.

Hagley fell into tutor mode. "A light spell is what we call a rudimental—the easiest kind of spell to master. Since light is basically aethers, changing them into light is the simplest of all spells. Any magus can master it, regardless of his specialty." He raised a finger. "Watch and listen. I apply the Law of Association, recite its words, and trigger the spell."

"I don't remember that law."

"If entities share a common element, their patterns interact through that element. In this case, the common element is light."

Hagley uttered the rudimental. Instantly a second globe burst into view. "Maintaining two at once is draining, but a single one requires little effort." A snap of his fingers and his second globe vanished. "You try it."

More light would help. Hagley walked him through the spell sequence. Confident he was ready, Gresham attempted his first rudimental.

Nothing. He was crestfallen, his first spell officially a failure. Wanting something and making it happen were clearly two different matters.

"Nobody succeeds on his first try. Do it again."

Gresham couldn't; he'd already forgotten the words. He now understood why Hagley rehearsed his spells before casting them.

Under Hagley's coaching, Gresham tried again; and again, and again and again. After uncounted unsuccessful efforts, he was about to give up when a second ball of glowing mage-light showered the cave. He'd done it! He'd cast a spell. He was a magus. He let out a whoop. The globe vanished.

"You lost your concentration. Don't worry, it happens to everyone. Later, when you get the knack, you'll learn to do other things and still be able to maintain a spell this simple. When you're learning, even that's hard. One more time now."

Gresham tried again, and another globe burst into existence.

"You did it again!" Sully yelled. "We be having two magic men now."

Gresham couldn't contain his grin. "I did, didn't I?" He shook his head in disbelief. Amazingly, the globe still held, even though he'd spoken.

"Good job. It takes most new students a fortnight to do this well," Hagley said, slapping his back.

His globe vanished when they heard Rayna's scream.

So frightened she could hardly breathe, Rayna stood, frozen in place. There, hovering near the shoreline not fifteen paces away, was the most grotesque creature she'd ever seen. A dull gray, it was gigantic; its length thrice that of a man. Huge eyes flanked its monstrous head. It had jagged teeth and too many arms to count. Worse, it looked poised to strike.

"Rayna! The trees!"

She snapped her head around. It was Gresham, crossbow in hand. Thank the gods, the men had returned.

The instant she dove for the trees, the thing struck. Something wrapped around her ankle. Its grip tightened, tripping her, the pain in her foot so awful she was sure it would be torn apart, or worse, that she'd get dragged into the creature's maw.

Fortunately, something was preventing that from happening. She looked. The beast had snared not only her leg, but the stout root of a nearby bush. It was all that was saving her.

The beast let loose with a beastly roar. It swung to face Gresham, a greenish-red ooze bubbling out its eye from a bolt wound. She tried to pry herself loose while the thing was distracted but couldn't.

"I'll do it!" Sully yelled, racing toward her, his cutlass waving above his head. Dodging under the beast's wildly flapping arms, he slashed at the limb that held her. Green gore splattered, and her leg broke free. Grabbing the boy's hand, she dove into the brush, pulling him with her.

They scrambled out the far side of the stand. The beast bawled its objection, slashing at them with other arms, but found only tree limbs, not theirs. The wooded grove had saved them. Howling, it ripped at the trees, leaves and branches flying every which way.

Tugging Sully along behind her, she ran up the hillside, getting as far from the threat as she could.

"The cave!" Gresham yelled, barely audible over the creature's howls.

Bolstered by her fear, she scrambled over rocks that would have seemed impossible to climb only hours ago. Heart racing, she clambered higher, distancing herself from that horrible monstrosity. Only when she'd reached the cave did she stop to catch her breath. "Are you all right, Sully?" she asked, turning to find him. Gods! He wasn't with her.

"I got the map!" he yelled, running through camp, waving it over his head.

With a new target in its sights, the serpent lunged at him, arms reaching to grab him. Somehow, the nimble scamp dodged their grasp, running for the cave. Before it could strike again, a second monster suddenly appeared out of nowhere. Gods! How could Sully escape two of them?

Seeing this new rival, the first beast attacked the second, embedding its powerful beak in its neck.

Hagley was standing just out of reach of the dueling behemoths, his hands dancing as if operating a puppet. He made a grabbing gesture with his hand. The new beast moved in concert with his motion, lashing, open-jawed, at its attacker.

Once Sully made it to the cave, Hagley ceased his gyrations and the second monster vanished.

Hagley looked up the hill. "Get our gear!"

The monster launched itself at Hagley, but before it could strike, a second Hagley appeared. Then a third, and a fourth. While the beast attacked those closest to it, Gresham dragged their bags out of harm's way. The original Hagley slipped behind a rock, hands still waving, his eyes riveted on the beast.

"I have them!" Gresham yelled, once he was well out of the creature's reach.

All the Hagleys but the one behind the rock dissolved, leaving only the original running toward the cave. Once he got there, they ducked inside.

Hagley dropped to one knee, wheezing, his chest heaving, looking strangely excited. "I've never been so scared in my life."

Rayna plopped herself against the cave wall, wondering if her heart would burst. "Me either!"

Gresham rushed to her side. "Are you injured?"

She held his hand, trembling. "My foot hurts a little, but aside from that, I think I'm all right." She shook her head, "I was sure I was about to die!" She frowned. "What happened to that second monster?"

Hagley sat up, beaming. "It wasn't real. Like those other me's, it was illusion to distract the real beast." He clenched his fists. "I just tried two new spells, and both worked on my first try." His eyes sparkled with a fire Gresham hadn't seen in them before.

Rayna went over and hugged him. "Thank you, my wonderful magic man," she said, kissing his cheek.

Sully scrunched his face. "I be thanking you too, Hagley, but I ain't kissin' you."

Rayna wheeled on the boy, grabbing him by the shoulders. "You foolish boy!" she scolded, hugging him close. "If Hagley hadn't used his magic, you'd be dead."

He twisted away, looking hurt. "But I saved you."

"Yes, you did," she admitted, squeezing him to her. "But don't do it again! I don't want harm to befall you because you're being my hero."

"She's right, little man," Gresham said. "One of my old sergeants had a saying: there are two kinds of soldiers, old ones and bold ones, but you'll not find any who are both. A good soldier must carefully choose when to be bold if he's to grow old." He squeezed Rayna's hand. "That said, this time you chose wisely."

Rayna wiped her eyes. "Thank you …all of you, for saving my life."

Hagley cast another spell, and debris started filling the cave's entrance, clogging it so that nothing else could get in, including light. He resolved the latter with another of his light spells.

Deciding the cave was the safest place to sleep, they spread blankets and turned in.

Gresham tossed fitfully all night, and was first to waken. A sliver of sunshine shone through the cave's opening. He removed enough debris to peer outside. Spotting nothing dangerous, he squeezed through the opening. Crawling out, he inspected the area.

Tracks were everywhere, many where they'd planned to camp. They were freakishly large, made by something dangerous. As horrible as the beast's attack had seemed at the time, it was most likely a blessing. What fate would they have suffered had they slept out here?

He scouted their intended route. Boulders blocked every avenue. There was no way forward. They'd either need to figure a way to cross over to the ocean side or return the way they'd come—and they hadn't food enough to do that. Their chances of reaching A'ryth or even returning to Portsmouth looked grim.

As he was pondering their plight, an idea struck him. He returned to the cave. Kneeling beside Sully, he nudged him awake. "Hey little man, how deep did you explore these caverns?"

Sully sat up and yawned. "Hagley made me a torch. I went way far after you was asleep."

"Did you find an end, or did the cave keep on going?"

"It be going on forever."

Gresham nodded. "I thought so."

Their chatter had awakened the other two. Gresham stood. "I just scouted outside. The path forward is impassable. It only gets more treacherous. Worse, there are tracks all over our camp. Big ones. I've not seen the likes of the creatures that come out at night here. Now I understand why the trail on the map was on the ocean side. We need to get over to that side, and I may have figured out how we can do it."

He had everyone's attention. "Last night Sully explored that tunnel. He never found its end. With luck, it might go all the way through the mountain—to the ocean side."

He stooped down and picked up the food pack. "This is all that remains of our food—one or two days' worth at best. We have two choices; hike back to where we landed and try to either find some way over that cliff, or back to Portsmouth. I don't like our chances of doing either. Our other choice is the tunnels. I like the latter, but you all have a say. What should we do, explore or backtrack; what say you all?"

"I wanna go the tunnel way!" Sully offered.

Hagley disagreed. "We have no idea how far or where these tunnels go. It makes more sense to backtrack and find our way to Tanner Point."

"There's no way I'm going back the way we came," Rayna moaned. "I barely made it here when I wasn't tired and exhausted."

"When aren't you tired?" Hagley complained.

"Oh, like you weren't," she snapped.

"Besides, I don't know how long I can maintain my light spell," Hagley added. "Think how happy it'll be to be caught under a mountain, unable to see."

It was the first time he'd seen Hagley show anything but deference to Rayna. Judging from her response, she was as shocked as him. She looked Gresham's way. "You're our guide, you decide."

Hagley's comments made sense, but there was no way Rayna could hike all the way back to Tanner Point. Besides, siding with Hagley would draw her ire. "How about we compromise and spend one, and only one day searching the caves. If we fail to find an ocean outlet, then we retreat to the quay."

Hagley and Rayna looked at one another. Eventually each nodded.

Decision made, each ate half of a ration and got ready to leave. "Since Hagley says there's a limit to how long a globe can be maintained…" he paused, grinning, "I'll help him out." He cast his newly learned spell, and glowing light appeared just over his head.

Rayna's jaw dropped. "You just made light!"

He winked. "A little trick Hagley taught me."

Everyone grabbed gear and they were on their way. Hagley led. Sully walked beside him, with Rayna and he right behind them. Gresham tapped the boy's shoulder. "Sully?"

"Yeah?" he said, looking back over his shoulder.

"Did you see caves like these in any of those bad dreams of yours?"

"No."

"Good. If you have any more nightmares, be sure to tell me about them."

Rayna sidled up closer, entwining her arm in his. "Hey, Soldier Boy, you didn't tell me you could make magic." She flashed that wonderful smile of hers. "And searching the caves was clever. I'm most impressed."

They continued, arm-in-arm, yesterday's transgressions hopefully forgiven.

They hadn't gone far when their tunnel forked. Which to take? "Since the ocean's to the west and were heading south, let's go right at every fork."

The height and width of the tunnel never seemed to vary. The one big exception was when they stumbled upon a bunch of strange-looking columns. Some appeared to have dripped from the ceiling, only to freeze in place. Others grew up from the floor, often joining with the ones coming down from the ceiling. Water pooled at its base. It seemed void of life which, given the tracks he'd seen the night before, was a blessing. Gresham wondered if that would be true of the rest of the tunnel. He touched his sword, taking solace from its presence.

Hagley insisted they trade globe duties again, far sooner than Gresham expected. If they drained themselves of the aethers they'd find themselves deep within the bowels of this mountain, unable to see. He shuddered at the thought.

Tunnel branches were appearing more and more often now. They kept to their rule, always bearing right. At one point they encountered a large cavern with a cone at its center that was five times a man's height. Its ceiling had caved in creating a hole, casting sunlight on its walls. Hagley went there and plopped down, basking in the sunlight. His weary companions joined him.

They'd rested only briefly when Rayna said, "I almost died yesterday. If I had, my life's story would have ended with no one really knowing who I am."

"That's likely true of all of us," Gresham countered.

She sat up straight. "Let's not let that happen. Let's each share something about ourselves the others don't know, so none of our stories remains a secret."

"I ain't got nothing to tell," Sully lamented. "I ain't been nowhere, and don't do nothin' but help Keep at the Dragon. He says I'm his waif."

Rayna flashed one of her smiles. "Then tell us what you want to do."

Sully cocked his head to one side, thinking. "I'd like to make magic like Hagley does!" He looked at Gresham, "Like he taught Gresham to do."

"You need to be born with the Gift in order to do that," Hagley cautioned.

Sully gave him a petulant look. "Maybe nobody ain't discovered my Gift yet."

"I'm sure that's it," Rayna consoled. "Now come over and sit by me." She draped her arm around him and cuddled him closer.

"What about you, Soldier Boy? You showed us you can do magic; what other secrets haven't you shared?"

He shrugged. "I'm just a lowborn orphan who's been lucky enough to be schooled by an orphanage and trained as a soldier."

"So you say," Rayna pressed, "but if that's true, why is it everything about you reeks of someone born high?"

"I agree," Hagley offered. "If you're an orphan, why are you so sure you're lowborn? What do you know of your family?"

"I spent my whole life thinking I had none, then recently, out of nowhere, an uncle—my mother's brother—paid me a surprise visit."

Rayna pressed, "What is his family like? Where do they live?"

Gresham squirmed. "I only met him that one time, and we spoke only briefly. Prior Rigby introduced him as Jarek Verity."

"Jarek Verity!" Hagley squawked, sitting up straight. "Gods Gresham, he's a Royal Magus, a member of King Aldridge's Court!"

Rayna shook her head. "You have royal kin and you call yourself lowborn?"

"One can hardly claim someone kin you've been with for less than an hour."

Rayna sat shaking her head. "It had to be."

Gresham had no idea what she meant. He looked at Hagley, "What of you, what don't we know about you?" he asked, anxious to shift the conversation elsewhere.

"Yes," Rayna asked, "what do magic men do anyway? How long have you been a magus?"

Hagley's face fell. "I'm not a magus, Lady, but I still hope to someday become one."

"So, tell us about the magi," Rayna pressed. "I know nothing of the gifted," she said, glancing toward Gresham.

He shrugged. "Mostly they spend their days refining their maistry. Some teach, but most hire themselves out. Selling their wares is how magi earn their keep. I've been studying the arts since my fourteenth year after a travelling magus, sharing an evening at my father's caravan, discovered my Gift. He seemed most impressed when I managed a light spell on my first try. He got most excited when I was able to cast other rudimentals too." He shrugged. "Apparently, it's rare to be able to do that.

"Amazed by my range of spells, and knowing how traders love profits, the magus convinced my father of the advantages of having a sorcerer at his side. He urged my father to enroll me in an arts university. My father is a rich and powerful merchant. Tight with his coin, I was amazed that the magus was able to convince him I was a good investment. A month later I was enrolled at our arts university. It's the best of its kind and quite costly." The sparkle in his eyes faded. "After three years of training, my magic still fails when I most need it. I failed my robe trials—twice. The only reason I haven't returned to the mainland is my dread of seeing the look in my father's eyes when he learns his son is a failure, or worse, a bad investment."

"Failure! How can you call yourself a failure?" Rayna challenged. "Yesterday you saved us from that beast. The day before you helped us escape wharf pirates by making them dance. How is that failure?"

"Rayna's right," Gresham said, "When have you been needed more? We'd all be dead if it weren't for you."

"I guess that's true," Hagley said, his eyes sparkling. "Perhaps I should amend my remark. I was a failure until I met the likes of you three. I don't know how or why, but my success is due to the lot of you. Whatever it is you've done for me, I thank you."

Sully patted Hagley's arm. "You be with friends is all."

"What about you, Rayna," Gresham said, "tell us what it's like to be raised a highborn."

"I'm told my father is some noble, yet as hard as this is to believe, I've never met either of my parents—at least not that I can remember." She shared how she was moved from school to school every year, escorted by this man named Robard. She recounted her meeting with the friar. "All I know of my 'highborn' parents is what he told me. I'm more imposter than high lady."

"What of this mysterious father of yours; what did the friar tell you of him?"

"Only that he's some High Lord in St. Pyre—one too ashamed of his daughter to openly claim her."

"A Lord! You can't get much higher born than that," Gresham argued.

"I agree," Hagley said. "Lady, your claim of imposter is without merit. You are a lady through and through. You speak like one. You dress like one, and carry yourself like one. Why, in Portsmouth, even dressed in rags, those lowly pirates knew you were a person of degree."

"Lady, you be a princess," Sully said. "And everyone knows they be highborn."

"You embarrass me," she said, her face burning red. She stood. "Thank you all for sharing your stories. I feel I know each of you better now." She was looking at Gresham when she said it.

They resumed their journey. Ceiling holes became more frequent, letting in so much light they no longer had to rely on globes. Despite the frequent openings, all were too high to provide an escape from the tunnels… until Sully's shout. "Look! There be a way out!"

Unlike the cave opening on the marsh side, this one offered no easy egress. They had to clamber up the debris formed when the opening collapsed. They wound up high on a bluff with a breathtaking view of the ocean. Even this high up, Gresham could smell the sea.

The sun was setting. Orange hues glistened off the water for as far as the eye could see. Even though they were far above the water, the climb down to the beach didn't look difficult. Still, fearing more beastly encounters, they spent the night camped on the ledge.

A morning breeze woke Gresham. The sun was up, and the others were stirring. Gone was the gloomy fog of the marsh. Even though the trail to the beach was still in shadows, they all rushed down to caper in surf and sand.

Discarding their boots, they waded through the tide pools looking for shellfish. Sully trapped and killed a fish at the expense of his cutlass edge. Others found mussels and oysters. They gathered driftwood, cooked and ate, savoring their bounty, fresh air, and blue skies overhead.

They set off down the beach hoping to find some sort of landmark that would help them gain their bearings. Their path was mostly hard sand with only an occasional rock to scale. The seaward side was far easier, far faster, and far safer than the marsh had been.

Late that afternoon the peninsula ended. Another land mass could be seen off in the distance, but they'd have needed their boat to cross over to it. "I guess it's time to search of our key-man," Gresham offered. He scanned the barren hillside. "Anyone see a cave?"

After a failed search, they pored over the map hoping to find a clue that might help locate the cave. Gresham scoured the bluff. "Maybe it's in another tunnel like the one we were in. Let's search up higher."

Those efforts fared no better. Disheartened, they gathered to rest and discuss what to do next. Trying to free his mind, Gresham took in the scenery. The salt air was invigorating, and he loved the roar of the surf as it crashed against a stone archway a short way up the beach. Wave after wave collided with the arch, funneling its way beneath, disappearing in the waters beyond. Or was it water? He sat up, seeking a better view.

Rayna squinted. "What is it?"

"That archway, is that water behind it or… …a cave!" He jumped to his feet and ran down the beach, the others in hot pursuit.

The sand ended at the base of the archway. Gresham climbed up it. The top was narrow, with water to either side. Keeping low, he crawled to its center and peered beyond it. A surge of water rippled back toward the sea, exposing a sandy entrance to a large cave. "I found it!" he yelled, waving the others over.

The group watched as another wave come bursting through, inundating the cave's entrance. The water roiled a bit, then retreated as the wave lost its force. "Now! Before the next wave."

They plowed through the shallows, fighting the tug of the receding water, and made it into the cave. Not far from them someone had fashioned a rock pathway that led into a giant cavern. They ran for it before another wave arrived.

It turned out to be another tunnel like the one they just travelled. Its rocks were worn smooth. Someone, or something, had walked this path many times. They headed inside.

It wasn't long before Hagley was forced to cast another light globe. Whereas their earlier tunnels had run in long straight lines, after a brief climb, this one spiraled downward so steeply that Hagley and Gresham had to link arms to help Sully and Rayna climb down it. Their whorled pathway eventually leveled out, emptying into a cavern several times the height of the one they'd rested in that first night. Sunlight flooded its insides through a hole in its ceiling.

Sounds of rushing water lured them to its far side where they discovered an underground river. Cheering, they splashed water over their faces and drank their fill. They were refilling their water bags when Hagley suddenly stood, scanning the cave.

Rayna tensed. "What?"

"I sense something."

"What do you mean by something? Something bad?"

"No, it's more like… …something powerful."

His answer did little to mollify Rayna. "Powerful like that marsh beast?"

"I don't know," Hagley said, perusing the area, "Let's go see. Stay wary."

Hagley led the way. They passed through another tunnel that emptied into an even larger cavern. "Gads!" Hagley yelled, jumping back.

Gresham slipped past him to see his cause for alarm. Standing immobile at the cave's center was a giant man-like statue. "Is that what you sense?"

"Yes."

Sully's eyes looked ready to pop out of his face. "What does it be?"

"I know." Rayna said, surprising everyone. They stared at her. "Well, I don't know what it is exactly, but I bet that's our key-man." She held up her map. "See, he looks just like the drawing."

They edged closer to it. Despite the power Hagley claimed it gave off, it remained motionless, regardless of how close they came. They circled it. It was as tall as two men.

Rayna pointed at its head. "Look at its forehead, do you see?"

Its forehead had a key-shaped depression. Rayna ransacked her pack and pulled out her mother's key. "I believe I'm meant to insert this into its head."

   Everyone stared up at the statue. Gresham shrugged, "This is where the map said to come. This thing may hold the secret to reaching A'ryth. I agree, let's try the key."

   The statue was so tall they'd need to stand shoulder on shoulder to reach its face. Gresham squatted, leaning against it. Hagley climbed to his shoulders. It took every bit of Gresham's strength to stand upright. "All right Sully," he grunted, "you climb to Hagley's shoulders and place the key."

   Sully stepped into the Rayna's cupped hands and she boosted him up to Gresham's shoulders. He crawled up Hagley, stood on his shoulders, and walked his hands up the statue. Balancing with one hand, he fished Rayna's key from his pocket and pressed it into the statue's forehead.

   Bright light burst from the statue, and its eyes glowed red. Sully screeched, nearly falling as he scampered down Hagley. All that motion was too much for Gresham. His legs gave out, and all three collapsed in a heap at the statue's feet. Scrambling on hands and knees, they distanced themselves from whatever had come alive. They were still scrambling away when it spoke. "Do you ride, Seeker?" it asked in a deep, rumbling voice. Its skin was glowing blue.

   Hagley spun around, wide-eyed. "It's a golem!"

   Gresham looked at him. "What in the gods' names is a golem?"

   "A statue animated by magic. No wonder I sensed such power. A'ryth's magi must be highly skilled to create such a thing."

   Gresham stared at it. "So, what do we do now?"

   "We answer it," Rayna said. She looked up at the giant. "Yes, we ride—to A'ryth."

A'ryth

Jarek shook Goodricke's shoulder, waking him. Goodricke sat up, looking around. "Is Caitlyn out hunting food?"

"She's gone. Judging from the amount of dew in her tracks, she left soon after we fell asleep."

Goodricke frowned. "Why would she lead us out of the swamp only to desert us?"

He shrugged. "She seemed awfully protective of her homeland. The reading you took last night said the Nexus was close. Perhaps we were too close for her liking."

"Should we try to follow her?"

"Trying to track a tracker would be folly. Best we seek A'ryth on our own."

After a foraged meal a quick pack, they were ascending the mountain again. Goodricke led the way, his eyes always on their path, hopeful of finding Caitlyn's trail. Jarek doubted he would. What concerned him were the incessant ups and downs, every dip followed by another. Sitting astride his capall had spoiled him. Now that he was afoot, the drudgery of a mountain trek became far more real.

The sun was high when they finally reached the summit. To his delight, the land flattened.

Goodricke squatted, examining the ground ahead, looking concerned. "This is a well-traveled path, milord. It may be a game trail, or perhaps some pathway Caitlyn's people use," He looked up at Jarek, "or we may be entering something's feeding grounds."

"Let me scan for signs of life." He probed. "How strange. Behind us, all seems what I'd expect of the hinterlands—yet in front of us I find no sign of life whatsoever. But if there's nothing in front of us, why the path? Something is amiss." Were the arts in play? Was it Caitlyn's Crone's doing—or perhaps the mysterious creature Lavan had warned him about?

"Do we proceed, milord?"

"What choice have we?"

They trekked onward, albeit far more warily than when they had Caitlyn as their guide. Fortunately, they encountered nothing out of the ordinary—until they came upon some foothills. Long, straight and vertical, they filled the horizon, stretching as far as the eye could see. Save for an archway where their trail ended, it looked impassable.

"What do you make of it milord?"

"It's too perfectly proportioned to be natural; it must be man-made. He probed again. "I find no life whatsoever." He stared ahead. "My gut tells me those hills ahead are the reason why."

Goodricke stared at it. "Dare we proceed?"

"It's that or give up on Lavan—something neither of us is willing to do."

Their footsteps echoed off its walls when they walked under the archway, into a tunnel, Jarek probing; Goodricke at his side him, hand on his sword. The tunnel was short, and they quickly found themselves at its other end, standing before a stream. Like the strange hills they'd just passed through, the river continued as far as they could see in either direction, its width never varying. Trees abounded on the opposite bank, and they could see where their path continued. What was lacking however, was a means for crossing the water.

Jarek probed, surprised to suddenly detect an abundance of life. Grabbing a stick, he stuck it into the water, testing the stream's depth. "I can't reach the bottom. A natural riverbank would taper off gradually. This one goes straight down. This is definitely magus-made."

"How do we cross it?"

Jarek looked him, grinning. "Using a little trick I learned from Lavan."

Goodricke looked uneasy. "Trick?"

"A feather spell."

Goodricke looked uneasy. "I'm most uncomfortable around the arts, milord. Did Master Lavan not mention that?"

Jarek couldn't help but laugh. "This from a magus' manservant? Cheer up, I've seen it done before." Then, with a twinkle in his eyes, added, "Once."

He tossed his stick into the water and watched it race downstream. He looked up at Goodricke, a twinkle in his eyes, "I hope you're a good swimmer."

Goodricke rolled his eyes. "I hope this is just that sense of humor Master Lavan warned me about," he said, watching the stick vanish from view. "Besides, rare is the sailor who doesn't swim."

"Good. Let's hope swimming skills aren't required. During this spell we need to maintain physical contact throughout." He offered Goodricke his hand. "Hold tight, and whatever you do, don't let go."

He spied a spruce on the far bank, its leaves dipping into the stream. He chose it as his target. Imagining the two of them standing there, he rehashed his incantation. Neither too much aether, nor too little. Most importantly, maintain his concentration throughout.

Jarek cast the spell, and was dimly aware of his feet leaving the ground. He felt as he were floating. He pushed that physical awareness from his mind to focus solely on the spell. They rose, drifting forward. Reaching the arc's zenith, they began to descend. The shift in direction disrupted Jarek's concentration. His control wavered, then fell apart.

Down they plummeted, splashing into the frigid torrent. A mass of bubbles shot up his nose, making his eyes throb. He coughed, desperate to rid his lungs of water. The icy current grabbed him, tugging him downstream.

Pain overcame panic when something suddenly wrenched his shoulder, halting him. Blinking, he cleared his eyes. There, beside him, was the blurry visage of Goodricke, clinging to a tree branch. He pulled Jarek toward him, "Grab on!"

Jarek's grasp found nothing but twigs, which snapped and broke, but he finally grabbed the limb, first with one hand, then a second. Raging water poured over the branch, pummeling his face, blinding him.

"Let's make our way to shore," Goodricke hollered over the din.

Walking hand-over-hand, Jarek worked his way along the slippery bark, the chilly water sapping his strength. A hand slipped!

His grip failed! The water had him again. Once again, a rescuing hand gripped the back of his tunic, catching him. "I have you!"

Goodricke's arm encircled his waist, dragged him up the bank, and plopped him down on hardened ground. Goodricke stood over him, smirking. "And here I thought it another of your jests when you asked if I could swim."

Jarek inhaled, catching his breath. "The trip was getting boring. I did this to rid us of that boredom." A cough spewed water. "Besides, do you realize how long it's been since you've bathed? Although risky, I deemed our swim a necessary task."

Goodricke cackled. "I was thinking much the same of you, milord."

While Jarek lay wondering if his arms would ever stop quivering, Goodricke poured the water out of their packs and hung them on a limb to drain. "Our gear's drenched, but everything seems to be here."

"It's been wet before."

Jarek finally felt strong enough to walk, and they shouldered their wet gear and renewed their trek. They'd just rounded the first bend when Goodricke stopped. "Look!"

Barring their path not fifty paces in front of them, stood three figures, a thin, fit-looking fellow, a second older man with fizzled gray hair, and Caitlyn.

The older fellow said something to the younger one, who ran off. Caitlyn and the other fellow came forward, meeting Jarek and Goodricke halfway. The stern-faced older fellow said something in a foreign tongue. Caitlyn nodded and looked at Jarek. "The Lore Master is unsure if he should berate you for entering our lands uninvited, or praise you for a most clever arrival. He says your lore is strong."

Jarek bowed, trying to appear composed, despite his sopped clothing and clinging hair. "I thank him for his praise, but fear he must not have been watching too closely. Also, Lady, tell him we beg forgiveness for our rude entry into your lands. Had we known how to properly ask we would have done so."

Caitlyn translated. The fellow chuckled and answered.

"The Lore Master agrees you had no way to announce your arrival. He says you're the first Outlanders to breech A'ryth's borders, something he fears will not sit well with the other Elders."

"Other Elders?"

"Our rulers. Lore Master Dalbhach sent Mendore to tell them of your swim. His tale will cause much discussion."

"How did you know we were here?"

"Our scouts have been watching you the entire day." She gestured toward her companion. "Magus Verity, Goodricke Loddvar, please meet Lore Master Dalbhach, one of our Elders."

Jarek looked around, "Are we in A'ryth now?"

"Very nearly. The river marks our boundary, but the city is some distance yet." She giggled. "Also, when we come here, we do not swim, we use the bridge."

Even the austere Lore Master cackled at her translation.

Goodricke looked around. "Bridge?"

She led them back to the water and stepped onto—nothing. Their bridge was invisible. She walked across, turned, and rejoined them, grinning.

However, the best means for getting here was of secondary importance to Jarek. "Have you warned your Elders of Zakarah; that he may be present at the upcoming Nexus—which incidentally will happen very near your city?"

"I have. The Lore Masters spent much of last night discussing that very matter. They are sure what you call the 'Nexus' is *Ama de Cumhacht,* the Time of Power. The Council of Elders debate the matter now."

She gave Goodricke's damp clothing the once- over. "You are a strong swimmer, Goodricke Loddvar," she said, winking at a puzzled Goodricke.

Jarek laughed. "Do not befuddle the poor man, Caitlyn."

"I do not know this word 'beefuddel,' but still, I think you are right." She turned. "Come," she said, motioning them to follow. "Lore Master Dalbhach says the Council will want to speak with you. The place you seek is sacred, so do not hope so much."

Dalbhach whispered something to Caitlyn, and she nodded. "Be aware. Now that you are here, the Elders will be deciding what to do with you."

They followed their reluctant hosts through a wooded area, past an open field to another archway, a twin of the one they'd entered earlier.

"Arches protect all entrances to our city," Caitlyn explained, "and ward off evil."

They passed through the tunnel. Jarek had no idea what to expect of a city hidden in the hinterlands, but whatever those expectations might have been, they would have been woefully wrong. What he now beheld was a wonder beyond anything he could have imagined.

They stood on a ledge overlooking a deep valley. Gold-tinged brown and white rock walls surrounded it; the array of colors breathtaking. Spiraling up from the valley floor, stretching toward the sky, was a score of stone pillars with houses carved upon their tops. To call these majestic columns 'carved' didn't do them justice, however. Sculpted would be more accurate. The bases of these homes jutted far wider than their supporting columns, making them seem precarious, but a closer look revealed each was solidly attached to its base. All were decorated with intricately designed terraces and obelisks.

Equally elaborate homes jutted from the cliff walls, each adorned with columned terraces and tall pilasters. Cabled archways connected the spirals to the homes on the walls, forming a complex web of pathways, all leading to a trail that wove down to the valley floor. More houses were below, equally eloquent in design, and artfully blended with their dazzling neighbors above. The place was a wonder.

Caitlyn beamed with obvious pride. "What do you think, Outlanders?"

Goodricke stood, taking it all in. "Such beauty, hidden here in wilderness. It's a marvel."

Jarek was no less awed. "Yes Caitlyn, it's marvelous. Your people used the arts to build it, didn't they?"

She looked confused. "Of course."

Jarek studied their handiwork. "It would take the lifetime of every magus in the Outland to build cities such as yours."

Her brow wrinkled. "What is meant when you say every Lore Master?"

"We are few in number and have many cities."

"Do you mean you have few lore masters?"

Now it was he who was confused. "Yes. Most people are mundane; very few are born with the Gift."

Her eyes widened. "Are you saying most Outlanders are *gan draíocht*?"

"If that's your term for those lacking the Gift, yes."

Her eyes went wide. "That is hard to believe. It is rare that one in A'ryth is born so."

It was Jarek's turn to disbelieve. "You're *all* gifted?"

"Sometimes a child is born *gan draíocht*—with no magic, but not often. I felt sadness for Goodricke Loddvar when first I met him because his *draíocht* seemed weak. But to be without *draíocht* at all…" she shook her head, "such a terrible thing I cannot imagine. I am glad not to be an Outlander," she said, giving Goodricke a pitying glance.

It took a while to wend their way to the valley floor. Curious onlookers stared at them as they passed. One brave little girl ran up to Goodricke. Giggling, she reached as high as she could and said something in their strange language. Caitlyn laughed. "She asks if you are a giant."

Goodricke smiled at the girl and held his hand very low. "Please ask if she's a pixie." When Caitlyn did so, the girl shook her head, giggled, and ran away.

They were taken to a lavishly decorated building styled in the fashion of those above. It was centered in a courtyard, surrounded by plants and colorful flowers, the likes of which he'd never seen. To either side of its entrance were a pair of pillars carved in the image of warriors. The combination seemed tranquil—yet intimidating.

A dignified-looking white-haired man stood waiting for them. Caitlyn ran over and embraced him, and waved them over.

"Magus Verity; Goodricke Loddvar; meet Bardán, my grandsire."

Bardán bowed. "My pleasure, I'm sure," he replied in crisp Common.

"The pleasure is undoubtedly ours," Jarek said, matching his bow. "And I compliment you on your command of our language."

"That is most gracious, but having lived much of my youth in the Outlands. I've as much practice as could be hoped for."

Caitlyn stroked Bardán's arm, beaming with pride. "Grandsire was once a Seeker. It is he who taught me to speak with your tongue," she said, her verbiage making Bardán wince.

"It is my granddaughter's desire to become a Seeker too, but there is much to learn besides learning to speak Common. Outlanders have many customs and courtesies to understand; and religions, and she must know how to use the travelways, then return from the Outlands. She is near to earning her key."

"Key?"

Caitlyn answered for him. "Each Seeker is given a key for use in the travelways. About that, I can speak no more. Come, the council awaits us. Grandsire and I are to translate."

"Lady, could you tell us more of this Council?" Jarek asked before they went inside.

"They are our Elders, or as you Outlanders would say—the most powerful of our magi—wisest in the ways of *draíocht*."

"The arts," Bardán clarified. His smile faded. "Before we go inside, it is only fair to warn you that the Elders were quite angered by the news of your having breeched our city's defenses."

Jarek and he exchanged worried glances. Was his companion feeling as ill at ease as his was?

Bardán escorted them inside. The serene setting seemed in sharp contrast with the peevish looks of the men sitting before him. Six stern-faced men sat waiting, sitting on one side a long table. Lore Master Dalbhach was one of them. Their dour expressions made their displeasure with the Outlander's presence clear. Four empty chairs sat empty opposite them. Bardán and Caitlyn sat in the outer two and signaled for Goodricke and Jarek to take the remaining two.

Goodricke couldn't shake the sense they were on trial. If they were, what consequence might they face?

Bardán introduced them, and the inquisition began. The Elders demanded to know how and why they'd come here. Jarek told Malg's tale, that it was how he knew of A'ryth. With Bardán and Caitlyn translating, the process was excruciating slow. On more than one occasion arguments broke out amongst the Elders. Bardán chose not to translate those conversations.

Finally, Odhran, the Elder in charge, asked Jarek to explain how he'd gotten them over the stream. His relating of his feather spell evoked puzzled looks.

Eventually the all-important question of why they'd dared to enter A'ryth arose. Jarek gave a recounting of the tragedy of the first Nexus, and said that two more would follow; the first very near to A'ryth. He described his encounter with Zakarah. When he spoke of Lavan's abduction, the Elders glowering expressions turned to ones of concern. Whispered side conversations ensued.

This hadn't lasted long before Odhran called Bardán over. After a whispered comment, he returned. "Odhran says the Elders have much to consider. They offer you shelter for the night; but one night only."

"What is it they're trying to decide?" Goodricke asked.

Bardán looked grim. "When abominations breech our sacred borders, we put them to death. The Elders ponder whether or not the same should be done with you. You are to learn your fates in the morning."

Stunned, he and Jarek stared at one another.

The Travelways

The audacity of the answer Rayna had given the golem stunned Gresham. He was even more astounded when it answered. "Yes, seeker."

The golem shambled past him, veering toward the river, the weight of its strides vibrating the ground. The normally timid Rayna chased after it. "Anyone wanting to go, come with me." The others followed, albeit with far less fervor.

The golem shuffled to a nearby wall, reached for an overhead shelf, and grabbed a log raft four times a man's length and several ells wide. It was more barge than raft. Despite its obvious weight, the golem lifted it high above its head.

Sully watched, bug-eyed. "That thing be strong!"

Hagley put a hand on the boy's shoulder. "Yes, golem strength is legendary."

Holding the boat aloft, the brute carried it to the river and dropped it. Water sloshed everywhere, but before the current could steal it away, the golem stepped off the bank, sinking waist deep in the water in front of it, and pinned the barge against the bank. It turned to Rayna. "Seeker ride."

"It seems to think I'm this Seeker person, whoever that is? In case it leaves when I board, you three get on before me."

Sully hopped in first. Hagley followed. Tripping over his robes, he very nearly tumbled overboard. This wasn't the first time Gresham had seen him stumble. What was making him so suddenly clumsy? Gresham stepped onto the boat and helped Rayna board.

"A'ryth," the golem rumbled. It took hold of two ropes tied to the raft's front. The craft lurched as the ropes went taut and they were underway. The golem started slowly, but quickly had them moving so fast that Gresham had to sit to avoid falling.

Awed, they sat watching the creature trudge forward. The tunnel walls gave off an eerie blue light that shown so brightly that globes weren't necessary. Whoever built the raft had given careful thought to its design, including a knee-high rail that enclosed a two-benched seating area.

Rayna turned to him. "Ready to see A'ryth, Soldier Boy?"

"You keep calling me Soldier Boy. When did my name change?"

She laughed. "When I heard Shay call you that. I thought it fitting."

He rolled his eyes. "You've waited your whole life to meet your mother. It'll happen soon. Have you thought about what you'll say to her?"

"I have. I worry over it constantly, yet nothing I come up with seems quite right. I suppose I'll decide that when I see her. Part of me is angry with her for deserting me. But another part weeps for her suffering at losing both husband and babe. If it were you, what would you do?"

"I think my need to see her would win out over any anger."

"It will likely be so with me too" She sighed. "I'll know soon enough."

Their tunnel resembled the one they'd used escaping the marsh, save that these walls were perfectly formed. Gresham wondered if they'd been created from the same magic as the golem.

After a bit the golem stopped. A huge gate blocked their path. It pushed the gate open, pulled the barge beyond it, and closed the gate behind them. It pulled a lever and the water began to lower, taking them with it. Gresham looked over the side. The golem was standing on a slowly descending plank. Rayna and he exchanged nervous glances as the walls beside and behind them grew higher. A second gate appeared below them, with the river continuing beyond it. Once they reached it, their descent stopped. The golem opened the second gate, pulled their raft beyond it, closed the gate, and started walking again.

The same process repeated itself whenever time they encountered a new gate. At one point the pattern reversed, and instead of going deeper, it began rising, as did every gate after that.

Aside from these endless locks, the scenery never changed. Eventually, even the locks vanished. The trip grew boring. So much so, that when they spotted daylight in front of them, everyone cheered.

As they drew nearer however, they grew quiet. What lay ahead of them? Was it good or bad, or even worse, dangerous? Their collective gaze stayed riveted on the approaching light. As they slowly approached it, they were finally were able to make out a few details. Unlike the cave they'd started in, natural sunlight shimmered in this tunnel's end. A dock came into view. Rayna squeezed Gresham's hand, her nails digging so deeply they hurt.

They emerged from the tunnel to find perhaps twenty or so people standing on the shore, watching their approach. Their arrival had been anticipated.

"Seeker home." The golem said. It halted, and its blue glow vanished.

The people on the dock stood gawking—mostly at Rayna. She turned to her travel companions. "Is it just my imagination, or are they staring at me?" She was equally surprised to find her companions doing the same thing. "What? Why are you looking at me that way?"

Gresham pointed to their greeters. "Doesn't anything about these people strike you as odd?"

Rayna looked again. "Well, they look enough alike to be kin. Why?"

How could she not notice the obvious? "Rayna, they look like you."

Her jaw dropped.

A gray-haired man bowed to her. *"Fáilte abhaile seeker."*

She tipped her head in kind. "I'm sorry, but I don't understand you." She turned to Hagley. "Hey magic-man, you speak several tongues. Do you know what he's saying?"

Hagley shook his head. "No, but I think he just greeted us."

The man's gaze took in the rest of them. *"Cén fáth ar thug tú Outlanders chuig A'ryth?* He waited for a response. When it became apparent he wasn't being understood, he barked an order at a nearby lad. The boy ran off. The rest of their greeters stood silent, watching. Waiting. For what, Gresham had no clue.

The boy returned, accompanied by a woman with flaming red hair. Her eyes widened when she saw them. She came down to their raft. "Welcome back, seeker," she said to Rayna in highly accented Common.

Rayna stood there, looking confused. "Thank you, Lady."

The woman said something in her native tongue and several greeters scurried down the dock, grabbed gear, and helped the arrivals off the barge. One threw a grapple at the golem's head. He set its hooks, and while he held the rope taut, a second man shinnied up the line and extracted Rayna's key from its forehead. He returned and gave it to her.

Freeing his grapple, the first man yelled, *"Tarraing siar."* The golem animated again. Making a wide turn, it headed back up the tunnel, raft in tow. Another golem stood motionless beside a second boat.

"I am Caitlyn," the redhead offered. Once introductions had been made, she beckoned them to follow. "Come with me," she said, leading them away. "Please do not be offended by the stares of my people. You are the first Outlanders most have seen."

She led them up a ramp and through a stone archway. Hagley tripped over his robes again. Gresham finally realized why he'd suddenly become so ungainly. All their trudging had trimmed his girth, making his robes hang too low.

Gresham was so intent studying Hagley's clothes that when the man stopped, he nearly ran into him. The others had halted too. All were staring. Once Gresham slipped past them, he understood why. A'ryth was the most astounding place he'd ever seen.

Fate Learned

A gentle shake awakened the napping Jarek. It was Goodricke. "Milord, Bardán has come for us. The Elders beckon. He says they've made their decision."

The walk to the council area felt like a trip to the gallows. They arrived to find the seven stern-faced Elders awaiting them. This time no seats were offered, which didn't bode well.

Bardán bowed and spoke something in A'rythian. Odhran nodded and answered. Bardán turned back around, his expression hard to read. "Your lives are to be spared." An audible sigh escaped Jarek. "However, you have been banished from our city. Return here, or tell others of our existence, and that decision is rescinded. You will be hunted down and killed."

A long silence followed the pronouncement as the Elders let the gravity of their verdict sink in. "Agree to those terms and I will take you back to the place you entered our city where you'll be free to go."

As grateful as he was to have his life spared, Jarek could not agree to those terms. The Nexus was imminent, and Lavan's life was at stake. "My companion agrees to your terms, but I do not."

He wasn't sure who his response surprised more, Goodricke or Bardán.

"Milord, you cannot…" Goodricke began, but Odhran's shout of *"tost!"* silenced him.

"Translate my words for him, Bardán," Jarek demanded.

"Magus," Bardán pleaded, "do not say such a thing. Please reconsider."

"I cannot. I must be present at your *Ama de Cumhacht* or my friend's life is forfeit. Did your granddaughter not deliver my message? Did she not warn them that a great evil comes that must be confronted?"

His mention of *Ama de Cumhacht* had the Elders' murmuring, and Bardán's translation spurred an even more boisterous exchange. Just then Caitlyn arrived, begging an audience.

Odhran beckoned her forward, and she whispered something. He jumped to his feet with a shout, clearly angered by what he'd been told. He repeated her message to the other Elders, spawning other equally stunned expressions. Their gazes wandering from her, to Goodricke, to Jarek, and …to four arriving people.

Jarek's jaw dropped. "Gresham? Hagley?" With them was an A'rythian woman and her child.

Gresham rushed over and the two embraced. "Uncle! I found you!"

Jarek stepped back, looking him over. "How in the gods' names did you manage to follow me?"

Before Gresham could respond, a loud slap on the council table demanded their attention. Odhran was standing, his face a beet red. He shouted something at Bardán.

"The Elders demand to know why you dare bring other Outlanders here."

Jarek spread his arms. "I did not. I'm as puzzled by their arrival as he is."

"But you clearly know them, at least this one," he said, nodding at Gresham.

"Yes. His name is Gresham. He's my nephew. But how he got here is as much a mystery to me as it is you. I also know the stout fellow. He's a magus in training. But I'm as puzzled by his presence as I am Gresham's."

Bardán's translation did little to quell Odhran's anger, but did give him pause. His ire shifted to Caitlyn, questioning her no less as harshly.

Gesturing to the new arrivals, she answered at great length, sounding apologetic.

"What did she tell him?" Jarek asked of Bardán.

"That a seeker returned through the travelways bringing her child and two Outlanders with her."

"Seeker?" Gresham whispered. "That's what the golem called Rayna."

"You must not speak unbidden," Bardán hushed. "Your life and that of your friends are in great peril."

Wide-eyed, Gresham said no more.

Shouting broke out amongst the Elders. Their bitter exchange involved a lot of pointing and accusing gestures, most directed at Lore Master Dalbhach, as if the Outlander's presence here was somehow his fault. Shouts were also directed Caitlyn or Bardán's way. No translation was offered. Finally, Odhran motioned the A'rythian woman forward, making demands of her too.

The woman simply stood there looking confused. "I'm sorry, but I can't understand you," she said in upper class Common.

Confused, Jarek turned to his nephew. "Who are this woman and her child?"

"Her name is Rayna. She came with Hagley and me. The boy's name is Sully, and he's not her son."

Bardán was close enough to overhear. "Young man, for the child's sake, it would be wise to not repeat what you just said."

Caitlyn translated Rayna's words, which fostered even more puzzled looks. Odhran motioned Rayna forward, looking her over, then said something.

"He wants you to explain," Caitlyn said. "I will interpret."

※

From the moment Rayna showed them her mother's key, she felt under attack. She told her story, a long, slow process with all the translation involved. When she was asked how she knew of the travelways, she pulled out her map and handed it and her key to Caitlyn.

It was hard to hear with both Bardán and Caitlyn firing questions her way. Many concerned something called *draíocht*. Whatever it was, it apparently held great sway here. She did her best to provide answers, repeating the story of her mother's letter a second time.

She soon grew weary of it all. She had pressing questions of her own. "Caitlyn, may I ask something of them?"

Caitlyn's translation quieted the Elders. Odhran nodded. "What is your question, Lady?"

"My name is Rayna. I'm here to find my mother. Her name is Akaisha. Could someone please tell her that her daughter has come to see her?"

A silence fell over the group at the mention of her mother's name that gave way to a whispered discussion. As they talked, each of the old men glanced her way at least once, making her feel conspicuous. She heard her mother's name bandied about a few more times, then all grew quiet.

Caitlyn turned to her; her expression grim "I am sorry Lady. The Elders say your mother is not among us. She was what we call a seeker, one who goes among your people to learn your ways. She left many years ago. As is true of many seekers, she never returned."

Rayna felt as if her stomach had been struck. "No! That cannot be. Look!" She pulled a parchment from her purse and handed it to Caitlyn. "She wrote this. It says she was returning home. It was she who gave me map and key and asked me to come find her." Tears blurred her vision. "She must be here." She sank to her knees. "She must." How could the gods be this cruel?

Although Caitlyn spoke Common, she apparently didn't know its written form, so handed it to Bardán. A long silence followed his translation, after which Caitlyn was called to the Elder's table. After a few quiet murmurs she returned Rayna's letter to her. "I am very sorry for you, Lady."

Rayna tried to respond, but her voice failed. She inhaled, composing herself. The Elders were clearly men of importance and she was keeping them waiting. She stood. "Please thank the Elders for this audience," she offered, her voice cracking, "but with their permission, I would like to be alone now."

After more conversing Caitlyn asked, "Would it please you to have someone show you where your mother lived."

She wiped her eyes. "Yes, I'd like that very much."

"We send for a guide now."

As she stood waiting, Bardán came over and joined her. "Lady," he whispered, "the Elders believe the child to be yours. It would be best for his sake to not let them know otherwise."

"Thank you for telling me," she said, glancing Sully's way.

Soon, a middle-aged woman arrived and led Sully and her away. Although friendly, the woman spoke no Common, but that didn't deter her from trying to communicate. "*Seanmháthair,*" she said, smiling.

She forced a smile of her own. "I'm sorry, I can't understand you," was the only response she could offer. After repeating the word a couple more times, the woman gave up.

Rayna walked hand-in-hand with Sully. Passers byes spoke to her along the pathway, seemingly greeting her. Not understanding a word anyone said, all she could do was smile and nod in return.

They came to a spot where several pathways intersected. The woman veered onto a smaller trail, and Rayna soon found herself amongst several buildings. From a distance they seemed an assortment of intricately designed cottages, but as she drew closer, she saw people going about their daily chores. These were people's homes.

Her guide stopped in front of one such place and pointed, grinning widely. "*Seanmháthair,*" she said, tugging Rayna toward its entrance.

An elderly woman looked up as they entered. Old, her skin was wrinkled, and she was dangerously thin. Her eyes went wide when she saw Rayna. She struggled to her feet with a grunt, and then ever so slowly reached out a trembling hand and touched Rayna's cheek. "Akaisha?"

Sully looked up. "She be thinking you be your mother."

Rayna pursed her lips. "Older folks confuse easily." She took the woman's hand, shaking her head. "No, not Akaisha." She pointed to herself. "Rayna." The woman looked puzzled.

How could she make her understand? "Sully, cross your arms as if you're cradling a babe, and rock it back and forth." He did as she asked. "Yes, like that." She pointed to herself. "Rayna." She pointed at Sully. "Akaisha." She pointed at the mock baby again, imitating a crying babe. "Akaisha and Rayna."

She waited, hoping the old lady would puzzle it out, but it just seemed to confuse her more. Her guide intervened. "*Mátair Akaisha. Babaí Rayna,*" she said, pointing to Sully and the pretend baby. "*Is iníon Akaisha é Rayna. Is é Rayna do gharinion,*" she explained.

Realization painted the old woman's face. "*Ghariníon?*" she asked, tears flooding her eyes. She took Rayna's hand and kissed it.

The guide was weeping, too. She wiped her tears on her sleeve, looked at Rayna, and pointed at the old woman. *"Seanmháthair."*

Rayna turned to Sully. "Remember that word so we can ask Caitlyn what it means."

She smiled at the old woman and withdrew her hand. "I'm sorry, I don't understand."

"Seanmháthair," the old woman repeated, her hands pressed to her heart.

It was then realization stuck. Rayna started trembling so badly she had to lean on Sully for support. He who looked up at her. "Lady, you look to be sick."

She reached for the woman's hand. "You're my grandame."

The woman nodded, saying *seanmháthair*, tears rolling down her cheeks.

Oíche na Cumhacht
Night of Power

After Rayna and Sully's departure, Hagley and the remaining Outlanders were banished from the city proper. "Make sure to repeat my warning that *Oíche na Cumhachta* brings with it unexpected evil," Jarek urged Bardán as armed guards led them away.

They were being taken to a place high above the city, to where the magus and Goodricke had first entered A'ryth. The climb to get there was arduous, Hagley's feet growing heavier with each stride.

About half-way there, Master Verity stopped and leaned against the wall, steadying himself. "Are you all right, Magus?"

"I find the climb a bit dizzying is all," he said, shutting his eyes. "I've no fondness for heights. It felt the same when I walked down this horrid path. I managed it then, I can do it now."

After a brief rest they resumed their climb. Master Verity's dread was understandable. Their path was steep and only a few feet wide, with no protective rail. Any misstep could prove disastrous. By the time they finally reached the top, Hagley found himself sharing the Magus's concerns.

They were led through an archway to an open field, after which the escorts returned to the city. As soon as they were gone, Magus Verity started interrogating them. "Why in the god's names did you two fools bring a woman and child with you?"

They recounted their tale of their journey here, and why each was here. Their explanation took the better part of an hour. "You baffle me, Hagley," Master Verity said after hearing it. "You claim you couldn't pass the university's trials, yet your command of the arts now includes not just light globes, but a variety of illusions and some sort of dancing compulsion. Do I have that right, or did I mishear?"

"Yessir, I can't explain it. It's been this way since I joined up with my friends."

Jarek thought a bit, then nodded. "I have a theory that might explain your sudden command of such diverse spells."

"You have?"

"Later." His attention turned to Gresham. "As for you, my good nephew, how is it you're suddenly creating light globes? Did you not tell me a soldier has no use for the arts?"

Gresham related what happened at the university with Masters Kagen and Vardon.

Jarek scratched his chin. "They claim you to be a Battle Mage, eh?"

"Yes. They even gave Hagley a spell book to teach me from," he said, nodding toward Hagley's pack.

"What!" he said, twisting to face Hagley. "You're traipsing through the wilderness with a precious spell book in your possession?"

"I… I didn't want to leave them behind for the pirates."

"Them?" He snapped his fingers. "Show me!"

Hagley reached into his knapsack. After sifting through it, he handed a book to Jarek. "This one contains illusions. I used some of them on our journey here." He handed over a second book. "This has only two spells, one for moving things from afar, and a counter-spell that prevents them from moving at all."

He handed Jarek another. "This one is called *Hands and Arrows*. Master Vardon said to give it to Gresham. He claimed that with a bit of training Gresham could master its spells. The last one is a rune primer to help him read it."

Jarek thumbed through *Hands and Arrows*. "Most of these require the use of your hands." He handed the book to Gresham. "We'll start with those and work on the arrow spells later."

"Start Sir?" Gresham asked, nearly choking on the words.

"Vardon wanted you trained, so trained you'll be. While we wait on the Elders, I want you two to master as many spells as you can. If we're to face who I came here to face, we'll need any advantage we can gain."

"Who might we face?" Hagley asked.

Jarek cleared his throat. Goodricke stared at the clouds, whistling. "His name is Zakarah. He's the one who took your headmaster," he answered, then recounted all that happened at the Nexus.

Hagley feared he might vomit. "The headmaster was taken by a demon, and we're to face it?"

"It's not as bleak as you think. Goodricke here is quite adept with a sword, and the one he carries is enchanted. He's here to guard our backs. A second Nexus is to occur this very night—here in A'yrth. That's why I'm here—to confront Zakarah, to somehow get your headmaster back, the A'rythians permitting."

Finding the topic too horrific to think about any further, Hagley changed the subject. "Sir… you said you might be able to explain how I'm suddenly able to cast spells that I couldn't before."

Jarek paused, contemplating. "I believe the main reason you failed the university's tests is because you're intimidated by authority. But this lack of confidence is only partly why Kagen failed to identify your facet." He scratched his chin. "If my conjecture is correct, it explains this wide range of spells you've somehow managed, but I'm not sure you'll like what I have to say."

Master Verity sure had a knack for dampening one's excitement. "Why is that?"

"If I'm right about this, you'll likely never cast spells with the skill of a Master."

It was the worst possible news, although down deep, he'd suspected it all along. "May I hear your theory?"

"I believe you're a Pervader, a type of magus that is most rare. In fact, there have been only a few in recorded history."

His comment perked Hagley's spirit. "What, exactly, is a Pervader?"

"Someone fluent in all facets of the arts, yet master of none—a generalist. You know enough of magic to know how rare it is to be multifaceted, right?"

Hagley nodded. "I'd settle for simply for being proficient in one."

"You'd be selling yourself short if you did. You've seen how inept even a Master can be with spells outside of his facet. I'm fortunate in that my Gift is multifaceted, yet I'm hard pressed to preform spells out of those specialties. Take Gresham for instance. I've a passable Wind Blast, but I'm hopeless with most combative spells. You'll never have that problem. Your spectrum is so broad that once you get beyond your confidence issues, there may be no such thing as a spell you can't perform with an appreciable competency. Do you follow what I'm saying?"

Hagley flushed. "I'm not sure." He wanted to feel elated but wasn't sure if what he'd just heard was good or bad news. But the fact that the magus who discovered Hagley's gift was so surprised to discover he could cast more than one rudimental, gave Jarek's Pervader theory a ring of truth.

Jarek kicked Hagley's spell books. "You stole these from Master Kagen's library, right?"

Hagley's face flushed. "I considered it borrowing. I always return them."

"Bah!" Jarek said with a dismissive hand. "Kagen told me he left them lying about on purpose, knowing you'd take them." Jarek shook his head. "I can't believe you never figured that out. He was trying to help you find your facet. The reason he never succeeded is because you don't have one—you have them all." He picked up one of the books. "Did you use any of this book's spells?"

"I used one to block our cave the night the marsh monster attacked Rayna."

"Lift that rock," Jarek said, pointing.

Surprisingly, Hagley managed to lift the rock from afar, even with Magus Verity watching.

"Great." Jarek flipped over to the book's second spell. "Now let's try the binding spell." He told Goodricke to walk across the field. "Bind him; prevent him from moving."

Hagley tried, but failed.

"DO IT!" Jarek shouted.

Fearing a Royal Magus's wrath, Hagley tried again. Goodricke froze in place, twitching nary a muscle.

"Just as I thought. If you think your well-being is at stake, your concentration goes way up. Now release him and do it again." Jarek kept at him until Hagley could do it every time.

Next, he turned his attention to Gresham. "Let's check out this 'attunement' of yours. I'm sure you'll find warring spells far more useful than creating a light globe. First however, let's teach you some control. You're useless until you master that."

Hagley was surprised how quickly Jarek was able to teach Gresham control. But then, he was a Royal Magus. "Could I see the spell book Vardon gave you?"

He thumbed through it. "Most of the spells in this book require the conjuring of a phantasmal hand—ones that appears to be real, but are not. Some attack, others defend. You control a conjured hand by moving your own." Jarek extended his hand and flexed his fingers. "As your hand moves, so does the phantasm. Let's give this Interposing Hand a try."

It took the better part of the day for Gresham to master that single spell, but since the remaining spells relied on similar principals, he mastered those more quickly.

Their practice was interrupted when a messenger arrived. "Magus, the Elders request your presence."

"You two practice without me."

This time when Jarek arrived, the Elders offered him a seat—he hoped that boded well. Surprisingly, the day's topic had nothing to do with Outlanders. That very morning the Elders detected a taint at their Place of Power, the site of the upcoming Nexus. Fearing it might be due to the presence of Jarek's beast, they wanted to know more about it.

"Zakarah is a demon, an underworld creature of unimaginable evil." Jarek recounted the events of the first Nexus. "My plan is to be there and offer him something in exchange for my friend. He covets magic of all types. If he refuses whatever I offer, I'm prepared to do battle with him. I'll want to enlist your aid if it comes to that."

As usual, Bardán's translation sparked a heated debate. "*Ní féidir linn é sin a dhéanamh,*" Odhran, calmly announced.

"He says they cannot do so," Bardán told him.

"They must!" Jarek insisted. "Left to his own devices, this creature will wreak the same havoc here that he did in the Outland!"

"I did not say they will not, Magus, I said they cannot."

"What spells do your people use when battling the Crone?"

Bardán gave him an odd look, then translated the question. A discussion ensued, after which the embarrassed-looking translator bowed to Jarek. "Every A'rythian is born with a natural resistance to the Crone's magic. Although limited, it has proven useful. But we have no spells we use against her. Perhaps our ancestors knew of such things, but if so, such knowledge has been lost to us. What *draíocht* we use is to protect us from the Crone, not do battle with her."

How could they survive in such a dangerous place if that were true? "Surely some of your spells inflict damage on her abominations."

Bardán pursed his lips. "I wish it were otherwise. It is why we have guardians."

This was grim news. "What magic have you?"

"As I told you, our magic's primary purpose is to help us persevere against the Crone. Having lived in the Outland, I would say our ability to heal surpasses all but your Clerics. We also are at one with the woodlands, attuned to any plant or creature not tainted by the Crone." He gestured toward the cliffs. "And as you've seen, we also mold stone, but only during *Ama de Cumhacht*, and only by using *ceangailte*."

"*Ceangailte?*"

"The channeling of the collective power of the group into a single individual."

"Tell me more of *ceangailte*."

"It is a joined circle of Lore Masters, where each channels his *draíocht* to a chosen person, significantly increasing that individual's abilities."

"This *ceangailte* gives me hope. Can you demonstrate it?"

As usual, and conference of the Elders ensued. "First," Bardán said, "the Elders wish a demonstration of Outlander magic; of how you'd fight this demon. They ask that you show how your friend floated a rock at your Nexus." A young man approached carrying a head-sized rock, and placed on the ground in front of Jarek.

Jarek wasn't sure he could do it. "In the Outland each magus has different skills. We call them facets. We are quite inept with spells outside our facets. I am not very good at doing what it is they request."

"That is a good thing if we are to demonstrate the power of *ceangailte*. Please proceed."

Having just practiced it with Hagley, the spell was fresh in his mind. Concentrating on the rock, he cast. The rock rose, albeit barely—a paltry effort. Judging from the looks on the Elders' faces, they were nonetheless impressed.

"The Elders will now channel their *draíocht* into you using *ceangailte*."

The Elders formed a circle and clasped hands. Jarek joined them, and one of them initiated the chant. The surge of power that rippled through the circle made Jarek's arms tingle.

"The Elders have channeled their power to you. Please try your spell again."

Jarek triggered it. The rock soared. Although not nearly as high as Lavan had done at the Nexus. *Ceangailte* was amazing. With it, he might be able to meet the demon on equal terms. But how? He had a fledgling Battle Mage in his nephew, and a Pervader in Hagley. Although still untrained, with his guidance and the Elders' *ceangailte*, they might just have a chance to save Lavan after all.

"The other Outlanders have skills I do not," he offered. "One is a warrior. The other's gift is most unusual. If the Elders are willing to teach that one *ceangailte*, I believe that together, the three of us might be strong enough to confront Zakarah."

Another discussion ensued. "Odhran wishes to see their skills too. If they prove convincing, we will teach your magus *ceangailte*."

A messenger was sent, returning shortly with Gresham, Hagley and Goodricke.

"What have they decided, Uncle?" Gresham whispered. "Are we being sent home, or are they going to let us try to save the headmaster?"

"Do exactly as I say as it might just be the latter. Which of the spells in your book have you mastered?"

"Mastered? None. The one I do best is the Gripping Hand."

"Then we'll use that one."

"Use it how?"

"We're about to demonstrate to the Elders what a powerful Battle Mage you are."

"But…"

Jarek interrupted him with, "No buts! I want you to prepare yourself for a huge influx of power. You're no good to any of us if you faint."

He had Goodricke stand fifteen or so yards in front of Gresham. "Now lift him off the ground—and don't fail."

Gresham's unease was obvious, but Jarek hoped the Elders wouldn't notice. Gresham closed his eyes, his mind churning. Jarek could almost hear him reciting the spell. His eyes popped open—his former nervousness displaced by intense concentration. He reached an arm forward. The Elders gasped as the monstrous hand and fingers appeared out of nowhere to encircle Goodricke. When Gresham raised his arm, Goodricke lifted off the ground. The stunned Elders applauded.

"The Elders are impressed, Magus," Bardán confided. "Show them which man they are to teach *ceangailte* to."

"This one," he said, turning to Hagley. "It's time to show off your Pervader skills. The Elders are about to teach you a spell unlike any I've seen before. Your headmaster's life rests in your ability to master it, so pay attention."

Hagley's mouth opened, but before he could utter a sound. "Hush! Act like you've been doing this your whole life."

Praise the gods that Hagley's nimble mind was able to comprehend what was being told through a translator. A nervous glance Jarek's way was followed by a nod.

The Elders reformed their circle and channeled *ceangailte* into Hagley. Shock registered on his face as he felt their power. Next, they tried having him initiate it. He failed the first couple of tries, but the nods of the Elders made it clear he'd been successful on his third try. They practiced it two more times for good measure, after which Gresham was asked to join the circle.

Gresham repeated his spell under *ceangailte,* causing Goodricke to yelp. He'd gripped him too tightly.

"Toss him into the air," Jarek ordered.

Goodricke gave him an incredulous look that turned to surprise when he flew fifteen or so feet into the air. Gresham opened his palm and the giant hand caught the poor man, and gently lowered him back down. More applause.

"What of him?" Bardán asked, nodding toward Goodricke. "The Elders wish to see his *draíocht*."

"He has none. He is what Caitlyn called *gan draíocht,* but his weapon has *draíocht*."

Odhran asked to see the weapon. "All we know of it is that it glows when evil is near."

Odhran's hands roamed the sword's surface. After a long silence, he said something to Bardán, but raised his hands before the man could translate. Odhran looked closely at the sword's pommel. He nodded and smiled. Gripping hard, he twisted it. The pommel came off. He tipped it and a vial slipped out. He opened it and sniffed its contents, then handed it to the Elder beside him, who examined it and passed it down the line. A discussion ensued.

When they were done, Odhran replaced the vial and reattached the pommel. He motioned Goodricke over and handed him the weapon, saying something in A'rythian. Bardán translated. "Your sword resists the effects of ill *draíocht* much as our city's archways do. Whoever holds this weapon gains that protection. They believe the potion inside can reverse the effect of an evil enchantment."

Jarek now understood why Odhran was first among the Lore Masters. He bowed to the man. "Please thank him for sharing his wisdom." He smiled at Goodricke. "Now we know. Use your gift wisely."

"Odhran says the four of you may attend *Oíche na Cumhachta*. Until then, you are to remain outside our city. A runner will be sent when you are needed. Bardán cleared his throat, after *Oíche na Cumhachta,* you are to leave our city and never return."

<hr />

Gresham was surprised when a young woman arrived to escort them back to their field. She so resembled Caitlyn's she could pass for her younger sister. "I am Brin. I am seeker student," she looked up at him. "I am to study you and learn Outlander ways. Caitlyn says you study to become Lore Master, yes?"

"Yes, I'm training to become a magus; that's the Outlander name for a Lore Master."

"You shall be of much interest to me."

She led them back to their field. Once there, Magus Verity recounted what went on at his meeting with the Lore Masters before the rest of them were summoned. "Unlike us, A'rythian magic doesn't vary from person to person. Everyone's Gift is identical. Its facets include the ability to mold stone; commune with the natural world, and an aptitude for healing. They're also born with some innate resistance to magic. That's the limit of their arts, none of which is useful against Zakarah. I'm afraid that means I'm going to have to rely on you two to help rescue Lavan."

Hagley jumped to his feet. "Us? You jest! We're beginners."

Gresham felt equally ill at ease.

"There's logic to my request. Let me explain." Jarek paused, gathering his thoughts. "We have to assume Zakarah will come to this Nexus too. The taint the Elders found at the Nexus site suggests his touch. If they're wrong, whatever we plan is moot. If he shows, my plan to free Lavan is to bind him to our world and not free him until Zakarah releases Lavan. Unfortunately, there's only one magus in A'ryth capable of casting such a binding." He looked at Hagley.

Hagley pointed at himself. "Me, bind a demon?! You said he's the most powerful sorcerer you've ever encountered. I couldn't even earn my robes!" He traipsed back and forth, his face a darkened red. "How could you even think such a thing?"

Jarek didn't relent. "Yesterday you proved yourself capable of casting a binding, something I can't do. Nor can Gresham or any of the Lore Masters. That leaves only you."

"There's no way I can do what you ask."

"Sit!" Jarek barked.

Hagley flinched, and sat back down, looking pale.

"Let's form a circle." Done, he had Hagley invoke the *ceangailte* spell. "We need to get used casting under it." He looked up at their escort. "Brin?"

"Yes, Lore Master?"

"You said you wanted to help. Please walk across the field and don't let Hagley stop you."

As she left, Jarek turned to Hagley. "Initiate *ceangailte* and bind her."

Hagley nodded. Seconds later Brin stood frozen in her tracks. "Outstanding!"

Jarek's praise did little to bolster Hagley's spirits. He looked so pale Gresham thought his friend would faint. It was obvious to Jarek, too. "Remember how disappointed you were when you learned a Pervader could never achieve advanced proficiency with any spell?"

Hagley looked up at him but said nothing. "This is your one chance to gainsay that prediction. Tonight, you'll be drawing upon a score of magi, not just two. You'll most likely be more powerful than any magus since the Great Age."

That had Hagley's attention. "What if Zakarah tries to harm me while I'm binding him?"

"One of my facets is Protection. I'll be guarding you. Not only that," he nodded at Gresham, "our friend here is a Battle Mage. Who better to have at your side?"

It was Gresham's turned to be stunned. "But Sir, I only just learned the few spells I know. How could I contest the likes of Zakarah?"

"Like Hagley, you'll be part of a circle, calling on its collective strength. As I said, all you have to do is initiate a spell and let the circle do the rest. Let's rehearse."

They continued working under *ceangailte* for the better part of the afternoon. The difference *ceangailte* made was astounding. Under it, Gresham cast all of his book's spells with relative ease—at least those he could remember. Jarek had won him over—he'd willingly help. He only hoped the same was true for Hagley.

※

"Who's your friend?" Rayna asked, spotting Sully with a strange-looking fellow no taller than him.

"This be Dzojek. He speaks our talk!"

"You speak Common? Excellent," she said, offering her hand. "A pleasure, Dzojek. I'm Rayna."

The little man bowed. "It is my pleasure, I am sure."

His accent was thick, differing from the other A'rythians. "Do you live here?"

Dzojek frowned. "Dzojek does not live with *máistirs*. Dzojek is Jacaí. He's here because his bultúr was killed. With a bultúr, Dzojek would fly home. Without a bultúr, I cannot."

The little man's strange references baffled her. Fortunately, Sully came to the rescue. "A bultúr be some sort of bird; a really big one. Dzojek flies on it. *Máistirs* be his name for the people who live here. Jacaí is the name of Dzojek's people. I don't think the two folks be getting on real well. Leastwise, Dzojek don't fancy them all that much."

How odd, Rayna thought. She'd ask her grandmother about it. "It was a pleasure meeting you, Dzojek. Perhaps we'll meet again."

Second Nexus

Around dusk, Brin arrived, leading Hagley and the rest down and through the city to a small canyon at its far side "It is this way." Soon they were walking a narrow canyon with a small creek at its center. They hadn't gone far when the walls narrowed, welling the brook's waters so high they found themselves sloshing through knee-high water. What had started out as a warm evening cooled the deeper into the canyon they trudged. It widened when its brook emptied into a sandy pool at the canyon's end.

The Elders were already there, along with a whole host of other A'rythians. Bardán greeted them. "Welcome to *Áit na cumhachta,* the Place of Power. The Lore Masters await you."

The mere mention of the place's name had Hagley's gut twisting. Jarek placed a hand on his shoulder. "It's important that you understand that every person here is adept. All will participate in your circle. The Lore Masters will be using a variant of *ceangailte* that allows anyone in the circle to tap into its power." He glanced Gresham's way. "That means it's available to either of you if and when the need arises. We also stand at the focus of a Nexus, amplifying the circle's strength even more. You two will have access to power that exceeds what the world's most powerful magi get to experience."

Hagley knew Jarek's speech was meant to bolster his confidence, but he was more concerned with holding his bladder. He was about to face the very demon who'd spirited away the headmaster of an arts university, not some acolyte who couldn't earn his robes.

"If Zakarah appears, it will be when the Nexus focuses. You'll have no problem recognizing when it happens. If he materializes alone, I'll try to bargain Lavan's return. Such a plan has little chance to succeed, but I'll try. If he arrives with Lavan, ignore Zakarah and bind the headmaster. It is paramount that you keep him here no matter what else happens."

Hagley tried to swallow but his mouth was too dry.

"Lavan tells me Zakarah seeks magic, be it an item or a person. If he doesn't free Lavan, we'll deny him what he seeks. Expect trickery if that happens. If we frustrate him enough to drop his guard; bind him. Release him only if he produces Lavan. Bind Lavan in that case; we don't want to lose him again. If all goes awry, whatever you do, don't let him spirit away anyone else."

Bile roiled up from Hagley's stomach. It tasted sour. He choked it back down. Jarek patted his shoulder. "With luck and wiles, we'll outwit the bastard. Remember, no matter how frightened you get, do not break the circle. Do so and we'll all likely wind up in Zakarah's thrall in some gods' forsaken elsewhere."

Hagley almost vomited.

"You watch for an attack," he told Gresham. "If Zakarah even looks like he's casting, attack him. I know you fear this is beyond you, but tonight you're not novices, you are part of a full circle of power unmatched since the Great Age." He pointed to the Lore Masters as they formed a circle around the pond. "Now, go join the circle." He then left to confer with the Bardán.

Hagley grabbed Gresham's arm. "I can't do this. I couldn't pass my trials with five Masters watching me. How does your uncle expect me to bind Zakarah in front of thirty of them, say nothing of dealing with some underworld demon?"

Gresham leaned so close Hagley could smell his breath. "This is about daring Hagley, nothing more. You proved time and time again you can be relied upon in getting us here. Now we need you to do more of the same to keep us here. You're far more experienced than I am, and I plan to do everything I can to get your headmaster back. Don't let Zakarah beat us. You can do this."

Gresham's courage humbled him. He'd practiced the arts for less than a week and here he was ready to confront a mighty wizard. How could he do any less?

By the time darkness fell, most of the A'rythians were seated around the pond, close enough to grasp hands. But Hagley couldn't bring himself to join them, even when Gresham did. Instead, he stared at the heavens, trying to fathom what a Nexus was. The moons were so close they almost appeared as one; something he'd couldn't recall having seen before. They gave off so much light that torches weren't needed. Their light seemed strangely bright. Then it struck him. He was seeing aethers, not moonlight. It was as if someone had placed a giant light globe in the sky.

He glanced around. Goodricke was placing crystals all around the pool. He remembered Jarek saying they'd done that at the first Nexus. Finished, he sat at the far side of the pond, well away from the circle, with his sword draped across his lap. Hagley wondered what good a mundane weapon would be against the likes of Zakarah.

Suddenly Goodricke's crystals came alive, blasting light everywhere. The temperature dropped so much Hagley could see his breath.

Jarek rushed to the pond. "Form your circle, the Nexus has begun." Each man had been instructed to bring a blade. "Keep your knives at the ready, and whatever happens, do not touch the water."

Bardán relayed the message in A'rythian. Hagley vomited. Fortunately, no one was looking. He wiped his mouth on his sleeve, and defying his body's every instinct, forced himself to join the circle, taking a place between Gresham and an elderly A'rythian.

Light rainbowed from the crystals, bathing the canyon walls in shards of colored light. Goodricke was on his feet, his sword at the ready. It was glowing blue. Everyone stared at the pond. The image of a face had materialized on the water's surface. Hagley feared he'd throw up again. *I can't do this. I'd rather die than be spirited off to some demon's lair.*

Its hooded cowl prevented him from seeing Zakarah's features, for which he was grateful, but he knew the image forming before him had to be the demon. Warm liquid trickled down his thigh.

Jarek joined the circle. "Link up!"

Everyone joined hands. Power like Hagley would never have imagined rippled through him. His trembles ceased as a sense of wellness engulfed him, only to pass him by and come rushing around the circle again and again, swelling in intensity each time it returned.

The pond turned a bright aqua as foreign words blasted Hagley's mind. *Beannachtaí draoithe eile.* Zakarah was mind-speaking A'rythian.

You use the wrong tongue, Zakarah! It's me you face.

Master Jarek and Zakarah were using mind-speak, and Hagley could hear it. He wondered if the others could too.

Ah, we meet again, 'Royal Magus.' Have you decided to join your friend and me? The demon's ensuing laugh made Hagley shiver.

Hardly. I'm here for Lavan. What have you done with him? Present him!

The demon smiled. *You assume he's with me, but do you see him?* His smile vanished. *Even if he were here, why would I send back someone so useful; lose a mind so informative? What gain is there in that?*

What gain is it you seek? What is it you'd take in exchange for him?

The demon pushed back his cowl, scouring the area, his gaze finally settling on the sword Goodricke held. A forked tongue escaped his mouth, testing the air, wagging like the tail on an excited hound. *Mayhap that glowing sword. What does it do?*

Give us Lavan and it's yours.

I'm afraid your friend is indisposed. But rest assured I am …hosting him.

Prove it.

Will this suffice? Something shot out of the water, hovering high above the ponds. It was a rock, covered with tiny speckles. Reflecting aethers, it showered the area with countless beams of light. Hagley remembered Jarek saying they'd lost a similar stone at the first Nexus.

I said to show me Master Lavan, not a rock he once owned.

I'll show you what I choose, when I choose. He paused, looking around. *That sword will do.*

He waggled his fingers in Goodricke's direction. Turpin's sword rose from his lap, and floated toward Zakarah. His smile transformed into a grimace the instant he touched it. Screeching, he flung the sword back toward Goodricke, who had to dodge aside to avoid getting impaled. Jarek smiled. *I gather you didn't find it to your liking?*

Zakarah snarled. *No, but these new friends you've brought me will do quite nicely.*

Hagley felt himself being dragged toward the pond—as was the rest of the circle. Panic set in as he envisioned the lot of them being taken to Zakarah's elsewhere. A sudden blast of *ceangailte* surged through him and the sliding stopped. The circle had countered the demon's spell.

You're out numbered and outmanned, Zakarah. Give me Lavan.

Jarek glanced Hagley's way. *Now!*

Magus Verity had just ordered him to bind the demon. Hagley, the bumbling acolyte who couldn't earn his robes. 'I can't, I can't, I can't', raced through his mind, only to be countered by Gresham's earlier urging, 'You *can* be relied upon. You proved it in getting us her. Whatever you do, don't let Zakarah beat us.'

Gresham, Goodricke, Jarek, the Lore Masters; all were counting on *him*. His dream of becoming a magus was on the line. Dispelling all else from his mind, he cast the spell.

The demon started as the binding locked onto him. He'd done it! A blundering merchant's son had just bound a demon.

Zakarah snarled, his gaze flitting around the circle, trying to identify this new foe. *Fools!*

Hagley's spell faltered briefly, only to be strengthened by yet another surge from the circle.

You're trapped, Zakarah. Give us Lavan and we let you leave. It's the only way you're leaving here.

We'll see about that!

Once again Hagley felt the pull of the demon's spell. And once again, the circle answered.

Zakarah growled his frustration, sounding like some cornered beast. Snarling, he raised his arms. His lips moved. He was casting!

In the same instant sparks erupted from Zakarah's hands, a gargantuan hand appeared, absorbing them. The sparks sputtered, then stopped altogether. Gresham had done his job. A wand appeared at Zakarah's side, but the spectral hand grabbed and crushed it.

No! Accusing eyes scanned the circle, seeking yet another new adversary. Hagley wouldn't have changed places with Gresham for the world.

Magic ebbed and flowed. Back and forth. Neither side winning; neither giving in.

The tugs suddenly ceased. *So be it Royal Magus, you are too many. I yield; you shall have your wizard back.*

Relief washed over Hagley. They'd won. Hearing Zakarah yield, the circle relaxed. In that weakened moment, the demon broke free of Hagley's binding and with a cry of *Be at the final nexus with the relics I need if you want him alive,* he vanished, the pond suddenly void of his image. The hovering rock fell, splashing into the pond, sinking from sight.

Goodricke dove in after it. What was he thinking? All eyes fixated on the water. Hagley held his breath, waiting to see tendrils encase their friend like happened to the headmaster. But after what seemed an eternity, Goodricke surfaced, holding a skull-sized rock high over his head. He sloshed ashore, water streaming off his clothing, and held up the rock. "It's the headmaster's agate."

Jarek ran to him. "You fool! Zakarah could have seized you."

Goodricke shook his head. "The sword had ceased to glow and the waters had dimmed. I knew he was gone."

Jarek stared at Goodricke for several moments. Finally, seeming more relaxed, he held out his hand. "Give it to me."

With Zakarah gone, the circle disbanded; the A'rythians chattering to one another in their strange tongue.

Gresham joined his uncle, who'd pressed the rock to his ear and raised a hand. All grew quiet. "Gods!" he said, his eyes widening.

He handed the agate to Gresham. He listened, his eyes growing equally wide. Hagley joined them, listening too. The rock was chanting *Beware the witch. Beware the witch,* repeating it over and over. "That's the headmaster's voice!" he said, handing the rock to Bardán. After a listen, he translated it for the other A'rythians.

Despondent, Hagley watched the agate pass down the line, each person listening to its whispered warning. His binding had failed. Worse, after all their planning, they'd failed to rescue the headmaster, who now warned them now of yet another evil. Most terrifying of all was the possibility that Zakarah might know who had bound him. Would he exact his vengeance? Who'd have guessed Zakarah's departure would depress him, but that's exactly what it had done. A night that had begun full of hope had ended in disaster.

Head down, hands behind his back, Hagley paced. First wharf pirates, then marsh beasts and demons, say nothing of Headmaster Lavan's warning of yet another unknown threat. Why hadn't he returned to the university with his wagon that day in Portsmouth? What had possessed him to join this danger-wrought adventure? More importantly, would he ever return home?

Commitment

With the Nexus over and the demon gone, Gresham and the other Outlanders reconvened with the Elders in the council area to discuss what had just taken place. Uncle Jarek had stopped to pick up his map along the way. "Uncle, what did Zakarah mean with that last message? Will you face him again? Will we have another chance to rescue the headmaster?"

"Magus," Bardán added, "Odhran asks that same question."

"Tell Odhran I will do whatever is necessary to save my friend. Lavan says Zakarah covets ensorcelled items—magical relics like the one Goodricke carries." He forced a wry grin. "Albeit ones more to his liking. I didn't mention this earlier because I didn't think it important, but there's to be one more Nexus. It occurs days from now. And yes, I plan to be there."

Bardán translated. As usual, it triggered a debate among the Elders. When it ended, Bardán gave them its upshot. "The Elders are in your debt. They say your warnings likely saved many A'rythian lives, and ask how they may aid you."

"Tell them I'm most grateful for whatever information or assistance they can provide." Jarek spread the map on the table before them. "We have only four days to reach the final Nexus, which occurs here," he said, bouncing his finger on the image of a volcano. "It is paramount that I get there in time. Ask them how I can do it."

After Bardán's translation, a runner was dispatched. Bardán explained. "The Elders say the island you seek is in waters too dangerous to reach by boat." He paused. "They say the best and only way to reach your volcano on time involves great luck and even greater risk, and that it relies upon the help of another. We await the man who is key to your success."

Jarek turned to Hagley and him. "You two pay close attention. I want you privy to my plans. Hagley, tell the magi at your university what happened here, and that I still hope to save their headmaster."

Minutes later a runner returned with a half-sized man they introduced as Dzojek. He looked nothing like the A'rythians. No taller than Sully, he was rawboned, with large piercing eyes. Seeming none too pleased to be there, he engaged the Elders in a heated debate. He calmed when shown Jarek's map, his demeanor changing from surliness to curiosity. A far more civil conversation ensued that involved a lot of pointing at the map. Finally, Odhran stood, and he and the little man exchanged nods.

Bardán shared what had just transpired. "What this man Malg told you of our history is incomplete. There were two peoples stranded when our ancestors shipwrecked, the Jacaí and us. Those ancient Jacaí served us."

"They were your slaves." Dzojek snapped. The dwarfish man spoke Common as well as A'rythian.

Bardán shrugged. "Suffice it to say our ancestors did not treat the Jacaí as equals. Both our peoples were marooned. The Jacaí chose to live in the mountains rather than with us. Their people are uniquely gifted with animals. They have tamed the bultúr, the great birds of the high peaks, and use them as steeds. The birds fly riders to the outer islands for trade with Outlanders, thus their fliers learn Common." He glanced at Dzojek. "One of the Crone's beasts felled Dzojek's bultúr. Fortunately, he escaped and made his way here."

Dzojek's nodded. "The witch has flying minions now. They took down Rajko and his bultúr. I must warn my people."

"So you have said, Dzojek." Bardán turned back to Jarek. "Without a bultúr to fly over the Crone's realm, the only way for Dzojek to return home would be to cross her Haunt. Any escort we might offer would be forced to cross The Haunt a second time to return. A single crossing is dangerous; a second is folly. That is why he's still here. What Lore Master Odhran has suggested, and Dzojek just agreed to, is that you escort him to Jacaioi. In exchange, Dzojek promises the Jacaí will fly you to the volcano on their *bultúrs*. It's the only way—if at all, for you to reach the volcano in time."

Jarek stood. "It's decided then. He and I shall depart immediately."

Bardán held up a hand. "It's not that simple, my friend. The Haunt is infested with abominations in far greater numbers than what you encountered in the marsh. We venture there only in patrols, and only in times of great need. Even with the considerable *draíocht* of your magi friends, I fear it unlikely you'd survive its perils."

Dzojek stamped his foot. "It is promised. We go. My people must be warned."

Bardán spoke true, Jarek and Dzojek stood no chance going it alone. They'd need help. "I'll go with you, Uncle."

Jarek's eyes widened. "Think on what you just said. Not only do we risk an encounter with this witch they speak of, but we'll face Zakarah again; this time without the aid of the Elders."

"Sir, your friend needs you, and you need me. Even if my magic is of little aid, I'm a trained soldier. I can be useful in other ways."

"I'll go too," said Goodricke, stepping up beside Gresham.

Jarek stared at them a while before placing a hand on each of their shoulders. "Thank you." He looked Gresham in the eyes, "You two make me proud to call you friend and kin."

Jarek turned to Hagley. "Tell Master Kagen everything that happened here."

Hagley shook his head. "Brave marsh beasts and wharf pirates all by myself? No way! If I go with you, we'd have two swords and three magi." He sighed. "I find those the better odds than going home alone. I go with you too."

Despite Hagley's lament, Gresham knew returning home was the safer option. Offering to join Jarek was likely the bravest thing the young magus had ever done. He squeezed the back of Hagley's neck. "You're a good man, my friend."

Jarek nodded. "Yes, well done. We leave at dawn."

Bardán asked that they remain in the council area for a bit. Odhran wanted to contribute too—by outfitting them the same way they would a guardian. Women soon arrived to measure them.

Gresham asked Bardán if it was all right to speak with Rayna before he left. He was granted permission, albeit only if accompanied by a guard. Outlanders were still Outlanders.

Soon a guard arrived and took him to her. He found her sitting in front of a hut talking with an elderly woman. Gresham imagined that's what Rayna might look like in her final years.

Spotting him, Rayna ran to him and threw her arms around his neck, albeit only briefly before stepping back, embarrassed by her action. "Apologies. I forget myself. It's just that… it's been so long since I've seen you."

"Praise the gods for your forgetfulness then," he said, grinning.

"Come, meet my grandame," she said, tugging him back to the old lady. "As Mother Healer, she's a woman of great importance here."

"You found family after all. How wonderful," he said, truly happy for her.

"I did!" she bubbled. "Gresham, meet Nirtae," and gesturing toward him, said, "*Seanmháthair, is é seo an fear a dúirt mé leat faoi.*" He had no idea what she just said, but she'd obviously been learning the local language.

"*Tá sé an-dathúil,*" came the woman's grinning response.

Rayna smiled. "She says you're very handsome."

"Tell her thank you."

Rayna did. Then, looking him up and down, the woman said something that made Rayna blush.

"What did she say?" he asked, curious.

"Never mind," she said, turning even redder. "Come, let me show you around."

"I don't know if that's allowed. See that fellow," he said, looking at his escort who stood a polite distance away. "He's to go everywhere I go."

"Then let him follow."

She said something to her grandmother, who turned and scowled at Gresham's escort. Taking his hand, Rayna continued along the pathway he'd come to her on. They found a bench, sat and talked, her filling him in on all that had happened with her since she'd found family. Rayna openly wondered if Yudelle had returned to the mainland yet. Gresham laughed. "If she has, I hope she took the Inquisitor and his troopers with her; and maybe Quinn, too."

She laughed. "So, Soldier Boy, what have you been doing since I last saw you?"

He inhaled. "That's mostly why I'm here." He related the events of the previous night, albeit leaving out the fact he'd be leaving with his uncle.

She listened, saying nothing until his tale ended. "Weren't you terrified?"

He thought a bit before answering. "I don't think terrified is the right word. Apprehensive yes, but I was concentrating too hard to be all that scared. Maybe it was my soldier's training, but for the most part I just did what my uncle asked of me."

"You're far braver than I am." Her brow furrowed. "What happens now, and why do you have an escort?"

He doubted she'd like his answer. "The Elders refuse to allow Outlanders to remain in their city. We're to leave tomorrow morning—under threat of death if we ever return to, or divulge A'ryth's existence."

She'd stiffened at the mention of the word 'leave.' "What of the Chevaliers? How can you go home with them still there? If you return to Stalwart, you might get arrested. If they do to you what they did to your mother, we'd never see…" Pursing her lips, she didn't finish the thought.

"I'm not returning to Stalwart—at least not yet. Zakarah claimed he'd bring the headmaster to a third Nexus. My uncle plans to be there." He paused. How best to say this? He took her hand. "And he'll benefit from having a Battle Mage there to aid him."

Rayna jerked her hand back, disbelief painting her pretty face. "Don't even think it! One fight doesn't make you this Battle Mage. It's way too dangerous. It would be better to risk the Chevaliers!"

"I wasn't a Battle Mage last night, yet with the aid of Lore Masters I did what was needed. Rayna, you weren't there. This Zakarah is evil. Last night I was who I'm meant to be. With my uncle's guidance, perhaps I can become that person permanently." He let out a long, slow breath. "You've found your grandmother. Just as you need to stay with her in order make yourself whole, I need to become this Battle Mage for me to do the same. It's what I was born to do."

"That's folly!" she barked. Jumping to her feet, she turned her back to him, her face buried in her hands, her shoulders shaking.

Standing, he gently turned her around. "Why are you crying?"

"Because you're leaving, going on a dangerous mission. We may never see one another again," she said, meeting his gaze. "Oh, hells!" Rising to her tiptoes, she wrapped her arms around his neck and kissed him.

The world surrounding them vanished. Rayna was kissing him. That was all that mattered. He pulled her tight against him, relishing the bliss of it.

When the kiss finally ended, he just stood there, his mind totally jargogled. Eyes sparkling, she reached up and tweaked his nose, and then pulled his face back to hers. Their lips met again. This time he lifted her off the ground, spinning her in circles as they kissed. Their embrace continued long after he set her down. *The guard is watching.* He squeezed her closer. *Let him.*

"If things go wrong," he said, finally breaking their kiss, "there's something I want you to know. I'm not sure how best to say this." He took a deep breath, hardly believing he was about to confess his love to a woman, "I…"

She clamped her hand over his mouth, throttling his words. "I know… me too. Now come with me."

Hand-in hand, they returned to her grandmother's hut. They found her sitting in her chair just outside its door. Rayna whispered something to her, and Nirtae looked up at Gresham. Breaking into a grin, she motioned for him to join them, telling them to hold hands. Rayna smiled, albeit only briefly, before breaking into tears.

"*Céard atá cearr?* Nirtae asked, seeing her granddaughter's distress.

The two women shared a short exchange, after which Nirtae stormed over to Gresham's guard and started berating him. Looking like he wanted desperately to be someplace else, the man bowed, turned, and made his escape. Apparently, one did not challenge the Mother Healer.

"What's wrong? What's happening?" Gresham asked.

"I told Nirtae the Elders are forcing you leave," she pulled his hand to her lips and kissed it, "and that I didn't want that to happen. I asked her what I should do."

"What did she say?"

"*Ligfimid don draíocht cinneadh a dhéanamh*. It means, let the magic decide."

Nirtae returned, and pointing to a bench, ordered them to sit. She went into her hut, returning with some herbs, a bowl and pestle. Using a knife, she cut off an inch or so of Rayna's hair, then did the same to Gresham. Using bowl and pestle, she ground the herbs to a fine pulp, added their hair clippings, and set fire to the mixture. Holding the bowl in front of Rayna, she blew the smoke at her, indicating she should breathe it in, then did the same with Gresham.

The instant he inhaled it, his spirit was outside his body, observing the scene below like it had during his berserker rage. He watched Rayna rise to her feet, and with a longing look, lead him inside of Nirtae's hut. Lying on a mat, she pulled him down with her.

Watching from the doorway, Nirtae whispered, "*Ligfimid don draíocht cinneadh a dhéanamh.*" Smiling, she closed the door and returned to her chair outside the hut.

Gresham's spirit-self drifted down to join Rayna's, as arms entwined, they melded as one.

The Haunt

Goodricke crouched beside Dzojek, studying Malg's map. They were about to enter The Haunt, and the little Jacaí was suggesting the best route to take. The A'rythians seemed to fear this place beyond all else, but Goodricke struggled to fathom how any place could be any more vile than Foul Marsh had been. He'd love to get Caitlyn's opinion, but he hadn't seen her since before the Nexus. Had she returned to her guardian duties?

Dzojek asked him a question. Enough of such thoughts, you've a task at hand. "Beg pardon, what was that?"

Before he could answer, Hagley and Gresham arrived. He was pleased they were coming along. Their efforts at the Nexus had been what kept the demon from capturing the lot of them. And Gresham was also a trained a soldier. With the little Jacaí man to lead it, their party was well rounded.

"Welcome, young sirs." Goodricke pointed to the two piles of boots, leggings, tunics, vests, and surcoats on the ground beside him. All made of the thick pliable hide, the A'rythians had made a set for each of them. "Try on Odhran's gifts. His clothiers were up all night tailoring them." He and Dzojek were already wearing theirs.

As they dressed, Goodricke spotted Jarek approaching, similarly bedecked. "Excellent," Jarek announced, "you found your new attire."

Their hosts had provided not only clothing, but provisions, too. Smoked meat, packs, water skins; everything a guardian normally carried.

Once everyone was ready, they headed to the council area to bid their farewells. Bardán and Brin waited beside the Elders, but there was no sign of Caitlyn. Goodricke had hoped to say goodbye.

Bardán bowed. "Magus Verity, the Elders wish you good fortune in your encounter with the demon, and offer special thanks for warning us of him. Even in *ceangailte*, an entire circle was almost drawn into its clutches." He bowed to Hagley and Gresham. "And they offer special thanks to the young Lore Masters. Without them, all would have been lost."

Flushing, Hagley tipped his head. "We all contributed, Sir."

Bardán smiled. "True." His gaze took in the entire party. "Despite his gratitude, Lore Master Odhran reminds you of your banishment and your vow not to return to or speak of A'ryth to others."

Jarek touched fingers to lips and then heart, "So it shall be."

Farewells made, Bardán escorted them out of the city, under another archway, to the river encircling their city. A few curious townspeople awaited them. Word of their departure had apparently spread. Sully and Rayna were among them. The boy looked forlorn. "You shouldn't be adventuring without me."

Hagley walked over and ruffled the lad's hair. "It's too dangerous for you, Lucky Person, but know that I'll be relying on all those tricks you've taught me." The boy smiled.

Gresham hugged Rayna. "I shall never forget last night."

"Nor will I," she said, tearing. "Stay safe."

Brin elbowed her way to Hagley and draped a necklace around his neck. "This charm is for you Lore Master Hagley, to bring good fortune on your journey."

It was a piece of yellow cliff-stone. "Many thanks, Brin."

"Traveling mercies, Outlander."

When their guide bade them to follow, Bardán led them to the river, spoke a few words, and stepped onto another of those unseen spans. "The bridge is open. Fare well my friends."

Goodricke approached the 'bridge.' Extending his foot, he probed the invisible walkway. Jarek did the same. "It seems a far better way to cross the river than your way, eh milord?" Laughing, they walked across it, through another archway, and out of A'ryth.

They hadn't hiked long before being halted by a familiar voice. "Is it not foolish to walk when one could ride?"

Goodricke turned to find Caitlyn sitting astride another of those beautiful white horses. Two others pranced behind her. She trotted over. "Goodricke Loddvar, it is folly to risk The Haunt without a guardian to guide you. It is lucky for you that I go with you."

Guardian or not, Caitlyn was still a woman, and worthy of a man's protection. "I shall keep you safe then."

Laughing, she said, "Only an ignorant Outlander would say such a thing, but I thank you anyway." Despite her remark, she looked pleased.

She turned to Jarek. "What say you to having me guide you, Lore Master?"

"I must confess, not knowing what we face or where to go are of great concern. If you offer guidance, I for one, am grateful."

She smiled and nodded. "And you Jacaí, can you abide the presence of a *máistreás*?"

Dzojek scowled. "Only a fool would refuse the aid of a guardian."

She turned her attention to Hagley and Gresham. "Do either of you ride? There are six of us and only three capall, so we ride doubled."

Gresham nodded. "Lady, I'm a trained soldier. Riding is a simple matter for me."

"Then Dzojek rides with you. As skilled as the Jacaí are at riding a bultúr, their legs are too short for a capall."

Goodricke was paired with Hagley, Caitlyn with Jarek.

They made far better time on horseback. Caitlyn led them as unerringly as before, seeming familiar with every turn or twist of the trail. It smelled of the woodlands and was alive with chattering wildlife. Such peacefulness belied the danger that lay before them.

At mid-day they rested near a brook. Goodricke joined Caitlyn as she refilled her water skin. "Lady, the Magus and I are concerned."

"And why is that, Goodricke Loddvar?"

"Wasn't the purpose in us returning Dzojek to his people to avoid someone risking The Haunt a second time? We're worried how you'll manage it."

Caitlyn smiled. "Do not worry." She pulled a necklace from her bodice; a key dangled at its end. "The Elders proclaimed me Seeker. I do not return through The Haunt; I go to the Outland with you."

The sun was setting when they reached a high bluff overlooking a deep canyon. Trees shrouded the valley below for as far as the eye could see. Vast and foreboding, steep escarpments bordered both sides. Thinking about the hidden dangers that lie ahead had the hairs on Goodricke's arms tingling.

"What you see before you is the Crone's Haunt," Caitlyn said. "We must survive it in order to reach Jacaioi. We release the capall now. They refuse to enter the place where so many of their kind have perished."

The pathway down was narrow, with rocky cliffs on one side and sheer drop-off on the other. Any misstep could prove fatal. The multitude of curves and switchbacks limited their view. At the pace they were descending, Goodricke figured it would take them the better part of the day to reach the bottom, and they had only three days to reach the final Nexus.

Dusk made their descent even more treacherous. Caitlyn made frequent stops to confer with Dzojek. Their exchanges involved a lot of pointing skyward or to spots on the valley floor. It was after one such exchange that Caitlyn slipped off her pack and announced, "We spend the night here. It's high enough to be safe from attack below."

They were at a wide spot on the trail. Eroding rains had carved a small grotto in the hillside, making it suitable for encampment. Gresham slipped off his pack. "I'll gather brush and start the fire."

Caitlyn held up a hand. "No fires until after we've crossed The Haunt. We dare not let our presence be known."

Darkness fell, bringing blinding blackness and an eerie quiet with it. Nary a cricket nor night bird's song could be heard. Gresham thought back to his soldier's training. In situations like this, one's enemy could be on you before being seen.

Dzojek and Caitlyn spent the evening at cliff's edge, scouring valley and sky, murmuring in their native tongue. Gresham recognized only two words, Crone and bultúr. Any mention of the great flying birds inevitably spawned an argument. After one such disagreement, Dzojek stomped away. Gresham curled into his bed, wondering at the source of the Jacaí's anger.

The party ate at first light, broke camp, and were well down the trail before the sun crested the far hill. The rocks had darkened; as had their mood, particularly Caitlyn's. Gone was the jovial, smiling guide of yesterday. The closer they came to The Haunt, the quieter and more ill at ease she became. What had once appeared to be a broad and vast woods was closing in on them now, restricting their view, exposing them to unseen dangers.

The trail flattened as they neared the valley floor. Its curves vanished too. Gresham was surprised at how quickly they'd reached the bottom. Loose rocks were strewn everywhere, making their path hard to discern. He'd have expected a woodland to be rife with the sounds creatures make. Instead they were greeted by an eerie silence.

Caitlyn halted the party short of the trees and conferred at great length with Dzojek and Jarek. Done, his uncle beckoned the rest to join them. "We're about to enter The Haunt. The Crone's abominations prefer darkness to daylight. Unfortunately, Caitlyn says the forest's canopy is so thick that even in daytime little light reaches its floor, meaning we must be ready for attack at all times."

Gresham cast another nervous glance at the woodlands.

"Fear not," Jarek assured them, "we have ample arsenal to deal with them. I'll use my Gift to blend us with our surroundings, but beasts have ears as well as eyes. Since it's very difficult to maintain more than one spell for any length of time, Hagley will mask our sounds."

Hagley stood straighter, drying his palms on his pants.

"Stay calm, Hagley," Jarek soothed. "It's simple illusion. You've already managed far more difficult spells; you'll handle this one with ease." Gresham gave Hagley a pat, "Which leaves Gresham free to defend us if we're attacked."

It was Gresham's turn to dry sweaty palms.

Jarek tapped Goodricke's sheath. "You all saw Goodricke's sword glow at the Nexus, that's because its ensorcelled to detect the presence of evil. He'll be monitoring it to assure we have no surprises. And he's quite capable of wielding it as a weapon, too. Caitlyn's a guardian. She's dealt with these monstrosities her whole life, as has Dzojek. We're a force to be reckoned with." His gaze bounced from person to person. "We enter The Haunt now."

Hagley cast his silence spell, and they marched forth, the thicket closing in on them, seeming to swallow them. Gresham had never experienced absolute silence before. He'd didn't realize how much he relied on sound. Not hearing his own footsteps was bothersome. Fearful of tripping, he watched the ground as much as the surrounding woodlands. Twice he thought he spotted distant movement, and hearing nothing to reinforce his suspicions had his gut churning.

The Haunt's perpetual dusk and dense trees challenged his sense of direction. It made simple things like seeing your pathway nearly impossible. Time and time again, someone in the party would stumble on a tree root, or get struck in the face by a limb released by the person in front of them because they didn't hear it coming. With no path to follow, Caitlyn and Dzojek made frequent use of Goodricke's compass, pointing, gesturing, and mouthing words, struggling to communicate within their soundless bubble. Gresham lost all sense of time or bearing, and prayed their guides knew where they were going. His soldier's training made relying on others difficult.

They plodded on, the thick undergrowth slowing their progress. Holes in the canopy were rare. Whenever they found one, they'd stop and savor its sunlight. During one such break, Dzojek spotted a huge vulture-like bird hunting the treetops. He shook Caitlyn, pointing. She stared, disbelief on her face. It had a long beak and massive wings with huge claws trailing behind. The back of its head extended almost as far as its beak. Was this a bultúr?

They bolted for cover as more flyers came into view; two small raptors and a third bird as large as the first. Dzojek was beside himself, making frantic gestures, dancing and yelling as if someone could hear. A flailing arm hit Hagley.

"Ow!" The unexpected blow disrupted Hagley's concentration. His spell failed, his pained yelp echoing through the trees.

Horrific screeches reverberated from skies as the giant predators circled and dove, speeding toward the troupe. Jarek extended his arms, fingers waggling. "Defend!"

The largest of the raptors headed straight for Dzojek, its horrific cry echoing throughout the wood. Its fast-beating wings rustled tree leaves as it swooped past them, talons extended, about to seize the fleeing Jacaí.

Gresham reacted. Extending his arm, he chanted. A phantasmal hand appeared in the path of the unsuspecting bird. Gresham opened his palm, spreading his fingers. The phantasmal hand did the same. The creature squawked as it crashed into it. A swat of Gresham's hand batted it sideways. Flapping furiously, the giant vulture struggled to stay aloft, but crashed as colossal fingers pinned its wings to its body. Branches, twigs, leaves, and feathers flew everywhere. Goodricke leaped on its back and drove his sword through its neck with a two-handed thrust. It flopped briefly, then panting, the gargantuan avian ceased all movement. Goodricke slid down its side. The dead carcass beside him lay shoulder high with the big man.

Gresham scanned the area too. One of the smaller birds chased after Hagley, but just like in the marsh, his adversary found not one target, but many. Gresham had no more idea who the true Hagley was than the raptor did. As it scooped up the nearest Hagley image, Gresham leaped on its back and drove his blade into its neck. It sliced through the bird and hit the captive Hagley. All three tumbled in a heap. Frantic, Gresham jumped to his feet, scouring the area. Relief washed over him. Other Hagleys still scampered about. That couldn't happen had he killed the real one. Caitlyn was spinning her rawhide weapon, seeking targets. Freeing his blade, Gresham searched, too. Jarek stood over a third bird, his hands extended, pointing at it, watching it in its death throes.

Dzojek yelled, pointing skyward. Their fourth assailant was airborne, fleeing, a small rider clinging to its neck. It disappeared above the canopy.

"Is everyone all right?" Jarek asked.

Hagley stood beside Gresham, smiling. "I'm alive, but I wouldn't be had Gresham not killed that abomination."

Goodricke and Caitlyn were stooped over catching their breath. Dzojek was kneeling beside the bird Goodricke had killed, bobbing back and forth, cradling its head in his lap.

Jarek walked over. "Why do you grieve?"

He looked up, his eyes moist. "It's Jorrel."

Caitlyn explained. "Jorrel was his bultúr—before the Crone infused it with her evil. That poor creature lying there, although born a bultúr, died an abomination."

Dzojek jumped to his feet. "No! He was no longer her minion." Red-faced, he wheeled on Goodricke. "You killed my Jorrel!"

Caitlyn stepped between them. "That is not so, Dzojek, you know the Crone's devilry when you see it."

Dzojek's anger succumbed to grief. He looked down at the dead bird. "No, he was still breathing when I reached him. When he looked, he knew it was me. He was no longer minion, he was Jorrel."

"Stand aside!" Jarek spoke the words with such authority that Dzojek scrambled out of his way. Kneeling, his uncle placed a hand on the animal's head and closed his eyes. Everyone watched. After a moment, Jarek spoke to the little Jacaí. "You're right, it died as Jorrel, not as a minion. He recognized you before his life force left him. Do not despair, he preferred death to serving the Crone."

"Bah!" Dzojek scoffed. "How could you know such a thing?"

Jarek gave a gentle smile. "I spoke with his soul."

Dzojek threw his arms up. "You don't even speak Jacaí. You only say what you think I want to hear so my people will help you." He turned his back on the magus. "That will not be. I will never aid those who killed my Jorrel."

Jarek's tone was soft. "Souls communicate through senses the way we do words, and are often very exact." Dzojek looked dubious. "Perhaps I can convince you. Ask a question whose answer only Jorrel would know."

The little Jacaí stared back at him, doubt in his eyes. "Tell me how he was taken."

Jarek pressed his palm to the bird's skull. Everyone watched in silence. "Is see you and Rajko scouting, you upon Jorrel, him riding… Thundar. Flying minions attacked, crippling Thundar's wing. When you tried to help, Jorrel went down too. You were the only one to escape."

Dzojek said nothing, but his stunned look told everyone Jarek's accounting of events was true. The little man knelt beside Jorrel, rubbing fingers over its scarred wing. "Jorrel took this wound." He looked up to where the bird and rider had escaped. "Poor Rajko."

"How so?" Caitlyn asked.

"It was he and Thundar who flew away. It's what I was trying to tell you when no one could hear."

Jarek stood. "Jorrel is at peace in death." He looked skyward. "But I fear his cohort has gone to warn his mistress. We should leave."

With their presence no longer a secret, stealth gave way to speed. They ran when the terrain allowed and hurried as best they could when it didn't. They kept up their blistering pace despite their weariness. Exhausted, they trudged on.

They had no more encounters that day, save for an isolated creature or two that turned and fled upon seeing them. Jarek halted everyone when they came upon a knoll. "Caitlyn says we're well past where the Crone has been sighted in the past, making an encounter with her less likely. We still need to remain vigilant however, because we won't make it out of The Haunt until tomorrow at best. We dare not sleep in the open, and this is the first place I've seen that's defensible. We spend the night here."

They explored the small hillside, seeking the best possible hiding place, eventually choosing an open area in front of a rocky alcove. Small, it offered protection from above and behind and a clear view to the front.

Jarek removed his pack. "Remove yours too, but keep them close. And no bedding tonight, lest we need to flee at a moment's notice. I'll mask our camp in the image of thorns. With luck, it will discourage wandering beasts."

They decided upon two-person watches that would allow the others to sleep. Goodricke and Caitlyn took first watch; Gresham and Hagley were assigned the second. Knowing he wouldn't be able to sleep, Gresham found a somewhat comfortable place where he could scout the area, but eventually his eyes grew heavy, and weariness claimed him.

Goodricke's gentle shake woke him. The big man held a finger to his mouth. "Something prowls nearby," he whispered. Gresham had never seen the big man this wary. "Lots of somethings."

While Goodricke woke Hagley, Caitlyn did the same to Jarek and Dzojek.

Gresham took a calming breath, his hand drifting to his sword. He could hear them, whatever they were. The occasional crack of twigs was unnerving; but not as much as the sniffing sounds. Those sent a chill up his spine. Jarek and Hagley had masked for sight and sound, but nothing had been done to hide their scent.

The sniffing drew louder, ultimately stopping just outside their burrow. Gresham held his breath. The noises resumed as their stalkers fanned out, surrounding them.

"All right everyone," Jarek whispered, "We've been found. When I light the area, attack with your best."

Sword or spell? Gresham ran through what few spells he knew. Hand spells had worked twice before; he'd best rely on them.

Jarek conjured a light globe, brightening the area. A dozen or so hideous-looking creatures blocked the cave's entrance. Growling and snarling, their rancid breath both frightening and nauseating. The closest were dog-like monstrosities resembling huge hunting hounds, but far larger and broader of chest, with huge, frothing fangs. Other abominations crowded behind them. One was two-legged, almost man-like in appearance, with hideous growths marring its misshapen face.

Gresham lashed out with his spectral hand, grabbing for the closest threat, but his hand crashed into nothingness. Some invisible force was shielding the mongrels. The others' attacks fared no better. Sword held high, Goodricke charged a nearby beast, only to bounce off this unseen barrier. He crumpled and fell, dazed. Dzojek rushed to aid him.

Gresham's limbs suddenly went sluggish. He was hardly able to move. Their assailants appeared similarly suspended. Leaves crackled. Something new approached. What? Rancid bile filled his mouth. He forced it back down, but its taste remained.

The once-bultúr they'd seen earlier came into view with a Jacaí-sized shape straddling its neck. Behind it sat a hag. Long and skinny, her scraggly unkempt hair hung low over pointy shoulders. Deep blotches and pocks marred her wrinkled face and jagged nose. She cackled. The Crone had found them.

Gresham found himself suddenly able to move again. He started walking. His limbs felt heavy, as if he were sleep walking. But a part of his mind knew this nightmare was real.

"Gresham! Take my hand!"

His uncle's voice broke his trance. He'd been walking right toward the Crone. The Magus pulled him down, joining hands with him. Caitlyn and Hagley did the same as they formed a circle. Power surged through him. Linked, their strength countered the Crone's enchantment, and his urge to join her vanished.

The Crone had one arm stretched out in front of her, gripping a stick-mounted black skull roughly half the size of a human head. She barked some command he couldn't fathom, and her snarling beasts attacked. But as with his own assault, something blocked them. "I've shielded us too," Jarek huffed.

The Crone hissed. Sliding off the once-bultúr, she strolled over and calmly fondled Jarek's invisible shield. Ignoring her foes, she studied it intently before walking to where Goodricke and Dzojek lay—outside of the shield's protection. Dzojek gave what had once been Rajko a pleading look, but his once former friend simply stared back through emotionless eyes that had Gresham shuddering.

The Crone screaked and two beasts grabbed the horrified Dzojek and dragged him to a nearby tree. Two others attempted the same with Goodricke but jumped back howling. His sword was glowing. After another shrill command from the Crone, they renewed their efforts, only to cry out again. The witch stormed over and grabbed the sword. It flared blue, and she too jumped away.

She looked around, assessing, then strolled over to Dzojek. His captors had pinned his arms behind the tree. The poor little man twisted and jerked, desperate to break free. She pressed a hand to his forehead and his struggles ceased. His face went slack, his blank stare mirroring that of Rajko.

Leaving her limp victim, she returned to Goodricke and held out the skull, mumbling. Goodricke's muscles jerked. He looked stunned, albeit alert. She spoke again, and his face briefly took on Dzojek's numb expression, but a shake of his head had him glaring at her again.

"Help him!" Caitlyn begged of Jarek.

"I cannot," he answered. "It's all I can do to maintain our shield and provide enough light to see. I can't believe the potency of her Earth Magic." He nodded toward the skies. Stars twinkled above. "At least we're not under a canopy. Come sunrise, her strength will wane while ours grows. We need to somehow endure until then."

The standoff lasted well into the night. To their horror, Dzojek's transformation continued before their eyes as the Crone stood before him, grinning, with her hand pressed against his forehead, slowly changing him from Jacaí to minion.

Sores had developed on Goodricke's face, and saliva oozed from the corners of his mouth, but he continued to defy her. Could daylight save them if they lasted that long, or were they getting a preview of their respective dooms?

Suddenly all went black.

<hr>

"Gresham!" It was Hagley, shaking his shoulder. He must have dozed off. He sat up with a start, his heart hammering. It was dawn. "Gods! Did I break our circle?"

"The circle was broken, but I did it, not you. Look."

The Crone and all her minions were asleep, their grotesque bodies sprawled on the grounds before them. So were their friends.

Hagley grinned. "Although flesh and blood couldn't penetrate her shield, my sleep spell could. Magus Verity said her strength wanes in daylight, so I thought it might buy us time."

Gresham surveyed the area. Dzojek looked even worse than before. Warts similar to those of the other minions adorned his face, and his features now drooped, making him appear more minion than Jacaí. He looked for Goodricke. "Goodricke's gone!"

Hagley nodded. "Yes, I saw him leave."

His explanation was cut short by the Crone's screech. Had their talking awakened her, or perhaps the dawn light? Whichever, her cry roused her minions. She rushed to the beasts who'd had been guarding Goodricke and grabbed them by their necks. They jerked backwards, their bodies shaking. Blood oozed from their mouths.

After a moment, their thrashing stopped. They stilled. She'd killed them with no more effort than that.

She whirled, facing her captives. No taller than Caitlyn, and thinner than any living creature ought to be, she nonetheless looked formidable. Her look of loathing made Gresham wince. She stood before them, her bloodshot gaze floating from person to person, her glare menacing. She raised a hand, shadowing her face from the rising sun, something not lost on Jarek.

The comforting surge of the *ceangailte* coursed through Gresham. "Be ready," Jarek whispered. "The moment those rays touch me, I'm dropping our shield. Strike when I do. There's no way she could have kept her shield active while asleep. Let's hope she hasn't restored it."

Gresham felt the warmth of sunlight. "Now!" Jarek hollered.

Gresham swung his sword at one of the dog-like creatures crouching before them, severing the head. Turning about, he plunged his blade through the eye of another. Yet another fell to a vicious swipe. His companions were attacking other minions, and had them leaping about, howling their hideous barks. Powerful gusts bowled over other attackers, victims of his uncle's Wind Blast. Hagley stood beside him, wielding Jarek's short sword. Although causing little or no damage, he was nonetheless keeping the beasts at bay. Caitlyn used her disks on anything still moving. Their surprise attack soon had every creature downed or stunned, save for the Crone.

Hair flapping, she stood holding her mounted skull at arm's length, using it to part the maelstrom Jarek was directing her way. Gresham added phantasmal arrows to the mix, but those too, were diverted by the black skull. Seeing Gresham's attack, the Crone pointed a bony finger at him, her ominous cackle filling the area. He lost awareness of all but her, and sat unmoving, sure he was about to die.

But the anticipated attack never came. Instead, blood gurgled from her mouth as a glowing sword emerged from her chest. Goodricke stood behind her, twisting Turpin's blade.

Her hideous face contorted. Falling to her knees she grabbed the blade, its touch evoking a horrific scream. She lurched forward, pushing the blade backwards. It came free. She twisted to face her adversary, hate pouring from those loathsome eyes. She lifted a hand as Goodricke moved to impale her again. Whatever she did stilled him.

She struggled to her feet, the skull absorbing any attacks directed toward her. Blood poured from lips and nose. She staggered back to her bultúr. Snarling, she swatted Rajko from his seat. The once-Jacaí landed in a heap, unmoving. Taking his place, she bawled a command and the raptor lifted off the ground. Shrieking a thunderous caw, it pumped its massive wings and flew away, disappearing above the canopy with the Crone clinging to its neck.

———

Boomaaker stood before the pond, taking comfort from the shimmer of the moons' reflections. One-Who-Hunts fed only in daylight.

He awaited the God-man's appearance. Why hadn't it revealed itself yet? Perhaps it desired a sacrifice, some show of the people's worth. Surely that was it. He waved a claw, and two warriors dragged over a squirming female, laying her at his feet, her neck exposed. Fangs foaming, she thrashed, resisting her fate. Had she been worthy she would have willingly given herself. Her loss would be meaningless.

Boomaaker withdrew his blade. A swift slash opened her neck. He grabbed her mane, watching the blood gurgle from lips and throat. Her jerking ceased and her body stilled. Releasing her mane, he sliced downward. Despite her hard scales her chest cavity opened, exposing her heart. He made quick work of anything attached, and pulled out the still warm organ. He held it high overhead his head, keening. The peoples perched in the rocks above echoed his cry. Their wails swelled to excited shouts when he tossed the dripping flesh into the pond.

———

Zakarah watched the offering sink to the mud before holding out his arm, fingers dancing. Instantly his visage appeared in this other world pool. The beast fell to its knees, bowing. Too feeble-minded to have value; he wouldn't gather this one. He smiled. That didn't mean it and its ilk wouldn't prove useful, however. The beast looked up. It was time to instruct it.

Turpin's Boon

With the Crone's departure, her surviving minions lost their will to fight. They tried to flee, only to be cut down by iron and magic. What were once snarls, became pitiful death wails. In no time all had been downed. Caitlyn watched as her companions went from body to body, assuring each was dead.

Caitlyn knelt beside Dzojek. The poor Jacaí hadn't moved since the Crone's attack. He simply sat staring blindly, not even blinking.

"Rajko is still alive," Gresham hollered, checking out Dzojek's friend.

"This one too," Goodricke called, standing over the man-shaped beast. Caitlyn walked over, studying it. Although it lacked the horrific markings the Crone's spells had given Dzojek, its face drooped, looking deathly pale. "Stand aside," Goodricke warned, raising his sword, preparing to end the thing's life.

"No, not this one!" Caitlyn enjoined, holding up a hand. Falling to her knees, she cradled the creature's head. "Ewan, it's Caitlyn. The Crone is gone; you are saved."

"That thing has a name?" Goodricke said, lowering his sword.

"Yes! Look," she said, pointing to tattered remnants of what appeared to be cloth. "Beasts do not wear clothing. And this," she said, tapping a colored spot, "is Ewan's family crest. This 'thing' you see was once as you and I. His patrol went missing moons ago. We thought them dead." She stared at what had once been a man. "Perhaps that would have been a better fate."

"Dzojek is no better off," Jarek observed. "We can't leave them like this. Killing them would be more merciful."

"Nay," Goodricke said, drawing his sword. "You forget Odhran's counsel," he added, unscrewing the pommel and extracting its vial. "What better use for Turpin's potion than this?" he asked, taking a sip. The instant he swallowed, color returned to his cheeks. Facial muscles that had gone slack under the Crone's ministrations once again tightened. He looked like the Goodricke of old.

They laid Dzojek, Rajko and Ewan side-by-side. Caitlyn propped Ewan into a sitting position and opened his mouth, allowing Goodricke to feed him the potion. They watched in wonder as Ewan's features slowly changed. The unsightly warts that covered his face and hands began to dissolve, and some of the sores faded, but not all. Many festering ones still remained. Although he no longer appeared to be a Crone minion, he didn't look totally human either.

Caitlyn offered him water. He swallowed, staring at her the whole time. "It's all right, Ewan, you're back among us," she said in A'rythian. He closed his eyes, tears trailing down his cheeks. The potion may have healed his body, but what had enduring life as a Crone abomination done to his soul? "I must attend the others. I'll be back."

Dzojek, although dazed and shaken, made a full recovery, and was ministering to his friend Rajko. Although faring better than Ewan, Rajko had yet to speak. Unlike Ewan, who still had sores, Caitlyn found little wrong with Rajko. "Give him more water," she instructed, leaving the Jacaí in Dzojek's care.

She joined Goodricke and Jarek. "Thank you, Goodricke Loddvar. Your gift has returned us three lives."

Goodricke shook his head. "The gift was from a wizard long dead and a sword given over to my care by Master Verity. I deserve no thanks."

She smiled and stepped between them, holding each by the elbow. "Then I thank you both, and the dead wizard too." She watched Dzojek attend to his friend. "Your sword's magic has done much for them."

"Let us hope," Jarek said, checking the skies, "for we must leave. The Crone may be gravely injured, but she survived."

Caitlyn looked over at Ewan. "But Dzojek is the only one well enough to travel."

"Goodricke and I were just discussing that very matter. We can make litters out of blankets and tree limbs. Goodricke and I can carry one, Hagley and Gresham the other. That leaves you and Dzojek free to guide us. With food and a night's rest, perhaps they'll fare better tomorrow."

They assembled their makeshift litters, gathered their belongings, and were once again on the move. Whenever Jarek's probes sensed something in their path, Caitlyn altered course, but carrying stretchers slowed them. She openly doubted they'd make it out of The Haunt before nightfall.

Their minion encounters were few and their battles brief, happening only when they stumbled upon some unsuspecting beast. Their superior numbers made short work of those encounters. They kept well under the canopy too, avoiding flyers. But as Caitlyn feared, day's end still found them still in The Haunt.

They pitched camp. Jarek masked their presence with phantasms while she helped Goodricke and Gresham set perimeter traps, and all but the first watch bedded down.

Escape

Rajko was speaking now. After those first spoken words the two Jacaí hadn't stopped talking since. Envy stabbed her; she longed to speak in her native tongue instead of talking like a child in Outlander speech. But she was Seeker now, this was her new language.

She examined Ewan. The potion had transformed him back into something recognizable. Before swallowing it, had it not been for his clothing, she wouldn't have known he was human; she'd have let Goodricke kill him. Despite his recovery, he refused to speak.

She knelt beside him. "Ewan! Talk to me," she said, speaking A'rythian. "Tell me what became of the others, and of your horrors." She looked around their camp. "It's me, Caitlyn. We have been friends since we were babes. Share your pain with me."

Ewan stared at her, opened his mouth, only to shut it again. He held up his hands, examining the growths that blighted his skin. "I'm still her beast."

He spoke! She grasped his hands. "No, you are free, you're no longer hers to command. Inside you are as you always were. Maybe the outside can be healed, too. The Mother Healer knows far more of such things than me."

He pushed her away, albeit gently.

"What of the others?" she asked. "There were seven with you. Taryn was one of them. What became of your wife?"

"She's dead. All of them are."

"What happened?"

He buried his face in his hands. "We killed them. I killed them."

"Ewan, no! Whatever happened was the Crone's doing. You would never have done such a thing otherwise. You must not think that way."

"It is what happened. I cannot bear the thought of it."

"Release it, lest it consume you."

"You don't understand, Caitlyn."

"Help me do so then; tell me."

"I was scouting ahead when pain suddenly flooded my mind, and all went black. I don't know how long I lay there before waking, but when I did, the Crone stood above me, grinning her awful smile. She reached out and touched my head, and then..." Ewan buried his face in his hands again.

"Then what?"

"At first, I felt pain, then a numbness in both body and mind. A distant part of me remembered who I was, always. Even when we came into your camp last night, I recognized you. But this new part of me was greater, stronger, this beast within me.

"As I awakened, I felt blood lust. The beasts around me shared it. Former men or beasts, I knew not and cared not. I just wanted blood. And it was blood we went after. The Crone controlled my mind, including that portion that had been a man, that knew where my party was heading. She used me to lead her to them, and..." Caitlyn started to say something but stopped when he raised his hand. "we killed them all, Taryn included."

"No, the Crone killed them, you were just her weapon. You said the beast was in control, not you. You must forgive yourself."

"You don't understand," he said, tears pouring down his cheeks. "We didn't just kill them; we ate them." His voice cracked so badly she could scarcely understand him. "How can I forgive myself of that?"

Caitlyn had no answer. She sat holding him for most of that evening, listening to his sobs. Thankfully, he eventually fell asleep.

Caitlyn left him to take up her watch. Through the night they heard several traps trigger, but one at a time and never one after the other. Come dawn, they examined their traps. Although nothing had been killed or captured, footprints and blood were proof of visitors.

Ewan and Rajko were stronger that morning, allowing them to abandon the litters. They hiked in pairs for safety. Holes in the canopy became common, and mountains appeared off in the distance. Limbs aching and weary beyond belief, they mustered up what little of their strength remained.

Finally, they reached foothills. Escape was at hand. The open terrain between the woods and hills resembled the grounds where they'd first entered the Haunt. This time they'd have to climb the cliffs. Its boulders and hills offered places to hide, but to reach them they needed to cross two hundred paces of exposed meadow. Their joy at reaching the end of the haunt abruptly died. A band of abominations occupied the final field they had to cross. Of all shapes and sizes, their numbers were too vast to count. All looked hideous—say nothing of dangerous. There was no way their exhausted party could do battle with them. Worse, there was also no way to slip past them without being seen. Caitlyn's heart sank. Had they come all this way only to die with escape seemingly inches away. How could the gods be this unkind?

There was one bit of good news in that Jarek's probes had sensed them before they unwittingly stumbled into their midst. Dzojek and she returned to tell the group the gloomy news. They discussed options and possibilities, Caitlyn translating for Ewan, Dzojek doing the same for Rajko. It was Ewan who finally posed a solution, one that sent chills up Caitlyn's spine.

"Ewan says he knows the abominations' minds and ways, even their language." Ewan gave her a wry smile, nodding for her to continue. "He says at least some good came from having been among them for five moons." Ewan interrupted her again, holding up his mottled arms. "He says he still looks like them, too."

"So, what is it he proposes?" Jarek asked.

"That he enter their camp as one of them. He says they are easily incited. He will tell them he has found us coming up the trail and lead them to us. When they leave, we're to run for the foothills. Once there, he says it's unlikely they'll follow. Leaving the Haunt risks falling prey to guardians. Ewan can then slip away and join us."

They sat silent, contemplating Ewan's proposal. "And he thinks this will work?" Jarek asked.

Caitlyn repeated the question and translated Ewan's response. "He makes no promises but asks if you have a better plan."

Jarek looked at the others. No one spoke. "All right, tell him we agree. Ask him when best to try it."

She translated.

"*Láithreach bonn*," he said, smiling.

"Right now."

Staying under the cover of bushes, they edged their way back to the meadow. Peek holes in the scrub offered unfettered views of the minions. Caitlyn and Ewan hugged. "Thank you. Be careful," she urged.

Ewan slipped off into the brush. Soon they heard his cry as he charged toward the abominations, yelling, pointing back the way he'd come. The excitable abominations grew hysterical, dancing about, jumping and screaming. Those not hopping about were frothing at the mouth. Ewan let out another scream and raced for the woods, to a spot a good distance from the humans. The abominations gave chase, screaming their lust.

With the beasts gone, they burst from their hiding place, racing hell-bent across the field to the shallow canyons at its other side. Using knolls and boulders to shield them, they wound their way up the hillside, not resting until they were well up the slope. While the others struggled to catch their breath, Caitlyn peeked back down the valley, searching in vain for Ewan.

After a short respite, they resumed their climb, every so often stopping to check for him. On their sixth such stop they finally spotted him, talking with the minions. Even from their lofty position they could tell there was contention. Instead of trying to sneak away as promised, Ewan appeared to be taunting them.

"What's the matter with him?" Gresham asked. "Why doesn't he shut his mouth? He's going to get himself killed if he keeps that up."

Jarek looked at Caitlyn. "That's his wish, isn't it?"

The truth of his words stung. "*Dias!*" she cried, pressing her hands to her mouth. "No! Ewan, it wasn't your fault! Oh no, please; Ewan, no!"

Sobs stole her voice as the abominations mobbed Ewan. He made no effort to run or defend himself as he vanished beneath a pile of teeth and claws. Caitlyn wailed. The others prayed.

———

Boomaaker lowered an eye fold, shielding the sun's glare. The people had formed into groups the God-Man called scods. They stood side-by-side, one people for each toe on Boomaaker's claw.

The God Man had decreed that scods would make the warriors mightier. With his back to both pond and cliffs, Boomaaker surveyed the meadow before him. The people's scods stretched as far as the eye could see, each armed with pointed sticks and sharpened rocks.

Prey! popped unbidden into Boomaaker's mind. The people shrieked as One-Who-Hunts swept in low, scattering the scods. Boomaaker tried to run, but as always, One-Who-Hunts' magic prevented it. None could move. All he could do was watch in dread as One-Who-Hunts landed and crunched a people in its mighty jaw. Leaping skyward, it circled and dove again. *Prey!*

Although their terror was great, the people were still frozen, weighted down by fear and magic. One-Who-Hunts flew low over a scod, grabbed a people in each claw, and flew from sight. With One-Who-Hunts' magic gone, the peoples could run again. Boomaaker did.

Jacaíoi

Jarek bent over, leaning on his knees, struggling to catch his breath. After a nearly sleepless night, today's steep ascent was hardly bearable. It was late afternoon, and they'd been climbing without pause since escaping The Haunt. Watching his younger companions climb with relative ease underscored the fact that he was growing old.

The higher they climbed, the more arduous the terrain became. Occasional scrub grasses were the mountain's only vegetation. Gullies dotted the landscape, likely rivulets during the rainy season. In dry season these gravel-strewn trenches simply made footing more treacherous. Still, distancing themselves from The Haunt had brightened everyone's spirits. Even Caitlyn was faring better. He wondered what nightmares had driven Ewan to seek such a ghastly end. And what of the Jacaí, especially Rajko, who'd endured life as an abomination for more than a moon? The pair had been leading the climb all day, and neither seemed depressed. Jarek had his own worries. The final Nexus was two nights hence, and any opportunity of rescuing Lavan fading. There'd be no fourth Nexus.

Goodricke looked down the hill, checking on him. Caitlyn did too. He'd best catch up. Ignoring his body's complaints, he resumed his climb.

They camped at sundown and did little else but rest. Staring at the valley below, it was hard to believe something so beautiful could harbor such horrors. When he'd first learned of the Elders' reluctance to return Dzojek to Jacaíoi, he'd thought them callous. Now he understood.

Caitlyn was conferring with the Jacaí. Although he wasn't quite sure what to make of her audacious plan to accompany them to the Outlands, he was nonetheless relieved that she wouldn't have to risk a return journey back through The Haunt.

Gresham and Hagley gathered kindling, and Goodricke prepared a meal. The prospect of finally eating heated food sounded wonderful.

Caitlyn joined him. "Rajko and Dzojek say if we keep our pace, we might make Jacaíoi by nightfall tomorrow, but they warn the climb steepens the higher we get."

Not good news. "Is there no way to get there sooner? The Nexus is imminent."

Dzojek was there too. "I am sorry Máistir, it is not likely."

Jarek bedded down, too glum to converse. Wrapped in his blanket, he studied the moons. Juno and Ceres looked close enough to create a precursor event—and perhaps generate sufficient aethers to contact Lavan. He closed his eyes, fondling his ring.

Lavan! Can you hear me?

Jarek! The gods be praised, you've reached me. I have important news. Zakarah will use the upcoming Nexus to enter our world in the flesh. He's after the university's relics and anyone Gifted.

Lavan, I'm coming for you, do not despair. I'll get you home yet.

Such false hopes are more than I can bear. There was a brief silence. *Zakarah knows we're communicating. He comes. I must go.*

Jarek lay back on his bed. The impending arrival of Zakarah was grim news indeed. Stewing at its portent, he tossed and turned well into the night. Come morning, he shared Lavan's revelation with the others.

As the Jacaí had warned, the hills grew steeper; so much so that Jarek had to grasp shrubs or rocks, anything anchored, to keep from sliding. Where the previous day's climb had been filled with boisterous chatter, today's was solemn. Between the steepening ascent, thinning air, and thoughts of Zakarah's plans, hardly anyone spoke. Still, they made reasonable headway—until the cliffs became too steep to climb.

While the Jacaí scouted for an alternate route, the others rested. He could not. Every moment of delay decreased chances of saving Lavan. Despite his despair, he refused to give up.

Darkness finally forced the Jacaí's return. Dzojek looked grim. "I am sorry Máistir, but we find no other pathway."

After eating, they bedded down. Jarek's troubled mind had him tossing and turning all night, unable to blank out his worries.

Ultimately, however, his weary body succumbed, and sleep claimed him.

"Máistir Jarek, awaken!" Dzojek was shaking him. It was morning.

"What is it?"

"Look! Bultúr!"

Circling above were two raptors, each bearing a rider. These new arrivals landed their birds in an adjacent field. Rajko and Dzojek rushed to greet their fellow Jacaí, hugging and chattering with the new arrivals. The others held back, granting them privacy, even Caitlyn, who shared their language.

Jarek was waiting for Rajko and Dzojek to introduce them when all four Jacaí suddenly mounted their bultúrs and flew away.

Hagley chased after them. "Wait!"

Stunned, Jarek grabbed Caitlyn's elbow. "Have they truly forsaken us? Do the Jacaí despise your people that much?"

She watched them depart. "I would not have thought it, yet it seems so."

Everyone watched, speechless. It was no longer a question of whether they'd make the Nexus on time, but rather if they'd make it anywhere. They sat, despondent, discussing their options. With cliffs in front of them and The Haunt behind them, they came up with none. Lacking a meaningful plan, all they could do was wait and hope the Jacaí returned.

Around midday, six bultúr appeared on the horizon, wings pounding. One had two riders, each of the others one. This time, everyone rushed to the field when they landed.

Although Jarek had seen Dzojek's bird when Goodricke killed it, it was dead, lying on its side. This was his first close-up view of a living, breathing raptor. Chests heaving, loud puffs escaped their gasping mouths as they struggled to regain their breath. Long of neck, it was their huge wingspan that was most impressive. If two men were to lay head-to-head, they wouldn't span its wing. Their pointed beaks were nearly the length of a man.

"Greetings, my friends," Dzojek said. He sat behind another Jacaí on the lead bird. "I beg pardon at leaving you to wonder for so long, but my people had many decisions to make where you are concerned. As Máistreás Caitlyn knows, we Jacaí have little love of her people, but Rajko and I explained how you saved us. For that they grant you audience to plead your case to be flown to the volcano. But you are large, much more so than we Jacaí. We are unsure if the bultúr can carry such weight. We are here to see."

Goodricke, Gresham and Hagley mounted the largest three bultúr, with Caitlyn and him assigned to smaller birds. Caitlyn's rider did a test flight. Although the bird struggled to get airborne, once in the air, it seemed to bear the added weight well. One by one, the remaining birds joined it. They were finally heading for Jacaíoi.

Jarek had never considered himself cowardly, but sitting on the neck of a bird, staring down at sure death exceeded his bravery. With eyes pinched shut, he clung to a man half his size.

Angry at himself over his fear, he opened one eye. From this height, not only could he see The Haunt, its green canopy filling the valley beyond, but he could make out what had to be A'ryth off in the distance. But as astounding as the view was, he closed his eye again. He'd remember what he'd seen and peek no more. He gripped the Jacaí flyer even tighter.

Things worsened when they reached Jacaíoi. His bird swerved and dove, plummeting toward its perch. Jarek tasted bile as he clung like a frightened child to his diminutive guide's waist. Fanning its wings, the bultúr landed abruptly on a perch, nearly tossing Jarek. It folded in its wings and its rider leaped off. Jarek slid off too, wobbling on shaking legs.

Having landed, his friends babbled on about their miraculous rides, clearly having found it exciting. Not him. Even with his feet safely on the ground, he was convinced his stomach was still somewhere aloft.

Bultúr perches lined their rocky ridge. A stone's throw below was Jacaíoi. It was little more than a village. As with A'ryth, its homes had been carved from rock, but these had been forged with sweat and hammer, not A'rythian magic. Doorways had been fashioned by stuffing wooden planks into craggy openings. Stacked stones formed chimneys, and clothing hung from vines strung across crude balconies. Jarek counted no more than three score of huts. The Jacaí were few in number. Villagers stood outside their homes, staring at the new arrivals as Jarek and the others followed Dzojek down the trail to meet them.

The afternoon was spent relating their experiences to the Jacaí council, a group tantamount to the A'rythian Elders. The council's foremost concern was whether or not they'd killed the Crone. Most other questions concerned the tribulations of Rajko, Dzojek and their birds. Only after a full recounting of those adventures did they question Jarek on his encounter with Zakarah, albeit with limited interest. It was obvious that reaching the Nexus was his concern, not theirs. He was promised a morning decision as to whether or not the bultúrs would attempt the long flight to the volcano. That meant he'd not make it to the Nexus on time.

Their hosts treated them well. Evening found them well fed and rested but did little to assuage Jarek's horror at having failed in his quest. He sat cleaning tobacco from his pipe, watching the moons converge. Suddenly a brilliant rainbow of aethers burst from the moons to some distant place. Colors sparkled, then faded. He'd just witnessed the final Nexus and he wasn't there. He'd failed the person who relied on him most.

He tried to reach him. *Lavan!*

There was no response.

Lavan, we didn't make it on time, but we're still coming. Lavan!

Still no answer. Jarek buried his face in his hands, wondering if this was how Ewan felt. *Forgive me, old friend.*

Bolcán

A very excited messenger interrupted Jarek's sleep. "*Máistir* Jarek, I bear great tidings. The council has consented to fly you to the *Bolcán*."

To finally hear good news lifted Jarek's spirits.

A short time later, Dzojek escorted the travelers to the bultúr corral, informing them that neither he nor Rajko would accompany them, explaining that each rider trains his own steed, to be flown by no other. "Rajko and I will visit the nests today to select our chicks. We will not fly them until they are fully grown and seasoned."

A bultúr and flyer were assigned to each of them. The Jacaíoi had rigged the bultúrs with saddle and harness. Once all passengers were aboard, the giant birds took flight. They were on their way to the volcano.

Cool winds buffeted Jarek's face. Thankfully, he felt far more secure sitting in a harness, enough so to brave a peek below. It seemed as if he could see the entire world from up here. Despite his apprehensions, he found it exhilarating.

By mid-day they'd quit the mountains and were soaring over the sea. Reefs dotted the seascape everywhere below. No wonder the Portsmouth seamen refused to enter these waters. Seals basked atop the rocks. The sight of normal-looking creatures was comforting after the abominations of The Haunt, but it did nothing to lessen his anguish at having missed the final Nexus—Zakarah had threatened to kill Lavan if Jarek wasn't there with the desired relics.

The flight took half the day. "*Bolcán*," his flyer yelled over the wind, pointing. A large island loomed in the distance, a smoking mountain at its center.

The riders soared inland to a small lake. Landing, the thirsty bultúr drank their fill. While Goodricke checked his previous night's bearings, Jarek joined Caitlyn in refilling their water skins. "Do you think the Jacaí might fly us to the Nexus site?"

Caitlyn looked over at the riders. "I fear not. The day wears long, and bultúrs don't fly at night. The Jacaí will want to return home, but I will see."

As she headed over to discuss it, the bultúrs started flapping their wings and hopping about, cawing, clearly agitated. The riders grabbed the birds' reins, trying to calm them, but the frantic birds grew even more agitated, leaping and pulling so hard that the Jacaí were forced to jump into their saddles. When one of the distressed animals suddenly took flight, the others followed.

Prey! Entered Jarek's mind. It was mind speak! Was Zakarah near?

A huge serpent came flying low across the lake, eyeing the fleeing bultúr. It gave chase, and flying much faster, caught the trailing bird. The terrified bird let loose a pitiful wail. It was silenced with a chomp from its attacker's jaw. Its body went limp as its rider fell out of his saddle, plummeting into the sea below. The Jacaíoi now numbered one fewer. Jarek wondered which of the fliers had been lost. Was it his? By now the remaining bultúr were little more than fading specks on the horizon.

With the dead bultúr clutched in its maw, the beast descended, splashing into the lake near to shore.

"To me!" Jarek yelled, ducking behind a log. The others came running, but before they could reach him, a mind-blast overwhelmed him. His muscles froze. The others tumbled to their knees. It was a binding spell! The creature was gifted.

Hagley and Caitlyn had fallen only feet from him. Gresham lay next to them. "Join hands!" Jarek urged, resisting the binding enough to crawl to them. They linked. "Initiate *ceangailte*, Hagley!"

Feeling the now familiar surge, Hagley countered the binding. Jarek's lethargy vanished. The others were moving too—save for Goodricke who knelt in the dirt, watching the avian walk out of the lake, its long-barbed tail whipping the air behind it.

It eyed them. Supporting its weight on two powerful-looking hind legs, it spread its giant wings to either side and lowered them to the ground, balancing itself on elbowed claws attached to its wings.

It snorted, then shook its body. Muscles rippled front to back, spewing water everywhere. Intelligent eyes with vivid golden irises encased its dark oval pupils scoured the area. They made looking anywhere else impossible. The creature was as magnificent as it was terrifying.

"What sort of beast is that?" Gresham whispered.

"I believe it's a dragon, something I'd not believe existed were I not seeing it with my own eyes."

The beast rose, his gaze shifted to Goodricke. Snapping its head back and forth, it shook the bultúr's carcass. *Prey!* Then, tossing the bultúr aside, it waddled toward a trembling Goodricke.

Goodricke's dread was palpable. His eyes fluttered shut when the beast brought its enormous head close, sniffing, smelling him. It reared back, shook its head, and sneezed, spewing spittle all over Goodricke, then turned toward Jarek and the others. It blinked. The binding vanished. Even Goodricke was able to move now. Screaming, he leaped away.

"Goodricke! No!" Jarek shouted. "Remain still!"

The dragon reared, bellowed a frightful roar, then waddled back to the dead bultúr. Gripping it in its jaws, it flapped its massive wings and lifted off the ground. They ducked as it passed overhead and veered out over the lake. Driving its great wings, it sped off with its catch, back in the direction from which it had come.

"Praise the gods that it already captured a meal," Jarek said, letting out a puff of air. He turned back around, "Did the rest of you hear its mind-speak?"

Caitlyn nodded. "It called us prey."

"It felt like the thing was inside my head," Gresham added, watching the dragon fade from sight.

Hagley was on his knees, cradling his head. "It's still in mine."

"You're still hearing it?"

"No," he said, rocking back and forth, "It's just that… well, I know it's still within me!"

Jarek was learning to trust the young magus's instincts. "Tell me if you sense anything unusual."

He walked over and placed his hand on a rather pale-faced Goodricke's shoulder. "How about you… are you all right?"

Goodricke swallowed. "I believe so, milord. Although moments ago, I'd not have said the same. From the moment that thing arrived I found myself unable to move."

"It was the same of the rest of us until we countered its spell." He scratched his chin. "Interestingly it continued to think of you as prey, but not us. Perhaps it's because you're not gifted." He looked up. "At least it's gone." He tapped Goodricke's tritant. "Can this thing locate the Nexus in daylight?"

"No, but it still has last night's readings. Although not exact, they should get us fairly close." Kneeling, he checked the settings. "It's lies in the same direction that creature went. Dare we follow?"

Jarek sighed. "What choice have we? Let's hope it and the Nexus aren't too close."

Donning their gear, they worked their way around the lake. Flat sands and waist-high ocean grass blanketed their route, making for an easy skirt of the water. Once past the lake, those scattered shrubs and small trees gave way to thicker, taller foliage. By the time they reached the foothills, the dense underbrush all but stopped their progress. Lacking a means to cut through it, they backtracked, seeking an easier route. While doing so they stumbled upon a creek flowing in the right direction. The walked it. Although soaking their feet, it proved a far easier walk—until they reached the waterfall.

Their stream cascaded over and down a cliff-side, its roar echoing off the surrounding cliffs. Jarek crawled to its precipice and looked. The others joined him. The creek laced its way over a pair of rocky ledges, emptying into a huge pond perhaps forty paces below. A small creek flowed out its other side, creating a fen on the pool's far side. Although considerably larger than the pools at the first two Nexuses, its resemblance to them was uncanny, leaving little doubt that they'd found the final Nexus site.

However, laying near the water's edge beside its half-eaten bultúr, was the dragon, looking their way. A half dozen other carcasses lay nearby, most little more than picked over skeletons.

"It sees us, Uncle," Gresham whispered.

"Yet it doesn't threaten. It could have harmed us at the lake, but did not. The gods willing, it won't here either."

"Magus," Hagley interrupted, pointing. "Look! A body!"

Laying among other much larger corpses, right at the cliff's base, was what appeared to be human remains. "Gods no, please don't let it be," Jarek whispered. "I'm going down for a closer look. The rest of you stay here. If that thing comes after me, run like hell!"

He'd need to traverse both ledges to reach the bottom. He climbed over the boulder that had been shielding him, and after a few slips and scrapes, managed to reach the middle layer. Another twenty paces below was the second ledge. It was far easier to manage, and he made it the bottom without incident.

Wary, he crept toward the corpse, eyeing the dragon. Would it continue to simply watch, or was he walking to his doom? The corpse lay face down. Kneeling, he touched it. It felt cold. Whoever it was had been dead for some time. He rolled the body over, "No!" he gasped. The dead eyes staring up at him belonged to Lavan. Cradling his friend, he rocked back and forth, tears rolling down his cheeks. "Gods! I failed you my friend. All that risk I put my companions through was for naught. I didn't get here in time. Oh, to speak with you one more time and tell you how sorry I am."

Suddenly the impact of that thought struck him. How long had Lavan been dead? Did his soul yet linger? Could he still commune with his friend like he'd done with Rajko's bultúr?

Lavan! It's, Jarek. Can you hear me?

Nothing!

A shadow suddenly blocked the sun. Heart pounding, he whipped his head around, fearing he'd be face-to-face with the dragon. He wasn't. His friends had joined him. "Gods! I feared you were the beast."

Goodricke knelt beside him. "It's the headmaster!"

"Yes, we were too late."

Hagley's head snapped around, looking toward the dragon, his face pale. "What's wrong?" Jarek asked.

Hagley gave him odd look. "Aren't you seeing it?"

"Seeing what? Out with it boy, what's happening?"

Hagley looked back at the dragon. "It's sending images—of you removing a chain from the headmaster's neck and talking into it."

Of course! Lavan's orb. How had the creature known? He reached inside Lavan's shirt and pulled out his pendant. He touched his ring to it. *Lavan! It's Jarek. Can you hear me?*

Jarek? Is it really you? came a distant whisper.

Hagley's eyes widened.

Jarek saw it. "Can you hear us?"

Hagley nodded, his stunned gaze returning to the dragon.

How had the Hagley heard without an orb? Did the beast have something to do with it, or was this part of the lad's strange gift? "You're a most interesting young man, Hagley."

Jarek! Are you still there?

Lavan's plea drew him back to the task at hand. *Yes, old friend, it's me.*

Where am I? I feel empty, as if I'm floating.

Did he not realize? Jarek closed his hands around Lavan's pendant. *You're with me, my friend.*

But where?

You're dead. You're are merely an essence now; locked within your ruby. I'm holding it now.

A long pause. *Yes, I remember now—Zakarah slew me.* Another pause. *That necklace was supposed to bring good fortune. Where was its luck when I needed it most? I clearly wasted my coin.*

Despite the situation's gravity, Jarek couldn't help but chuckle. *Not so—it still holds your orb. Because of that, we're still able to speak—to say our goodbyes. For how much longer, I cannot say.*

Even though I'm dead? You really can talk with ghosts then. A long pause. *Does that mean I can only speak with you? If so, I truly am in hell—a high price for my life's misdeeds. So, I now reside in a jewel, eh? How did that come about?*

I wish I knew. There's a creature only just paces away that likely played a role in all this.

A creature?

A dragon—there's a living, breathing dragon here at the Nexus site. Its Gift astounds.

A dragon? Yet another pause. *To see that wonder would require sight—which I have no longer have.*

I should never have helped you with that foolish experiment of yours. This is my fault.

Bah! You speak as if I had no say in my life's choices? Did I merely live in your shadow? You always were one to take blame that wasn't yours. No, you cost me nothing. Had it not been for my own folly, I'd still be there in the flesh. Say no more of such things.

Do you know where Zakarah went?

A long pause. *He's with me.*

No, you're with me.

Yes, both things are true. I'm with you; and with Zakarah—at the place where he captured me.

The first Nexus?

Yes, he's there now.

How did he get there?

He opened a portal. I heard him cast the spell. He's come to steal the university's relics. He hopes they'll help him survive in that hell he brought me to.

Do you remember the spell he used to open the portal? Can you recite it?

Have you ever known me to forget a spell? Yes, I remember it, but it requires a facet neither of us owns.

I have someone here who might be capable of casting it—someone from the university.

Who?

Hagley, the young fellow hoping to be granted a third try for his robes.

If he can't even earn his robes, how can he possibly cast a spell this complex?

Because he's a Pervader—capable of casting any spell.

Really? You're sure of this?

I am. He's here with me now.

One more thing; a body of water is needed in order to open the portal.

I understand. Thank you. Here's Hagley now. Teach him the spell.

"You heard, Hagley. Learn the spell."

"Just because I'm this Pervader person doesn't mean I'm capable of opening a portal."

"You've said the same of other spells, and none has surpassed you yet. You can do this."

"Right, just talk with a dead man who lives in a piece of jewelry while learning a spell that only a half dozen wizards in the world could master—oh and cast it successfully." He sighed, shaking his head. "I'll try, Sir."

Lavan recited the spell over and over until Hagley knew it by rote.

Thank you. I'll try to devise a counter to this, Jarek offered, *to prevent Zakarah from using it again.* Placing Lavan's amulet around his neck he said, *Goodbye my friend, I'm keeping you with me. May we someday be together again on the other side.*

Do not rush that meeting. The other side's not nearly what it's made out to be. Defeat the bastard instead.

Nervous, Hagley turned to The Magus, seeking direction. Eyeing the dragon, Jarek gave him the headmaster's necklace. "Put this on. It might help communicate with the dragon."

Communicate with the dragon! Was he jesting? "Why?"

"Lavan said water is needed to open a portal. That means we need to get past that thing, and get to that pond. Now, how about you exploit this bond you seem to have with this beast and see if it'll allow us by."

"How?"

Jarek faced him. "By asking it."

He was serious? "What if it eats me?"

The Magus shrugged. "Then it'll eat the rest of us once it's done with you. I can do the asking if you prefer, but it's far more likely to kill me than you. How well off will you be if that happens?"

Hagley shuddered at the thought. Becoming a magus no longer held the appeal it once did. "All right, I'll try."

He headed toward the dragon, Jarek at his heels. The dragon's huge eye watched their approach, unblinking. Back in A'ryth, Hagley was sure nothing could frighten him more than facing Zakarah, but the dragon had just proven him wrong.

So far it had made no overt threat. The closer they got, the more imposing the beast became. He could hear the dragon's heavy breathing, and smell its putrid breath, likely from chewing on rotting bultúr flesh. Even lying down, it was several times Hagley's height—much larger than the bultúrs, both in thickness and height.

He took a deep breath, and heart pounding, edged even closer. Was this bravery or foolhardiness? He looked down at the grisly remains of the bultúr. He scrunched his face, unable to imagine eating such a thing.

Prey.

He flinched, startled by the unexpected mind-speak. "Yes, very dead prey. Was it tasty?"

"Hagley!" Jarek chastised, "I doubt it will understand human speech. Use mind-speak."

Was it tasty?

Tasty?

In man-speech, it's when we eat something that we find pleasing.

Man-speech?

The sounds we humans make in order to share our thoughts. "It's the noise I'm making now."

The dragon cocked its head, studying him.

What should we call you? What is your name?

Name?

Conversing with this creature was tedious. *When your prey see you, what's in their minds?*

One-Who-Hunts comes!

Of course, you hunt them. Hunter would be a good name for you.

Its monstrously large eye blinked. *Hunter.*

"Yes, I shall call you Hunter."

"You named it?" Jarek squawked. "Stop wasting time and get to the point."

The dragon glared at Jarek. Did it understand human speech?

"Ask 'Hunter' how Zakarah bested him. How he managed to steal Hunter's prey? Was Zakarah's magic too powerful for him?"

Snorting, it turned its attentions back to Hagley. *Eat prey; sleep. Wake. Prey gone.*

"Tell him we want to bring them back," Jarek urged.

Can?

It definitely understood him. "Yes, we'll bring back your prey," Jarek promised, having no idea how that could possibly be done. "But to follow he who took them, we need use of your pond."

The dragon's huge eye flitted from him to Hagley. Then, lying down, it closed its eye, as if suddenly having lost interest in them. Had it just granting them permission?

"Well, Hagley, may we?"

"I think so."

"Then let's do this before that thing gets hungry again. After all, there's not much left of that bultúr."

Jarek waved the others over. They came, albeit cautiously. Once past the beast, they hurried to the pond.

"Now Hagley, before your new best friend there changes his mind."

Hagley spoke the spell. The waters before them shimmered a blue green, glowing like *Llochán de Cumhacht* had done upon Zakarah's arrival. At its center was a whorl of shimmering water, reminiscent of a cyclone Hagley had once seen, albeit this one was made out of water. Within it was a hole wide and tall for a man to walk through.

Gresham let out a whoop. "You did it!"

Hagley grinned. "I did, didn't I?" He looked at Jarek, "Now what?"

"What else? We go through it," Jarek said, wading into the glimmering water. The instant he stepped into the swirling vortex, he vanished. Gresham went next. The others followed, with Hagley going last. Before he stepped into the waters, he turned to face the dragon. *Gramercy, Hunter. We go to find your prey now.*

Prey!

Hagley's next step had him spinning and whirling, flying out of control in a tunnel of nothingness. He soiled his pants.

Chaos

Quinn entered Marshal Booker's office and found him sitting at his desk, his nose buried in papers. "Sir!" he announced, saluting.

The Marshal looked up. "Yes?"

"You asked that I keep you apprised of the Inquisitor's plans."

"And…?"

"The Chevaliers show no signs of readying to leave. In fact, they practice maneuvers as we speak."

The Marshal stroked his beard, contemplating this new information. "Thank you. I know you have regular duties, but I'd consider it a personal favor if you'd continue to keep an eye on them for me. Report anything out of the ordinary directly to me."

"Yes, Sir."

"That will be all."

As Quinn turned to leave, the Marshal's aide burst through the doorway. "Apologies Sir, but you need to see this. Right away!"

Quinn followed them outside. The sergeant pointed toward the long line of people streaming into the fort, all looking disheveled. "Who are they Sergeant? Why are they here?"

"Most are from Pembok. Others come from as far as Eynshawkshire and Holyshire. They claim their villages have been besieged by devil monsters. They talk of human slaughter."

"Get Captain Dyson. Now!" The Marshal turned to Quinn. "You get the Inquisitor. Tell him we need his troops."

Quinn started to leave. "Wait!" the Marshal barked. Weren't you part of the Inquisitor's Portsmouth escort?"

"Yessir."

"Good, he knows you. Tell him that since his people are unfamiliar with our island, I've assigned you as his Cornet and guide. We might as well get an eye-witness accounting of his Clerics' skills."

Quinn delivered the message, and before long, both church and garrison cavalries were mustered in the fort's main yard. Quinn sat saddled beside Grand Inquisitor Kolton, or more accurately, 'Aren't-

I-Grand' Inquisitor Kolton. Quinn had never met a man so enthralled with his own self-grandeur, which was undoubtedly why Quinn's father so unabashedly curried his favor. He was on the Inquisitor's other flank, fawning over him. "Your Grace, are you ready to show these godless beasts what happens when they test the righteousness of the Church and the steel of the Kingdom?"

Having to deal with two such vain men tried Quinn's patience, but if he could bring down this pompous buffoon by spying on him, perhaps it would be worth it.

The Inquisitor sat taller in his saddle. "Well said, Captain Dyson. It's time the people of this island see God's wrath in action. Shall we proceed?"

His father nodded, as if acknowledging an equal. "Your Grace, Kinsmen's Highway splits into three forks at Pembok. Perhaps it would be best if we split our force there."

Deftly done father. Not only did you assert your strategic brilliance, but you prefaced it with 'perhaps,' properly deferring to one of superior rank. The pandering continued.

"Since reports say Broughton is all but deserted now, why don't I take my men to Eynshawkshire and root out the devils there, while your troops rid Holyshire of its vermin? Quinn knows the road well and will prove a most able guide." His father looked over at him. "I'm proud of you, son."

As you've told me so many times in private. Quinn tipped his head. "And I of you, father."

Looking regal, his father spun his horse about and led his guardsmen out the main gate. As soon as their dust settled, the Inquisitor's force followed, Quinn among them. He spied Marshal Booker watching from his doorway. Quinn nodded as he rode past. The Marshal smiled and went inside.

Anxious-looking peasants streamed past them on either side of the road, seeking the safety of the fort. But by the time they reached Pembok, not a soul could be seen—the town was deserted. "Which way, Cornet?" the Inquisitor demanded when they reached the three-way fork.

"The road left goes to Eynshawkshire; the right one to Holyshire. Broughton is straight ahead."

"Captain Dyson," he shouted to Quinn's father. "What say you take your troops that way," he said, pointing toward Eynshawkshire, "while I go this way, and as you so aptly stated earlier, root out these godless devils."

His father nodded, and the two cavalries parted ways.

They were almost to Holyshire when they first encountered the so-called devil monsters. Monstrous creatures, the likes of which Quinn had never seen, came charging out of the woods from either side, their beastly snarls and growls sending chills up his spine. The creatures charged, racing toward him on all fours. When they reached the horses, they rose on hind legs, mouths open, attacking with tooth and claw. One bowled into his steed, the force of its attack knocking his horse back a stride or two. Mouth open, with jagged teeth as long as a man's thumb, it lunged at Quinn's thigh, but a swift spin by his warhorse drove its heavy buttocks into the beast, tumbling it aside. A scream to one side of him told him not all riders had been so fortunate. His horse reared, kicking the devil beast's face as it tried to rise. Quinn drove his Cornet's lance into its open mouth. It let out an agonized bawl as the blade sank deep within its skull, spewing reddish gray gore in all directions.

Having dispatched it, he spun the horse around, seeking other attackers. One had sunk its fangs into the upper arm of the lancer beside him. The man's horrified scream parroted that of the beast Quinn had just killed. The devil shook its head side-to-side, like some hunting hound capturing a kill. Drawing his sword, Quinn drove it through the back of the beast's neck.

What had originally been a dozen or so attackers was quickly pared to less than half that. Lancers dispatched the rest in short order. One horse was down, kicking, screaming its terror. A merciful lance ended its agony. Two lancers leaped off their steeds and retrieved its dead rider. Several of their comrades sat slumped in their saddles, bearing wounds.

A loud ruckus drew Quinn's attention. A score more of the devils came charging out of the woods, with more following behind. Realizing he was outflanked and outnumbered; the Inquisitor ordered a retreat. The cavalry's swift horses easily outran the devil creatures, who gave chase anyway.

They'd been harried by their pursuers ever since, and periodically turned to engage them. They'd dispatch their closest pursuers, then escape before enough others arrived to overwhelm them. This fight then run strategy was all that was keeping them alive.

Holyshire had been built at the base of Holy Peak, making their escape a downhill chase. Finally, after gaining adequate separation, the Inquisitor ordered his troops to turn about and re-engage.

Quinn reined in his panting mount, readying for another stand. Sweat dripped off his forehead, stinging his eyes. He spun around, the wind whipping the flag atop his Cornet's pole. It felt odd to be wielding the Cavalier's sigil, but a Cornet's duty was to bear his troops' standard, regardless of who those troops his flag stood for.

While near to Holyshire the forest had offered intermittent concealment. Now that they'd reached the plains, they were fully exposed. The Tarangini River lay not far ahead. Fording it would slow them even more.

"Chief Clerics to the front!" the Inquisitor ordered. Several blue-robed riders trotted to the front of their line.

Quinn had been sent to spy on Cleric magic. So far, he'd seen plenty of it, for which he was grateful. Without it, they'd have been overwhelmed more than once. Initially, the Inquisitor impressed him as an able commander, but this latest maneuver had him questioning that. He prayed the man knew what he was doing.

By now the creatures were pouring down the ridge the troops just abandoned, less than a half a league behind. Inquisitor Kolton held up his hand. "Hold! Hold." Their pursuers drew ever closer; dangerously so. "Now!"

Arms held aloft, the Clerics began a chant. Quinn's horse shied as the ground beneath them rumbled. Ignoring their own frantic steeds, the Clerics concentrated on their spell. The smell of horse-lather and fear filled the air as the vibrations crescendoed into a full-fledged quake. Quinn gripped his reins as his stallion bucked and whinnied.

The hillside the devils were on collapsed. A hundred or so of them fell with it, crushed beneath an avalanche of boulders. When the dust settled, only a few remained.

The Inquisitor spun his horse around. "Ride!"

They charged at full gallop until they reached the Tarangini, where they turned to assess the enemy. Those few devils who'd survived the avalanche were giving chase. "Swordsmen to the fore!" the Inquisitor ordered, eyeing their approach.

That was Quinn's queue. Drawing his blade, he and the squad he was in charged into a score or so of charging beasts. The fact that this was Quinn's third such foray this day did little to settle his nerves. At least this time they weren't outnumbered. The good news was, that despite the beasts' ferocity, they were as dumb as livestock.

He and the rider beside him attacked the same foe, which leaped up, trying to unsaddle them. Quinn's stallion kicked, sending the devil somersaulting. It crashed in a heap. Before it could rise, Quinn drove the sharpened tip of his Cornet pole through its neck.

He spun around in time to see his less fortunate companion get knocked off his mount by another clawing, biting beast. As they tumbled to the dirt, two lancers came to the rescue. Quinn joined them. They quickly dispatched the devil, and leaping off their mounts, helped the injured man onto his horse, a bloodied arm dangling limply at his side.

The skirmish was short. A second Chevalier had been downed, as were all surviving enemy. When the sides were even, the devils were no match for the cavalry's swift horses and the rider's sharp blades. Two Chevaliers scooped up their fallen comrade, and raced to rejoin the main force.

The Inquisitor waited, sneering. No pursuers were in sight. "That should keep those heathen beasts at bay for a while. Let's ford this river and set up a hospital."

Quinn decided he'd been wrong about this man. True, he was still vain beyond comprehension, but he looked after his men. None were ever left behind, dead or wounded. Soldiers were always sent to retrieve the fallen. Whatever political intrigue existed between Church and Court was beyond Quinn's grasp. What counted was that this man was battle savvy and honorable in the field. He could follow such a man—at least until they made it back to the garrison. He wondered how his father's troops were faring. Did they face devils, too?

The wounded were laid out in the field. Healers rushed to minister them. Quinn dismounted, offering what help he could. The torn flesh of most of the injuries looked far too severe to survive. He gave them water or encouragement or prayers, whatever he thought best met their needs. When he'd done all he could, he gave way to the healers.

What followed could only be described as a miracle. Wounded man after wounded man that Quinn had been certain wouldn't live to see the morrow, were now walking about. Gashes that should scar for life, dissolved into faded red lines. Perhaps these Clerics truly did commune with their god.

"How many, Evander?" the Inquisitor asked of his surgeon.

"Seven." The man crossed his chest and touched his forehead.

"Preserve them as best you can and tie them onto their horses. We take them with us. Their bodies shall be returned to their families."

"Yes, Your Grace."

Wounded tended; they rode again. As guide, Quinn rode beside the Inquisitor. "How far, Cornet?"

"Just beyond that ridge, Sir."

They pushed their mounts, riding them hard. Quinn would need to tend to his stallion once they reached the garrison.

That plan was crushed when they cleared the ridge and saw the valley below. Countless devils filled the valley before them. Not only did they bar access to the fort, but the arts academe as well. Worse, their numbers seemed too great for even the Clerics' formidable magic. Reaching the garrison looked impossible. Quinn studied the Inquisitor, wondering at his plans.

Sojourn's End

The spinning, weightless feeling that engulfed Jarek came to a sudden, watery end. Inundated by water, he could see light above him. Seconds later he burst through its surface. Treading water, he looked around. The portal had returned them to the site of the first Nexus. A few strokes and a short crawl had him out of the water, onto wet sand. He took in his surroundings, marveling at how different the place looked in daylight. Lavan had the right of it, the place was serene.

The others soon arrived too, save for Hagley, who came bursting out of the pond seconds later, and swam to shore.

"Next time Hagley, how about placing us on dry land."

Hagley crawled out of the water and sat next to him. "I'm hoping there won't be a next time, Magus. I for one, am just glad to be free of that dragon." He looked up. "Besides, it's raining," he said, holding his hands out, letting raindrops splash his palms. "We'd have gotten wet, anyway."

Caitlyn and Goodricke were on the opposite side of the pond. She parted wet stringy hairs from Goodricke's eyes. "There you are." She looked around the tiny canyon. "So, this is the Outland, eh? It's much smaller than I expected."

Goodricke chuckled. "Welcome to your new home, Seeker."

She scanned the colorful vertical rock walls. "This place looks very much like *Llochán de Cumhacht*."

"And Hunter's pond too," Gresham added. "Perhaps the magic makes all Nexus sites appear the same? But I'm with Hagley; I'm just glad to be home."

Standing, Jarek shouldered his pack. "I'd hardly declare us home. Come, let's get moving. We're beyond Pembok, almost to Broughton. Stalwart is halfway across the island. We'd best be on our way if we're to beat Zakarah to the university."

The walls of the shaft he'd descended via Lavan's feather spell were marred with scratches, lending credence to Lavan's claim that

Zakarah had been there. It appeared Hunter's prey had struggled to climb out of here.

Their own climb was equally arduous, but all managed it without mishap. Once out, Caitlyn walked the area, examining the muddy ground. "Their tracks lead that way," she said, pointing.

Dread washed over Jarek. "Broughton's lies in that direction. We'd best hurry."

They'd hiked for perhaps an hour when Hagley suddenly proclaimed, "In our rush to leave, I forgot to close the portal!"

"There's nothing we can do about it now," Jarek said, trudging on.

It was late that afternoon when they finally crested the bluff overlooking Broughton. They stared down at the town, the rain making it difficult to see. Nestled between two hillsides, the town's buildings filled the valley below. Nearly as large as Stalwart, it was the island's second biggest town. "Let's go get ourselves some horses," he said, heading down the slope.

As they approached town, they spotted strange-looking mounds. A closer look had Jarek shuddering. Most were fly-covered mutilated remains, their stench gagging. It was all Jarek could manage not to. Most were human, but some of the carcasses were Hunter's prey. He knelt beside one. Surprisingly, like most of the nearby human bodies, it had been gnawed upon. Did these creatures eat their own?

They wandered the town in silence, searching in vain for survivors. The town's buildings looked undisturbed, including one whose sign read 'Grocery.' They went inside. It's shelves were still fully stocked, apparently having been of no interest to the prey. They wandered around grabbing food from the shelves, stuffing it into their packs.

Having replaced their depleted rations, they set off in pursuit of Zakarah. The prey's trail led down Kinsmen's Highway toward Pembok. Jarek mulled over what he'd just seen. If Zakarah's horde had done this to Broughton, did everyplace between there and Stalwart face a similar fate? As much as much as he hated to lose even part of another day, risking the open road in darkness was simply too dangerous. "Let's find someplace to sleep. We leave at first dawn."

They bedded down in a vacant schoolhouse, out of the wet, and were up at first light. Thankfully, the rain had ceased, albeit the skies remained dreary.

It was nearly mid-day when they reached Pembok. It was as deserted as Broughton, but there were no signs of carnage here. Had its inhabitants fled in time, or had the dead already been buried?

Finding nothing living or dead, they chose not to linger, and resumed their march toward Stalwart. They weren't far outside of town when they heard the tramp of galloping horses approaching from behind. A dozen or so horses, most without riders, were racing their way.

"Those are garrison soldiers," Gresham said.

Moments later, disheveled riders arrived on lathered, wheezing mounts. Jarek waited for the prancing horses to settle before greeting their leader. "Hail, Corporal."

"Hail to you." The corporal looked them over. "Are all of you alright?"

"Yes, we're unharmed." He looked at the empty mounts. "Where is the rest of your force?"

The soldier's shoulders slumped. "Dead, Sir. We three are all that remains of the Fort Stalwart Dragoon. We were overrun by devils just outside of Eynshawkshire. Captain Dyson was one of many who fell. We can only pray that the Inquisitor's forces didn't suffer a similar fate. We hasten for the fort now to warn Marshal Booker."

"May we make use of your empty mounts?"

"Of course."

They were soon galloping toward home, the cavalrymen leading the way. Mud from the lead mounts pummeled Jarek's face. The only horse he'd had ridden in recent years was Caitlyn's capall, and he was once again paying the price of neglected skills. Every time his backside went down, the saddle rose to meet it, battering his buttocks. It was going be a miserable ride home.

If Gresham's memory served him correctly, Fort Stalwart was just over the next ridge. They galloped, heads down, anxious to warn the people of Stalwart.

A shock awaited them when they cleared the ridge. Not only was the valley below filled with Hunter's prey, but a group of mounted Chevaliers was there too, not forty paces away. Worse, Quinn was among them.

Reining in his mount, the corporal trotted over to a man garbed in purple robes and saluted. "Grand Inquisitor, I'm Corporal Fisk."

Gods! As if Chevaliers weren't bad enough, their Grand Inquisitor was among them, the very person Marshal Booker had warned Gresham to steer clear of. And Quinn was at his side.

The Inquisitor returned the salute. "Thank you, Corporal. You're one of Captain Dyson's men, aren't you?"

"Yessir."

"Where is the good Captain?" He gestured toward the valley below. "As you can see, we have a rather large number of devils between us and the garrison and could benefit from his services."

"Your Grace, Captain Dyson's dead."

Quinn flinched, his face blanching. The Inquisitor, apparently aware of who Quinn was, turned to him. "My sympathies, Cornet."

The shocked Quinn said nothing at first, then muttered his thanks, his composure somewhat restored. The Inquisitor looked their way. "Who are these other people, Corporal? They're clearly not soldiers."

"No Sir, only the three of us survived. We met these people on the highway on our return. One is a member of the Royal Court."

That caught the Inquisitor's attention. He rode over for a closer look, as did Quinn, whose eyes flared when he spotted Gresham. To Quinn's credit, he said nothing as the two sat staring at one another.

Curiously, the Inquisitor seemed equally surprised. He spurred his horse forward. "Jarek Verity, how surprising to find you of all people on this vermin-infested island."

The muscles of his uncle's cheeks went taut. There was no smile in his eyes. It had never occurred to Gresham that his uncle might know the Inquisitor. From their reaction to one another, he decided old enmities must exist between the two. "It's been a long time, Rance." Jarek hadn't used an honorific, but if the Inquisitor took umbrage; he hid it well. "But as much as I look forward to sharing old times," his uncle continued, "we've more pressing concerns at hand."

The Inquisitor twisted in his saddle, looking at the horde below. "That we have—that we have. I was just asking this young man," he said, nodding toward Quinn, "how we might get past these devils and into the fort." The Inquisitor leaned closer. "Please bear with him," he said, talking softly. "He's just received some rather shocking news. He's Captain Dyson's son."

Corporal Fisk overheard. He looked sick. He turned to Quinn. "My apologies. Had I known I would have found a more delicate way to break such grave news. Please forgive me."

Quinn tipped his head. "You're forgiven, Corporal. I'm new to the garrison. You could not have known. But we have more urgent matters at hand. Fortunately, there's one in our midst who might lend us counsel." Quinn looked Gresham's way, "Smithy, how surprising to see you, I somehow had it in mind you'd left this place for good."

Gresham couldn't help but wonder whose reunion was most chilly, his with Quinn, or that of his uncle with the Inquisitor. Still, the man had just learned of his father's death. "Quinn, you have my sincerest condolences, Captain Dyson was a fine officer and a good man."

Quinn took a moment to respond. "Yes, my father was an excellent officer."

Quinn's omission said volumes. How would Gresham have taken the death of a father who had treated him so? "As for my quick return, circumstance seems to have made mockery of all our plans. What can I do to help?"

Quinn offered up a condescending smile. "I direct the Inquisitor's question to you. Since you were raised a commoner here, I'm sure you're more familiar with Fort Stalwart's grounds than me. Do you know a way to get us past these devils and into the city?"

Quinn would never change. Gresham matched his mocking smile. "Actually, I do."

Homeward Bound

Rayna walked along the beach; the same one they'd used after escaping that horrid marsh. Sully was with her, as were Brin and the guardian charged with escorting them back to the Outlands. The Elders had made good on their promise to allow Rayna to leave A'ryth any time she wanted.

She stepped into the tidewaters, watching an inrushing wave wash over her feet, thinking about Gresham. She prayed to whatever gods would listen that he was still alive—that he and the others had survived the perils of the Crone's Haunt. Her grandame was right, she needed to tell him; he deserved to know.

The wave receded, and she rushed to catch up. "Look," Brin said, pointing. "The bay. We are close." The words were hardly out of her mouth when their guardian veered off the beach, heading up the adjacent bank. "He takes us to the Seeker's Cave."

Soon they were inside the cave. The guardian grabbed a rod off a pile stacked just inside the entry. He handed it to Rayna. *"Déan teagmháil leis le do eochair."*

Although Brin and Rayna had been tutoring one other in each other's languages, whatever the guardian said exceeded her grasp. Smiling, Brin pointed to the necklace Rayna's grandmother had given her to hold her mother's key. "He asks that you touch the slata with your seeker's key."

The instant she did so, light burst forth from the slata, flooding the area almost as much light as one of Hagley's globes. She looked around. It was more tunnel than cave. Water dripped from its ceiling.

The guardian led them down the tunnel. Before long, they were sloshing through ankle-deep water. Her boots were drenched by the time they reached the tunnel's end. It was another cave, reminiscent of the one that housed the golem. Sunlight filtered through an opening on its far side. A lone canoe lay beside the opening. A pair of sleeping bunks and long rock-carved shelves lined the cavern, many holding food stores. Someone had planned well. The place seemed more wayside inn than wilderness cavern.

Having already been given a day's ration of food, she declined an offer to take more. After all, she'd be in Stalwart soon.

Brin seemed equally impressed. "Although I learned much of this place in my training, it is my first time seeing the Seeker's Cave." The guardian said something, after which Brin led Rayna to a molded figurine. She pointed at its keyhole. "When you return, fit your key into this. Doing so will announce your arrival to the Lore Masters. Within a day's time a guardian will arrive to escort you through the travelways."

The guardian bent his slata in half and it ceased to glow. Bowing, he presented it to Rayna. "*An slata seo agat.*"

Brin smiled. "He gifts it to you, Lady."

"*Go raibh maith agat,*" she said, thanking him.

The guardian grabbed the canoe as they left the cave, and dragged it down to the marsh. "Only three can fit inside," Brin offered. "I will wait here for the guardian's return."

Rayna gave her a hug. "Thank you for your help."

"It is I who should thank, Lady. I have learned much of the Outland from you. And," she offered with a proud grin, "I speak much better Common now."

Rayna smiled. "Yes, you do."

As Rayna climbed into the canoe, Brin called out, "Rayna?"

"Yes?"

"Please tell Hagley that Brin says hello."

"Of course, as soon as I see him," she said, praying that would happen.

She sat, and Sully hopped in behind her, adjusting his cutlass so he could sit. The guardian pushed off and, hugging the shoreline, started toward the bay. "Look," Sully said, pointing at a rock jetty, "that be where our boat got all wrecked."

Instead of heading into the bay toward Portsmouth, they crossed the marsh before heading into open waters. Rayna was surprised at how quickly she spotted land. The guardian's route took a fraction of the time Gresham's had, with the added bonus of landing them far from Portsmouth. Rayna had no desire to see that horrid place again any time soon.

After beaching their craft, the guardian showed Rayna a cave where another canoe was stowed, then returned to his boat. "*Go dté tú slán,*" she said, waving goodbye.

"You be talking just like them, Lady," Sully said. He looked around. "Which way do we go?"

It felt strange to be the one being depended upon. She decided she liked it. "We need to find the Kinsman Highway," she said, starting up a nearby path, "Once we do, I'll know the way home."

It didn't take long to find the highway, and they were soon on the way to Stalwart. Any time she'd travelled this road in the past, it held other travelers. She'd hoped one might offer them a ride. But after travelling a considerable distance, she failed to see a single wagon.

Things got worse when the skies opened up, soaking them, making their walk insufferable. She chastised herself for not having brought a change of clothes. After half a day without seeing a single sole traveling in either direction, she felt a growing sense of unease. Something was amiss. Too tired and hungry to dwell on it, she pushed onward. If she had to walk in this wet all night to reach Stalwart, so be it.

Dusk was approaching when they heard strange grunts. What would make such sounds? They were coming from the adjacent woods. Sully looked nervous. "That be sounding odd, Lady. Think it be a marsh beastie?"

She shook her head. "Not this far from the water. Likely it's someone camping," she said, trying to sound reassuring. She forced a smile, her eyes never leaving the forest, the turmoil she felt inside, belying her confident words. "Who knows, maybe they have hot victuals they're willing to share." They'd eaten sparingly so far, and knowing Sully's ravenous appetite, she'd eaten little, saving most for him. She chastised herself for not having accepted the offer of more food. Gresham had taught her better.

Sully's face lit up. "Food? Beauteous!" Brightened by the prospect of eating, Sully scrambled up the bank at the side of the road and disappeared into the brush.

"Sully! Wait!"

Lacking the boy's vitality, her climb took far longer. She'd no sooner picked up his trail when his head popped out from behind a bush. His face was ashen, and he looked ready to cry. "Sh-h," he said, putting a shaking finger to his mouth. "Don't be making no noise."

She laid a hand on his shoulder. "What's the matter, you look as if you've seen a ghost."

He brushed her hand away. "Not ghosts, bogarts!"

"Bogarts? Here?" Resting hands on her hips, she eyed him. "You're just trying to scare me, aren't you, you little scamp?"

He shook his head. "No. Look over there!" he whispered, pointing. His face was pale and his lips quivering; this wasn't an act.

"You wait here while I have a look."

She crept toward where Sully claimed to have seen them, watching the ground the whole time, carefully avoiding twigs or dry leaves that might announce her presence.

She heard grunts coming from some bushes just ahead or her. Oddly, they had the rhythm of language. She froze. Her curiosity was piqued even more when she heard laughter. What in the gods' names were these things? Dropping to her knees, she crept closer, and ever so slowly parted the branches barring her view.

A sandy, treeless space lay in front of her. At its center were three pig-like creatures gnawing on a deer carcass. Powerful looking, they were half again the size of a man. They gibbered in some strange tongue as they tore at their meat with huge pointed fangs.

Fearing she'd be spotted, she eased shut the branches and crept back to Sully, moving as quickly as stealth allowed. "Let's get out of here!" she whispered.

They rushed back to the road and raced until weariness made further running impossible. Exhausted, they ducked under some bushes, out of the rain, resting as they caught their breath. They'd hardly done so when Rayna heard more of that frightening gibberish coming from the road. Placing her hand over Sully's mouth, she pulled him close. They watched as a half dozen more of the beasts wandered past, heading toward Portsmouth. Had Sully and she not stopped when they did, they'd have run right into their midst.

As soon as the creatures were out of ear shot, she led Sully deeper into the woods, getting as far from the highway as possible.

Eventually they stumbled upon a well-camouflaged gulley with an overhanging cliff. It was growing dark and they needed rest. This looked as safe and dry as anything she'd seen. They hunkered down, clinging to one another for warmth. It was well into the night before sleep finally claimed her.

Raindrops spattering a nearby rock woke her. It took a moment to remember where she was, and why. She bolted upright. "Sully, wake up!"

He sat up, looking around. "Do more beasties be coming?"

"No, but it's morning," she said. "We'd best get someplace safe before they do find us." Disoriented, she had no idea where they were. "Where are we? With all that running in the dark, I'm lost."

The rain continued to pummel them as they renewed their trek. As disagreeable as the wetness was, it did mask their noise and blur their tracks.

Eventually they stumbled upon a creek bed. By then the rain had relented, but enough had fallen that a rivulet had formed. "I think I know where we be." Sully said. "This be the creek bed what leads to Hagley's practice place."

"Are you sure? It doesn't look familiar."

He nodded.

"Good. I can't think of a better place to be with these creatures around than keeping company with powerful sorcerers."

Thus far the morning had passed free of beastly encounters. Taking the backwoods had been an excellent idea. Still, climbing over its slippery boulders was exhausting. They stopped to rest and consumed what remained of their provisions. Done, they resumed their trek.

The trickling water and ever-steepening canyon slowed their progress. Sully claimed they'd be able to see the university from the bluff up ahead. She decided they'd stop there for another rest—providing, of course, her aching legs didn't give out on her first.

"Come on," Sully encouraged, "we almost be there. I been here lots of times."

Unsure of how much more climbing she could endure, she prayed the boy was right. A huge rock blocked her path. "Here, Lady," Sully said, reaching out his hand. "Only one more rock and we be there."

He hoisted her up and onto it. She sprawled to her back as Sully crawled to the bluff. One quick glance and he snapped his head around, wide-eyed. "Come see!"

His anxious look frightened her. Mustering her strength, she crept over and peered down the slope. She gasped, her heart thumping. Beasts like they'd encountered the night before filled the valley below, blocking the university's entrance. "Gods! What now? How will we ever get inside?"

"By using Hagley's secret way," Sully said.

"You sure this is how to reach it?"

"Yep, this be Hagley's gulley all right."

"Then take us there."

They hadn't gone far when they heard something else walking the canyon behind them. "Hide," she warned, tugging Sully into a small crevice between two boulders. They clung to one another, shaking, listening, afraid to even breathe. The sounds grew louder. Not knowing what headed their way became too much to bear. She dared a peek.

It was a doe and two fawns. Exhaling, she stood. "It's just some deer."

Hearing her, the animals bolted, disappearing in the foliage. Had she just driven the poor things into the grasp of those hideous monsters? She sighed. If so, there was little she could do about it. Heart still thudding, she did her best to calm herself.

Sully was staring at her. "Don't be afraid, Lady, your protector be with you," he said, drawing his cutlass.

She hugged him, laughing. "I know you are. Thank you."

They hadn't slipped much deeper into the small canyon, when Sully pointed. "There, that be it!" She chased after him as he hustled ahead, stopping next to a wall of ivy. "It be behind this."

Rayna pushed the leaves aside. Sure enough, hidden behind the plant was Hagley's gate. She pushed the foliage aside and tugged, hoping to lift it enough to roll under it the way Gresham and she had done it earlier, but it wouldn't budge. "I need your help." But even with Sully's aid, it wouldn't move. She sat back on her haunches. "It's no use. It's too heavy."

"Wait! I seen Hagley use something to open it." He foraged through some nearby ivy, and pulled out a broken portcullis bar. "He used this!"

She wedged one end under the gate, the other over a boulder, and pried. The gate lifted briefly, then fell back in place. "It's heavy, I need your help." Even with Sully's help they fared no better. "It's no use; we're not strong enough."

She thought she heard something. Was it more wildlife; monsters; or her imagination? She scanned the area. Although she saw nothing, she knew they were making an awful lot of noise. The longer they remained here, the more likely it was they'd be discovered.

"I be having an idea!" Sully scrambled up a boulder. "Why don't I jump down on the bar. Maybe that will help lift it. If it comes up, slide a rock under it so it don't be closing again."

Could it work? She grabbed a foot-tall rock and knelt beside the gate. Sully leaped, landing on the bar like some caravan carnival flier. The gate lifted briefly, then fell again. It all happened too quickly to do any good.

She grabbed a second rock, pressed both against the gate, and leaned back, bracing her feet against the two stones. "Try it again."

"All right." He scaled the rock. "Ready?" He jumped.

The gate lifted. This time Rayna was ready. She shoved her feet forward, pushing both rocks under the gate, blocking it open.

Sully clapped. "It worked!"

The opening was small, but Sully had no problem crawling under it. But even after digging dirt away, Rayna barely fit—her clothing kept catching on the gate's jagged tips. By twisting sideways, she was finally able to scoot underneath.

They were inside the arts university.

She lay there panting, staring out the gate. "Anything coming down that gully will see the gate's open." She looked at him. "Since you crawl under it so easily, why don't you go out and cover the opening with brush? Stack boulders in front of it too."

"Don't need to," he said, moving to the wall. A chain pulley hung from the ceiling. "I seen Hagley use this."

He reefed on it, and the gate rose, the rusty metal screaking so loudly, Rayna was sure the whole countryside could hear it. She pushed the rocks out of the way. "Let it down!"

With the gate closed, only specks of light filtered through the ivy. How would they see to find their way? Then she remembered the slata the guardian had given her. She touched her key to it, and blue light burst forth, lighting the tunnel. She brushed the mud and grime off her hands and stood. "Now all we have to do is find our way out of this tunnel."

Passage

Gresham led the combined parties down a small ravine to his old childhood cave. They dismounted and walked their mounts inside. With a roof several cubits high, it was both tall and wide enough to house the lot of them, horses included.

The cave looked exactly as he remembered, right down to the torches stacked by its entrance and his old pitch barrel. He grabbed a torch and shoved it into the pitch barrel, rotated it in circles, soaking it with pitch, then lit it with his flint. A light globe would have been more effective, but with so many Chevaliers present, using the arts was out of the question. "With this many of us, we'll need more torches."

The corporal and two of the Inquisitor's men undertook the task of finding more wood.

Gresham pointed to a small opening at the back of the cave. "That tunnel leads under the hillside. Its outlet is near the fortress. When I was a boy, I climbed a tree just outside the city wall and used this tunnel to sneak away unseen. One needs simply to take this passageway to its other side cover perhaps thirty paces of open space to gain the tree, climb it, and leap from its limb to the wall. There's a stairway nearby the sentries use.

"Traversing the tunnel involves a lot of squeezing through small openings, so there's no way we can bring the horses." Quinn was standing beside his stallion. "Sorry Quinn, he's a beautiful animal. Maybe if we leave the horses here in the cave, they won't be found. There's water and grazing just outside the cave."

Quinn rubbed the animal's nose. "What say you? Think you can survive out there?" He looked around the cave. "Do we have another choice, or is this our plan?"

Gresham knew the decision wasn't his to make. "Uncle; Your Grace; what say you?"

Inquisitor Kolton answered first. "I doubt horses will be of much use inside a garrison. If the One God wills it, they'll survive."

"I'll stay here with the horses," Jarek said. "With my bad knees, I doubt I could climb a tree."

Gresham thought back on his uncle's confession about fearing tight places, doubting a sore knee was the true cause of his uncle's reticence.

Goodricke placed an arm on Jarek's shoulder. "I'm tall enough to help you up that tree, milord."

"I'll help too, Sir," Hagley chimed in.

Gresham bit his cheeks. Sorry Uncle, your ploy has failed.

Caitlyn strolled over to Quinn's stallion, looking concerned. Stroking his nose, she whispered something. Its ears perked up. She then wandered from horse to horse, repeating her ritual with each animal. Each responded similarly. Everyone, the Grand Inquisitor included, watched her strange antics. "The capall understand." she announced, once she was done. "They will stay wary."

The Inquisitor squinted. "What are you saying, young lady?"

Jarek stepped between Caitlyn and the Inquisitor. "Capall is the name for horses in her language. She's very sensitive to animals and wishes them well is all."

Caitlyn started to say something, but Goodricke interrupted. "Caitlyn, could you please check my horse, he may have taken a stone."

She looked confused. "Certainly."

As the men began unloading tack and gear from the horses, Goodricke whispered something to Caitlyn. Gresham hoped the big man was cautioning her of the Church's suspicious attitude toward others' use of the Gift.

His gaze wandered to Quinn, wondering why the man hadn't had him arrested, or at least confronted him. Had Captain Dyson not passed on word of his having turned berserker? He and Quinn had much to discuss, but now wasn't the time.

When all were ready, Gresham raised his torch. "This way, lady and gentlemen."

The hike was shorter than he remembered, and in a short time he spotted light streaming through an opening. "That's our egress. It's only a few paces from there to the tree, but I suggest we wait until dark before risking open ground."

That left time to kill before nighttime. The men paired off in twos and threes and found nooks in which to wait. Quinn was sitting by himself. Gresham joined him. "We should talk."

Quinn stared at him, as usual, his emotions impossible to read. "Not now, Smithy." He stood and walked away, leaving Gresham to wonder what had or had not been told, and to whom.

Later, after nightfall, Gresham crept back to the opening. It was little more than a hole in the ground. It was a snug fit as a kid; it would be an even tighter scrape for grown men. Pushing aside the dirt, he poked his head out, forced his shoulders through, and boosted himself to the surface. The small boulders shielding the hole were as he remembered them. A hole in the clouds was letting through enough moonlight to see the tree. Thankfully he saw no activity. Apparently, the prey were content to guard the gatehouse. He slipped back inside.

"There's enough moonlight right now to see the way, and the area looks clear. We should go now before the clouds move back in. Since Quinn and I are most familiar with the grounds, we should lead the way. I know which tree to climb, so I'll go first. Quinn can mark where I go and guide the rest of you to me. Goodricke, why don't you and the Magus come next. Just bring him to the tree. Between the two of us, we can get him onto the wall. Anyone else needing help should go early, too. I'll stay by the tree until everyone's safely inside. Any questions or disagreements?"

When the Inquisitor didn't challenge the plan, everyone else agreed. Gresham slipped out the hole. Quinn followed. "That oak behind the infirmary is the one I used. Send them there."

Quinn scoured the area. "Got it."

"One more thing," Gresham added.

"What?"

"You'll be last to cross; be careful."

Quinn looked away. "Worry about your own job, Smithy. I'll attend to mine."

Keeping low, Gresham scurried to the oak. Even in darkness, it looked an easy climb. He waited. After a bit he heard loud whispers. "I think he said it's this one, milord."

It was Goodricke. "Yes, over here," Gresham urged. Two shadowed forms emerged from the darkness. "I think it'll be an easy climb, Sir. Would you like one of us to go up first?"

Jarek assessed the ascent. "I think I can get up by myself, it's the hop to the wall that concerns me."

Gresham pointed at Goodricke. "You go first then."

Goodricke hoisted himself up a few limbs before offering a hand to Jarek. By the time they were halfway up the tree, Caitlyn arrived. Seeing the two men above, she scampered up to help.

One by one the others arrived, starting with Hagley. All was going well. Almost everyone had crossed over when Gresham heard shouts from inside the walls, followed by flashing lights and the sounds of men running. The garrison guards must have heard noise and thought it an enemy incursion. Goodricke's angry cry silenced them. "Douse those lanterns, you fools!"

The lights went out, but the damage was done; Gresham heard growls off in the distance, drawing closer; and quickly. "Hurry!" he yelled. "Send the rest now. You too, Quinn."

The stragglers made no effort at stealth, but their pounding feet weren't the only ones Gresham heard; untold numbers of prey were heading their way. He drew his blade.

He heard Quinn's yell. "That big oak." Moments later Quinn and four churchmen arrived, the Inquisitor among them.

The Inquisitor pointed up the tree. "Climb!"

The three troopers managed to scramble from sight before the brutes arrived, but there wasn't time for the Inquisitor, Quinn, and him to make it to safety.

A half dozen snarling beasts burst into view, closing fast. "Stand back, gentlemen, these are mine," the Inquisitor commanded. "Watch how a righteous god deals with devils and heathens."

He jerked a necklace from within his robes. It held a scepter. He began a chant. Gripping the scepter, he extended his hand toward the oncoming creatures. "*Caecitas*!" The charging beasts tumbled to the ground, flopping about. "You are blind to God's Way and all else," he decried. "Be judged!" He lifted the scepter high. "*Mortuus*!" His second injunction dispatched the beasts. He stared wild-eyed at their twitching bodies, his feral grin making Gresham shudder.

Finally, the Inquisitor pried his eyes from his victims. "Get up that tree before more arrive. I go last."

All three were soon atop a crowded wall. A dozen or so archers were there, firing volley after volley at arriving prey. Gresham headed down to where a garrison Lieutenant stood bellowing orders. "When you're done killing those bastards," he said, "fire that tree. I want nothing else breaching these walls."

Orders given; the Lieutenant gave the new arrivals a quick appraisal. His eyes widened when he realized the Grand Inquisitor was among them. "Your Grace," he said, bowing. "Welcome back." Then, without waiting for a response, he barked an order to Corporal Fisk. "Corporal, take these citizens to Marshal Booker's office, now!"

Command given, his attentions returned to his men on the wall.

The Horde

Kagen walked the university's battlements, peeking through the staggered merlons at the horde beyond. Perhaps a thousand paces beyond the wall, they were so numerous they filled the field. He had to squint to see through the driving rain. Sopped, he was delighted when he spotted Vardon stationed atop the next wall section.

A scowling Vardon caught sight of him, too. "What are you doing up here? It's too dangerous."

Kagen joined the Battle Mage and rested against the nearby turret. "And what am I to do, hide inside and let these children protect me?"

"Better that than expose yourself to these monstrosities. Besides, up here an old man is more liability than asset."

Kagen shook his finger. "Don't dismiss me yet, I still have worth." He scoured the walls. "I'm at least as useful as these striplings you have with you now. How many people have we inside our walls?"

"Thirty-one students and another score of hired hands."

Kagen eyed a nervous-looking youngster manning the position beyond Vardon's. "How many are old enough to fight?" He sighed, "As if any of them are."

"We chose age fifteen as the cutoff for defenders. The younger ones are sequestered inside the building—where you should be."

Kagen did the math. "So, it's thirty-odd defenders against their masses." He looked out at the beasts again. They kept their distance, rarely coming within a hundred paces of the walls. "What are they waiting for? Why don't they attack?"

Vardon shook his head. "Who knows? They're unarmed; maybe they await weapons." He sighed. "As if they need them. I've seen one up close; their claws could shred a man, say nothing of their bite. More likely they await orders from their leader."

"And who would that be?"

Vardon pointed across the field. "See how the rain fails to penetrate that one spot?"

Kagen shielded his eyes. "Yes, most unnatural; likely a protective shield. I'd lay odds we have a sorcerer in our midst."

"Precisely what Genevieve and I surmised. From this distance it looks very man-like, and the beasts defer to it."

Hundreds of monsters led by a wizard; not good. "So, what's your thinking; what will you do if they attack?"

Vardon leered. "My plan is to give them all they can handle. Twelve of my battle protégés man the walls. I've coached them on every spell I know, including some from Gresham's book."

Vardon's head jerked up. "Look! Our mage just came out from under his shield."

They watched a robed creature segregate his horde into small groups. Vardon shook his head. "This doesn't bode well. I recognize an attack when I see it. I fear we're about to find out what they're up to." His shouted warning was relayed around the wall.

A runner arrived. "Master Kagen, Mistress Genevieve demands your presence."

His eyebrows rose. "Demands? In that case, I'd best see what she wants. Defend us well Vardon, while I devise a mitigation strategy. If these things clear our walls, I plan to do all I can to protect these children."

The Sally

Inquisitor Kolton had been wrong, Gresham mused. They did have need for horses inside the garrison. In fact, they had far too few of them. Bedecked in light armor, he sat astride a warhorse. Quinn was beside him. They were part of a makeshift cavalry comprised of church troopers, garrison soldiers and townsmen. Limited by available mounts, they numbered fewer than forty. Positive the horde was preparing an attack, Marshal Booker had decided to strike first.

The horses were gathered just behind the gatehouse. Gresham looked atop the nearest wall, to where his friends stood watching. With no Clerics near them, they planned to form a circle and aid the riders by whatever means possible.

Chains jangled as the gate began to lift. His gut twisted. Although Gresham had faced wharf pirates and Crone minions, this was his first formal combat. The man beside him looked pale, his eyes haunted. Others were praying. Wild-eyed horses pranced about, spooked by the scent of Hunter's prey, their riders struggling to control them. The stench of horse stool and human vomit permeated the air. Going into battle held none of the glamour of Gresham's boyhood fantasies. He'd trained all his adult life for this moment, but that didn't make it any less horrifying. The gate clanked against its stopper. Out he rode, heart thudding.

Corporal Fisk rode point. Zakarah had organized the prey into small squadrons. Fisk's wedge charged the nearest one. The large warhorses bowled over the first prey, and trailing swordsmen cut them down. Those who ran were slain from behind. None escaped. The same was true of the next group they attacked; and the next. Despite being outnumbered, the cavalry was winning the day.

Gresham made a point to keep one eye on Zakarah. A prudent move, for the demon was casting. A lethargy overcame him, akin to what he'd felt when the Crone assailed them in her Haunt. His horse slowed, going from a gallop to a trot, and finally to a complete halt.

Apparently fearing the war horses more than soldiers' blades, the prey stopped running. At first, they kept their distance, but spurred by the cries of more distant beasts, they turned and charged the immobilized horsemen.

A stationary cavalryman was too easy a target for the tooth and claw of the prey. Knowing he was the only one equipped to disrupt Zakarah's spell, Gresham began his own incantation. A phantasmal hand appeared just above the demon's head, but without the aid of a circle, Gresham wasn't skilled enough to control it. Try as he may, all he managed was to force Zakarah to keep his eye on it—until he felt the familiar surge of *ceangailte*. Somehow the circle had reached him—giving him total control of his phantasm. His hand lunged at Zakarah. Although he missed, it disrupted Zakarah's concentration, forcing him to drop his spell. The horses were moving again.

He was so focused on his spell, he failed to see a fast-closing prey. "Gods man! Defend yourself!" Quinn screamed from the mount beside him.

His warhorse spun about, trying to avoid the attack. It shrieked as the beast's claws raked the poor animal's flank, as did Gresham when the prey's jaws clamped down on his exposed leg. Searing pain wracked his thigh as the creatures teeth found flesh. His mount bucked, tossing the beast over the horse's rump. It landed behind him. He spun around, weapon extended, only to find blooded steel protruding from its mouth.

"It's about time Smithy," Quinn yelled, plucking his weapon from the back of the monster's head before galloping away.

Although the horses could now move, so could Zakarah. Another spell was imminent. The corporal must have concluded as much. "Fall back!"

He led them in a wide swath, racing through the ranks of the prey, taking out two more squads before making a mad dash for the gatehouse. Heads down, the cavalrymen ducked under the lowering portcullis, into the safety of the city's walls. Archers made quick work of their pursuers as the gate clanked shut behind them.

"Form up and count off!" the corporal ordered.

All men were accounted for, but he and two others would need healers, as did five horses.

Gresham checked his thigh. Although it hurt like all hells, his wound didn't appear too serious. Quinn reined up beside him. "How bad is it?"

"It's only a puncture," he said, "thanks to you."

Quinn shook his head. "I'd never have guessed you'd be the type to freeze up in a battle, Smithy. You disappoint me. Do that next time and I might not be there to save your sorry hide. Now get that wound attended to." Hissing, he spun his horse about and trotted off.

"Nice chatting with you, Quinn," Gresham mumbled, turning toward the hospital area. "Did I mention I was busy saving your hide?"

Although their skirmish had done little to turn the tide of events, any victory would lift the defenders' spirits. After getting his leg tended to, Gresham searched the bulwarks for his friends—their circle had saved him, and he needed to thank them. Handing his mount to a stable boy, he sought them out.

Jarek stood in the Marshal's office. Kolton and Corporal Fisk were beside him, as was a blue-clad Cleric. The Marshal looked ill at ease. "Our sally into their ranks apparently took some heart out of them, for they've offered no threat since."

He paused, composing himself. "Inquisitor Kolton asked that I convene this meeting to discuss events." He gave Jarek an odd look before turning to Fisk. "Corporal, we'll start with you. What happened out there? All was going well when you suddenly stopped your charge."

"I didn't stop it, Sir; our animals simply quit on us, all at the same time. I could barely move my arms."

The corporal's account drew a wry smile from the Inquisitor. "That's because that heathen wizard unleashed a trick from up his ugly sleeve, but one of our men foiled it."

The Marshal nodded. "An interesting assertion, Your Grace; would you care to embellish?"

"Did you not see the giant hand?" the Inquisitor asked, matter-of-factly. The remark had Jarek's attention. What was Rance up to?

The Marshal stared at the churchman. "Hand?"

"It appeared out of nowhere, disrupting the heathen's spell. Someone used the Gift to foil the wizard's treachery." He glanced over at Jarek. "And, although this action originated on the battlefield, it was abetted by others." He turned to the Chevalier beside him. "Tell them what you saw."

The man tipped his head. "Sir, during the battle, one of the riders failed to draw his sword during the entire period the horses were stilled. His demeanor was similar to that of our Clerics when they cast spells. There's no doubt in my mind it was this man who initiated that hand."

Damn! They knew about Gresham, and perhaps even the circle.

The Marshal spread his arms. "So... who is this heroic Cleric?"

Kolton shook his head. "Not a Cleric—a soldier. His name is Gresham, the very one who led our troops back inside your fortress. He clearly engaged in sorcery." He looked at Jarek. "Upon his return, he immediately sought out Magus Verity and his party. Trust that we'll keep our eyes on this Gresham fellow."

The Marshal's glance flitted briefly Jarek's way before returning to the Inquisitor. "Your Grace, wouldn't it be more appropriate to thank the man rather than chastise him? After all, he likely saved both your troops and mine."

Kolton shrugged. "Perhaps; but it's my duty to assure His Gift is not abused, no matter how high-minded one might think the cause. As far as I'm concerned, Magus Verity's entire group is suspect." He glared at Jarek. "Grave circumstance will not deter us from doing our ordained duty."

Haven

Kagen found Mistress Genevieve waiting for him by the door. "What is it?" he asked.

She frowned. "We have visitors."

"Visitors? That's impossible, the gate is down and bolted."

"So I would have believed. Come see for yourself," she said, starting down a corridor. She led him to the refectory where Lady Rayna and a young lad sat waiting, soaking wet and covered in mud.

The boy jumped to his feet as they entered the room. "Hey mister, you be surrounded by monsters. They be everywhere outside."

As he placed a hand on the lad's shoulder, he acknowledged Rayna with a nod. "Thank you for that warning, young man. And who are you?"

"Sully, Sir. I be Hagley's good luck friend. I make his magic work."

An odd boast. It did explain why the boy looked familiar, however. He'd seen him riding Hagley's wagon. Kagen shifted his attention to Rayna, who looked understandably distraught. "Lady, as pleased as I am to see you again, I must confess, your appearance here dismays me. How in the gods' names did you get inside our university?"

Their story was long and fascinating. The good news was, through it, he learned Hagley and Gresham were with Magus Verity, alleviating his fears they'd met some ill fate in Portsmouth. Conversely, the Magus had failed to rescue Lavan, and had undertaken what sounded like a foolish venture to still try to recover him, aided only by Goodricke and two untrained acolytes.

Most alarming, however, was that these two had breached the university's defenses. If they could, so might those beasts. "Show me how you got inside."

Mind Speak

Sully led them down the corridor that led to Hagley's secret door. "It's here," he said, kneeling by the wall. He pushed aside the doorway's cinder block. "There be a stairway behind this hole what leads to lots of tunnels. One goes to Hagley's practice place. That's where we got in."

Genevieve stood watching, arms across her chest. "Show us."

Sully was about to climb through the opening when he sat upright. "Hagley?" Everyone stared at him. "Yes. I be hearing you. Where be you?"

Kagen knelt beside him. "What's happening?"

The boy seemed not to have heard him. "Yes, I hear you. Can you be hearing me?"

Kagen frowned. "Do you hear anything, Genevieve?"

"No," she said, her eyes glued to the boy.

Sully looked up at Kagen. "Don't you be hearing him?"

Genevieve frowned. "No. Tell us."

"Hagley be asking if I be hearing him. He keeps asking it over and over." Covering his ears, he gave them an odd look. "He ain't using real words though—he be speaking inside my head."

◈

Jarek stared at him. "Any response Hagley?"

"No Sir. Well, maybe." How could he explain it? "I received no answer, but I felt… as if I were… connected, kind of like what I felt with Hunter."

Jarek scratched his chin. "Perhaps Kagen heard you but doesn't know how to respond." He fell silent, deep in thought. "Let's assume they hear us but can't answer. Try it again, only this time, let Kagen know what Zakarah's after."

◈

Kagen gazed into Sully's eyes, half expecting to find them somehow altered, but he saw nothing but a perplexed youngster staring back at him. "You say you're Hagley's good luck person?" When Sully nodded, he turned to Genevieve. "Could it be that he and Hagley share some bond?" He looked back at the boy. "Do you still hear him?"

"No Sir, he ain't doing it no more."

Genevieve rubbed her chin. "We need to understand what's happening. I think we should test him," she urged.

Kagen agreed. "Sully, are you willing to let us see if you have magic inside you?"

Sully's eyes went wide. "Sure!"

With their intruders in tow, Kagen led them to the testing room. He took the boy's hand. "I want you to touch this jewel. If you have magic in you, you'll see lots of colored lights."

He placed Sully's hand on the prism. Instead of the anticipated myriad of colors, the room shone totally blue. "Does it being only blue mean I don't be having magic?"

Kagen placed a hand on Sully's shoulder. "No, it means yours is so special that we don't even understand it." His comment evoked a grin.

He looked over at Genevieve. "I've never seen this happen, have you?" he asked, giving Genevieve a curious stare.

"No, it's most unusual," she answered, looking equally perplexed. "Perhaps the single color suggests a limited gift?"

"An interesting speculation," Kagen agreed, scratching his chin. "I wonder…" he looked at Rayna, "could the boy's gift rely on another, perhaps a conduit? Lady Rayna," he said, waving her over, "would you mind if we test you, too?"

She stepped up, looking wary. "What is it you want me to do?"

"Exactly what Sully did."

She placed her hand on the prism but jerked it back as a full spectrum of light filled the room. "As I suspected. You, my dear, are gifted."

He was toying with his beard, trying to fathom their situation, when Sully gasped. "Hagley be talking in my head again."

"Is he saying the same thing?"

Sully shook his head. "No, he be naming the one who brought the beasties, saying he's here to steal your wrecks."

"Wrecks? Do you mean relics?"

Sully nodded. "Maybe that's what he be saying."

"Did he say who brought the beasties?"

"Zakra, or something like that."

"Zakarah?"

Sully's head bobbed. "Yeah, that be it."

Kagen turned to Genevieve. "Gods! That's that sorcerer who spirited away the headmaster." He squeezed Sully's shoulder. "Can you answer him?"

Sully shook his head. "I only be having my special kind of magic that hears."

"Try it anyway."

Sully held his hands over his ears. "Hagley? This be Sully; here at your magic school. Do you hear me?" He paused a bit, before looking up. "Hagley just keeps saying that same thing, over and over like before."

"Try talking to him again, but don't say your words aloud, speak them inside your head like Hagley's doing."

Sully looked stricken. "I don't know how."

"I guess we'll have to help you then," Kagen said, his gaze drifting to Rayna. "My dear, would you be kind enough to place your hands atop Sully's? If you're truly his conduit, he'll need your help." She laid her hand on Sully's. "Now try again, Sully, in whatever manner you feel is best."

"Hagley, I be hearing you. I be here at your magic school with Rayna. I told Master Kagen what you said about the bad man bein' after the wrecked stuff."

<hr />

Hagley was jubilant, shouting. "Sully just answered me! He's at the university with Rayna."

319

Kagen left Rayna and Sully in Genevieve's care. When Sully had shown them Hagley's secret entrance, he'd spotted several other offshoot tunnels. He wasn't sure whether to be elated or distraught. On one hand, each tunnel represented a potential means to gain access to the school, but each was also a potential means of escaping the school.

There seemed no end to the tunnels. He spent the morning searching for other outlets but found none. The day was getting on and he was feeling weary. While sitting, resting, a rat poked its head from some debris stacked beside him. Its escape hole looked too large to be rodent made. Kneeling, he peeled away the rocks, enlarging the hole. Behind it was another passage.

Strengthening his light globe, he widened the opening and crawled inside. Judging from the amount of dust and cobwebs, it hadn't been used in decades. Realizing it had sufficient space to stand in, he walked—and walked and walked. The tunnel seemed endless. Despite his weariness he explored on, determined to discover where it led. He gave up only after he'd gone far enough to realize that, regardless of where it led, it was a means to escape the school unseen. He had his mitigation plan.

By the time he made it back to his starting point, he was spent. It was all he could do to muster the strength to make it to the refectory where Genevieve and the others were huddled. "Everyone listen!" he extolled after catching his breath. "You're to follow me. We're leaving."

Chaos erupted, but the Mistress quickly restored order. Kagen led them to Sully's hidden doorway and pushed aside the cinder block. "Anyone capable of casting light please do so now." Light flooded the corridor. "Excellent. Now, everyone through this hole."

He led them down the stairway and into the tunnels. Pain wracked his chest, every breath seeming more difficult than the last. It seemed to take forever, but they finally reached his newly discovered tunnel. He paused, gathering enough breath to speak. His pains were worsening. "Who among you is fourteen?" Six students raised their hands. He nodded. "Remain with me a bit, the rest of you crawl through this hole. Quickly now, we haven't time to waste."

He pulled Genevieve aside as the children streamed through the opening. "This tunnel can take you out of here, exactly where, I'm not sure, but anywhere is safer that the university right now. Lead them as far as the tunnel allows. I'll get Vardon and the others and follow."

Genevieve nodded. "All right students, you heard Master Kagen, let's go. Let the youngest go first."

Kagen waited until all were out of sight. "The rest of you with me. We're going to the relic vault. Grab all you can carry. We'll take as many of them with us as we can."

They hurried to the relic room. Kagen lagging behind them, gasping for breath, struggling to keep up. One arm had gone numb. *Don't die now old man, you're needed.*

He dispelled the threshold and stepped inside, directing each student what to take. Hundreds of years of knowledge and they could only rescue a small portion. Worse, neither he nor Lavan knew the capabilities of most of the relics. He'd just have to guess at what best to take or leave. It was horribly frustrating, since anything left behind might be used by Zakarah.

Soon all had their arms full. "Good. Take them to the tunnel join the others. I'm going to find Master Vardon."

The worried youngsters hustled down the corridor. After stuffing a few smaller items into his robe, Kagen waved his hands over the doorway, mumbling an incantation. Door and wall merged, becoming indistinguishable. He headed for the bailey to find Vardon.

He stopped by the outer door, catching his breath. Listening, he heard what sounded like claps of lightening, the kind one encountered only in the worst of storms. Had a siege begun? Was the school now under attack? If so, it sounded as if Vardon was making the brutes pay dearly. He dared to feel hopeful.

That hope vanished when he opened the door. Beasts were leaping down from the walls, pouring into the bailey. Worse, several were at the main gate, cranking up the portcullis. The school had fallen. He prayed Vardon and his defenders still survived.

He no sooner entered the courtyard than he spotted Vardon. He'd abandoned the walls. Eight or so defenders were with him, forming a defensive circle not twenty paces from Kagen. He hurried to join them.

Vardon spotted him. "Get below you fool! There's nothing you can do here. Go protect the little ones."

"They don't need me!" he gasped. "They're gone. I've found a way out of here." Vardon's eyes widened. "Bring your lads. The school may be lost, but we still have our lives. Hurry!"

Vardon gave him a brief, questioning look before yelling. "Follow Master Kagen!" They backed their way to the doorway, casting spells as they moved.

The gate was up. Brutes poured in unabated. "Inside! Quickly!" Vardon ordered. He pushed Kagen through the doorway. "You first, you're the slowest."

Vardon's right! I'm feeblest. Gasping, he prayed to whatever gods might listen that his heart not give out before they reached the tunnel.

After bolting the door, Kagen led them to the sliding cinder block, and crumpled to his knees, pain wracking his chest. He nearly passed out. There was no way he could keep going.

He pointed. "Push aside that block. There's a tunnel behind and below. Go down the stairs, turn left, and head straight until you reach a pile of rubble. You'll find a small opening to one side. Get inside and seal it. I'll stay behind and fend them off."

Vardon slipped his arm around Kagen's waist. "Not likely, old man." Vardon half lifted, half carried Kagen through the opening, and set him on the steps.

"Seal the opening!" Kagen wheezed. "We dare not let them find it."

Blue flames blasted the cinder, melding doorway and wall. "Good. Now go."

Vardon shook his head, scooped up Kagen, draped him over his shoulder, and carried him down the steps to where the others waited. "Give me a hand."

Some grabbed arms, others legs or shoulders. "This way!"

The jouncing ride was painful, but Kagen realized it was his only hope. "That's it, just ahead!" he said, spotting his rubble heap.

They set him down. Vardon ordered his charges through and carried Kagen inside. Kagen peered back at the hole. "Can you do as good a job with this opening as you did with the last one?"

Vardon was puffing almost as hard as he was. "I can try."

Kagen closed his eyes, avoiding the glare of Vardon's cast. A sulfur-like odor permeated the air. When he opened them to look, the entrance was sealed.

Vardon knelt and embraced him. "You bought us time, you wily old bastard. You're a marvel!"

Kagen smiled. "Then I'm not yet worthless?"

Vardon laughed. "Not as long as you can draw a breath."

Kagen grimaced. If only Vardon knew. "I fear I'll soon be worthless then. Death courts me."

Vardon's smile vanished. "You four, pick up Master Kagen. Give the man who saved our lives the aid he deserves."

<hr />

Stunned, Hagley slumped to the floor of the solar room, trying to cope with news—Marshal Booker had just informed them that the university had been overrun. Sully, Rayna, Kagen, Vardon, Mistress Genevieve, his fellow students—all dead. Bile roiled up his throat.

Gresham had taken it hardest. The moment he heard the news he muttered Rayna's name and buried his face in hands. He hadn't twitched a muscle since. Hagley wanted to assuage his friend, but the proper words escaped him.

Master Verity's blind stare reminded Hagley of Rajko's before they'd cured him. His stunned gaze drifted to Hagley. "Gone. All of them. We're all that remains of the island's sorcerers."

"I'm sorry milord," Goodricke consoled.

Caitlyn draped her arms around Gresham's shoulders. "Should we pray for them?"

Jarek nodded. "Yes."

They joined hands and bowed their heads.

Hagley? Hagley looked up, shocked. It was Sully. *Hagley, do you be hearing me?*

Hagley concentrated. Mind-speak back, you idiot! *Sully, I hear you. Where are you?*

In a tunnel, like the one to your practice area. Master Kagen brought the whole school here. Bunches of beasties tried to be killing us, but we got away.

"They're safe!" he yelled, "All of them."

Whoops and cheers greeted his proclamation.

"Where are they?" Jarek demanded. Others were asking questions too. Hagley held up his hands, begging for silence. He closed his eyes, concentrating. *Where is this tunnel?*

I don't know, but Mister Vardon thinks we be under the fort.

Jarek knelt in front of him. "Tell me what's happening."

"Sully thinks they're below the fort but isn't sure where."

Master Verity ran fingers through his hair. "Tell them to remain where they are, that we'll find them."

Hagley relayed the message and the search began. Despite many probes, they searched the better part of the morning without success. Jarek claimed there were simply too many living auras to discern one from another. Jarek looked frustrated. "Have Sully describe his surroundings."

Hagley closed his eyes. *Sully, we're still searching.*

Hurry, folks be hungry and thirsty and scared.

We're doing our best, but we need your help. Describe where you are.

I told you, in a tunnel. Mister Vardon says it likely be some buried road. A bunch of stones stop us from going farther.

Stay where you are, we'll find you.

"They're in an underground roadway, blocked by rocks."

Gresham's eyes lit up. "The monument! It stood in front of the fort's original gatehouse before the keep expanded. What better place for a road to end? It's been lying under a pile of rubble for years."

It sounded too right to be wrong. They hurried to the fallen gate, and Jarek's probe found them. "Very good, Gresham, they're right below us. Have the Marshal send men with shovels."

Gresham recognized many of those climbing out the hole, Sully was the first to appear. Others followed. His stomach twisted; so far, Rayna wasn't among them. Gods, let her be safe.

After the students came the magi, starting with Mistress Genevieve. The last of them was Master Vardon, with a body cradled in his arms. A woman climbed out beside him, helping him lay out the body. It was Rayna!

He limped over to her. Seeing him, she jumped up and leaped into his arms. Far too soon she stepped back, glancing down at his bandaged leg, looking distraught. "Gods! You're injured!"

"I was bitten, but the Clerics assure me I'll be all right." Although true, it was still painful. "What's important is that you're safe," he said, pulling her to him again, hugging her tightly, savoring her touch and the smell of her hair. With Zakarah's horde surrounding them, he wondered if it might be their last embrace.

Requital

Trumpets blared, the call to man their posts. Gresham limped to his assigned place on the wall, and, peered through the crenels at the horde beyond.

Zakarah was organizing his brutes. It was the first they'd seen of the demon since the university's fall. Bunched in squadrons, the nearest prey gathered less than a hundred paces away. Twenty groups deep, their ranks ran all the way back to Zakarah's command post. They began spreading in either direction; an assault was imminent—the battle was about to unfold.

Gresham's station was to the right of the barbican, the jutting part of the wall designed to protect the gatehouse, the most vulnerable part of the city's wall. If the prey were to breach it, this was the most likely spot. Soldiers manned the floor's murder holes, ready to drop boulders or burning oil if the gate itself was surpassed.

To his right, soldiers manned arrow slits, with magus students dispersed in between each. Clerics manned the barbican's other side, with the Inquisitor in command. Master Vardon commanded the magicians on this side.

As usual, Quinn was with the churchmen. Only the gate's turret separated he and Gresham. For a king's man, he sure spent a lot of time in the company of the Inquisitor. Quinn looked his way. The Clerics and magi weren't the only ones keeping an eye on one another.

Men below were hoisting pots of oil all along the battlement walls. His uncle stood beside him, studying the clerics. "It seems we're about to finally see one another's methods. This should prove most interesting."

"Spread out along the rampart, fifteen paces apart," Vardon ordered, "and we'll link."

Forming a circle without having to touch hands was something Jarek contrived after observing Hunter. It was how the circle had reached him during his encounter with Zakarah. When Gresham asked how he figured out how to do it, his uncle explained, "Once we walked the spell to its logical conclusion, how to project it became obvious."

Hagley was there at the time. "That's why he's a Royal Magus and I've yet to earn my robes."

Vardon made his way along the battlements, offering encouragement. "Don't be alarmed when you feel the magic rage through you. It may make you dizzy, but it passes quickly." He pointed to the Clerics. "Since our Exalted Grace insists upon watching us, let's show him something worth seeing by giving those devils our best."

The magicians linked and Vardon triggered a spell. Storm clouds instantly formed over the prey, and wind spiraled among them like small cyclones. Lightning claps rippled within a thunderhead, raining a blackened deluge upon the alarmed beasts—smoke erupted from anything it touched. The creatures fell to the ground screaming. The mayhem continued until the spell finally ended. The violent winds eased, and the clouds wafted away, leaving behind lifeless, charred bodies. The magicians had finally dealt Zakarah a blow.

"Well done, Vardon," Jarek complimented, looking toward the Clerics. "That should impress our pious friends."

The words were no sooner out of the Jarek's mouth when the prey began shrieking anew. Flames engulfed those nearest the Clerics' wall, frying them where they stood. The Inquisitor had performed his own demonstration. Jarek nodded the Inquisitor's way. The smiling Inquisitor nodded in return. Jarek's eyes twinkled. "It seems we've a game afoot. Let's hope Zakarah winds up the worse for it."

The twin assaults had the beasts in disarray, racing pell-mell toward the back of their ranks. It all stopped when a flash erupted from within the demon's shield. The beasts prostrated themselves before him, foreheads touching the ground. He stomped to the prey who had fled their forward positions and pointed an arm. Pitiful wails erupted from his targets. Their bodies vibrated as their cries transformed into woeful death throes. One by one, they ceased to move. Glaring at the fortress, Zakarah shouted a command. The prey formed into two lines, marching in opposite directions, a hundred paces beyond the walls.

Gresham turned to Vardon. "What do you suppose they're doing?"

Vardon chewed his lip. "It's the same maneuver they did just before they overwhelmed the university. Zakarah spread his force so wide that we had more wall to protect than we had defenders, allowing their superior numbers to break through our defenses."

The horde now fanned to either side for as far as Gresham could see. How had this many fit on Hunter's island? Once the lines encircled the fortress, they stopped, turned, and faced the walls.

Gresham took stock of his post. Three bowmen and two of Vardon's acolytes shared his wall; just six men to defend a section of wall that stretched forty paces, facing more attackers than one could count.

The prey charged, closing on the wall with frightening speed. Baying like charging cattle, they thundered toward the wall. Mouths frothing, they started climbing it.

Gresham's pulse raced, his body readying itself for battle. A shaking hand drifted to his sword. *No! I'm a Battle Mage; I can inflict more damage with magic than steel.* He waited until the archers fired real arrows before loosing illusionary ones of his own, some of fire, others acid. Shafts of all varieties rained down upon the charging prey. Beast after beast fell to arrow or spear, only to have another take its place.

Soldiers dumped burning oil on those first arrivals. The howls below were hideous; the stench of their burning flesh revolting. Still, on they came, apparently fearing Zakarah more than getting charred. They were reaching the wall below him in ever greater numbers. Using claw and muscle, they scaled the walls with frightening ease. One cleared the battlement.

Gresham stopped casting and drew his blade. He lunged, his blade piercing its neck. The creature's eyes widened as blood gurgled from its mouth. The prey appeared far less fearsome while dying. Placing a boot against its chest, he withdrew his weapon. A push of his boot tumbled it off the wall.

An agonized scream drew his attention. A prey had its jaws clamped on the back of the bowman beside him's neck. The beast snapped its head from side to side, then flung the poor man off the parapet. Another beast joined it, flanking the magician beside him. Gresham pointed his hand, aiming with his fingers. Static crackled. Illusionary arrows pierced both beast's chests. Focused on those two adversaries, the young magus failed to spot a third one clear the wall beneath him. Gresham evoked an Interposing Hand, blocking the creature's attack, then transformed it into a Gripping Hand and tossed the attacker off the wall. Three more prey appeared, dooming the poor man, who toppled off the wall, screaming as he fell. At least he'd fallen inside the fort. Mayhap someone could come to his aid.

Moments later, the last of the bowmen met a similar fate, leaving just one acolyte and him to defend their stretch of wall. Then he too, disappeared beneath a swarm of snarling gray bodies as more prey gained the battlement wall. The smell of death was everywhere, and Gresham now stood alone; his wall overwhelmed. Would his death be next? Two prey, the one's who'd just killed the acolyte, turned, facing him. Jaws open, they crawled toward him, snarling like rabid wolves, saliva dripping from their jaws.

Seeking a means of escape, he backed toward the gatehouse, lashing at an oncoming beast. His sword seemed to gain weight with each and every swing. His arms now ached as badly as his wounded leg. More fiends gained the wall. The situation was hopeless. If he didn't get off the wall now, he never would.

He backed away from them until the brattice wall stopped his retreat. A probing foot found the stairs. He glanced down. The men manning the murder holes were no longer there and beasts were battering at the gate below him. Several prey had gained the grounds between the inner and outer curtains. The fall of Stalwart was imminent.

"It looks bad!" came a voice from behind him.

Gresham's head snapped around. There, covered in gore, stood Quinn, rounding the turret from its other side. Blood trailed down one of his arms. Gresham raised his sword. "Not good for them, you mean. After all, they face two champion swordsmen."

Quinn's face stretched into a feral grin. "Back to back like at practice?"

"Back to back it is."

Circling, they descended the steps, rotating in circles, leaving no angle unguarded. Who would ever have guessed their survival would someday depend on the other. "Ironic, isn't it?"

Quinn drove his weapon through a prey's eye. "You've the right of that."

Backs together, they descended the stairwell, always circling, swords never resting.

Goodricke had been put in charge of one of the groups of townspeople atop the garrison's inner curtain. While trained soldiers manned the outer wall, his group was comprised of farmers and tradesmen, most armed with little more than axes and pitchforks. Their mission, if the outer curtain were to fall, was to stave off the enemy long enough for the outside defenders to slip inside the garrison walls.

Caitlyn was at his side, as was Rayna, who'd volunteered as a healer. Sully was there too, cutlass in hand. Rayna had refused to let the lad out of her sight.

Goodricke's gut knotted as more and more prey appeared on the walls, especially those nearest the gatehouse. He feared the townsfolk's mettle was about to be tested.

Rayna cried out. "Gresham abandoned his wall."

His wasn't the only parapet being abandoned. Beasts were jumping into the fort all along the ramparts. A horn blasted. "They've ordered the garrison gate open," Goodricke hollered. "We've a job to do."

Caitlyn's leather thong spun in circles, her flying disks seeking and finding targets.

"Gods no!" Rayna wailed. "Sully, get back here!"

In all the excitement, they'd taken their eyes off the boy. He'd climbed off the wall unseen, and was rushing toward the main gate, waving his cutlass high over his head. The little self-imagined hero was racing to help his friend Gresham.

Gresham had the right man protecting his back. That same prowess that had tested him so during the cadet championships was now keeping him alive. They reached the bottom of the stairway only to be attacked by a half dozen more of the beasts. How long could they survive this frenetic pace? How many more brutes must they contend with? He scanned the area, arms quivering, gasping for breath.

His heart skipped. Sully was running toward him, brandishing his cutlass. "No! You little fool!"

He wasn't the only one to spot the oncoming boy. Three prey broke away to fend off this new adversary.

"Sully, go back!" he yelled, but there was no way he could be heard over this din of battle. The prey jumped Sully. Cutlass lost, the boy disappeared beneath their pile.

Rage consumed him. Time slowed. He was suddenly outside his body, observing the battle from above. He heard a savage howl, more forceful than those around him; more terrifying, too. It took a moment to realize it was he who had uttered it. His berserker had taken control.

His weapon became an extension of his fury. He cut, slashed and maimed, killing his way toward Sully, dimly aware of Quinn at his side. Onward he charged, cutting down beast after beast. What had once seemed too many enemies now seemed too few. Such paltry numbers couldn't deter him.

Gresham's fury multiplied. Within moments he reached Sully, slashing, cutting and tearing. Something within him remembered his Gift. An instant later spectral hands were ripping into the beasts, grasping foes, crushing them. Bodies flew. Gore spattered. They would feel the wrath of a Battle Mage gone berserker. He might die this day, but the price he'd exact would be huge. Hands grabbed and tossed until the only body remaining was a very small one, soaked in blood.

"Smithy! Smithy!"

The voice was distant. He searched for more foes but found none. Did those cowards fear the righteousness of his rage?

"Smithy! Gresham!" The voice persisted. "There are no more. You killed them all!"

It was Quinn.

His battle rage faded, a plea from Quinn once again restoring his senses. He looked around, dazed.

The defenders were rallying. Although many beasts were still inside the walls, they were quickly being dispatched. Cavalrymen and foot soldiers mingled in their midst, driving the surviving prey toward the wall. Flying weapons honed on targets, arrow and spear alike. No longer attacking, the prey scrambled for the outer wall, desperate to escape.

Gresham sheathed his bloodied sword. Gathering Sully in his arms, he headed for the hospital area, examining the torn little body he carried it.

Quinn walked beside him. "Is he alive?"

"I don't know."

Quinn darted ahead. "Follow me. I've seen what these Clerics can do. They brought back more than one man I thought would never live another day."

Quinn forced his way through the garrison crowd, Gresham chasing after. He slipped through a doorway. Gresham followed, twisting to and fro, careful not to bump the boy.

They were inside the field hospital. Clerics were tending wounded everywhere, the room seemingly too full to hold another. Quinn motioned toward him. "Over here."

Groans and cries filled the room. The stench of blood and fetid flesh hung in the air. Quinn seemed to be looking for someone specific. "There." He headed for an elderly Cleric attending a badly wounded soldier. "Evander, I need you!"

The exhausted man's hollowed eyes looked up at Quinn, and then drifted to Sully. "Let me see him," he rasped.

Gresham laid the boy down. Evander examined him, shaking his head. "I'm sorry, he's too far gone. I must save what little Effulgence I have left in me for those who have a chance to survive," he said, returning to the wounded man.

Quinn grasped his shoulder. "Evander, he's a boy! Surely a single spell given to one so young can't cost you that dearly."

Evander looked at Quinn briefly before scanning room, looking at the wounded. Closing his eyes, he nodded. "One only."

He removed Sully's tattered clothing, exposing raw, torn flesh. Blood gurgled from open wounds. The Cleric was right; Sully stood no chance. Gresham closed his eyes. How would he ever convey such dire news to Hagley and Rayna?

With one hand hovering over Sully's chest, Evander fondled a golden rod that hung from his neck, the image of the God Star carved in its front. The cruciate hummed as Evander prayed. He released his talisman long enough to gently turn Sully over, then repeated the process. The wounds, although still not healed, no longer spurted blood. "There, that's all I can do. Do not raise your hopes; he's very near to visiting The Light." Evander stood. "Leave him. He'll be taken to the tunnel with the other wounded. I must tend to others now." He moved on to his next patient.

Gresham followed Quinn outside. The battle had ebbed, most efforts now focused on tending the wounded. Gresham paused just outside the door. "Thank you."

Quinn leaned against the building, watching the chaos around them before finally speaking. "It was you who ruined that devil's magic in the field yesterday, wasn't it?"

Gresham nodded. "The magi tell me I'm gifted. They're trying to teach me how to control it." How much should he divulge? "That fit you just saw is called a berserker's rage. Clearly, I've yet to master their lessons."

"The gods be praised for that—your failure to do so likely saved our lives."

Neither spoke for a bit. "You never told the Chevaliers I went into a similar rage during our duel, did you?"

Instead of answering, Quinn pushed away from the wall. "I should go. Marshal Booker will expect a report."

Gresham watched him leave. Quinn was harder to fathom than any man he knew.

⁂

Jarek leaned against the wall, waiting. He'd been called to Marshal Booker's headquarters to discuss how to deal with the devil beasts, as had several others. University Masters, soldiers, the Inquisitor and his chief Clerics among them. Now that they'd seen the enemy in action, they were discussing next steps. "Who all are in the tunnel, Sergeant?"

"The wounded, all the women, and any man too young or old to fight. Their gate can be sealed from beneath."

"Excellent." The Marshal paced the area behind his desk. "We'll man the outer curtain for show only, to delay another attack, but as soon as an assault comes, we'll retreat to the inner curtain. The smaller garrison walls will be far easier to defend."

Inquisitor Kolton cleared his throat. "Marshal, might I offer an alternative approach? Abandon the outer walls immediately. Entice the devils inside and let my Clerics bestow God's wrath upon them. I'm sure their results will please you."

"Explain."

"None but a Cleric would understand. It would be simplest to describe our actions as creating artwork that dare not be disturbed." Runes, Jarek thought, he wants to draw runes. "Allow no others outside the garrison, however."

Marshal Booker turned to Master Vardon. "Are the magi amenable?"

Vardon inclined his head. "If His Grace's Clerics can do harm to these devils, by all means, let them do so."

"It's decided then." The Marshal circled the room, meeting each man's eyes. "This next stand will be critical, gentlemen." He pointed skyward. "If we fail, I fear we'll be explaining ourselves to the Inquisitor's overseer." The remark evoked chuckles. Even Kolton smiled. "I for one, prefer to forestall that inevitable meeting." He stopped pacing. "Regardless of the course of upcoming events, in the king's name, I thank each of you for the bravery you've already shown. But our work's not yet done; go out and win the day and may whatever gods you worship watch over you."

≈≈≈

Jarek returned to the wall. Everyone had been assigned a new post on the inner curtain. He stared at the horde beyond. Unlike the humans, their wounded remained untended and rotting. The main horde had reassembled just outside of the archer's range, their once-orderly squadrons wandering in discord.

The surviving magicians were guarding the walls to the right side of the garrison gate. Closest to him were those he held dearest: his nephew, brave and as self-assured as the most seasoned magus; Goodricke, wielding Turpin's sword. Hagley, with a skill-level no one had yet to fathom.

The hospital had been moved inside the tunnel. Rayna had gone there to help tend the wounded, but Caitlyn remained, the only woman left among the defenders. She'd come to the Outland to learn its ways, only to be besieged by monsters worse than those of her Haunt. Having spent the bulk of her life dealing with horrors, the fate she faced must seem unjust. Why couldn't Zakarah content himself with his relic plunder and leave? Or was he still here because he'd yet to find them?

Leaning against the battlement wall, he slid to his butt and pulled out Lavan's amulet, wishing he could somehow confide with his friend one last time. As much as he hated to admit it, the demon's powers exceeded his. In fact, they surpassed everyone's—save for Hunter's. But then, whose didn't pale when compared to the dragon.

Jarek toyed with that thought. Just because he couldn't outfight the miscreant, didn't mean he couldn't outsmart him. He took off his Masters' ring and removed the orb, then did the same with Lavan's amulet. He pressed the two together, wishing they could still be used get his friend's advice. After all, it was Lavan who'd warned that Zakarah was here for the university's relics—and he who had told of the demon's plan to return to his hell via portal.

He sat up. What if he couldn't? What if he could foil the demon's plans with a counter spell that prevented him from leaving? Zakarah might still defeat him, but at least his prisoners wouldn't dwell in his hell. It would be a way reap a bit of revenge.

As he sat pondering what Lavan might do, an epiphany struck him. Of course, how obvious! "Hagley!" he hollered, wanting to discuss his idea with the talented lad. Looking down at the orbs, he laughed. "Even in death you still look after me, old friend."

From the corner of his eye he saw someone approach. There, within ear shot of him, stood one of Kolton's high Clerics, watching him talk into the orbs. Scowling, the man turned and left—in a hurry. Jarek shook his head. Nothing good would come of this.

Coming up the stairs, nearly colliding with the fast-fleeing Cleric, was Hagley. "You called for me, Magus?"

"Yes. Do you still sense your link with Hunter?"

"I do. I can't seem to rid myself of him."

"Do you think you can contact him?"

Hagley seemed surprised by his comment. "I could try."

"Here, maybe these will help," he said, handing him the orbs. "Tell him you've found his prey, and that many have already died. If He-Who-Steals isn't stopped, perhaps all of them will die."

Hagley tried to mind connect with Hunter, sending him Jarek's message. "I'm sorry, but he didn't respond." Trumpets blared, announcing another attack. "I have to return to my post. Here are your orbs," he said, holding out his hand.

"Keep them. Hide them. Tell no one you have them."

Hagley left. He peered down the wall. Per Kolton's instructions the area had been emptied save for a group of Clerics still praying before their newly created runes. Had they not heard the horns? By now the prey had cleared the unattended outer wall and were in the fort—in the killing grounds between the two curtains. Still, the churchmen didn't move.

The first of the prey fell to archers' missiles, but others arrived to replace them, pouring over the walls in ever increasing numbers. Only when the horns sounded the signal to close the garrison gate did the Clerics finally abandon their runes and dash for cover.

Oblivious of the runes, the oncoming beasts charged forward. When they reached the drawings, a group of Clerics on the wall opposite Jarek's, raised their hands and chanted. The runes exploded, ripping apart anything in their proximity. More distant runes exploded too. Apparently other Clerics had made similar drawings. Beasts were down everywhere, either writhing in pain or wandering about with no sense of where they were. Shafts quickly took care of any still moving.

A cry of, "Archers, the gate!" was heard. Prey were raising the portcullis. Arrows rained down on them, but not in time. The gate lifted, and in marched Zakarah.

Every spellcaster and archer instantly targeted him, but strange winds whirling around him sent their attacks awry; the nearby beasts taking their brunt. Zakarah seemed not to care. Ignoring the chaos surrounding him, his eyes skimmed the bulwarks; until he spotted Jarek.

He walked to the foot of Jarek's wall. "So good to see you again, Royal Magus. But alas, despite my ever-growing fondness for you, I fear circumstance dictates that this must be our last such meeting." His jagged-toothed smile faded. "Things might have been different had you joined me and your companion."

It was Jarek's first up-close view of the demon. His sleeves did little to hide his thorny arms. With clawed hands and feet, he looked more prey than human. His cowl was back, his hideous face exposed. Pocked and pinched, save for its greenish hue, he could have passed for kin of the Crone. "You're more hideous than I'd imagined, Zakarah. Be gone! This is not your world."

Zakarah pressed clawed hands together. "Ah, such ungraciousness. And here I thought we'd bonded. But what can one expect from someone so feeble? Even your memory goes wanting. You forget that I take what I want, when I want." Zakarah's lip curled into a snarl. "Where are the relics?"

Jarek smiled; that fact he'd asked meant the relic vault remained undiscovered. Still, with refugees in the tunnel and defenders on the walls, many lives depended on the outcome of this encounter. If he surrendered the relics would Zakarah return to his hell and spare them? When he thought of what had happened to Lavan and the beast by the pond, he knew better. It was either defeat the monster, die, or be whisked away to his hell for a fate worse than death. "You receive no welcome, nor do you gain the relics. Leave now, and I spare your life."

The demon laughed. "We shall see the truth of that."

He started a chant. Was he powerful enough to hold his shield and cast another spell? Remembering how disruptive Gresham's phantom hand had been in the field the day before, he invoked his

Wizard's Hand spell. In and of itself, this spell didn't do damage, it simply allowed him to move things from afar.

A stack of rubble lay near the gatehouse door. Jarek's phantasmal hand grabbed a piece of broken masonry and flung it at Zakarah's shield. The demon easily side-stepped it, but dodging it prevented him from casting.

Zakarah tried again. Again, Jarek pummeled him with debris. Zakarah glared at him, hatred burning from those awful red eyes. Jarek smiled. He may not be able to enter the fray himself, but neither could Zakarah. Hopefully the others would prevail against this horde.

As their stalemate continued, Jarek's ability to maintain his attacks waned. He was depleting his aethers. His spells weren't the only ones faltering. All along the wall magi spells were suffering a similar fate as their store of aethers were spent. The same was true of the Clerics. He doubted anyone here had ever used his Gift this long or this fiercely. It wearied mind, body and spirit.

Soldiers jostled spell casters aside, replacing waning magics with sword and mace. Bodies were falling, beasts and humans alike. Before long, there were frighteningly few men guarding the walls. Despite the defenders' gallant efforts, the prey were simply too numerous.

More and more garrison walls were being breached. Jarek's heart sank. Beasts were gaining the garrison grounds unabated. With the Gifted's spells spent, it was man against beast, a numbers game the defenders couldn't win. Watching the scene unfold, Jarek resigned himself to the town's inevitable fate. As with all Zakarah's previous endeavors, the demon was winning the day, a bitter thought indeed.

Suddenly the cries around him took on a new tone—sounding more animal than human. Jarek scanned the area. The prey had halted their attacks, both in and outside of the garrison. They dashed about, paying little heed to their human adversaries with their eyes trained skyward. Jarek looked to see a giant raptor swooping toward the fortress, talons extended.

Hunter had answered Hagley's summons.

Garrison archers fired at this new threat, but their shots fell far short. Jarek felt a familiar surge, followed by an overwhelming lethargy, reminiscent of that he'd experienced upon his arrival to Hunter's island. Defenders and attackers alike froze in place. All but the Gifted. Still, with their aethers spent, they found themselves unable to cast, totally defenseless.

The great beast passed overhead. After flying a short distance, it banked and looped back toward them. Zakarah saw it too, and ran for the gatehouse, but Hunter landed in front of him, blocking his path.

He-who-steals! echoed through Jarek's mind.

Zakarah augmented his protective spell, the air around him now glowing a vivid blue. His eyes darted about, seeking a means of escape. It was the first time Jarek had seen Zakarah show fear. Relishing the moment, he decided hubris was in order. "Zakarah," he yelled, "let me make amends for my earlier discourtesy. Meet Hunter. He's been anxious to meet you ever since you stole these beasts you brought to my land. Actually, you might say he's 'hungered' for this opportunity."

Zakarah cast a venomous glance his way, but quickly returned his attention to the imposing dragon. His lips were moving. He was casting anew. Was he daring an attack or attempting to flee? Bright light shimmered above him. He floated toward it, his image beginning to fade. He was making his escape.

Jarek countered Zakarah's spell. An invisible barrier blocked the demon's ascent. Zakarah clawed at this new barrier to no avail, and cast yet another menacing glare in Jarek's direction. Hunter reared his head, and let loose a frightening roar that echoed off the buildings and walls. *Take prey!*

If Jarek lived a hundred years, he was sure he'd never again see anything as rapid as Hunter's strike. In the blink of an eye all that could be seen of Zakarah were his legs, frantically kicking from inside of Hunter's mouth. Suddenly, the squirming ceased, and green liquid oozed from the dragon's mouth. Hunter snapped his head back, opened wide, and lurched his neck forward. Zakarah disappeared into the dragon's mouth. Hunter sat back on its haunches, chewing.

Jarek watched, feeling neither relief nor bliss; just numbness. No one cheered; cast a spell; or as much unleashed an arrow. Those that could move, did not. All simply stared, watching the dragon consume the once mighty demon.

Hunter spat out a few bones and blinked. Everyone could suddenly move again. Chaos erupted near the gatehouse as the prey pushed and fought one another, desperate to escape the fort. Shafts peppered them. Seeing his prey under attack, Hunter blinked again, and the volleys stopped.

With a flap of his powerful wings, he leaped airborne, chasing after his panicked prey. Flying just overhead, he herded them out the gate. Those who went east were left alone. The others were hounded until, they too, were heading east. Hunter was shepherding his flock, driving them toward Pembok and Broughton. Jarek smiled. He was herding them back to Hagley's still open gate, taking home his flock.

Cheers echoed everywhere as they watched the dragon leave. Soldiers held weapons aloft, shouting and waving. Others hugged; many danced. Jarek took in the scene. Down his own parapet he spotted Vardon, laughing and celebrating with two of his students. Beyond them he spied Goodricke and Caitlyn, hugging and dancing in circles. Gresham and Hagley were locked in an embrace too. He thanked whatever gods that were listening that they'd spare those he held dearest.

The killing field below was strewn with bodies, human and prey alike. The battle's toll was almost too great to fathom. Drained, he watched the others celebrate; wishing Lavan could have been here to share this moment.

Suddenly a laughing Hagley appeared out of nowhere, leaping on Jarek, bowling him over. "I saw you!" he whooped. "You kept Zakarah from escaping!"

Jarek pushed the lad aside. "We each played our part. Remember, it's not about me or you, all share credit in our victory."

Hagley's eyes twinkled. "I think I'm finally beginning to understand that, Sir." He clapped his hands together, unable to contain his excitement. "Hunter heard me after all."

"Yes. Think back at how upset you were when you hadn't closed your gate. If you had, Hunter would never have gotten here. We'd all be dead."

"That was my plan all along," he said, winking.

Their laughter was disrupted by panicked shouts. People were pointing at the sky. He looked. Hunter was returning.

Swooping toward the fort, he was flying directly toward Hagley and him, showing no signs of slowing. Something was amiss. He passed over them, circled, then bore down on them, talons extended, clearly after the two of them.

Falling victim to the dragon was what Jarek had most dreaded since first seeing the beast—and now he was finally coming after him. Heart pounding, he ran toward the nearest stairwell, Hagley at his side, moving far faster than Jarek would guess a man of his bulk could possibly manage. Dread consumed him as he envisioned what had just happened to Zakarah happening to the two of them too.

Run though they may, the ghastly beat of its flapping wings was closing in on them with frightening speed. They weren't going to make it off the wall in time. "Hagley, get down!"

His warning came too late. Hagley let out a terrified scream as Hunter's huge talons closed around the young magician, his horrified expression bringing back visions of Lavan's look of dismay when Zakarah had spirited him off to his elsewhere.

"Hunter! No!" Jarek screamed as the dragon flew off with one last prey clutched in his talons, Hagley's look of horror forever etched in his mind. "No," he sobbed, dropping to his knees and cradling face in hands, weeping. The nightmare that was Zakarah had ended, but not without taking one last grievous toll.

Treason

Zakarah's defeat was first met with a dull silence, but realizing their ordeal had likely ended, Gresham heard cheers erupting one after the other from all around the city. But unable to shake the vision of what had happened to poor Hagley prevented Gresham from sharing their joy.

The townsfolk's glee turned out to be short-lived. It took but one glance and the death and destruction around them for a melancholy to set back in.

The ensuing days were spent attending the wounded and removing and burying the dead. The stench of rotting corpses made the task barely bearable. The highborn were interned in individual graves, but the common folk were piled together in a mass grave with but a single headstone commemorating their collective lost lives.

The ridding of the preys' carcasses was even more inglorious. Stacked in piles in a field a short distance from town, they were torched, burned and buried over. A strange silence hung over the town the whole time. He'd never heard the town this quiet. What few noises he did hear were too often the sobs and cries of those mourning some loss. It took two days to rid the town of the dead—the worst two days of Gresham's young life.

Rayna and Caitlyn filled their hours assisting in the field hospital. Goodricke had suffered a horrific wound, his arm now in a sling. Miraculously, Sully survived his wounds, and was recuperating under Prior Rigby's watchful eye, and when she could, Rayna's care too. People pitched in to help rebuild neighbor's homes and the businesses damaged in the battle. Ever so slowly, the town was coming back to life.

On the fifth morning after the battle, Gresham received a summons to Marshal Booker's office. He arrived to find Master Vardon, Mistress Genevieve, Uncle Jarek, and the new Captain of the Guard already there. Nodding a greeting, he took a seat beside his uncle.

"I'm sure you're wondering why you've been asked to come here," the Marshal began, once everyone was there. "First off, my special thanks to each of you for your brave efforts defending our town. Without them, we'd never have prevailed. Many of those who sought sanctuary here have already returned home. Still others fear to take to the highways. We're making them work in exchange for food and water, hoping to encourage their departure." He looked at Gresham. "I'm sorry that your magician friend was the battle's last victim."

The mention of the loss of his dear friend brought a flood of tears to Gresham's eyes. Manly though it might not be, it was beyond him to do otherwise.

The Marshal sat back. "Now... the reason I called you here is to discuss a matter of State—and before the Inquisitor arrives. He's due here shortly." He flexed his fingers. "It's difficult to know where to begin." His gaze drifted to Jarek. "Magus, is it true you were instrumental in bringing that demon here?"

Gresham frowned. What was astir? His uncle should be treated as a hero, not like this.

"Instrumental exaggerates my role. Although it's true I was with Headmaster Lavan when he first encountered that devil, his coming here had little to do with any action of mine."

"How then, did the demon know of the university's relics?"

Before Jarek could respond, a soldier poked his head through the doorway. "He's coming, Sir."

The Marshal stood. "Magus Verity, per my duties, I hereby charge you with High Treason."

Gresham started, unable believe his ears. How could his uncle be so accused? Anger roiled through him. This was unjust beyond belief.

Mistress Genevieve jumped to her feet. "That's preposterous!" she barked. "I would believe this sort of antic from the One Church, but not the King's Court. What's going unsaid here, young man?"

If her outburst vexed the Marshal, he hid it well. He simply sat there, tapping his fingers. "Mistress, you're the first one to call me young man in so long I can't remember who last said it. As to what's unsaid, I'm not at liberty to divulge the intricacies of Court politics, but I assure you Magus Verity will return with me to Suzerain to face these charges—and soon."

What little calm Gresham gained by the Marshals words vanished abruptly when the Grand Inquisitor Kolton burst into the room. Clad in formal purple robes, he was accompanied by four Chevaliers. The Marshal's aide entered behind them, and at a nod from the Marshal, turned around, departing the room.

The Inquisitor marched directly to Jarek, and grinning triumphantly, announced. "Jarek Verity, in the name of the One Church, you are charged with heresy!" He motioned his Clerics forward. "Seize him!"

"Stop!" The Marshal's shout froze them.

The aide returned, accompanied by several garrison soldiers, Quinn among them. Outnumbering the Chevaliers at least six to one, they circled the room, hands on weapons.

Marshal Booker stepped forward, insinuating himself between Jarek and the Inquisitor. He locked eyes with the churchman. "I'm sorry, Your Grace, but I can't allow that."

The Inquisitor's face darkened. His jaw went taut. "You can't allow? What makes a mere 'Marshal' think he can interfere in Church matters?"

"When royal concerns supersede them."

The Inquisitor banged his fist on the desk. "His Eminence rules over all lands, no kingdom's concern supersedes Church Law."

The Marshal kept his composure. "True in all cases but one; the Magus has been charged with High Treason." He snatched a parchment off his desk. "Here is the writ," he said, waving it in front of Inquisitor Kolton. "That charge, and only that charge, supersedes Church Law. You may consult with your magistrate if you wish, but trust that it's true."

The Inquisitor seemed at a loss for words. "I demand to see his Master's ring."

Gresham started. Had Kolton somehow found out about Lavan's orbs—that he'd used them to commune with the dead?

The Marshal shook his head. "His personal possessions are his own."

"Let him, Marshal," Jarek said looking calm, speaking for the first time since these curious proceedings began. "The Inquisitor is welcome to examine it. He likely wishes he had the skill to earn one himself," he said, handing over his ring.

The Inquisitor snapped open its bale, removed the ruby, and looked behind it. There was nothing there—the orb was gone. "You were seen wearing more jewelry under your robe. Show it to me!"

His uncle handed him Lavan's amulet. A search of its bale produced the same result. Kolton scowled at the Marshal. "This isn't the last of this, Booker," he barked, letting both ring and amulet tumble to the floor.

The Marshal matched his glare. "I'm sorry Kolton, but I'm afraid it is."

The Inquisitor wasn't about to give in. His eyes scoured the room, settling on Quinn. "Cornet Quinn, you were near the Magus during the battle. Was anyone here party to his blasphemy?"

It was Quinn's turn to scour the room. Gresham knew his search was feigned, that Quinn would choose him. Question was, where did Quinn's allegiance lie? Which Quinn would answer; the arrogant Captain's son who kept company with churchmen, or the compassionate one who'd helped rescue Sully?

His gaze fell upon Gresham. He smiled. "Smithy, you were there. Did you see anyone aiding the Magus?"

Whatever Quinn's game, it exceeded Gresham's grasp. "I saw nothing of the kind," he answered, wondering what would come next.

Quinn bowed to Kolton. "I'm sorry, Your Grace, but if the magus committed a crime, he did so without accomplices."

"Bah!" The Inquisitor spat, and barged out of the room, his Chevaliers in tow.

"I want the rest of you to leave too, save for Gresham and Master Jarek," the Marshal announced once Kolton was gone. His gaze settled on Gresham. "I've something to discuss with you and your uncle."

Gresham waited for the room to empty. "I don't understand, how can you charge Uncle Jarek with treason? You should be hailing him the hero he is."

The Marshal spread his hands. "I should think my motives obvious. Tell me, what would have happened had I not so charged him?"

Gresham pondered the question. "The Inquisitor would have arrested him."

"Precisely." He returned to his desk. "Sit," he demanded. "Fear not for your uncle's welfare, his work here is done and he's going home. Rest assured, the charges against him will be dismissed, but only after he's safely back in Suzerain."

"But why? What is it I'm not grasping?"

"The One Church is forever trying to expand its power. One tactic is to arrest and interrogate the Gifted, to build and enhance their own set of skills. Taking your mother was a prime example. Knowing this, we dare not let them seize someone as talented as your uncle and thus grow stronger through what they glean from him. The Grand Inquisitor has been central to most such arrests. It's the Court's goal to quash those aspirations."

The Marshal stood. "I'll leave you two alone now. I'm sure you've much to discuss."

Gresham waited until the Marshal left the room. "He said your work was done here. What does that mean? Do you work for the Marshal, were you aware of the charges he was about to bring?"

"Yes, and yes. There is much more to Marshal Booker than meets the eye. He's the cleverest man I know." Jarek sat. "I asked that he allow us this time together. As soon as Kolton leaves, which we expect will be soon, I'm to be taken to Suzerain. I'd like you to come with me, to live in the royal grounds where I can help further your arts. I planned to take Hagley too, but…" He grew silent for a bit. "So, what say you? I didn't come all this way to find family only to be separated again."

Live in the royal grounds and be tutored by a Royal Magus! He'd never have dared such a dream. "I'm honored Uncle, more so than you can imagine. But before I commit, there's someone I'd like to discuss it with first."

Jarek smiled, "Ah, yes, the A'rythian girl with the pretty eyes. Of course, go do so."

Gresham paused at the parish steps. Sully was inside convalescing under Prior Rigby's watchful care. It was hard to believe the boy had survived his awful wounds. Knowing how Rayna mothered the boy, he figured this was the best place to find her.

He went inside.

"Gresham!" she screeched, rushing to him, throwing her arms around him in a tight embrace.

He still marveled at the simple joy of holding her. "Is the scamp awake?" he asked, setting her down.

"Yes, mostly complaining how unfair it was that everyone but him got to see a real live dragon."

He laughed. "When will someone other than his favorite healer be allowed to see him?"

"Soon. But not yet. Prior Rigby insists he's still too enfeebled for visitors."

"I guess I'll just have to wait then. I'm just thankful he's alive."

She smiled. "Well, since you can't see Sully, I guess you'll just have to settle for me."

"Actually, you're the one I'm here to see. I have something I want to discuss."

The sparkle left her eyes. "As do I. I've been waiting for a private moment to tell it to you."

"Really?" He cocked his head, wondering what it could possibly be. "You go first."

She took a deep breath, and searching his eyes, brought his hands to her belly. "Nirtae says I'm with child."

Given a thousand guesses, he'd never have anticipated this. Gods, he was going to be a father. He spent his life longing for family, but it never crossed him mind he might do so by creating an orphan of his own. His face flushed. "She's sure? As a man, I know nothing of such matters."

"Knowing we'd lain together, she insisted on examining me. She said life is within me, that it was what the magic had demanded. As

Mother Healer, her sensitivity to such things is unequalled," she said, her eyes searching his face.

Rayna had finally found family of her own, and now his reckless behavior had ruined it. "Did Nirtae insist you leave A'ryth because we shamed her?"

Rayna broke out laughing. "Nirtae was hardly shamed. In A'ryth, when a man and woman beget a child, the Elders proclaim them husband and wife. She insisted I share the wonderful news with my husband." She took a deep breath, chewing her lower lip. "So, what is my A'rythian husband thinking? How does Gresham Smithy feel about this news?"

What he felt was a strange mix of dread and joy. Rayna was a high lord's daughter, and he'd begat a child on her. Would he suffer her High Lord father's wrath? Worse, would she? "Rayna, I love you. Were you not highborn, nothing would make me happier than to marry you, raise our child, and grow old together, but you're nobility, and I'm but a commoner."

"Commoner!" she snapped, her eyes flashing. "We've been over this foolishness before. The nephew of a Royal Magus who's been chosen by magic hardly qualifies as common." She took a calming breath, her eyes once again searching his face. "You still haven't told me how you feel about this?"

"Well, when you put it like that…" he said, scratching his chin, his eyes twinkling. Lifting her, he twirled her in circles. "I feel joy! Absolute joy. I can hardly believe it! You and I made a baby! We're to have family of our own."

Setting her down, he dropped to one knee and took her hand. "Nothing in this world would make me happier than to have my A'rythian wife agree to become my Outlander wife too. What say you?"

"Yes!" she said, clapping her hands, a huge grin painting her face. "And Prior Rigby says he'd be honored to be our Vow Master."

"How could he? I only just asked for your hand."

Twinkling green eyes bored into his. "A woman does what she must." She took hold of his hands. "Now, you said you had something to discuss too."

"It's not nearly so grand as yours. Uncle Jarek has asked me to return to the mainland with him; to tutor my arts." He stood. "What say you to raising our child at the Suzerain Royal Court?"

※

Their ceremony took place the day after the Inquisitor left. Rayna looked radiant in her beautiful blue dress bedecked in red jewels. He was wearing a tunic Kendal had loaned him, standing side-by-side with Rayna, facing the parish doors. Kendal, his groom's aide, stood on her far side. With Yudelle gone, and Caitlyn the only A'rythian present, Rayna chose her as her bride's maid. She now stood on Gresham's other side. His uncle, Goodricke, Keep, Zele and Marshal Booker were waiting inside. They'd allowed Sully to attend too.

Prior Rigby opened the doors and beckoned them in. Arms entwined, they went inside. Flowers lined the parish walls, their fragrance permeating the room. Seeing the couple enter, their witnesses stood.

Their ceremony was short and included an exchange of woven rings and spoken vows. As soon as it ended, Jarek stepped up beside them, bearing four glasses of wine. He gave one each to Prior Rigby, Rayna and Gresham. Wine was also being offered to their guests.

Facing their audience, Jarek spoke. "Life is strange. I came to these islands seeking family—someone who shared my blood." He placed a hand on Gresham's shoulder. "And praise the gods, I found him." He turned to Rayna. "And although today that family grows, my visit here has taught me how short-sighted my search was; that the sharing of one's blood is not nearly as important as the sharing of one's heart, as those of you gathered here have done with me. I thank each of you present for that life's lesson." He raised his glass. "A toast to what family truly is."

"Cheers," Kendal hollered, hoisting his glass.

Rayna turned to Gresham. "And cheers to you, Gresham Smithy, for sharing your heart with mine. You, Nirtae, and our baby, are all the family I'll ever need."

"And now," Jarek continued, "Keep has a feast awaiting us at his inn. Let's move these festivities there, and give this town cause for some much-needed glee."

Keep had renamed his inn The Dragon's Prey, and had mounted one of their skulls above its doorway. Although gruesome, the townspeople loved it. Word of their wedding feast had apparently spread, for the inn was chock full of people when they arrived. The impatient town folk had started the festivities without them. A minstrel was there, wandering about singing and reciting poems, delighting the audience. The room was full of laughter and cheer. His uncle was right—the beleaguered town badly needed this bit of glee.

Finding an empty table, they were about to sit when Keep rushed over. "Lady, please, this area is for commoners. You'll find the highborn seating above far more to your liking." He smiled at Gresham. "As will you, milord," he added, leading them upstairs. "Please be seated while I fetch you my special wedding tankards."

"It seems strange," Gresham said watching Keep go, "to be at here at The Dragon without Sully being here too."

"Yes," Rayna said. "And to think he'll be raised by Prior Rigby like you were."

Gresham laughed. "The gods preserve us."

She gave him a playful shove. "From what Prior Rigby tells me, he can't be any worse than you were."

Keep returned with a jubbe full of ale and two glasses. Seeing them, Rayna frowned. "Those glasses have rounded bottoms. How will we set them down?"

Gresham laughed. "I think it that's the general idea."

A few ales later a shout caught their attention. "I can't believe you got married and didn't invite me to the ceremony." It had come from the stairwell.

They turned to see a disheveled crop of shaggy brown hair emerge from the staircase. "Hagley!" Rayna screeched. Ale in hand, she raced to the stairs and leaped upon him, spilling her drink all over him. "You're alive!"

Setting her down, he laughed. "That I am!" He looked down at his sopping shirt. "How kind of you to toast my return," he said, wiping himself off.

Others joined in, slapping Hagley's back and ruffling his hair, welcoming him back. Gresham grabbed him by his collar and dragged him to their table. "Now sit and tell us how you're still alive you sorry bastard, else the cost of the ale is on you."

"A bargain that's hard to refuse."

Hagley plopped into a chair, took Gresham's ale from him, and quaffed it down. "After Hunter flew off with me, he told me I'd be his next meal. But wanting nothing to do with that, I pushed open his jaws and told him I had more important things to do, that he'd just have to settle for munching his prey."

Rayna hit his arm. "Don't tease, tell us what really happened."

"I'll get more ale," Keep said. "This round be on the house, but only if you hold off the tellin' of your tale 'til I return."

Hagley grinned. "It's good to know at least one person appreciates me."

Keep returned, handing Hagley a flat-bottomed tankard and refilled the bride and groom's rounded ones. Hagley took a swig and leaned back in his chair. "Remember my portal?"

"How could we forget," Gresham said, "I thought we'd never dry out after passing through it."

"What's important is, as the island's only available Pervader, I was the sole person capable of closing it, which made me indispensable to Hunter."

"You still remembered the spell after hearing it only once?" Gresham asked.

"Ye of little patience," he said, taking another sip. "Hunter flew me back to my portal. I spent the better part of the day there watching Hunter's loathsome creatures wallow through my gate. Once all were through, Hunter..." He raised a finger, "...remember, dragon's never forget anything—mindspoke Zakarah's spell into my mind, then went through the gate himself. Before I could forget it, I cast my spell and closed it behind him."

Gresham frowned. "If he could use your portal, why didn't he come through it earlier?"

"I asked that very question. Like the Crone, Hunter's Gift is Earth Magic. He draws his aethers from the volcano's vapors. If he's away from it long, his arts soon fail him—including his ability to fly. That said, you'd think he could have flown me out of the cursed canyon first before leaving. A bit of an ingrate if you ask me." He patted his belly. "Climbing up that shaft wasn't easy for someone my size. I'm not exactly slender if you hadn't noticed."

Gresham laughed. "That was days ago. It doesn't take that long to get from there to Stalwart, no matter how slow you walk."

Hagley took another sip. "It was sundown by the time I'd closed the gate. Not wanting to risk that awful climb in darkness, I spent the night there. The next day I made my way to Broughton." His smile faded. "Soldiers were there, as were several townspeople. Rotting carcasses lay everywhere. The stench was unbearable. I was conscripted onto a burial team and only managed to leave this morning. Fortunately, I enlisted a ride." He slapped his shirt. Dust went flying everywhere. "It's amazing how filthy one can get riding behind a pair of oxen."

The feast continued unabated throughout the afternoon, as did Rayna's ale consumption. Although a pheasant dinner sobered her up somewhat, dusk found her sitting sat at her table, both hands wrapped around her curved ale glass, staring off into nowhere, sporting a silly grin. Gresham doubted she'd ever consumed anywhere near this much ale before. "Perhaps it would be best if we stepped out for some fresh air?"

She stumbled trying to stand. Fearing she'd fall, he laid their glasses on their sides, picked her up, and carried her down the stairs, spawning hoots, cheers, and raucous comments from the crowd. It was their wedding night, after all. Once outside, he walked her around, letting her breathe in fresh air, hoping to clear her head.

"When encountering an officer, it's customary to salute," someone hollered.

It was Quinn, bedecked in a Lieutenant's uniform—he'd been commissioned. "Please Quinn, not this night of all nights. In fact," he extended his hand, "how about you and I quit squabbling and let bygones be?"

Ignoring the proffered hand, Quinn turned to Rayna. "Lady, you were the first to see merit in this man." Turning, he grasped Gresham's hand. "It took me far longer. Congratulations, Smithy, Rayna is a fine choice. Now," he said, releasing Gresham's hand, "if you two will excuse me, rumor has it there's a feast going on inside."

Gresham watched him enter The Dragon, shaking his head. "I swear I'll never understand that man."

"I know something you will understand," she said, her words slurred. Fresh air had helped, but she was still far from sober.

"And what is that?" he asked, laughing.

"Come, I'll show you," she said, pulling him by the hand.

A short walk had them standing in front of an inn reserved for highborns only. "Marshal Booker chartered us a room here. A rather nice wedding gift, don't you think?" She pulled on his arm. "Come, let's go see."

A call of, "Lady Rayna!" greeted them the instant they stepped inside. It was Robard. Rayna's nemesis had finally found her. He was short, slight of build, and graying, but contrary to the Rayna's portrayal of him, his carriage was that of a gentry, not a lackey.

He walked up to Rayna, bowed, and kissed her hand. "Well met, Lady. You're as stunning as ever." Rising, he offered Gresham a frozen smile. "I don't believe we've had the pleasure."

"Robard, this is Gresham," she said, then hiccupped. Robard's jaw tightened. "Gresham, this is Robard. He does my father's biddings because the man's too cowardly to do them himself."

Rayna was showing a side of herself he'd not seen before, but Gresham was wise enough to keep quiet. "So… what message does my father bring me this time?"

Her obvious intoxication had Robard vexed. "Given recent events here, he was most concerned about your wellbeing. He'll be most relieved to hear you're safe. He bade me to escort you to Suzerain this time, feeling it time for courtly instruction. Now that I've found you, I'll book ship's passage first thing on the morrow."

"There's no need, I'm booked already. But I go to Suzerain with my husband, not you."

Robard looked stricken. "Husband?"

"Yes. I'm a married woman now. Oh! And tell my father I'm soon to be a mother, and that if he wishes to see his grandchild, he should send a formal request, to…" she gave Gresham a questioning look.

"The Royal Academe of Arcane Arts."

Robard stood there, jaw agape, at a loss as to how to respond.

"If I deem his request acceptable, I'll grant my approval. You may go now," she said, dismissing him. "Oh, and when you return to St. Pyre, be sure to tell my father that Nirtae, Akaisha's mother, sends her tidings." Her eyes absolutely sparkled at Robard's startled expression.

"Yes, milady," he said, bowing and backing away.

"I can't tell you how satisfying it was," she whispered, leading Gresham away. "All my life I've wanted to say something like that to my father." She giggled. "Ah, to see the look on his face when he learns that, not only do I know where he lives, but my mother's name as well!"

Maybe Rayna was more clear-headed than he realized.

"And now, my love," she said, leading him up the stairs, "the bridal chamber awaits us."

<hr />

Jarek paced, awaiting Hagley's arrival. They were heading to Portsmouth this morning, and from there, on to Suzerain. Everyone agreed the newlyweds ought to have the carriage to themselves, so the Spymaster, Goodricke and Caitlyn were going by horseback. Jarek was supposed to ride with them, but given his affinity for horses, he'd begged a wagon ride instead.

Goodricke had convinced Caitlyn that the fastest way to see the Outland was by sea, and was taking her to the Sailor's Guild to arrange their voyage.

Jarek had spoken only briefly with Hagley at the feast, choosing to let him revel with his friends. But they'd spoken long enough for him to invite the boy to Suzerain with the promise of that third opportunity to pass his trials. Given Hagley's recent accomplishments, the trial would be little more than a formality.

Regardless of how he tested, after what Jarek had seen of Hagley's prowess, he'd make sure the lad received his robes.

Hagley finally arrived. After loading his belongings, Jarek climbed up beside him, chuckling at the purity of leaving Stalwart in the very manner he'd arrived—on a creaky old wagon with Hagley. His visit to the islands had come full circle.

"Good morning Magus."

"And to you."

"I'm at a loss as to how to thank you for what you're doing for me."

"Bah! You earned it. That said, we'll still need to convince the Suzerain Masters you're worthy of your robes."

"I'll do my best, Sir."

"I'll coach you before you're tested. In fact, if you'd like, we can do it on our way to Portsmouth. Or…" he broke into a big grin, "since I missed your explanation at the wedding feast, you can tell me how you survived being taken by Hunter. Your choice."

Hagley laughed. "As easy a choice as I'll ever make, Sir." He snapped the reins, spurring the horses forward. "Do you remember what it was like riding atop that bultúr?"

"How could I forget? I swear my stomach is still adrift somewhere above the Jacaíoi Mountains."

"Well, that pales when compared to being carried in a dragon's talons." And that was how Hagley began his tale.

Table of A'rythian Words and Phrases

Áit na cumhachta	Place of Power
Ama de Cumhacht	Time of Power (occurs only during a Nexus)
Beannachtaí draoithe eile	Greetings fellow wizards
Beithíoch	Foul Marsh's lurker beast
Capall	The white horses of A'ryth
Cara na foraoise, is féidir liom turas tú?	Friend of the forest, may I ride you?
Ceangailte	Joined magic
Céard atá cearr?	What's the matter?
Cén fáth ar thug tú Outlanders chuig A'ryth?	Why have you brought Outlanders to A'ryth?
Déan teagmháil leis le do eochair.	Please touch it with your key.
Draíocht	Magic
Fáilte abhaile seeker	Welcome home seeker
Gan draíocht	Without magic
Go raibh maith agat	Thank you
Is é Rayna do ghariníon	Rayna is your granddaughter
Is iníon Akaisha é Rayna	Rayna is Akaisha's daughter
Ligfimid don draíocht cinneadh a dhéanamh	We will allow the magic to decide
Ní féidir linn é sin a dhéanamh	We cannot do that
Oíche na Cumhachta	Night of Power
Seanmháthair	Grandmother
Seanmháthair, is é seo an fear a dúirt mé leat faoi	Grandmother, this is the man I told you about
sméar dubh	The berries of Foul Marsh
Stop, nó cosnóidh sé tú beagnach	Halt, or it will cost you dearly
Tá an tslat seo duitse agat"	This rod is for you
Tá sé an-dathúil	He is very handsome
Tarraing siar	The command for a golem to withdraw
Tost	Silence

RON ROOT, author of Nexus Moons, was born and raised in the Pacific Northwest. After a decades long career in Information Technology as a programmer, systems analyst and manager, he retired to pursue his three favorite hobbies: tournament bridge, whitewater rafting, and fiction writing.

Ron found stepping out of an IT world where strict logic dictates virtually every decision, into one dominated by unbridled imagination, to be fascinating, rewarding and enriching.